By Alexander C. Irvine

———

A SCATTERING OF JADES
UNINTENDED CONSEQUENCES
ONE KING, ONE SOLDIER
THE NARROWS

THE NARROWS

THE NARROWS

Alexander C. Irvine

BALLANTINE BOOKS • NEW YORK

A Del Rey Trade Paperback Original

Copyright © 2005 by Alexander Irvine

Published in the United States by Del Rey Books,
an imprint of The Random House Publishing Group,
a division of Random House, Inc., New York.

DEL REY is a registered trademark and the Del Rey colophon
is a trademark of Random House, Inc.

Library of Congress Cataloging-in-Publication Data
Irvine, Alexander (Alexander C.)
The narrows / Alexander C. Irvine.
p.   cm.
"A Del Rey trade paperback original"—T.p. verso.
ISBN 0-345-46698-5
1. World War, 1939–1945—Michigan—Detroit—Fiction.
2. Detroit (Mich.)—Fiction.   3. Factories—Fiction.
4. Rabbis—Fiction.   5. Golem—Fiction.   I. Title.

PS3609.R85N37   2005
813'.6—dc22

2005041338

Printed in the United States of America

www.delreybooks.com

2 4 6 8 9 7 5 3 1

Book design by Julie Schroeder

THE NARROWS

PROLOGUE

Midnight in the golem factory. Sweat and clay and blisters. Twitching pains in the wrist and the small of the back. The door to Moises' sanctum opens and closes. The motion of Moises' passing bangs the row of hanging platforms together, as if the unlivened molds were thrashing in whatever nightmares afflict clay that knows it must be born.

Twenty-three men work in what is now called Building G, a steel-and-glass afterthought of Albert Kahn's near the center of the Ford River Rouge factory complex, the rusting, monstrous alimentary canal of Henry Ford's empire, taking in raw materials and excreting Model A Fords by the thousand every day. Ford has refused all government contracts to build war matériel for the British, but someone somewhere agreed that Building G could be spared for an odd little project away from the Old Man's increasingly confused oversight. Nobody knows how this happened, and they don't much care as long as it works, which will be determined in about an hour. They think.

Inside Building G, the three-story space is ringed by a catwalk twelve feet above the floor. Two doors off the catwalk lead to over-

passes that in turn connect to other buildings. One of the doors, on
the north wall, is usually under tight surveillance by Building G's
crew because that's where Swerdlow comes from, and it's a poor
bunch of line rats that doesn't know where their supervisor is at all
times. On the ground floor three large bay doors face the train siding outside, and beyond it the canal slip that leads down to the
turning basin and the Rouge River. Spanning the ceiling, a spine of
girders supports a crane-mounted scoop bucket. Clay comes in on
trains, three or four open cars at a time backing down a spur off the
Detroit, Toledo & Ironton Railroad. When the locomotive detaches, someone has to go find a union guy to operate the scoop
bucket; the UAW fought hard to take the Rouge, and with their victory so recent they're hardasses about niggling little details. Usually
this entails a trip down to the canal slip, where the crane operators
gather to play cards and pass a bottle, and the union crane guys
don't at all like having to demean their profession by operating
Building G's little bucket. They draw straws to see who will miss
out on the rest of the liquor. Once the unlucky operator is dra-
gooned and herded back to Building G, the scoop bucket drops
giant clots of streaming, weedy goo onto a screen just inside Building G; the screener comes to life, shaking the bucketloads into
pieces small enough to fall through the screen onto a conveyor belt.
A work detail of a dozen men goes at this steady flow of head-sized
gobs of clay with pick and shovel, breaking it down and pitching it
onto the sorting line still squirming with swamp life. The break-
down and sorting crews are under strict orders to kill as few of
these worms and snails and crawdads as they can manage, on Moises' eccentric theory that the incorporation of these little lives will
make the golems that much stronger and more unpredictable in
battle. Nobody knows if this strategy will pay off, since the Golem
Line has just gone into production today, but every man on the line
has thought at least once that at the end of eight hours of shoveling
clay, it's hard to worry about the lives of snails.

It would be a hell of a lot more efficient to use the same clay pits that provided most of the Rouge's bricks; after all, some of them are still on the property. But even defending the Republic, Henry Ford is a tight man with a dollar. Good brickmaking clay is too useful to divert to a crazy Yid project like making golems, and anyway he's got God's own bounty of the stuff coming out of the swampy parts of the various parcels of Southern Michigan that he's busy turning into an industrial paradise. All of this raw stuff comes with impurities in the form of roots, rocks, rusted bits of metal, and enough cigarette butts to make the Army Air Corps' monthly ration—not to mention frogs, snakes, and occasionally fish, once in a while an unlucky muskrat. If this were a regular industrial operation, all of this stuff would be screened and pressed out of the clay, but Moises isn't rational on the topic, so anything that once had a pulse is supposed to be left on the sorting belt. At the same time the old rabbi is mortally convinced that only detailed human attention will get rid of all bits of metal. "You don't want to see what happens if I raise a golem that has a bent nail still in it," he says. The men on the line—that minority among them, in any case, who aren't refugees or immigrants from Eastern Europe—don't know what to make of Moises. He's skeletal and hunched and speaks English like a bad caricature out of *The Dearborn Independent* or one of Father Coughlin's nightmares, and since this is their first day of operation they haven't actually seen him come up with a golem. If he says that something bad would happen if they left a nail in the clay, though, they're all willing to go along with it.

The sorting crew, half a dozen men, works with trowels and rakes to break the clay down into clots that would fit nicely in your hand. At the end of the conveyor, these clots pass under a magnet with some kind of gadget attached that lights up if they've missed a piece of steel. If the gadget lights up, the belt stops until the sorters find what set it off. Under that part of the belt is a bin full of nails, train sprockets, broken watches, all kinds of stuff. At the end of every shift, they're supposed to roll the bin to the scrapyard behind the blast furnaces.

Every so often, more often than they would have figured given what the clay has been through to get to this point, a live frog springs out of the piles. If Swerdlow isn't in the neighborhood, they stop the line and chase around after it. Whoever catches the frog decides what to do with it; the line is about evenly divided among three opinions. Some hold that the frog should be immobilized in the clay for molding into a golem; others that any frog with the gumption to live through excavation, transport, shoveling, picking, and sorting deserves a get-out-of-jail-free card by way of the canal; still others that the primary function of live frogs is to become frog legs.

Snakes are by common consent preserved to be put into Swerdlow's desk. This is a tradition that predates the golem project, predates even the war. Before the Rouge went union, back in 1938 or so when Swerdlow was one of Harry Bennett's Special Service goons, he had once made a Pole by the name of Czerkawski eat a dead snake right at his station, and then fired him for holding up the line. Then, the old-timers like to say, putting a snake in Swerdlow's desk was like being blooded in combat. There were consequences. Now all he does is charge out of his office and scream at whoever is walking by, but even this small reward is enough to keep the practice alive.

Sorted clay tumbles down an incline to a conveyor that dumps it into a bin. From this bin, it's shoveled out onto long gurneys with shallow outlines of human forms stamped into them. The molding crew is all Jewish and all European; Moises won't have it any other way. Each golem is molded by a single man; if his shift ends while he's working on it, it's supposed to remain unfinished until he comes in the next day. All of this has been worked out over three weeks of retrofitting this empty little corner of the Rouge from its previous function, which to judge by smell had something to do with paint storage. For the last ten days they've done nothing but run through the sorting, screening, and molding processes, with Moises watching from a chair outside the door to his sanctum, which some of the guys on the line have taken to calling the Tabernacle.

Jared Cleaves likes that label. He's got an affinity for the mystical, and he takes a quiet satisfaction from being part of an operation centered on a ten-by-twelve room called the Tabernacle. Satisfaction of any kind is harder to come by today, though, because Jared's wife Colleen is pregnant. They thought they were being careful, they had every intention of waiting until the end of the war; but there you go. The baby's due in November.

Jumping Jesus, a baby. A boy? A girl? He's got to make something of himself. Can't have a kid growing up seeing his old man come home every night covered in riverbottom.

It's riverbottom with a purpose, at least. There aren't many ways that a twenty-six-year-old with no professional skills and two bad fingers on his right hand can contribute to the fight against Hitler and European fascism; Jared remembers with pride the day he was picked out of the line of men waiting outside the Rouge employment office. A midget walked up to him, wearing a tweed overcoat, sunglasses, and a hat. "Someone wants to see you," it said, and led Jared around the corner of the building to a long black custom Lincoln limousine. Jared had never been in a limo before, and hasn't since. Smoked glass partitioned the driver off from the two bench seats in the back, which were black leather tooled with patterns of what looked to Jared's untrained eye like elongated deer. The midget climbed up on the backward-facing seat, and Jared sat on the other and shut the door. "Where are we going?" he asked.

"There's some people at the Rotunda want to see you," the

midget said. It grinned at Jared, showing pointed teeth. So Ford has cannibal pygmies working for him, was Jared's first mystified reaction. Later that day he was to find out that the situation was—and is—much stranger than that.

The ride in the limo was short, just out across Miller Road and around onto Rotunda Drive, where Ford world headquarters stood like a monument to the future. Jared never saw the driver, and he wondered if the limo had extended pedals and a custom seat for a cannibal pygmy chauffeur . . . or maybe he just remembers wondering that. Jared Cleaves is a guy who sometimes has trouble differentiating what he really saw from the strata of recollection he later lays unintentionally over original events. Down in the subterranean parking lot, the limo eased to a stop and the pygmy led Jared along a row of parked Lincolns. "Harry Bennett's office," it said as they passed a frosted-glass door. "Makes it easier for him to meet the Sicilians." The pygmy had a slight lisp, which Jared belatedly attributed to its filed teeth. Then they were in an elevator, and then another hall, this one curving to the left. Everything was antiseptically clean. An air of efficiency and confidence radiated from the groups of suited men they passed, bantering about money and baseball. Nobody gave Jared or the pygmy a second look. "Wait in here. I'll be right back," the pygmy said, leaving Jared in a conference room, where he took a cigarette from a crystal jar and lit it with a silver-plated Ronson while he waited for whoever it was wanted to see him. A copy of the *Free Press* lay on the table, which threw Jared for a loop since he would have figured Ford executives for *Times* men. He smoked the cigarette and read about Hitler's latest outrages and the Tigers' loss to the Senators the day before. When he'd read all he cared to, he went to the window and looked south over the monstrous expanse of the Rouge, the steelworks and glass-rolling plant and turning basin carved into the Rouge River, the old Dearborn Assembly building, and the power station that fed parts of

Detroit and Dearborn in addition to the plant itself. The miles of railroad track, the acres of parking lots. If you were Henry Ford, and you could look out your office window at this, you could sleep at night knowing that you had damn well done something that people would remember.

Two men came in, along with the pygmy. They sat across the table from Jared and eyeballed him for an uncomfortable length of time. Each wore a black suit and a black tie, with a gold stickpin. The only difference between them was the amount of gray in their hair; the one on the left had none, while the one on the right was salt-and-pepper with a receding hairline. They looked like photographs of the same person taken fifteen years apart. "You sure?" the one on the left finally asked the pygmy.

"Hell, yes," the pygmy said. "It practically stinks, it's so thick on him."

"Hm," said the balding one.

"Mr. Cleaves," said the one on the left. "May I call you Jared?"

"Sure," Jared said. "But I don't know your names."

"I'm afraid it's going to stay that way. This is going to sound a bit strange, but do you have any family history of . . ." He trailed off and looked at the balding one.

"Where are you from, Jared?"

"I was born in Ypsilanti, and lived around here mostly except some time in Flat Rock."

"Where did your parents come from?"

"My father's from Detroit. My mother came up from Arkansas right at the end of the war."

"That would be the Great War?" Jared nodded. "Grandparents?"

"We're getting off track here," the one on the left said.

"Jared," continued the balding one. "Is there any history of clairvoyance or herbalism, folk healing and such, in your family?"

"Clair-what?"

The pygmy snickered.

"Let's cut to the chase here," the one on the left said. "How did you hurt your fingers?"

Without meaning to, Jared slipped his right hand from the table-top down into his lap. "Car accident," he said. "When I was a kid."

The pygmy started laughing out loud. It took off its sun-glasses to wipe its eyes, and Jared did a double take worthy of Curly Howard. Its eyes were pearl white, and before Jared averted his eyes he would have sworn he'd seen a little pattern of scales around the bridge of its nose.

Tattoo, he told himself. Guy files his teeth, he's going to have tattoos. He looked down into his lap and hid his fingers even from himself. "Why's he laughing?" Jared asked. It came out sullen. "I was in a car accident."

"He'll work for sure," the pygmy said.

"What we're looking for," the balding one said, "is people who have a family history of odd events. Things you wouldn't necessarily tell anyone else. Arthur here picked you out of the line of men over there"—he nodded in the direction of the window, and the rusted and sooty splendor of the Rouge beyond—"and told us that you were such a person."

Jared didn't say a word. *Things you wouldn't necessarily tell anyone else* was goddamn right.

"All you have to do is say no," the one on the left said, "and we'll put you right back in line."

Jared didn't say a word. After a silence interrupted by periodic giggles from the pygmy, both of the black-suited men began to ex-plain what they wanted Jared to do. He could hardly say no.

The guys on either side of Jared both have the same Rotunda story—not that Jared knows the details, which nobody talks about—but otherwise are about as different as two men can be. Jem, on his left, is pure hillbilly, from the coal country in eastern Kentucky. Eighteen years old, with a chip on his shoulder over his father being killed in a mine strike and memories of boiling shoe leather and grass for soup still fresh in his head. Jem is spoiling for a chance to get a snake into Swerdlow's desk. He swears he'll write his name on it first. Opposite Jem is Felton, who in Jared's estimate is about forty years old, been to one of the Negro colleges in the South and then come home to Detroit. Once Jared asked Felton why he was breaking up clay with a college degree, and Felton said it was better than working in the foundry. Which wasn't really any kind of answer at all.

The three of them form a kind of pod on the sorting line since they're just about the only native speakers of English in Building G, unless Swerdlow drops by to slander them all as malingering gold-bricks who by Gawd he ought to report as fifth columnists. Swerdlow seems to think America's already in the war—an odd conviction given the Old Man's public statement that he doesn't believe there's a war at all. It's a concoction of the bankers, is Henry Ford's position on the war in Europe, and he won't divert a man-hour or a lump of coal from the Ford Motor Company's mission to create better living through internal combustion. Somewhere in the middle is the truth, at least as far as Jared knows it: there is a war, but they're not in it. If they were, he for damn sure wouldn't be troweling clay. He'd be in uniform. His keeps his Selective Service registration folded in his wallet. And anyway, if anyone was going to report one of the boys in Building G, it would be the razor-cut gent in the black suit who stops by every day to look down from the catwalk and then step into Moises' office for a quick word. "If that ain't a spy," Felton says, "you can call me Franco."

Typically Jem and Jared call him Franco for an hour or so after every one of these appearances, just on general principles. Today, however, the spy comes and goes unnoticed by Jared because the only thought in his head is *Jumping Jesus, a baby.*

"Fellas," he says, "I have news."

"Roosevelt resigned," Jem says.

"Harry Bennett got religion," Felton says.

"Better," Jared says. "Colleen's in a family way."

Felton shakes his head. "Good Lord. Another Cleaves." He sticks out his hand and Jared shakes it, the pressure of Felton's grip sparking an ache in his damaged ring and pinkie fingers. Jem pounds him on the back. Behind them, the molders look up in puzzlement and ask each other questions in five or six languages.

Jem turns around and spreads his arms. "Jared Cleaves is having a baby, y'all!" he announces. "A baby!" He makes a cradle of his arms and swings it back and forth, and a cheer rises from the molders and the four other guys on the sorting line. Jared realizes he has a goofy smile on his face, and the realization makes him blush. He turns back to the belt and picks up his trowels.

Someone taps him on the arm, and Jared turns to see that it's Moises himself. He has, for no good reason, a moment of pure panic, as if he's just been touched by the Angel of Death. Then, when his heart starts beating again, he says, "Hey, Moises," thinking, what'd I do?

"You have a baby," Moises said. "Is a happy thing. Mazel tov."

Jared's nodding. "Thanks, yeah. Mazel tov to you, too."

Moises cracks a smile and shuffles back to his chair. Jared pries a tangle of roots and what looks like the eyelet of a boot out of a piece of clay. He's distracted with thoughts of pregnancy and fatherhood, and feels like the hands in front of him wielding tools belong to somebody else—until, that is, he gets a rusty fishhook through his left thumb. Then they're his hands, all right. He stomps around for a while cussing. "Can't talk like that when your baby's born," Jem says. "Shouldn't talk like that anyway."

"Shut up. I don't need no Bible-thumping hillbilly telling me how to talk."

"You got your shots?" Felton asks.

Jared is hunched over his injured hand, slowly working the fishhook the rest of the way through. "Goddammit. Yeah. I had my shots."

"Hate to see you get lockjaw with a baby on the way."

"Well, at least he wouldn't cuss around the baby," Jem says, and breaks up at his joke.

"Jem, I'm about to stick this fishhook in your eye, you don't shut up," Jared growls.

Swerdlow chooses this moment to appear. "Come on, ladies. . . . Cleaves, you got something better to do than make golems?" He notices Jared pressing his thumb against the one dry spot on his coveralls. "Fingers hurt, Cleaves? Poor baby."

"Jared stuck a fishhook through his thumb," Jem says.

"Oh no," Swerdlow says. "A fishhook, give him a Purple Heart and send him home. Boy gets a fishhook in the thumb, he's done his duty. Gawd. What a bunch of goldbricks." He throws up his hands in disgust and leaves.

Jared is wishing he had some kind of death-ray vision. He wills it to happen, focusing on a mole just above Jem's left eyebrow. "Why can't you keep your mouth shut?" he says.

Jem gets sullen. "I was explaining."

"All right," Felton says. "How about we make some golems?"

They were supposed to be home an hour ago now, but nobody wants to leave without seeing whether it'll work. Earlier, the clay came in late because of a short wildcat strike by railroad switchmen on the Detroit, Toledo & Ironton; then the magnetic directional doodad malfunctioned and Moises shut the whole line down until an electrician could come over from the power station and clean it. So now, at a little after one in the morning, they all stand caked in riverbottom, fiddling with their tools, a little nervous at the silence that has fallen in the building. Sixteen vaguely human-shaped piles of clay lie on sixteen gurneys, which is all they have. A Hungarian by the name of Ferenc pushes one of them over to the far wall, where a series of hooks hangs from a track on the ceiling. Ferenc hooks four of them through the rings welded onto each corner of the gurney. With each group of four hooks dangles a switch; he throws it, and the gurney rises up about six feet off the ground. When Ferenc rings a bell on the wall of Moises' office, a portion of the office wall slides open. With a rattle the gurney moves through the opening, and the wall closes behind it.

The men wonder aloud how long it will take, in five or six languages. It's a different experience for them, at least for the majority of them who have come from a Europe where war is a reality rather than an ambivalently contemplated possible future. Swerdlow reappears up on the catwalk, and even he is curious enough that he doesn't immediately scream at them to get the line moving again. The Golem Line isn't strictly a Ford project—Henry Ford is maybe the last man in Detroit, except Father Coughlin, who would put his own money into Jewish magic, and Ford has resisted Roosevelt's efforts to get him building engines for British bombers. Somebody somewhere had enough clout to carve out this little piece of the Rouge for a secret enterprise in kabbalistic magic, over Ford's farm boy outrage. It's subcontracted by some military agency or other, nobody is sure who; Swerdlow probably knows, and just as probably is holding back. The men on the line are quietly glad to see him. They hate him, but he's their leader, and deep down they want him to have feelings like they do. After a few minutes of watching them watch Moises' door, Swerdlow gets impatient. "If you ain't going to run the line," he growls, "at least get this place clean for the men who'll be here in the morning."

* * *

Looking over their shoulders at the Tabernacle, Building G's night crew take their tools over to the long sinks that line the wall near the ground-floor doorway opposite the scoop bucket. Apart from any interest in whether Moises will actually create a golem, they all know that nobody will be in there in the morning if the kabbalistic hocus-pocus doesn't work. So they go to the sinks, Jews from countries where there aren't any Jews anymore, hillbillies from Kentucky, Finns and Cousin Jacks from up north, and even a few men who grew up in Detroit. None of them is quite sure what Moises will do, and Moises has sworn to kill anyone who opens the door while he's got a mold in there. While they sweep and hose and scrub, every man in the room listens. Restaurant-style spray nozzles hang like dying steel-and-rubber sunflowers; Jared cranks the hot water up all the way and blasts clay down the drains that empty into the canal slip. A billion little silty bits of Washtenaw County, Jared thinks, finding their way to the Detroit River, and maybe after that Lake Erie and the St. Lawrence and who knows, maybe someday all the way to Europe, arriving transformed like the golems themselves, if there ever are any golems. At the end of eight hours breaking up gobs of clay, these are the kind of thoughts that run through Jared's head; the blast of the water and the steam rising in his face wrap him up in a sensory cocoon, and he falls into an easy reverie. A baby. There's a thousand babies born every day, maybe every hour. It's the most natural thing in the world—but he has a bone-deep conviction that it is happening to him in a way that it's never happened to anyone else. His Selective Service notice weighs a ton in his back pocket. If there's a war, how long will it last? What will he miss?

Jared starts imagining what the baby will be like when it's real, when it cries and waves its stubby hands and grabs on to his finger like he knows it will. Please let it change me, he thinks. I'll still just be a guy who spends his days breaking up clay, but I'll have a baby. He won't care about my fingers.

"Hey, Felton," Jem says. Jared looks up and blinks the steam out of his eyes. Jem is standing by the magnetic doodad. They check it at the end of every shift. "Did you turn this off?" Jem asks, and that's when all hell breaks loose.

There's a shout from Moises, and a roar that rattles every window in Building G. Bang—a huge dent appears in the tin wall of Moises' office next to the door. Bang—the dent bulges outward. And bang—the whole sheet of tin leaps away from its frame and a golem charges out onto the floor.

Something about the golem raises the hairs on the back of Jared's neck. Maybe it's the skin the color of old plaster, maybe the eyes like a drowned man's, maybe the just-askew motions of the body as it walks and turns its head to take in its surroundings. There's a charge coming off it, like the psychic equivalent of whacking your funny bone. It twitches; its head rolls back and forth as if it doesn't know how to move its eyes; and when it bangs into one of the empty gurneys, it rears back and slaps the gurney all the way across the floor to bang into the sorting line. Then a strange calm falls over it as it notices the expanse of concrete floor and the cluster of men around the sinks. Its head lowers and it walks toward them.

There are moments when you don't have to understand a language to know what someone is saying. This is one of them, as half a dozen versions of *Let's get the hell out of here* tangle in the weirdly charged air. People scatter, and the golem must be getting used to its body because it moves with sudden decision and focus, barely missing Ferenc before the Hungarian makes it out the door and down the railroad tracks, trailing a string of gibberish that Jared doesn't think is words even in Hungarian. This diversion gets nearly everyone else enough room to clear the building; even Jem and

Felton hightail it out through the bay doors facing the canal slip. Swerdlow is long gone out the catwalk door.

Jared can't take his eyes off the golem. It veers away from the door Ferenc went through and bangs into a nearly finished mold. An expression of odd confusion passes over its face, and it scoops up a handful of clay. For a long moment it works the clay in its palm; bits fall to the floor. Then the golem stuffs the handful of clay in its mouth. Jared has a dislocated memory of his mother, maybe? grouching at his little cousin Chucky. *God, kids like you, you'll put anything in your mouths.* The golem is distracted. It chews the clay, looking thoughtful.

Over its shoulder Jared sees Moises emerging from the shambles of the Tabernacle. He doesn't look injured, but he walks with the slow rigidity of a man so afraid of what he must do that he has absented himself from his own mind so that he may do it. While the golem munches the almost-flesh of its—brother? cousin?—Moises walks toward it like a man sleepwalking, and as if soothing it rubs a hand down the left side of its forehead. Until then, Jared hasn't noticed the letters inscribed over the golem's eyebrow; now he's taken with the way it looks strange as Moises obliterates the fourth letter. *Truth* becomes *dead,* and with its mouth open, weedy clay dribbling down its chin, the golem collapses into a heap of riverbottom.

You'll put anything in your mouths. Jared's mother's voice won't leave his head.

Moises takes a long, shuddering breath. Then he crouches next to the remains of the golem, taking an old man's care getting his balance on his haunches. His hands slide over the heap of dead clay, and pause. He digs one hand into the clay and comes up with a chunk of rusty metal. He holds it out in one upturned palm and with the other hand points an accusatory finger at Jared. "You. Thinking of baby," he says. "You don't pay attention."

A rifle shell? A nail from the sole of a boot? A belt buckle? Holy moly, Jared thinks. Moises was right. He is also hoping that the next golem turns out better than this one did. But when he opens his mouth, what comes out is, "The magnetic thing is broken."

Moises throws the piece of metal at him. It misses, pinging off the wall over the sinks. He stands there for another moment, then returns to his office. A moment passes. Then the chains rattle and the crane motor groans, and another gurney passes inside. If Jared took three steps to his right, he'd be able to see what was happening. Right then, though, that's the last thing in the world he wants to see.

"Hey, uh, Moises?" he calls. "If the magnet's busted, you sure you should do that?"

No answer.

He understands, not with any great flash of insight but with quiet satisfaction, as if he's made a perfect tracing of his own face in a mirror. The hell with whatever Swerdlow is going to say, or whatever news gets across to the Rotunda—Moises is making offspring, and through them making his dream of a world risen from the broken rubble of the Europe that cast him out. One little piece of metal, one clay-buster who can't pay attention, makes no difference.

Various sorters and molders are coming back in. Jem and Felton peer in through the bay door. "Where'd it go?" Jem asks.

Everyone's looking at Jared, and he feels like he should say something, but he's filled up. Again he opens his mouth with no idea what will fall out.

"I'll be damned," Jared says. But what he's thinking is that fatherhood is going to be a hell of a thing.

It is October 27, 1940, and the Frankenline is up and running.

CHAPTER 1

At three minutes before three o'clock on Tuesday, as Jared is buttoning up his coveralls in the locker room, Felton comes in and says, "Draft Marshal's here again."

Jared slams his locker and heads for the stairwell that leads up to the overpass from Building G over the scrap bins to a parts-recovery division, where broken parts are either retooled or sent back to the furnaces. Sure enough, the Draft Marshal's black Lincoln limousine is parked diagonally across two of the loading docks. He does this just to piss off Swerdlow, who can be counted on to come out of his office and rail about the Marshal jamming up the works. Swerdlow's got to be careful, though; the Marshal has the authority to pick men right off the line and disappear them into the OEI office. He's the reason they're all here; he's also connected, and he's also vindictive. Swerdlow has to yell or he'll look like he doesn't care enough about production efficiency, but he can't yell too much or he'll look like he's sheltering his men at the expense of troop strength at the front.

The guys on the Frankenline read the papers, and they listen to the radio, and they get stories from the returning vets who wash up at the Rouge. Today Winchell says that II Corp has finished off the Axis forces in Tunisia, but who knows? Everything they get is filtered in one way or another, and they know this, so their real sense of how the war is going comes from one source only. When the Draft Marshal comes through more than once a month, it means the OEI is twitchy, and that means things aren't so hot. Jared runs through his memory. He thinks it's been eight days. The back of his neck starts to prickle. He punches in and relieves Morten Gutersen, who as usual hasn't kept the station's tools clean. Irritation with Morten's dumb laziness takes Jared's mind off the Draft Marshal for the two minutes it takes him to hose off the trowel and rake. By the time he's back to the line, the Draft Marshal is coming out onto the catwalk.

The Draft Marshal is huge, bursting from his ancient uniform with its spangling of medals from San Juan Hill or some other mythological place. One of the Czechs over in the glassworks calls him Sergeant Vanek, after a character in a novel Jared's never read. Jared has a standing request of God that the catwalk will fail under the Draft Marshal's weight; he reconciles his hatred by categorizing the Draft Marshal's many evil qualities. Pomposity, snobbery, bloodlust, avarice, and so on. Individually they don't merit a sudden death, but Jared's a big believer in collective assessment when it comes to sin. The Draft Marshal is flanked by weak-chinned adjutants with clipboards, and his cold blue gaze falls on Jared as they pass overhead. Fourteen times the Draft Marshal has come in and marched along the catwalk before leaving Building G to plague the other lines. Each time he has looked at Jared, and each time Jared prays to be taken and prays to be left. After two years of hacking clay apart, the bloom is definitively off the rose of working on a secret munitions project. Jared's tired of feeling ashamed whenever he sees real soldiers.

The Frankenline grinds to a stop while the Draft Marshal conducts his appraisal; it's just impossible to work while he's up there dictating notes to his flunkies, and anyway the shift change is just finished. Swerdlow storms in screaming that the Marshal is killing fine American boys in Europe and the Pacific by stopping the lines to waddle along the catwalk looking for malingerers who aren't there. The Marshal ignores him, which is also part of the pageant. Jared is comforted a little by the sameness of it all.

Then the Marshal says, "That one there," and Jared knows it's him. "You. What's your name?"

Jared looks up at him. "Jared Cleaves."

"Why aren't you at the front, Cleaves?"

Jared holds up his right hand. The ring and pinkie fingers are crooked. When he wiggles the other fingers and thumb, the two fingers move from the knuckle only. They have strength enough, but he can barely bend them. "Nerve damage," he says. "I can't hold a rifle."

"Two fingers are holding you out of this war?" The Marshal draws the words out, freights them with contempt.

"I've been to the draft board every six months. Every time they turn me down." Shame heats up on Jared's face. Every recitation of those bare facts is like confessing to robbing a blind old woman. There's also the little matter of him not supposed to be going to the draft board, since the Frankenline is an essential wartime project with OEI stamped all over it, and even if the draft board wanted him they wouldn't take him—but nobody can blame a man for wanting to serve.

"We'll find something for you. Report first thing in the morning," the Marshal says. He pivots with some grace and locks eyes with Swerdlow, holding the gaze as he walks trailed by his flunkies out the door.

The Jeweler walks up to Jared with a wide grin and his hand extended to shake. Jared feints, then pulls his hand back for the traditional smoothing of the hair, prompting a burst of laughter. It's not so much that what he's done is funny, more that when the Marshal leaves, the men of the Frankenline overreact to everything until they've purged their tension. The handshake gag is already Frankenline tradition, since nobody shakes the Jeweler's hand.

The molders revolted against Moises' dictum that a single man had to make a golem from start to finish when the rabbi demanded they make the golems what the textbooks called anatomically correct. "What the hell," Jem wondered at the time. "We haven't made no women golems." It hadn't made any sense to them then, and still doesn't, but Moises stood his ground and finally a tubby Latvian whose name Jared never learned was elected to specialize in golem family jewels. Immediately Felton dubbed him the Jeweler, and all kinds of superstitions sprang up around him. They didn't shake his hand, they learned all of the Eastern European slang words for *queer,* they bought him a loupe at Hanukkah after Felton went and looked up when it was. The Jeweler took it all in good humor, or pretended to, because the other molders paid him ten dollars a week for his trouble; everybody else just chalked it up as one more thing about Moises that a rational man couldn't figure out.

Jared finishes his shift in a state of near exaltation. For a second time he has been tapped by the Draft Marshal, who everyone knows was behind the original selection of the Frankenline's crew. This is the big leagues, Jared thinks. I've been groomed. I'm ready.

Is he ever. The initial thrill of taking part in a top secret project to slow Hitler's advance across Europe—and using the magic of the *Untermensch* to do it—has long since worn off during the two and a half years Jared has been busting clay. When he started work on the Frankenline, the war was distant; now it is every day's headlines. Jared knows four men who have died, one in Tunisia and three in the South Pacific. He doesn't want to join their company, but he wants to be able to tell his daughter Emily that his service to the free world involved more than troweling clay and hosing out freight cars. And he's man enough to admit that he's rankled by the fact that his wife has a better job than he does. Colleen strips damaged engines at Willow Run; she's in the UAW, she makes more money than he does, and he can't even tell her the details of what he does. Sometimes being in on a national secret doesn't quite make up for all of that.

Jem and Felton drag him out after work to a bar Felton knows in Hamtramck across from Dodge Main. It isn't clear how Felton knows a bar in Hamtramck, where bored gangs of teenage Poles spend their evenings looking for coloreds to beat up, but that's Felton for you. The only Negroes in this part of Detroit come to work at the Dodge plant and get the hell out when the whistle blows, especially now that Poletown's all riled up about the Sojourner Truth housing project out on Fenelon. Maybe Felton worked at the plant? Jared doesn't know. Whoever runs the bar either doesn't know that Prohibition was repealed or is waiting for it to be reinstated; from the outside, all you see is a blank door in a windowless part of an apartment house. Walk in, and you find cable-spool tables, a bar hammered together out of scrap lumber by a carpenter unconcerned with finish work, and two or three gloomy survivors of another second shift building tanks. Large swaths of the plaster walls are rotted away, with newspaper pages thumbtacked straight to the wall studs. Their corners ruffle as the door closes behind Jared, and he's thinking to himself that he'll be lucky to finish a beer before the whole building falls down. Some place for a sendoff to the war.

"Look smart, here!" Jem shouts. "Our boy Jared is off to the war tomorrow, by God! Let's show him a good time tonight!"

Somehow this works. As if Jem has sent out a homing signal for anyone within ten blocks who's thirsty and wants to show Jared Cleaves a good time—which might be the case, since Jem is one leather-lunged hillbilly and his voice probably carried through the heating ducts into every apartment in the building—all of a sudden people are crowding through the door. Glasses tall and small come to their table. The music gets loud, some women show up, people dance. Jem has performed a mystifying act of conjuration. The goodwill is thick enough that nobody even complains about Felton being in Hamtramck. The women want to dance with Jared, and he goes along with it even though he doesn't like dancing. He likes the feel of a body close to his, though, and the way things are with Colleen lately . . .

Alcohol gives Jared a kind of safety hatch when his thoughts turn in that direction. The hatch clangs down now, and he relaxes into the succession of embraces, the brush of hip and hip, the slide of a partner's breasts across his chest—and the look in her eyes as she watches his reaction. He won't go with one of them, of course not; no man has ever been as married as Jared Cleaves. That doesn't stop him from enjoying the sweetness of the desire. Later the girls go home, and as Jared and Jem and Felton head for the door the bartender reminds them to keep Felton east of Woodward—but not too far east—if they don't want trouble. Felton says something back to the bartender that Jared doesn't quite catch, and the bartender is still laughing when the door bangs shut behind them.

They drop Felton at his place in Paradise Valley, in a four-story building with a jazz club called El Sino on the ground floor. Music is still coming from the open door when Felton hops out of Jem's car. "Give them Japs hell, boy," Felton says, and then he's gone.

"Goddamn, ain't Detroit a hell of a place." Jem is laughing as they head down toward Grand Circus Park and across to Fort Street. "A nigger just called you boy."

"That's not a nigger, that's Felton," Jared says.

"I take your point, but still. Detroit is a hell of a place." Jem roars down Fort Street past the old train depot, squealing his tires around the corners that lead to Jared's house. Jared weaves up his sidewalk, head full of the squeal of tires and whoever it was he heard on the radio talking about conserving rubber: *Is this trip necessary?*

Then he's home, to the silence of Colleen and Emily sleeping. Jared stands inside the door, inhaling the silence. The house smells like baking, and he goes into the kitchen, where sugar cookies sit in rows on spread towels. Colleen, possessor of a ferocious sweet tooth and corresponding dedication to baking, churns out cookies of every variety whenever she can get the sugar; must have been a good day for shopping. Jared eats one cookie, and then another, and then regrets both as the beer in his stomach reacts with the sugar. A belch rises in him. Trying to stifle it, he shoots it up into his nose instead. Eyes watering and nose burning, he drinks a glass of water and remembers to take his boots off before his footsteps wake Colleen. Emily sleeps the sleep of a two-year-old; she wouldn't wake up if he blew a trumpet in her room. Moving with the painstaking care of the experienced drunk—one of the few useful things he has learned from his father—Jared removes his boots and leaves them on the back stoop. He pauses in the open doorway, looking out into his postage-stamp backyard. A lot of work to be done back there. For a minute he almost decides to go weed out the flower beds, fix a hole in the fence, restring the clothesline after one of the neighbor kids snapped it last week. Now that he's going to go into the Marshal's service for real, he hates the idea of leaving it for Colleen to do.

He'll have to take a streetcar down to the recruiting office. And Colleen's going to give him hell in the morning; she'll know exactly why the car isn't home even if he spends an hour showering and eating cloves. Hell with it, Jared thinks. I did it. I'll take the medicine. Something else he learned from his father. He shuts the back door, softly, and unbuttons his shirt as he walks slowly down the hall toward the bed he shares with his sleeping wife.

Tonight, his dreams begin with his father.

Marty Cleaves had been a Ford roadman for nearly six years in 1919, when Highland Park was spitting out Model Ts like watermelon seeds at a Belle Isle picnic, Henry Ford was building the Rouge on the land where he'd watched birds as a boy, and Ford dealerships were sprouting up all over the country. Everyone said that the roadmen's day was over, that to sell cars you needed to prowl the parking lot of a dealership and rope credulous Polack steelworkers in off the street. Marty Cleaves had been a roadman since 1912, though, with a yearlong break to serve in the American Expeditionary Force in France, and he figured he knew how to sell cars.

He also knew how to make the roadman's life work for him in other ways. Prohibition came early to Michigan, in 1918, and rum-running became the dark sister of the auto industry. Each needed the other: the Black Hand, and later the Purple Gang, needed cars and trucks to move their goods from Canada, and the teetotaler Ford needed liquor to smooth the minds of the men who broke their bodies in his factories, abrade their discontent so they didn't notice that the Five-Dollar Day came at the cost of hands maimed in presses, backs torn heaving axles, fingers grown crooked and stiff from performing the same motion a thousand times a week. Ford took no liquor, but he let Harry Bennett lubricate his Special Service with Volstead nectar so they wouldn't get introspective while they bloodied union agitators with ax handles and tire chains.

Prohibition also kept Marty Cleaves alive as a roadman. When he picked up his latest car from the freightyard behind the paper mill off LeForge Avenue in Ypsilanti, where the Michigan Central wound along the Huron River, Marty also made sure to stop by a certain farmhouse off Munger Road south of town. Then he roared off, usually west on Michigan Avenue, the longest road in America, toward Saline or Clinton, Jackson, once even as far as Battle Creek. His real destinations were the villages in between, places too small for a dealership and too far off the beaten path to make the trip to the nearest Ford franchise easy. Quart bottles clinked on the floorboards next to the gas cans Marty kept handy on long trips. He'd stop every so often along the way, at a machine shop or small factory that turned out furniture or nails or paint, timing his arrival to a shift change, when the men were tired and looking for something to take their minds off the fact that the next day they'd be back doing it all again. In the smallest burgs the Model T itself would be enough to draw a knot of interested men, and while they opened the hood and poked their callused fingers at the engine or the planetary transmission, Marty Cleaves put his tongue to work. It was a rare day that he didn't empty the car of quart bottles before he sold the car itself. Alcohol was the informal combustion that drove Marty Cleaves' livelihood. It fired men's dreams and threw off recklessness like waste heat.

And rum-running was Detroit's oldest industry, older even than furs. Cadillac had been a bootlegger, after all; after him, Lewis Cass' rum and Joseph Campau's whiskey made the city run when its factories turned out stoves and carriage bodies instead of cars and steel.

When Marty sold the car, after a day or two or sometimes three, he rode in the passenger seat while the new owner drove him, lurching inexpertly on the Model T's planetary transmission, to the nearest train station, where Marty rode back to Ypsilanti to do it all over again.

Jared went with him for the first time in July 1919, a few days after his fifth birthday. His father had meant the trip as a birthday present, but the car didn't show up on time. On this day they roared through Depot Town and south to the farmhouse, where the barn door slid open before they'd turned off Munger Road into the winding dirt driveway. Inside the barn, Jared's father shut the car off and got out. "Stay here," he said.

Smells of hay and manure, oil and exhaust, a drift of cigarette smoke. Shafts of dusty light fell from windows set high in the walls. Up in the rafters a bird fluttered. Shadows resolved themselves into three men coming out of one of the empty stables, each carrying an open-topped box full of bottles. The boxes went behind Jared's seat, and one of the men said, "Hey, kid."

Jared looked over his shoulder into a stubbly face and a fall of black hair. The man winked. "Don't take any wooden nickels," he said, and chucked Jared under the chin. His accent stayed in Jared's mind long after his father had gotten back in the car and driven them out the other side of the barn and back toward Michigan Avenue.

They turned east instead of west, and Jared looked up at his father. He knew Dad's territory was west and south. "Where we going, Dad?"

"Thumbward!" his father said. "I'm gonna try something new today. Plus there's a show in Mount Clemens I want you to see."

Where was Mount Clemens? In Jared's mind, he could see the big mitten of Michigan. He knew where Ypsilanti was on it, and Detroit, and Ann Arbor was next to Ypsilanti, but the rest of the state was blank. Canada was near Detroit, he knew, and there was talk of a bridge.

"Fun town, Mount Clemens," his father said. "Spas, lots of girls. Before I married your mother I used to go up there when I had something needed curing."

Half an hour later they turned south and drove for a little while, windows down, enjoying the smells of forest and farm. Jared's father whistled a tune that was on the radio a lot. Jared practiced whistling, too. He was getting better at it. They made a turn and stopped. "Look at that," Jared's father said. "River Rouge."

When Jared has this dream, which is often, his dreaming mind awakens a little at this point. The Rouge in 1919 was one huge steel-framed assembly building and a blast furnace nestled against the rebuilt river. With the windows rolled down, they could hear the roar of the furnace. At this point in the dream Jared thinks: I can still hear that. He rolls over in his sleep, looking for Colleen.

"Biggest factory in the world," Jared's father said. They drove on, through Detroit, past Navin Field, and north to Mount Clemens on Route 25. Traffic jammed up as they came into the center of town. The park next to the courthouse was covered with cars, and clusters of photographers erupted in flashes whenever someone entered or left the courthouse itself. The day was sunny and hot; everywhere Jared looked were white shirts sweated through at armpits and between shoulder blades. Hot, curious men, lounging in the shade and waiting for something to happen.

A blast of music distracted him, and when Jared tracked it to its source he saw something that in the stroke of an instant made the world a hundred times bigger. A troupe of dark-skinned men and a few women paraded around the park. The men wore tight black pants and pointed hats with huge brims; the women were in white dresses with colorful embroidery. At the front of the group were five men playing horns and guitars and singing.

"Those are Mexicans," his father said. "Old Henry Ford has himself tied up in a lawsuit, and he's got these Mexicans up here parading around to impress the reporters."

Jared watched the procession. "What's a lawsuit?"

"Some newspaper said something about Ford he didn't like, and now he's trying to make them pay for it."

Jared mulled this over. Talking could cost money. He wondered if he'd ever said anything that someone would want money for, and then he wondered if he'd have to get Mexicans to play horns.

"That's what money gets you," Jared's father said. They drove on, north and east out of Mount Clemens. Pretty soon they were out into farmland again, and Jared never did see a mountain.

Five or six times they stopped along the road, wherever there was a group of men or a shop with cars parked in front. Jared's father talked and laughed, and men reached into the car and took bottles from behind Jared's seat. Some of them said, "Hey, kid," like the man in the barn. Some of them ruffled his hair. All day they drove, until sometime in the afternoon they got to a town on the edge of the biggest lake Jared had ever seen. It was a bright day, and hot. The water went on forever, dotted by rowboats close to shore and sailboats farther out, and near the horizon the low gray shape of a cargo ship. Jared's father explained to him the difference. "That freighter, she's probably on the way to the Rouge," his father said. "I'll bet she's loaded up with iron ore from the UP. Remember that tall building with the smokestacks? That's a blast furnace. Put iron ore and coke in it, and some limestone, and you get steel. Henry Ford owns that plant, the Rouge. If he ain't the richest man in the world, he will be. Pretty soon all his cars'll be built there. He'll bring iron from the UP and Wisconsin, coal from Kentucky, rubber from Brazil, timber from up north. Feed it all in one end, out the other you'll see a Model T." Something in his father's voice changed. "Be so damn many cars on the road that he won't need roadmen, that's for sure."

They were leaning against the side of the car, and Jared's father reached past him to pick a bottle out of the last box. He uncorked it and took a swallow. "This town is called Port Austin. All the way out at the tip of the thumb. 'Bout a half hour from now they're going to call it a day at a machine shop down the road. Bet you a nickel I sell the rest of this liquor, and bet you another I sell the car, too."

He stuck out his hand. "I don't have a nickel, Pop," Jared said.

"We'll make it what we call a gentlemen's bet. You can owe me the nickel, or the dime. I won't try to collect too soon." His father grinned, and so did Jared, even though he was thinking about how a bet was another kind of talking that cost money.

"Okay," he said, and stuck out his hand. They shook.

The bottle was nearly half gone by the time the whistle blew at the machine shop. Jared's father put the car into gear and rolled up to the side of the building. Five minutes later all the other bottles were gone, and Jared's father was folding a roll of money into the pocket of his coat. Sometimes when you talked it cost other people money, Jared thought.

"You broke even, kid. No hooch left, but I couldn't get one of them halfwits to cough up a down payment on this car. So I owe you a nickel and you owe me a nickel. Let's drink to it." He tipped the bottle to his mouth, and then handed it to Jared. "One little sip, son, and don't ever tell your mother about this. She'd have me on the road for good. But my daddy told me, and I'm telling you: it's good to get to know the demon early. Go ahead."

The bottle was heavy in Jared's hands. He held it with two hands the way his mother always told him to hold a glass, and tilted it slowly. Even before the liquor touched his tongue, his eyes were watering from the smell of it. It was the worst thing he'd ever tasted, crawling like fire over his tongue and up into his nose. He coughed it out, then breathed in too quick and got a noseful of it again. His father snatched the bottle away before Jared could drop it, and then thumped him on the back until he'd stopped coughing. "There you go, kid. There you go. Now you know to stay away from the stuff. That's one way you don't want to be like your old man."

Jared barely heard him. He was rubbing the sleeve of his shirt across his tongue, trying to scrub away the taste. His nose was running, too, and he swiped the snot away. His father put the cork back in the bottle and stuck it between Jared's legs while he got out to crank the car. When it was running, he tossed the crank in the back and they drove on. The sun was setting, and Jared started to get mad when he saw that his father was trying not to laugh. "It's not funny," he said.

"No, you're right. It's not. I'm sorry, son. I was just thinking that I did the same exact thing when your grandpa gave me my first taste. Wish I'd listened to him."

And here dreaming Jared remembers all the nights he's spent in bars, and is shamed at repeating his father's mistake. His shoulders hunch, and Colleen reaches behind her to rest a hand on his thigh. It's night, and now it's night in the dream, too.

The road was narrow and straight, trees close on either side. The bottle was empty. Jared's father whistled an aimless melody. When it trailed off he said, "You don't mind sleeping in the car, do you?"

The rush of summer air past the windows made Jared sleepy. He shook his head.

"Good, 'cause I think I can sell this car over toward Saginaw. Dealers up there don't know what they're doing. Always a place for a good roadman." Jared's father twisted his hand, and the car sped up. Wind pushed Jared deeper into his seat. Sleepily he watched the branches of trees appear and disappear at the edge of the head-lights' glow. "No; now I got it," his father said. "We'll go down around Brighton. Shep Elder has the dealership there, and he don't know the first thing about selling a car." Sometime later they turned south, and Jared fell asleep. He woke up when the car slowed to a halt, and looking out he saw buildings around them.

"Figure I'll drop you at home and then head out again," his father said, and Jared understood. His father didn't want to go home.

On their left was a factory, and before his father could say any-thing Jared spotted the Ford logo. "Highland Park," his father said. "That's the old Ford. Once he gets the Rouge up to full speed, won't be anything left for this place." Still looking at the factory, his father pulled out onto Woodward Avenue again, and Jared, who had roused himself so he could see Detroit go by, goggled at the expanse of brick and steel. Unconsciously he held the neck of the bottle in his lap and picked at the cork. He'd never been to Detroit before. So many buildings, so much light. Jared leaned out the window to look up at the sky, and he couldn't see any stars.

"Jesus!" his father cried, and hit the brakes so hard that Jared's head cracked into the door frame. He'd had enough time to throw up his hands, and he felt a crunch in his right hand. When the car stopped he fell onto the floor in front of his seat, feeling around for something to hold on to and pull himself back up. His father was saying something, but Jared's head was fuzzy and the words didn't come together. His right hand kept slipping when he got hold of something. When he got back up onto the seat and looked out, his mouth fell open and he said, "Pop?"

Standing in front of the car was a hunched-over little man, with skin that shone dark as dried blood in the headlights and bright red hair hanging in tangles over his shoulders. The little man jumped up and spun around, hair and beard flying out from his head. He landed on the narrow hood of the Model T and waved his penis at them. It was gnarled like a tree root, and his testicles bounced like twin paddleballs between his spread legs. The little man crouched on the other side of the windshield from Jared, and Jared could see little fires dancing in his eyes. With a grin the little man sprang away to hang on a streetcar cable, and swinging from one to the next like a monkey he disappeared into the night.

"We saw the Dwarf," Jared's father said, like he was trying to convince himself. "We saw the Nain Rouge." The car had stalled, and Jared's father's hand shook as he reached back for the crank. He got out and started the car, and stayed outside for a long time, looking in the direction the Dwarf had gone. Jared's head started to hurt, and something was wrong with his hand. He wasn't afraid; he'd never been afraid when his father was around. He was tired, though, and unsure, and the day had filled his head with so much that was new. He wondered if he was dreaming. He wondered if he'd really seen a naked red-skinned dwarf with burning hair.

Back in the car, his father said, "Nain Rouge means bad luck. I never knew anyone who saw it before. It's an omen, Jared. I need to give up this being a roadman. It's back to the salt mine for me. Soon as I sell this car, I'm going back in the salt mine. There'll come a day when dealers sell all the Fords that get sold, but people will always need salt. That's what this is about."

His father kept talking in that disbelieving tone, and as they drove away down Woodward Avenue into the heart of Detroit, Jared remembered something else his father had said that day.

Get to know the demon early.

He found his voice and said, "Dad."

"Goddamn, I can't believe we saw the Dwarf. What, kid?"

"Dad, my hand hurts."

CHAPTER 2

Colleen doesn't say a word about it when Jared gets up in the morning, which makes him nervous as all hell when he can gather enough brain cells together to feel nervous. Mostly he just moves slowly and wishes he could spread aspirin on his toast. Emily is her usual chatterbox self, learning a new word every minute and just about wearing it out before she tries another one, and even with a railroad spike hammered in between his eyes Jared is enchanted by her. Unlike her mother, she does want to know where the Hop-Frog, which is Emilyese for "shitbox green '35 Ford coupe," has gone. Jared explains that the Hop-Frog is still at Daddy's work. Still Colleen withholds comment. At breakfast Jared always sits across from Colleen, with Emily between them, and like she does at least once every morning Emily reaches out to him and takes hold of his crippled fingers. She's fascinated by them, the way they don't move with the rest of his fingers. Sometimes she pretends that the fingers of her own right hand don't work, and Jared has to fight down an angry reflex to snap at her. He only gets mad because he's ashamed. Two fingers shouldn't keep a man out of the war, the Draft Marshal is right about that—and today when his daughter grabs his fingers Jared smiles through his hangover and says, "Daddy's got funny fingers, doesn't he?"

She smiles like a model in a toothpaste ad. "Daddy funny," she says.

"No, Emily funny."

"No, Daddy funny."

They go on like this for a while, until Colleen says, "You're both funny."

"Mommy funny, too," Jared says. Emily smiles so wide that Jared can count all fifteen of her teeth. She's cutting two others but is in remarkable good humor about it. The first half a dozen or so had her up howling at night, and Jared has a Pavlovian kind of confused mistrust when a new tooth doesn't keep her up. It's one of those good things that he hasn't been able to appreciate lately.

"Mommy's going to go be funny at work," Colleen says as she gets up to put her dishes in the sink. She works at Willow Run, stripping damaged bomber engines and cannibalizing them for parts. Some of the parts go straight into new planes at Willow Run; others are trucked to the Rouge and fed into the Pratt & Whitney assembly line, where many of them were first machined. There's a standing joke that if any of the Liberators coming out of Willow Run fly back over the plant, they'll only fly for five minutes at a time until someone stops them to check specifications. Colleen carpools out to Ypsilanti with two other women, Arlene Bannister and Nadine Erskine. The Three Eens. Arlene's husband, Joe— recently ex husband, Jared reminds himself—is home from North Africa with a disabling wound, and Nadine's Clyde is somewhere in the Pacific. Jared wonders what they think of him. When they're at the house they're all smiles, but mostly for Emily. They ask him about the Rouge, but he's not supposed to talk about Building G, so he tends to stick to generalities and the conversations don't get far. Plus Jared has an uncomfortable yen for Arlene, which she has done nothing to discourage and Colleen has had the good grace not to comment on.

Now she won't have to dance around me and the Rouge, Jared thinks. Now she'll have a husband in the service like the rest of them. I'll make her proud.

Emily lets go of his fingers to chase after Colleen and shut the door when she leaves. "Bye, honey," Jared calls. She blows him a kiss and heads out. Emily shuts the door too hard and runs back to the kitchen to climb up into his lap. She eats his toast while he finishes his coffee, and since he's feeling just about human by this time he gets up to do the dishes. Emily helps him by bringing each dish and item of silverware individually to the sink, burbling all the while about the individual history of each article. Mommy's fork, Daddy's plate, Emily's cup: each has a history, and Jared hears all of them. Emily Cleaves is a girl who can tell a story.

When the dishes are done and dried, Jared says, "You're going over to Mrs. Pelletier's a little early today, honey."

"Daddy go to work?"

"Daddy has to go to a meeting. I'll be back before Mama gets home from work, so I'll pick you up at Mrs. Pelletier's in a little while, okay? Let's get you dressed."

Emily runs squealing from the kitchen, then reappears in the doorway, peeking around to see if he's going to chase her. "I'm coming to get you, baby girl," Jared says, and she runs down the hall. He goes after her, playing the game until eventually they both get tired of it and he wrestles her into a clean diaper. She picks out a jumper and puts it on backward, then collapses into heartbroken wails when he turns it around the right way, then leaps up to go find her new shoes. It only takes about fifteen minutes to get her presentable.

Normally Jared would drop Emily at his mother's, about half a mile away, but today is her day to volunteer at her latest charity.

CeeCee Cleaves is a serial volunteer, constantly helping somebody but unable to stick with any one philanthropy. Jared doesn't know what she's doing now, but he knows it happens on Wednesdays. So Mrs. Pelletier it will be.

Mrs. Pelletier is one of those women so fiercely maternal that the sight of her makes Jared wish he was eight years old so she would make him lemonade and send him out to her garden to pick the beetles off her tomato plants. She's all flowered dresses and welcoming smiles and cushiony old woman's bosom. Her husband is nine years dead, and all three of her boys are stationed overseas, so she devotes her days to caring for the children of neighborhood defense-industry workers. Her house, a pale yellow bungalow nearly obscured by three spruce trees and a gargantuan rhododendron, teems with children (one of whom, Jared isn't sure which, is the culprit in the clothesline-snapping incident). Every once in a while someone in the neighborhood decides that they need to do something else with the kids, and Mrs. Pelletier gets indignant. What else, she wants to know, is she going to do with herself? She can't spend all day gardening and reading *Life* magazine, can she?

Today she is wearing elbow-length yellow garden gloves, standing in front of the rhododendron with a pair of rusty pruning shears. Emily runs up to her and says, "Hi, Mipettee!"

"Emily Cleaves, you stay away from these shears," she says with mock severity. "They've been so rusty since Wilf passed that they'll give you lockjaw just looking at them."

Which of course makes Emily reach for them, which of course makes Mrs. Pelletier say, "Aren't you a dickens?"

Jared puts a hand on Emily's head in case she really plans to go for the shears. "You mind taking her for part of the morning? I have to go to a meeting over at the plant."

"What else would I be doing? Of course I'll take her."

"I can grind those shears for you tomorrow," Jared says.

Whenever he offers to do something for her, Mrs. Pelletier's gaze flicks down to his fingers. She always agrees, but there's always that reminder. This morning when she does it, Jared thinks that after today she won't be looking at his fingers — or him—the same way anymore.

"That would be wonderful. That old Indian keeps trying to get me to pay him for work, but I don't want him anywhere near my things." She's talking about the wizened article who lives one house to the west and across the street from her, a decrepit Indian everyone on the block calls Plenty Coup because they don't know his real name and he hasn't volunteered it, "I think Wilf's files are still in the garage, if you'd like to use them."

Old Wilf Pelletier added a kind of lean-to garage onto the side of the house about thirty years ago, from the looks of it. It can fit a Model T if the passengers are thin enough to get out without opening the doors all the way, and at the back is a workbench piled with the kind of tools that Henry Ford goes on hunting expeditions to find for his Greenfield Village.

Jared nods. "I got a file I think'll do the job, but I might look around in there."

"Well, you go on to your meeting. Emily, come inside. We'll plan our attack on this rhododendron over a glass of milk."

"Bye, Daddy!" Emily sings out. She and Mrs. Pelletier go inside, and Jared starts walking down to Fort Street to pick up the streetcar. Plenty Coup, bald-headed and stooped, his emaciated ancient body draped in a flannel shirt and canvas pants holed in both knees, is standing out in his yard with his walking stick. He shakes it as Jared passes, and the iron rings bored through its head clank. Jared isn't sure how to respond, so he lifts one hand in a perfunctory wave and walks faster.

It's eight o'clock, and the streetcars are jammed. Two pass by without even stopping. Ordinarily this circumstance would set Jared to grumbling, but this is the best day of his life. He's minutes from the fulfillment of the only thing he's wanted since Pearl Harbor, which is to serve. Thought I had it when they picked me out to bust clay, he thinks, but it turns out that when something more meaningful is on offer, existing circumstance sours pretty damn quickly. When he does get on, there's a discarded *Free Press* stuck behind one of the seats, and Jared picks it up and tries to get a look at it without elbowing the men and women around him. Turns out he's gotten two papers for the price of one—folded into the *Free Press* is a copy of the *Chronicle,* the Negro paper. He can get a little racial justice with his Iffy the Dopester.

The Tigers have lost three of their last four and are barely clinging to a .500 record. The Seventh Infantry Division has landed on Attu Island, in the Aleutians. How the hell, Jared wonders, did the Japs get to Alaska in the first place? Wasn't anyone watching American territory? Guadalcanal is all wrapped up. Churchill's in Washington for a conference. Someone is still complaining about Negroes moving into the Sojourner Truth housing project, which happened in February and you'd think people would be over it by now. It's warm for May, but there's supposed to be rain for the next couple of days. Jared loses interest in the papers and leaves them on the seat. He fights his way to the door at Grand Circus Park and walks a few blocks to the Draft Marshal's office in the Guardian Building. The Marshal doesn't work out of the regular recruiting offices, and when he calls, you never know where you're going to end up. Jared has known maybe a dozen people inducted by the Marshal, but he's never seen hide nor hair of any of them after they ship out. It's as if the Marshal drafts people for service on the moon.

The glass in the door bears the sign OFFICE OF ESOTERIC INVESTIGATION. Now Jared knows what *OEI* stands for. He isn't quite sure what *esoteric* means, but you don't need a dictionary to peg the connection with golems and psychic pygmies. While he's thinking about it, the door opens and three men walk out. They are wearing identical black suits, and one of them ushers along some kind of spindly midget, also in a black suit, whose presence tweaks memories of the Rotunda. The midget looks up at Jared and says, "Run while you thtill can, kid." Right about the time Jared's ears register the lisp, his eyes note the forked tongue. The imp looks sick. One of its feet drags, its eyes aren't quite focusing, and it looks like it wouldn't be upright without one of the OEI suits holding on to its collar.

"Were you the—?" he starts to ask, but the imp is already gone into a waiting car.

Hot damn, Jared thinks. Is it possible that this same pygmy or imp was consulting with the Marshal about him? No one else has noticed it; at least no one is standing on the sidewalk pointing and wondering what the hell that little fork-tongued critter was that just got into the government Lincoln. They just don't know, Jared thinks. It amazes him sometimes that he's in on a secret as big as the Frankenline, let alone the foundry imps or the invisible rustling watchers up in the Rouge's I beams. Two million people in Detroit, and not even two thousand of them—maybe not even two hundred—know what goes on in Building G. Jared Cleaves does know, and when he walks into this sandstone building he'll pick up a few more things to add to his collection of secrets. He bounces up and down on the balls of his feet a few times, out of exuberance. Time to step up and join the big leagues. Time to make his mark.

A sergeant is stubbing out a cigarette as Jared enters the office. He looks up. "I'm Jared Cleaves," Jared says. "The Marshal told me to report this morning."

The sergeant lights another cigarette as he flips through the files on his desk. Jared wants a cigarette, but doesn't have any, and they're not always easy to find. Usually he buys them from guys at the Rouge; the Yooper who collects scrap from the bins under the sorting line has some kind of deal with someone and is a pretty reliable source of Lucky Strikes. Jared's a Pall Mall man himself, but war's a time of sacrifice.

"Don't see a Cleaves," the sergeant says.

"The Marshal told me to come down here," Jared says.

"If he wanted you here, I'd have a file. No file. Beat it."

"Beat it," echoes a squawk from somewhere up near the ceiling. Jared looks up at the voice and sees a crow—or maybe raven, he never could tell them apart—perched on the transom over the interior door, one more refinement in Jared's evolving definition of *esoteric*.

"He pointed right at me last night," Jared insists. "Came to my work and told me this wasn't good enough to keep me out of the war." He's holding up his right hand now, as if he means to take an oath right there, and that's more or less his intention. If he's going to go to the war, he wants to do it now, before Colleen or his father or anyone else can talk him out of it.

His fingers don't interest the sergeant. "Look, kid," he says. "You know how many people come in here with cockamamie stories about the Marshal fingering them at some factory?"

"No, I don't know," Jared says. "Ask him. Is he here?"

"Doesn't matter if he's here or not. If I don't have a file, you can't sign up. The Marshal's a particular man."

"Well, you—can you give me a piece of paper? I'll leave him a note. Maybe there's a mistake."

The sergeant is shaking his head. "The Marshal doesn't make mistakes."

"Well, somebody did. What did he come down last night for?"

"You're starting to get on my nerves, kid," the sergeant says. "Hit the bricks."

"Hit the bricks," the crow or raven says.

Jared feels like he's in one of those dreams where you try forever to perform a simple action—tying your shoes, opening a door—and can't quite make it work. "He came to the Rouge," he says again, repeating himself out of pure helplessness. "You don't get it. The Marshal picked me once, and now he did it again. I'm ready."

"Take it up at one of the regular offices." The sergeant stubs out his second cigarette, lights a third. He notices Jared following the motion. "Here," he says, tossing a half-empty pack of Chesterfields across the desk. "Keep 'em and get out of here."

Jared walks back out onto Woodward at eight thirty in the morning. For the second time in less than twelve hours his horizon of expectation has altered violently. It seems impossible that after he's been singled out by the Marshal, and given a raucous sendoff in Hamtramck, that he will have to go back to the Rouge as if none of it had ever happened. He's glad he didn't tell Colleen; in that respect, at least, it turns out he did the right thing. Even if he didn't know it at the time. When he left the house that morning, there was a real possibility that the next time he talked to his wife, it would be via letter from an APO address. Jared shakes his head as he walks back to where he got off the streetcar. That wasn't right, he thinks, but it turned out okay. At least I didn't tell her and get her worried. She's got enough to worry about.

The minute he thinks that, he wonders if it's true. Seems to him lately that he's the one doing all the worrying. About Swerdlow, about the Marshal, about not fulfilling his obligation to his country, about being considered something less than a man because he can't go to the Pacific and kill people. About the distance he feels opening up between him and Colleen. They're about as lucky as two people in the middle of a world war can be: they have jobs, a house, someone to watch Emily. Still, the war hangs like a dream over everything, turning Jared's family life into something to be ashamed of. Lately he's started to wonder what Colleen—encouraged, no doubt, by his in-laws, who think Jared is some kind of deadbeat—thinks about him. Does she think he could fight? Does she think less of him because he's not good enough for the war? Her cousin is with the Eighth Army, waiting to storm Sicily; what kind of marriage can they have if Jared can't measure up to that example? He knows it's foolish to think this way, but that doesn't make it go away; in fact it makes it worse because he's a fool in addition to being a 4-F worrywart.

What am I going to tell Emily when she's a little older and she asks me about the war? Jared wonders. How am I supposed to look her in the eye?

He's fingering the scar that angles across his palm. Of all the things that could have happened, it had to be cutting his hand on the broken neck of his father's whiskey bottle. He didn't even remember it happening, and the effort to remember jerks him into the strange space between memory and dream. Sometimes he has to fight the impression that he imagined the whole thing, invented it as a story to cover something else that doesn't bear telling. All he has to validate his memory are the knots of scar tissue on the palm of his right hand.

Jared starts walking; he can't stand waiting for the streetcar. He walks through the city, fighting off memories of the Dwarf by picking out other childhood recollections to dwell on. Maine. Seals in the harbor at Portland, the smells of salt and fish. The slanting afternoon light against granite walls somewhere far north, and the strong brown river below. His father saying, *You know that's what Detroit means, don't you? The narrows.* A strong urge wells up in him to go back, and as he lets himself imagine it he realizes that in his mind he's there alone. Colleen won't go to Maine. All of her family, except a handful of random Illinois cousins, is within thirty miles of their house in Detroit. Still the urge to flee pulls at Jared; if he has to face not being good enough to fight, at least he could do it among people whose opinions don't matter to him.

Walking makes him feel a little better. He picks up his pace and outdistances the impulse to leave his wife and child. This improves his mood—he may imagine doing it, but he doesn't want the idea to be so attractive, and he's glad when it loses some of its luster—and a couple of hours later, when he comes up Mrs. Pelletier's front walk, the grin on his face at seeing Emily is genuine. "Daddy!" she crows, running up to him. Her knees and hands and face are black with dirt from Mrs. Pelletier's garden, and there's even dirt on her teeth, and she is the happiest two-year-old in all of Detroit. Jared sweeps her up and she wraps her arms around his neck. How could you even imagine it? he wonders. You couldn't leave this little girl.

Colleen came home a little after two, early because of some kind of wildcat strike that cut off the supply of damaged engines to her department. This happened often enough that the Emily handoff became a kind of ritual alternative to dropping her off at either Grandma CeeCee's or Mrs. Pelletier's. Jared was surly again by this time, and he could tell by Colleen's demeanor that she was picking up on it. He got angry when she didn't ask him what was wrong even though he wouldn't tell her if she did, and to avoid saying something that he knew he'd regret Jared walked out of the house barely fifteen minutes later. There was a little tin of hard candy on the Hop-Frog's dashboard, and Jared's heelishness suddenly made him tired. Too many ups and downs in the last day or so, and now this sneaky little act of kindness from his wife had him completely discombobulated. The only thing he could do was drive and rack his brains for something nice he could do for her, but if Jared knew anything about himself it was that he couldn't match her natural cunning when it came to gift giving. He gave up, waiting for inspiration to strike, and was in the Building G locker room putting on his coverall twenty minutes before his shift started. Since he had to unload on someone, he decided to go see Swerdlow.

Maybe Swerdlow would know why the Marshal changed his mind, and in any case Jared figured he should let the boss man know that he still worked on the Frankenline. He was also hopeful that Swerdlow would be his usual asshole self and refocus all of Jared's frustration.

Swerdlow's office was in the main assembly building, a hundred-foot-tall glass-walled architectural marvel. Jared stomped into it and found Swerdlow with his feet up on his desk. Shoe stamps weren't a problem for Swerdlow; his black wingtips gleamed in the light from his desk lamp.

"Cleaves," Swerdlow said with a gap-toothed grin. "What a surprise."

"I went down to see the Marshal this morning and they turned me away," Jared said. "Thought I'd let you know I'm still here."

"Oh, I knew you were still here."

Swerdlow waited after this, obviously enjoying Jared's angry confusion. Jared hated him, hated his little pussy-tickler of a mustache and the dyed hairs he plastered across the crown of his head and the flab under his chin and over his belt. Hated the white shirt he wore to pretend he was better than the line rats he tormented.

"What?" Jared said.

"You want to know why you're not in the war, kid?" Swerdlow said. "Because I'm keeping you out. Every time the Marshal comes for somebody, I let 'em go, but for you I went right to the fucking wall with the essential-industry crap. You think I couldn't find someone else to pick shell casings out of clay? For chrissake. Truth is, your fingers wouldn't keep you from any kind of rear-echelon job, but I got equal priority here. So the next time you're out with your wife on Sunday, spare a thought for old Swerdlow."

Now this was new. Swerdlow asking for pity? It couldn't be straight. Something else was going on. "Why?" Jared asked.

"Because you have something I need. Simple. It ain't because I like you. Your wife's out at Willow Run, right? There's a situation there that needs to be taken care of."

The shift-change whistle blew. Jared started to get up. "Sit down," Swerdlow said. Jared did. "I did you a favor, but there ain't nothing free. Right?"

Jared nodded.

"Okay," Swerdlow said. "You're late. Keep this under your hat and talk to me when you're off shift."

It was a long walk from Swerdlow's office past the tire plant and across the overpass into Building G. By the time Jared took his place at the sorting belt, it was twenty after three. "The hell you doing here?" Felton said.

Even if Swerdlow hadn't said to keep quiet, Jared would have been nervous about saying anything. The FBI had guys in every department at the Rouge, both human and not. Most of what sounded like birds rustling up in the plant's girders were actually little winged spies of one kind or another, created by the stupendous industrial atavism of the Rouge and co-opted one by one . . . victims of the OEI as much as Jared himself apparently had become. Ford was particular about the Special Service—they had to be human—but the feds and the OEI took any advantage they could get, and one of their imps could have a man off the job and facing charges faster than goose shit through a tin horn, as Jared's father would say. "Looks like the Draft Marshal didn't get me," was all he said.

"There's a first," Jem said.

The shovel buzzer sounded and the three of them went out to the rail siding. Jem took wheelbarrow duty, and the first time he left with a load, Felton said, "What really?"

"I don't know. And what I do know I can't tell. I need to keep this job, Felton. Let it be right now, all right?"

Felton nodded. They shoveled out the cars in silence until Jem came back and said, "You feel that one, J? Boom!"

A month or so after the Frankenline had gone active, Jared had transgressed the cardinal rule of the clay-buster, which was not to talk about yourself. According to Swerdlow, this policy existed to prevent hypothetical fifth columnists and provocateurs from learning personal information that they might use to squeeze Building G's workforce for classified information. It had sounded shaky to Jared at the time, since they'd all been vetted by the OEI and Ford brass, but he'd gone along with it for a while, until one Wednesday night Jem started talking about his father. The kid was so pathetic that Jared's guard had come down, and he'd talked a bit about Marty Cleaves, who true to his word had stayed at the salt mine for the last twenty-four years. Jem was flat astonished by Jared's revelation that a vast salt mine extended for miles below Detroit and Melvindale and the Rouge itself, and had since been obsessed by the idea that he could feel the explosions in the mine, twelve hundred feet below the concrete floor of Building G. After more than two years, it wasn't funny anymore.

"Give it a rest," Jared said.

"I ain't kidding," Jem said. "You sure you can't feel that?"

"You're about to feel the backside of this shovel, you don't shut up a minute," Jared said.

Jem and Felton both stopped working so they could stare at him. "Just let me work, all right?" Jared said, and that was about it for conversation. Jared hosed out the cars by himself and took the time to smoke one of the sergeant's Chesterfields all the way down before he went back in and started making little pieces of clay out of big pieces of clay again.

What he couldn't figure out was how Swerdlow had the pull to face down the Draft Marshal. He wasn't even sure how Swerdlow had any kind of say over it, or over him, since the Frankenline wasn't a Ford operation. The Rouge built a lot of wartime matériel that didn't go out with Henry's signature on it—Pratt & Whitney engines, Willys jeeps, tank parts, all kinds of stuff—but as far as Jared

knew, the Frankenline had no traceable connection to the Ford
Motor Company. The Old Man didn't much like Jews, and Jared
didn't figure he'd have started up the Frankenline on his own. The
feds had come to him needing to lease some space for an operation,
was what must have happened, and Ford was stringing Roosevelt
along on converting one of the Rouge's lines to build Rolls-Royce
engines for RAF bombers because he didn't want to sully his billion-
dollar industrial offspring by making armaments. Looking back on
it, Jared was pretty sure that the Old Man had already been senile
then, or close enough to it that only a doctor would notice the difference. In any case, somebody's arm got twisted, and Ford had
come up with some square feet near one of the railroad spurs not
too far from the canal slip. Jared picked up his pay at the same place
as the other eighty thousand Rouge rats, but he never had a union
checkoff, which meant he didn't work for Ford. The UAW had
taken their cut from everyone for two years now . . . not too long,
now that Jared thought about it, after the Frankenline had started
up. A man in a paranoid mood would be tempted to make something of this coincidence.

Jared hadn't ever looked into the union question since he made
the same money as everyone else doing similar work, and he didn't
figure he'd ever be filing a grievance, and anyway Colleen was in the
UAW and had hospitalization from Willow Run. Swerdlow, though,
that was tough to figure. He'd been one of Harry Bennett's goons
who beat women and put Walter Reuther in the hospital at the Battle of the Overpass in '37, and Bennett had pushed him into management after the UAW took over the Rouge in '41; foremen and
management didn't have to join the UAW, and Bennett wanted some
of his men on the inside looking for ways to torpedo the union.
Bennett and Ford were both figuring (insofar as the Old Man figured anything anymore) on busting the UAW as soon as the war was
over and they could afford a long strike; Jared knew that from gossip on the Rouge's bus line, overheard on those rare days when

he had to park at one of the outer lots. It would be a lot easier if they had enough people on the inside to throw monkey wrenches around, and Swerdlow was every inch a Harry Bennett cat's-paw.

"Making the union look bad, boys!" Swerdlow liked to sing out when he caught someone missing quotas—which the Frankenline had begun to do, these past few months. "Can't have goldbricks in the almighty Bolshevik UAW!" Jared was starting to be troubled by the increasing frequency with which golems never got up from the gurneys, or just stood around by the rail siding—sometimes for days—until Moises came out and wiped away their lives.

Swerdlow's in with Harry Bennett didn't explain how he could go toe-to-toe with the Draft Marshal, though. Or why he'd want to. Did he have some kind of arrangement with whatever fed tentacle had leased the space?

"You look like your dog died," Felton said.

Jared watched a worm writhe in a broken clod, then fall out onto the belt. It rolled away and fell into the molding bin. "I don't have a dog," he said.

"How about we take a walk when the whistle blows?" Felton proposed.

Jared considered this. He didn't have anyone else to spill his guts to, that was for sure. Colleen was home, his father was twelve hundred feet underground blasting salt out of the earth, and Jem was naïve as a puppy. Felton was older, and had been to some colored college in the South, and had X-ray vision where bullshit was concerned. Jared figured he knew more about politics than anyone else on the Frankenline . . . except maybe Moises, and Jared wasn't about to take his personal problems to a cadaverous little rabbi who could barely speak English.

"All right," he said, and went back to picking .50 casings out of the piles of European river delta on the sorting belt.

When the whistle blew, Jared put down his tools, sauntered over to pick up his lunch pail, and followed Felton up to the catwalk and across the east overpass. Back on the ground again, they wound past a conveyor feeding scrap rubber into the tire plant: bald tires, torn galoshes, even the curly strips of windshield wiper blades, all destined to become gaskets and tires in the jeeps that came together in the old Dearborn Assembly building, or vibration dampers in the bomber engines for the B-24s rolling—finally—off the line at Willow Run. They crossed a turning platform and followed the canal slip to the pits between the water and the foundry. Clever, Jared thought. Felton was taking him to the one place in the Rouge complex where the FBI didn't go: the foundry. Even Hoover's robot zealots didn't have the dedication to spy in that hellhole, and none of the G-fairies would go anywhere near it. It was the perfect place to carry out a conversation requiring some privacy. The only thing was, Jared would be the only English-speaking white man there, which would draw attention. If anyone asked him what he was doing there, Jared doubted he'd be able to come up with a reason that would pass the smell test. Not that it was against the rules to take a walk through the plant, but nobody in his right mind would go to the foundry on purpose.

Each as big as a football field, the pits held coal, iron ore, and limestone, sand and bentonite clay: everything you needed for steel except heat and men. The roar of the blast furnaces, elemental and hungry, rose up and erased every other sound. Still two hundred yards from the foundry's open doors, Jared could already feel the heat, and the sound had become feeling, a steady thrum in his bones and in his heart. He walked past the open hangar door, big enough for four trucks abreast, and paused near the base of the grab-bucket tower. From the top of the tower, a steel track spanned the pits, braced by another tower on the other side and extending out over the water, where a five-hundred-foot freighter down from Wisconsin was offloading iron ore. Between the steelworks and the freighter, floodlights caught the billowing bentonite dust devils pouring out of the foundry.

Jared sat on the bottom step, and Felton came around the rim of the pits. He looked into the foundry, his orange-lit face all fascinated revulsion, and Jared had the belated thought that this might not be the best place to have come. The foundry was notoriously the dumping ground for Ford's colored workers, especially now that the Rouge was union and the Old Man didn't have to pretend to love the black man anymore. In the 1930s Ford had hired more blacks than the rest of the auto and steel companies in Detroit combined, making a great show of his color blindness as a way of drawing attention away from the fact that all of his workers made less than their counterparts at General Motors or Chrysler. Now, with the war on and the UAW on the job, Ford left the racial politicking to the union. Felton was lucky not to be working in the foundry.

The penny dropped, and Jared thought: that's Swerdlow, too. If Felton worked for Ford, he'd be in there, or sweeping a floor somewhere. This put things in a different light. Had Swerdlow made some kind of offer to Felton, too?

"Felton," he asked, "you got picked for this job same as I did, right? Went up to the Rotunda and everything?"

Felton stopped and leaned against the railing. He took a sandwich from his pocket and tore the waxed paper off it. "You sure got a way of putting a man at ease," he said around the first mouthful.

"Come on, you can tell me," Jared said. "I went and told Jem about my old man and nothing came of it, remember?"

"Maybe nobody cares about your old man," Felton said.

Jared had forgotten all about eating. He started in on his own sandwich—chicken and cucumbers, on bread that was soggy where the mayonnaise had soaked in and stale near the crust—while he considered what to say. Before he could work up an approach that seemed both discreet and impervious to misunderstanding, Felton gestured with his sandwich and said, "Let me guess. Swerdlow told you he called the Draft Marshal off."

All Jared could do was nod.

"Oh, man," Felton said. "You're gonna wish you were in the war before this is over."

A high-pitched squalling cut through the roar of the furnaces. Jared was facing the doorway, and he watched a foundry worker come out with a pair of tongs held at arm's length. Wriggling in the tongs and howling like a banshee was one of the imps that plagued the blast furnaces, a stringy potbellied little goblin with a bullet head and a fouler mouth than Jared had ever heard on any human. With every howl came a torrent of sparks that bounced around the worker's feet. It had both hands wrapped around the tongs, but it couldn't reach the man's hands and couldn't force itself free of his grip on its head.

"I done told you goddamn imps to stay out of my ladle, didn't I?" he was shouting as he came across the packed gravel toward Jared and Felton. "I'm sick and goddamn tired of you spark-eating sonsabitches getting in the molds. It don't obtain, hear? I'm sick of it."

Jared cleared out of his way when he got within twenty feet. The imp yowled and kicked and forked its legs around the stair rail. The worker squeezed the tongs and its yowling went up an octave; with a heave he got it loose and went up and across the footbridge built onto the bucket rail. "Sick of it!" he yelled again, and the two of them shrieked their way across to the platform, where the worker held the imp out over the water near the bow of the offloading freighter. Sparks danced in the night as he dropped it, and a few seconds later a plume of steam shot up around the freighter's mooring line.

"I sure am glad I stayed out of the foundry," Felton said.

Jared nodded. "I hear you." Nine hours of a 110-degree sandstorm: that was the best-case scenario in the foundry. Worst case was you were standing in the wrong place when a kettle full of running steel cracked.

The imp's executioner looked to have found the middle ground.

As he came back to the ground and dropped his tongs to free both hands for a cigarette, Jared saw that one of his arms was piebald with deep scars from fingertips to elbow. At least they could smoke and sit down now that the Rouge was a union shop. Until 1941 there hadn't been a single chair in the complex outside of the offices, and tobacco was banned even from the foundry, where the air was so fouled with bentonite dust and God only knew what else that a Chesterfield was like a breath of fresh air.

"Goddamn those imps," the steelworker said. "That one's been blowing molds for two weeks. I told the steward about it, said sooner or later one of them imps is going to blow the plug right out of B furnace, and what do you think he said?" Exhaling a cloud, he went on. "Said the union doesn't engage in supernatural counter-measures. I told him explain that to the marines when we can't cast the blocks for their amphibious fucking vehicles. It don't obtain."

"You need the steward to tell you to drop them in the canal?" Felton asked.

"No, I need him to get a goddamn houngan down here and hex those little motherfuckers out of here. I ain't fought Harry Bennett so I can cook my ass when an imp blows a mold. No, sir." Churning out a contrail of smoke, he strode back into the foundry.

They both watched him go, ducking into their collars when a blast of sand billowed out the door. "So Swerdlow's keeping you out of the draft," Felton said.

"What do you figure?"

"I figure the Marshal should draft some of those imps."

"Come on, Felton."

"Ease up. We're all here because OEI saw something they liked. For all I know, Swerdlow could come for me next, and I don't know what the hell I'd say. Maybe Swerdlow's just sick of the Marshal coming in and kiting off with his men." Felton chewed and swallowed, then added, "But I did hear him mention your name the other day, when one of the OEI boys was by to check up. Put two and two together."

It took a minute, but Jared did. "They're planning this? That's crazy, Felton."

"Telling you what I heard, is all. Up to you what you make of it."

"So they weren't planning it?"

Felton shrugged.

"Shit. What should I do?"

"How should I know? It was me, I'd be nervous as hell about owing Swerdlow a nickel, never mind him keeping me out of the war."

Jared finished his sandwich. Colleen had put a bottle of Coke in his lunch pail, and he set it against the stair rail and popped the cap off it. It was warm, but still tasted good chasing the sand out of his throat. "You want?" he asked, tipping the bottle toward Felton.

"You're looking for trouble with the crackers around here, you go sharing a bottle with a colored man," Felton said, but there was a smile in the corner of his eye and he took a drink.

Crackers in the foundry, Jared thought. Colleen's mother would find a word for Felton, and that word would be *droll;* he knew this because she'd applied it to one of Colleen's uncles once when he was making jokes that you couldn't tell right away were jokes. She was a great one for improving the vocabularies of people around her in such a way as to make them wish they knew no words of more than three syllables. Jared and Felton finished the Coke, and Jared stuck the bottle in his pocket to drop in one of the recycling bins. The Rouge rolled miles of glass every day, and throwing away a bottle was a good way to get a lecture about the war effort. "You got the time?"

Felton checked his pocket watch. "Time to get back."

"Hate to waste your lunch like this."

"Hell, I ate. At least I didn't have to fish an imp out of the furnace, you know?" They started walking back. While the foundry's roar was still loud around them, Felton added, "If you want to talk about Swerdlow again, I'll listen. Whatever he's doing now, he could do to me."

"Soon as I know anything," Jared said. They made it back a whole thirty seconds before the start-up whistle blew.

It wasn't an hour before Sakiewicz, Ilgauskas, and Nowak, three vets from the tire plant, showed up on the catwalk to hassle Jared. All of them were old hands at needling the guys who hadn't been in the war. The kind of guys who felt like a Purple Heart entitled them to take a shit on anyone who was unlucky enough to never have been shot. "Hey, Cleaves," Sakiewicz called from the catwalk. "Flunked out of the war twice, you're some specimen. Once for each crooked finger. I bet your old man's just about busting, he's so proud."

Jared took it, like he always did. The one time he'd lost his temper and gone after them, they'd worked him over and he'd missed four days of work. Colleen was still angry about it.

They saw that he was going to play punching bag and settled in for a long stay. Two of them lit cigarettes, and they all came around to lean on the railing directly over the ramp and sorting belt, where they wouldn't have to raise their voices. "You might still make a good typist," Nowak said. "You ever think about that? Lots of guys get by only using two fingers, and you've got eight still working."

Ilgauskas' turn. "Fellows, it ain't his fingers at all. Hell, I had two toes shot off and was fighting again the next day. I think the head doctors won't let him in."

"Could be you're right about that. You suppose he's a Quaker?"

"Queer, maybe."

"Communist is my guess. Hey, Cleaves, which is it?"

"Y'all talk awful big from up there on the catwalk," Jem said.

All three of the vets looked at him. Sakiewicz flicked his cigarette down into the clay. "You say something, hillbilly?"

Jem picked the butt up and drew on it. "I said y'all are like crows in the top of a tree, quarreling like a bunch of old women." He savored the smoke. "But you can't be all bad. I appreciate the cig." He planted it in the corner of his mouth and went back to work with his hoe.

Sakiewicz stood up, and Jared waited for him to work through his standard repertoire of threats so the whole thing could blow over and they could all get back to making golems. And it might have happened that way if Jem hadn't found a fragment of an artillery shell on the belt in front of him. "Say, Ilgy. Where'd you lose them toes?"

Ilgauskas drew himself up. "Tunisia."

Jem grinned around Sakiewicz' cigarette. "Well, I'll be. This here is from Tunisia."

Which it wasn't, unless they had somewhere along the line gotten a shipment of clay from the Nile Delta, and were there Jews in Africa? Jared imagined golems in whatever you called the headdresses the Arabs wore. Or Egyptian golems, walking sideways toward the front with their arms crooked out in front and behind.

Jem flipped the fragment, spinning end over end like a coin, up toward Ilgauskas. "This here is from Tunisia. Least I can do since your pal give me a cigarette."

Ilgauskas caught the fragment. "Okay, hillbilly. Next time I see you, you're going to eat this."

Rummaging through the clay some more, Jem found a dead frog. "Let's do that. I'll hang on to old Frog here and use him as a chaser." He twisted the frog's legs off and dropped them into his coverall's breast pocket. "We'll see you around, Polack."

If it wasn't war before that, Jem's last words put up the red flag. Ilgauskas was Lithuanian, and Jem knew it. This was going to be like the wildcat strikes over the winter, when everyone went in groups to their cars because the wildcatters went after people who didn't join in with ax handles.

The three vets went back to the tire plant. When they were gone Felton said, "Son, you need to learn when to keep your mouth shut."

"I know when to keep my mouth shut," Jem said, "and it sure as hell ain't when three old women like them are picking on a friend of mine. I ain't scared of them."

Jared was thinking about how he was going to get to Swerdlow's office without taking a beating. He had another three hours to think about it, with Jem running his mouth the whole time and Felton stepping in every twenty minutes or so to bounce an ineffective *shut up* off the exuberant torrent of Jem's boasting.

The whistle blew. Jared went to the sinks and cleaned his tools, hosed off his apron, and hung it up. He stopped at the rock cart and filled his lunch pail with rocks.

"What's that for?"

"If Sakiewicz comes looking for me, I plan to get one good one in," Jared said.

"You're gonna bust his head with your lunch box?" Felton took the pail away and emptied the rocks back into the cart. "That's trouble you don't need. Listen, I'll come with you far as the office. Whatever it is Swerdlow wants, he'll keep you long enough that even if they are waiting for you—which they ain't—they'll get bored by the time Swerdlow's done flapping his gums." He handed the pail back. "Let's go."

Swerdlow was pacing at the top of the stairs in front of his office when they got there. Felton turned and left without a word. "You got a bodyguard now?" Swerdlow cracked.

"We were just passing the time," Jared said.

"Got to cure you of that habit. Way you line rats gossip, it's a wonder the Germans aren't running things here already." Swerdlow opened the door, and Jared went in. He sat without being asked, too tired to care whether Swerdlow would get his back up about it.

"Tough day rooting around in the mud, huh?" Swerdlow said. He sat behind his desk and lit the stub of a cigar. There was a glass on his desk, half full of whiskey despite Old Man Ford's well-known dislike of liquor. When you'd been one of Harry Bennett's men for fifteen years, you didn't need to worry so much about what Mr. Ford thought.

"How can I help you, Mr. Swerdlow?"

"That's it, get to the point. Something I have to ask you, though. Did you want to get drafted?"

Again the feeling of confessing to something shameful. "I tried to enlist, Mr. Swerdlow," Jared said. "They wouldn't take me on account of my hand."

"Well, we're gonna have to clear the air here. I can't have you going around with a chip on your shoulder because I kept you from getting your ass shot off. The army turned you down for good reason, kid. If they wanted you, they'd come calling, and don't make the mistake of thinking that the army wants you just because the Marshal does. Ask me no questions, I'll tell you no lies, but I will tell you that the Marshal and the army aren't always pulling in the same direction."

"Yes, sir," Jared said, more to acknowledge what had been said than to agree with it. The fact was, he didn't know anything about the Marshal.

"The Marshal works for the FBI," Swerdlow said. "Hoover's boys have their own ideas about who should be doing what, and they don't much care what Henry Stimson thinks, or what Eisenhower thinks."

Judging from what Jared had seen that morning at the Office of Esoteric Investigation, he doubted that the Draft Marshal had anything to do with the FBI. Not that the FBI wouldn't use supernatural assets when they could find them; just that G-men couldn't be so casual as the sergeant had been and keep their jobs. The way Jared had it figured, the FBI would give its collective left nut to have some of the stuff the OEI was working on.

"I wouldn't know anything about it," he said.

"No, and you don't want to." Swerdlow's cigar had gone out. He lit it again and loosened his tie. Jared could see a red line curving across his liberated chins. "Okay. Enough beating around the bush. There's a new wing went up a year ago at the Willow Run plant. It's right on the outside of the corner of the ell where Ford bent the plant. You know why he did that, by the way? So the building wouldn't cross from Washtenaw County into Wayne, where he'd have to pay more taxes on it. Cheap bastard—and he hollers about Jews. Go figure. Now he's got a giant wheel in the floor most of the way through the line where they have to turn the planes because he's more worried about Wayne County Democrats than the war effort. If you ever tell anyone I said that, I'll make sure you spend the rest of the war with your dick rotting off in Borneo. What I need to know is what's going on in that new wing."

"Mr. Swerdlow, if you need something from me, ask me. Keep my wife out of this."

"We're not negotiating, Cleaves. I'm telling you what you're going to do for me if you want to keep your job, and if you want your Colleen to keep hers."

A cold knot formed in Jared's gut. Swerdlow would do it; he'd slip a word to someone, and Colleen would be out of work. Both of them would end up sweeping floors somewhere. You cold-blooded bastard, Jared thought. Why are you bringing this to me? What's this really about?

He swallowed and said, "We need our jobs, Mr. Swerdlow."

This was shading the truth, since Jared knew—even if he did everything in his power to forget—that the Cleaves family could survive solely on what Colleen made at Willow Run. But Swerdlow didn't challenge him. "I know you do. That's why we're not going to argue about this anymore. You go home, put a bug in your wife's ear. Talk to me on your break day after tomorrow."

"What if she doesn't hear anything by then?"

"If you don't come talk to me day after tomorrow, she's going to hear from me the next day. Count on it." Swerdlow stood and put on his hat. "I don't have to tell you this, but I'm going to. I'm not asking you for myself. This has to do with the war. You can do more good finding this out than you'll ever do packing clay for that crazy Yid. Or going off to the Pacific. Which, trust me, if the Marshal got hold of you, you wouldn't be doing anyhow."

Jared followed him to the door. Swerdlow held it open for him, but crowded him as he went through; typical intimidation, you saw it all the time from people who had only enough power to be domineering with peons like Jared. As he went out, Swerdlow said, "Day after tomorrow."

The Hop-Frog was slow to start, and a fog of exhaustion settled over Jared as he ran through a mental checklist of possible reasons. Ignition, fuel pump, water in the lines, who the hell knew. It caught, and he hammered the accelerator, frustrated and angry for reasons that in his fatigue he couldn't quite articulate. The engine's pitch rose to a whine and Jared eased off, forcing his foot up until the car dropped into a comfortable idle. He drove home feeling at every intersection like he could just turn left instead of right, go straight instead of left, make any choice that wouldn't lead to him going home. Plenty of men did it. Shockey on the Frankenline had disappeared a couple of months ago, trailed by vague gossip that he'd lit out after getting cold feet when he found out his wife Lil was pregnant. Colleen wasn't pregnant, though. She couldn't hardly be, when since Emily came along more than two years ago she put him off every night until he gave up asking. Tired, she said, but wasn't he tired, too? All he wanted was some comfort, to know that she was there. To feel her body with his and know that she was there.

At the last turn before home, Jared ran into three fire trucks blocking the street. Their lights were off, but he could see arcs of water behind them. Whose house? What had happened? He went around the block and came down from the other end, stopping in the street when he'd gotten close enough for a good look. The firemen were hosing down the remains of old Plenty Coup's house.

Jared remembered driving by the other way, on his way to work, seeing the old Indian in his yard with his walking stick. Leaving the car where it was, he walked up to the closest fireman. "Hey," he said. "The old man get out?"

"We didn't find him," the fireman said. "Place was about gone when we got here, though. If he's still in there, we'll be sifting him out with a sieve."

Old Plenty Coup. Hope he's okay, Jared thought as he walked back to the Hop-Frog. He hadn't talked to the Plenty Coup much, but the neighborhood consensus was that he'd come from out west somewhere, and he was old enough to have run with Sitting Bull. Some stories he must have, not that he ever told any of them. Nobody in the neighborhood even knew his name. He was just the ancient Indian, skinny sunken-chested guy with a big nose and thin gray hair straggling over his shoulders. Rumor was he'd been some kind of warrior, fought Custer when he was a boy. Other rumor was he'd been a lumberjack up in the UP after putting down his tomahawk. Nobody knew. Jared had a bad feeling about what the firemen would find in the morning. Plenty Coup was ninety if he was a day; it was hard to imagine that he'd been out of his house at one in the morning.

Although he did spend a hell of a lot of time standing out in his front yard waving his stick at people. Maybe he'd just seen his house burning and walked away. That was a choice Jared could under-stand.

Jared sat for a long time after he'd eased into his driveway and shut off the car. A plane went over, the drone of its engines fading into the fuzzy whine in his head. Out the passenger window, beyond the cemetery to the west, he could see the fierce glow of the Rouge steelworks. He held up his crippled hand, silhouetting it against the light, flexing it and watching the ring finger and pinkie struggle to bend. I do good work, he thought. The golems kept going until they were literally shot to pieces, was the whispered word that filtered back via uncertain channels from people who swore they'd seen golems everywhere in the European theater; Jared watched the newsreels over and over, scouring them for clues that he was look-ing at a golem. He imagined seeing them marching into machine-gun fire with bits of their bodies flying away. He imagined them infiltrated onto the beaches of Sicily to soften up the Germans, or parachuted in to stand with the last Jews in Warsaw.

Truth was, though, he wasn't sure he'd ever seen a golem on a newsreel. They were supposed to be a secret, sure, but one of the things about the world that kept catching Jared by surprise was the way that certain secrets actually stayed secret. This was one of them. Nobody Jared knew seemed to have any inkling that there were creations of kabbalistic magic fighting the Nazis in Europe. Not to mention fighting the Japanese on Attu and bird-dogging German spies in the United States.

If any of that was true. Jared had invested a lot in believing it, even though if the golems were in fact wreaking havoc on the Axis in Europe, it was mostly due to Moises' superhuman dedication. All Jared and Felton and Jem and the other men on the Frankenline did was dig through clay. At least Colleen worked with machines, strip-ping damaged engines. She had real tools in her hands all day, and he had gardening tools in his all night. Jared shook his head. Maybe he should tell Swerdlow to piss up a rope; he and Colleen could get a fresh start somewhere else. If he wasn't going to move up in the OEI, do something more worthwhile than breaking up clay, it was time for a change.

He looked the other way, away from the Rouge and the firemen hosing down Plenty Coup's house. Three blocks down Logan Street was his father's house, the old man sleeping inside with CeeCee. Like the steelworker said to the imp, Jared thought to himself in Groucho Marx' voice: it don't obtain. Whatever it meant, it felt true. Jared could no more face his father after losing his job than he could fly to the moon. Marty Cleaves maintained an extensive list of actions that were indicative of character weakness in others—even if he had routinely indulged in each item on the list himself—and high on that list were losing a job and complaining about it. There was no whining around Marty Cleaves unless he was going to do it himself.

Jared got out of the car and looked up at the sky, its stars faded in the glow from the Rouge. The western sky grew brighter. They were making a pour. More molds would rattle away on the donkey engine, or more ingots to be rolled, and more engines and vehicles and armaments would come off the lines to kill men. If they worked properly, Germans and Japanese would die; if they didn't, if a manifold cracked or a rivet popped loose, Americans and British. Either way, once you built an engine for a B-24 or the treads for a tank, you made sure that someone would die.

Or a golem.

Jared wondered if he could get on at the salt mine. He'd gone to work at the Rouge wanting to be part of the war effort, and now it gave him no satisfaction. Better to ride the bucket down into the earth and blast loose the remains of ancient oceans so roads wouldn't be slippery in the winter. Could he work alongside the old man? They got along better with Jared at twenty-eight than they had when he was sixteen, that was for sure.

Quit your woolgathering and go to sleep, he thought.

The house was quiet. Sometimes, if Colleen happened to wake up around midnight, she'd sit up and wait for him to come home. She had to get up at five thirty in the morning, though, before Emily woke up at six, to get ready for her day at Willow Run. It only took about half an hour for her to get there, since the superhighway, but even to spend the day stripping burned-out and blown-apart (or just defective, which was too often the case with engines coming out of the Rouge) bomber engines, Colleen liked to look right. Jared liked being married to a woman who had room in her heart for frippery even in the middle of a war. The thought reminded him to do something nice for her. They just weren't seeing enough of each other, was the fundamental problem. The things Jared knew he loved about his wife had become kind of abstract because, between Emily and two jobs, they'd lost the time they'd once had to enjoy each other's company. There we go, he thought. Item one: spend more time with Colleen.

All of this ran through his mind as he slipped off his shoes and walked through the living room and down the hall to Emily's room. His daughter was sleeping on her back, both arms thrown up over her head like a referee signaling touchdown and fingers curled into loose fists. Jared wanted to slide in next to her, gather her into the crook of his arm and fall asleep with her drooling on his shoulder. She probably wouldn't wake up, but he smelled like river muck with an overlay of foundry, and he was grimed with clay. He kissed his fingertips and laid them gently on her forehead. One of her hands opened, then curled slowly back. "Night, baby," he whispered, and went into the bathroom to take a shower. When he came out, he looked at himself in the mirror. His cuticles were still black, and he could never get all of the clay out of his ears and nose. I'm turning into clay, he thought. Moises won't even have to say the words. They can just pack me up and ship me over.

Halfway to dreaming, he imagined it: to be a man of clay. Bullets thudding into his body with no more effect than hailstones,

Nazi stormtroopers fleeing before him. He dozed right there, leaning on the bathroom sink, and snapped out of it only when Emily murmured something in her sleep.

"Day after tomorrow," he said to the man in the mirror. "What am I gonna do?"

CHAPTER 3

He slept badly, and came fully awake when Colleen got up, feeling like his head was still full of sand and bentonite dust blown out of the foundry. Rolling onto his back, Jared looked up at the ceiling. It was just light out, and little feelers of sunlight were creeping through the curtains. There was a water stain in the corner of the ceiling by the closet; come some weekend, he was going to have to get his dad to help him patch the roof. Maybe Jem, too, depending on how bad the leak was.

That was that; Jared couldn't go back to sleep once he'd started thinking about the roof. He flipped back the covers and got up, padding out into the kitchen in his shorts to put on some coffee for Colleen, who was already in the shower. He had ten minutes before she came out and discovered that he was up. Then he'd have to tell her about the situation with Swerdlow. How, he had no idea, and the ten minutes passed without any inspiration presenting itself. WWJ said that the last remnants of the Afrika Korps had surrendered yesterday, May 12, and Pantelleria Island between Tunisia and Sicily was under heavy bombardment. Allied antisubmarine tactics were starting to pay off, with shipping losses way down. The British were evacuating Burma ahead of the monsoons. The Tigers beat Tommy Bridges and the Athletics, 3–2. There was no coverage of the disillusionment of Jared Cleaves.

"You're up," Colleen said when she saw him sitting at the kitchen table.

"Can't get a thing past you, can I?"

She gave him a halfhearted whack on the shoulder as she went by on her way to the coffeepot. He watched her, a little surprised like always how good she looked in her work clothes. It wasn't every woman who could turn heads wearing denim coveralls, a work shirt, and a kerchief over her hair, but Colleen Stuart Cleaves could. She was nearly as tall as Jared, about five foot nine, and slim through the hips. Willow Run had put some muscle on her arms and shoulders, and to his constant befuddlement Jared found he liked it. Watching her get ready for work, Jared was fiercely proud of his wife. He got up and hugged her from behind as she sipped her coffee and looked out the kitchen window into their little patch of backyard.

"Honey," he said. "You work near the new wing of the plant they put on?"

"Hm-mm," she said, her lips still on the rim of her cup. "All the way at the other end. And it's not that new. It's been there a year."

"What are they doing in there?"

She turned around. "I don't know. Everything over that way is classified. Why?"

"Boys at the Rouge are talking, all kinds of wild stories. There's a pool together, fellows have put up twenty dollars if I can get you to find out."

"Twenty dollars? Jared Cleaves, what is wrong with you? Even if I could find out, and even if I wanted to, what if one of the men in your pool is FBI? Or a spy or something? You know what kind of trouble we'd be in?"

He spread his arms in a show of innocence, but the deception gnawed at him. "Simmer down, honey, come on. Only reason I'm asking is because one of the guys in the pool is Swerdlow. If I don't come up with something he's going to be on me like white on rice."

Emily toddled into the kitchen, face still puffy with sleep. Jared picked her up and she laid her head on his shoulder. "Daddy," she said.

"Good morning, baby doll." Jared looked at Colleen. "Just ask around, is all I'm saying. There won't be any trouble. Gossip at the Rouge moves faster than an Italian retreat, and I bet Willow Run isn't any different. Anyone says anything, just tell 'em you heard it from some girls in the washroom or something. Twenty dollars."

She looked at him for long enough that he'd about given up, and when she spoke she changed the subject. "Where were you yesterday, by the way? Mrs. Pelletier said she had Emily all day."

"Only from eight to about ten thirty. There was a meeting over at the plant." Pangs of shame were shooting up and down Jared's stomach, both for the lies he was telling his wife and for the OEI's duplicity. Goddamn Swerdlow. He stroked Emily's hair and scratched her back a little through the cotton pajamas with sunflowers on them.

"Me want go potty," Emily said, reaching out for Colleen. Jared set her down, and Colleen led her into the bathroom. He stood leaning against the stove, listening to their voices drift in the house. Even apart from lying to his wife, now he was going to have to get twenty dollars. Maybe Swerdlow will give it to me, he thought, and chuckled. Fat chance.

Emily shrieked in two-year-old delight and came running naked into the kitchen, showing all of her teeth in a grin that would have cracked Jared's jaw if he'd tried it. "Emily naked, Daddy!" she yelled.

"Yes, you are, honey." He picked her up again. When Colleen came back for her coffee, he said, "How about this baby girl?"

Colleen rolled her eyes. "Oh, she's something. Say bye to Mama."

"Bye, Mama," Emily chirped.

The other two Eens arrived with a honk in Nadine's car. Colleen kissed Emily, then Jared. "I sure hope you've seen that twenty dollars," she said to him with a warning arch of one eyebrow.

"See you tonight," he said, and waved in unison with Emily's little hand as his wife drove away to Willow Run. "Could be that'll work," he said, while part of his mind galloped off into a daydream of joyriding through the country with Arlene Bannister.

"What work, Daddy?"

"Could be it would work if I hung you upside down like a bat," he said, and with her peals of laughter the day had really begun.

The specter of the Rouge couldn't be avoided forever, though, and Jared walked out of the house at two o'clock feeling like the sky was going to fall on his head. Emily trundled along beside him, keeping up a running commentary on the number and size of the puddles left by a thunderstorm that had swept through around noon. She wasn't wearing her galoshes, but Jared let her stomp the puddles. She'd be barefoot at Mrs. Pelletier's anyway. She broke away from him and ran the last fifty feet or so to Mrs. Pelletier's sidewalk; as she slowed down to make the turn, her steps shortened but her legs pumped just as fast, and her left hand reached out to the lawn jockey Mrs. Pelletier painted every year on the first Sunday in May. The picture imprinted itself on Jared's mind with that shock of immediacy he always felt a moment before he knew he'd just seen something he'd never forget. Emily made the turn, head down, arms pulled in tight, hair catching the sun as it bounced in time with the thump and squish of her footsteps. Keep this one, Jared thought. He was sad with the knowledge that by next spring she wouldn't run like that anymore, broken into pieces by the sight of her and the immense pressure of time about to begin passing again. Mrs. Pelletier was at her door in her sun hat; she swept Jared's daughter up in her freckly old woman's arms, and Emily took the hat and plunked it on her own head, disappearing from the shoulders up.

"Bye, honey," Jared called. Emily wriggled back to the ground and ran back to give him a kiss. She hugged him and then pulled away, delighted with herself for being such a big girl. Then she was gone into the house, looking for Mrs. Pelletier's grandnephew Warren.

"Terrible, what happened to that old Indian's house," Mrs. Pelletier said. To Jared's knowledge, she was the only person on the block who wouldn't call Plenty Coup by his popular moniker.

"Did they find him?" he asked.

She shook her head. "The firemen asked me if I knew where his family was, and so help me I almost said Little Big Horn. I think that was old Wilf trying to talk through me. He always did have a coarse humor about him. Not that that's an excuse for me, but I just never trusted him. The Indian, not Wilf. Although I didn't always trust Wilf, either." She shooed away the cloud of disconnected thoughts. "Anyway, no, they didn't find him. But I don't know where he could have gone."

Both of them had been looking down the block at the sodden ruin of Plenty Coup's house, but now Mrs. Pelletier looked up at Jared. "Do you know how old he was?"

"No idea," Jared said. "Wouldn't be surprised if he was ninety, though."

"He had an awful big nose," said Mrs. Pelletier. "They say your nose never stops growing. Shame on me; that poor old man. I wonder where he went."

"Maybe he's got kids somewhere," Jared said, just to say something.

Warren and Emily set up a racket in the house. "That's my cue," Mrs. Pelletier said. Before she let the screen door bang shut behind her, she added, "You be careful, Jared," just like she did every working day. Not knowing anything about the racial makeup of the Rouge steelworks, she thought he worked there because he'd said something about clay once; being from Detroit and therefore through osmosis having a skeletal understanding of industrial processes, she figured he meant the bentonite used to make green-sand molds. He'd never bothered to correct her since the Frankenline was a deep dark secret. Swerdlow was a pure maniac about secrecy. Moises, too; he rarely said anything to any of them, but when he did it was typically an admonition to keep quiet. "Loose lips," he'd say, having seen the phrase on propaganda posters. Jared couldn't figure Moises out. The one time Swerdlow had hired a Russian to work the gurneys, Moises had locked himself into the Tabernacle for sixteen hours, until every single gurney was racked and the whole line had to shut down. Swerdlow fired the Russian, and Moises came out and did nothing but animate golems for thirty-six hours. Even so, it was four days before the line was back to normal.

Funny you should have been thinking about the line shutting down, Jared mused at about eleven that night when the screener seized up. It had already been a lousy shift. Four of the seven golems Moises had animated weren't within spec, which where golems was concerned meant that they never came to life, or occasionally that they did get up off the gurneys but then just stood there or wandered around bumping into things. Tonight one of the golems had sat on the edge of its gurney like a hospital patient, methodically scratching its balls, until Moises came out and wiped it. The Jeweler had caught hell for that one. "What, did you get poison ivy?" Jem wanted to know. Then he cocked his head and said, "Boom, J! You hear that one?"

"Goddammit, Jem, shut up," Jared snarled. He was persecuted by Swerdlow, frustrated by Colleen, uncomfortably filled with pity for the Jeweler, and generally lacking in tolerance for Jem's prankster bullshit.

Jem ignored him and went back to hassling the Jeweler, who stood with his hands in his pockets like he was ashamed of them, which he probably was, although Jared would have figured two years molding clay privates was already enough to crush the pride out of any man. Maintenance guys crawled over the screener, taking the cowling off its motor and once in a while taking a mallet to it just on general principles. One of them just stood off to the side twirling a screwdriver through his fingers and gnawing on a cigar.

"Might be time for us to look for another line of work," Felton commented.

"Looks that way, doesn't it?" Jared said. "You think Moises is losing his touch?"

Felton considered this. "Could be."

"I'm thinking about that salt mine," Jared said.

"How about those Tigers?" Felton said.

That night, after he'd stood aching in Emily's room for the best part of an hour, Jared did wake Colleen up. "Honey," he murmured, nuzzling into the back of her neck. She rolled away from him and pushed his hand away from where it had come to rest on her hip. Jared had a moment to savor the irony that if by some lightning-strike coincidence she had chosen this night to open her body to him again, he would likely have forgotten to ask her about the new wing at Willow Run and they would both have been out of work. Sometimes it was better to be turned down, but God, it still ate at him. She might as well sleep in a burlap sack.

"Honey," he said again. "Remember what we talked about this morning?"

"Go sleep," she said. "Morning."

So morning it would be. Jared lay spooned with his wife, hand unchallenged on her hip again. If I'm going to be a man of clay, he thought, might as well have a wife of stone. As he drifted into sleep, he was wondering what it would be like to work in the salt mine with his old man.

In the morning Jared dragged himself out of bed when he heard Emily's footsteps outside the bedroom door. Usually she crawled under the covers with her parents after she got out of her own bed, and they rested in a drowsy pile for a few minutes before starting the day. Most mornings, Jared let himself drift away again when Colleen got up, but today he got up with them, shaving with one eye open while Emily sat at the kitchen table asking Colleen what she was doing—which was the same thing Colleen did every morning. Break eggs (when there were eggs), brew coffee (ersatz when they couldn't get the real thing), get herself ready for work, prod Jared out of bed. Only this time when she came to prod him he was already in the bathroom grumbling over a nick under the hinge of his jaw.

"If I'd known twenty dollars would get you out of bed this early, I'd offer it to you every day," she said.

He laughed even though there was more than a little needling behind the joke. "You Ford workers think your money makes you the queen of England."

Colleen tore off a small piece of toilet paper and pressed it over the nick. "Remember to take it off before you go to work," she said.

Emily ran in and said, "Daddy shaving!" She set down the teddy bear she'd been carrying and squatted on the floor. "Emily watch." The look on her face after she said this always killed him; she was a parodic exemplar of fierce determination, mouth set in a line and a little crease between her eyes.

"You watch, honey," he said, and kept on shaving. When he was

THE NARROWS — 75

done, Emily bounced up and ran back to the kitchen. He picked up the teddy bear and tossed it on her bed before heading for breakfast, and when he sat down, Jared made a point of being appreciative of the eggs and toast Colleen had ready. He never meant to take her for granted, but sometimes it happened. Today, with Swerdlow waiting on the other side of his shift, couldn't be one of those times. "So, what's the mystery building?" he asked after he'd complimented the golden brown of the toast and the perfect yolks of the eggs.

His wife shot him a look that let him know he hadn't fooled her a bit. Not that he'd expected to. This was one of those situations in which you made the gesture, and hoped that the making of the gesture was enough.

"People are talking about it, that's for sure," she said. "If the FBI's going to arrest people for talking about it, Willow Run will have to shut down."

"Talking how?"

"Well, for starters they're saying that nobody who works there is a Ford employee. It's a fed project, subcontracted somehow." She looked at Jared across the table, giving him a chance to comment. Since the only thing that popped into his head was a comment about the OEI and golems, he kept his mouth shut, and she went on. "There's a train spur to it, runs right into the building, but the only thing that ever goes in is cattle cars. At first people thought that Ford was starting up a slaughterhouse and he was going to feed everyone, but we've still got the same old lunch-box concession we've had since we started."

This was one of the ways Harry Bennett kept in good with Detroit's mobsters. They let him know ahead of time when someone was planning to kidnap one of Ford's grandkids, and he gave them sweetheart concessions at the plants; most Ford workers bought their lunches from the Black Hand. Jared had also heard around the Rouge that Bennett was running black-market parts out the back door, but nobody could swear to it.

"So where does all the beef go?"

Colleen shrugged. Observing closely, so did Emily. "The cars are closed. Maybe it goes right back out. But the cars aren't refrigerated, so it's not going far. Maybe they're doing something with it in there. Ford's got that Chemurgical Society making plastic out of soybeans; maybe he's trying to make cars out of beef now."

"Cars metal, Mama," Emily said.

"Yes, they are, baby girl." Colleen wiped egg from Emily's mouth and looked up at the clock. "The girls should be here. Kiss Mama good-bye."

Emily did, and Nadine blared her horn outside. After Colleen left, Jared watched Emily gnaw the butter off one side of her toast and wondered how he would make it all sound good enough for Swerdlow not to fire him. She didn't kiss me, he thought.

When he drove to work that afternoon, Jared was thinking about Arlene Bannister. In a concerted effort to stop thinking about Arlene Bannister, he changed his mental channel and started working over the Dwarf Dreams. He seemed to have them whenever something was on his mind that he wasn't sure how to deal with, and had over the years constructed an elaborate way of interpreting whatever elements didn't belong in the core Dwarf story. When he was in high school, he'd written a history paper on the Nain Rouge's appearances: to Cadillac before he was drummed out of Detroit in 1701, to British troops before they were slaughtered at Bloody Run in 1763, to people all over town before Detroit burned in 1805, to General Hull before he surrendered Detroit during the War of 1812. The essay had earned him one of the few As of his school career, which was ironic because in writing it he had simply transcribed the dreams he'd been having since he was five. One disaster after another, all following immediately after a Dwarf sighting—and here was where the Dwarf had thrown the Cleaves men a curveball. In another couple of months it would be twenty-four years since Jared and his father had seen it in Highland Park. Since then all kinds of bad things had happened in Detroit—Ford's cash crisis in 1921, the bank holidays, the Depression, mob massacres, labor strife—but none of them had been catastrophic for Jared or, in the long run, for the city. Even Marty Cleaves, in whom natural human adaptability tended to manifest itself as a tendency to insist that problems didn't exist, had rolled with the worst of what the Depression had to offer, hanging on to his job in the salt mine and keeping Jared and his two sisters in clean clothes and Christmas presents. They'd even taken a vacation in Maine when he was a kid. Usually Jared could brush it all off, figure that his father had just been drunk and he himself had been dreaming or susceptible because of the way he'd had his bell rung on the door frame. When malign influences like Swerdlow or sexual deprivation preyed on his mind, though, Jared started to feel like the Dwarf had just given him a lot of advance notice.

At some point during the Depression, maybe when he'd graduated high school in 1932, Jared had come to the final conclusion that the Dwarf had appeared to him instead of his father. The old man felt differently; every time the car broke down or the roof sprung a leak or one of the kids needed to go to the doctor, Marty Cleaves got disconsolate and crawled into a bottle for a while. He always held himself together, but while he was in these funks he talked about the Dwarf the way Henry Ford talked about Jewish bankers, hinting that he'd known that little red bastard would get him, and this was it happening now. Only it never was; the Cleaveses had come through the Depression just fine while people lined up by the thousands for the mirage of a job or a loaf of charity bread. Jared had never known how lucky he was until he'd started working on the Frankenline and heard some of Jem's stories. Jem's childhood made Jared feel like Henry Ford II.

* * *

For once, he'd anticipated a Swerdlow interaction being worse than it actually turned out. He found the man in his office and started right in before Swerdlow could derail him. "The new wing is a fed project. Nobody knows what it is, except there's a lot of cattle cars going into it. Maybe it's a slaughterhouse. Could be Mr. Ford needs one; there's an awful lot of people working out there, and a year ago it was a soybean farm."

"I thought it was a summer camp for poor kids or something," Swerdlow said.

"I guess you'd know better than me."

Swerdlow squinted at him. "That's what you got?"

"That's all anyone has, Mr. Swerdlow. That's what I could find out."

"Okay, Cleaves. You can take a deep breath. But keep listening. I'm going to need more than cattle cars before long."

CHAPTER 4

Sunday morning, Colleen went off to visit her parents at Fortress Stuart in the hinterlands south of Ypsilanti, a trip Jared avoided only after promising that on the thirtieth they would all go for the day. If it had been up to him, he would have limited his interactions with the Stuarts to Christmas and maybe Thanksgiving, but it had long since become clear to Jared that when you married a woman you married her parents too—even if those parents considered you a deadbeat with a suspicious strain of hillbilly in your blood. Jared could get along with Theo Stuart as long as the conversation stuck to hunting, baseball, and home improvement, but Deirdre Stuart maintained toward her son-in-law a policy of subtle denigration that survived Jared's every attempt to ingratiate himself to her. In addition, she routinely committed what Jared regarded as the cardinal sin of pedantry: a retired teacher of English, she rarely wasted an opportunity to show off the fact that she had a vocabulary that would humble Clarence Darrow. So offering up a fine Sunday, their only day off from work, was to Jared's way of thinking a pretty serious concession (although he was conscious as she left that Colleen didn't share this assessment). He resigned himself to it, and made himself feel better by reiterating to himself the point that Emily should know all of her grandparents. If he couldn't be a good son-in-law, he could at least be a good dad.

Having no car, and impatient with his own company, Jared took Emily to his parents' house over on Logan Street. Grandma CeeCee was the real reason for the visit; Jared's dad loved Emily, but Jared often had the feeling that Grandpa Marty might have loved a charming dog the same way. Other people, with the occasional exception of his wife and son, were mostly entertainment for Marty Cleaves. Grandma CeeCee, on the other hand, not having any other grandchildren, devoted much of her life to the pursuit of Emily's happiness. It was a marvel to Jared how two people with such radically variant perspectives on life had stayed together for thirty years and raised a kid—a marvel that lately he hadn't wanted to examine too closely, since he and Colleen had started to have trouble. And it was time to admit that there was more going on than just a rough spot; at some point they had passed that and gone into the land of serious problems. Jared's mother knew this, and with exquisite timing always tried to bring it up at exactly those moments when he was least prepared to discuss it. Then his reticence annoyed her, and she took Emily off somewhere and let Jared and his father sit together in their collective willful ignorance.

Today was no different. "You should have gone out to Theo and Deirdre's," CeeCee chided him. "This little girl sees us all the time; she needs to be around both sides of her family."

"Mom," Jared said. "Are you seriously telling me that you want to see less of your granddaughter?"

"No, I'm telling you that you should spend more time with your wife."

"I don't know that she wants to spend any more time with me," he said.

"What you talk about?" Emily piped up.

"Nothing, baby girl. Grown-up stuff," Jared said. He looked

back to his mother, hoping she'd take the hint, but CeeCee Cleaves
had been an obstinate girl and was an even more obstinate woman.

"I think what you need is another baby," she said.

"Me, too," Jared said. "Colleen says after the war is over."

"Well, she knows what she wants." CeeCee sighed. "Better than
you do, I think. Too many only children in this family."

On this topic, as well as a great many others, Marty Cleaves had
a theory. Two theories, really: the first that Jared and Colleen had
first gotten interested in each other because they were both only
children, and the second that all of their domestic aggravation came
about because they unconsciously wanted their family to look like
their parents', but also wanted to be different. "If you could settle
whether or not you were going to have another kid," was Marty
Cleaves' opinion, "all this other stuff would clear up. A three-legged
table will stand up, but there's a reason people build 'em with four.
Triangles and squares." Jared considered it a great misfortune that
his father had ever read a book about psychology, if he ever had. It
was just as likely that he'd heard someone talk about psychology on
the radio once and now figured that he knew as much about it as any
man needed to know.

My pop, Jared thought, looking at the old man with his can of
beer and his feet up on the empty lawn chair that sat facing his. Not
really old, just fifty-one, but already far beyond his former self. The
Marty Cleaves who had blasted around Michigan back roads selling
whiskey out of the back of a borrowed Model T was dead as the
pharaohs. He'd now been back in the salt mine for nearly twenty-
four years, long enough that his life before 1919 must have seemed
as if it belonged to someone else. This never seemed to bother him,
though. He put in his eight hours a day blasting salt out of a prehis-
toric ocean; twice a week he had maybe one drink too many at the
VFW; once a week he bowled at the Oakwood Lanes; once a week
he and CeeCee went downtown for a movie. During the summer he
saw at least a dozen Tigers games, and during the winter he trans-

ferred his passion to the Red Wings, who after losing the Stanley Cup finals to the hated Maple Leafs in '42 had savaged the Boston Bruins to win the Cup this year. Since the start of the war, Marty Cleaves' favorite topic of conversation was the debasement of both baseball and hockey. His current discontentment of choice was the fact that the Red Wings' leading goal scorer during the past season was a journeyman named Mud Bruneteau. "Thank God Syd Howe had more assists, or the Wings' best player on a team that won the Stanley Cup would have been a guy named Mud," he was saying now.

"Come on, Pop," Jared said. "It's baseball season. Tigers beat the Sens eight to one yesterday. Live it up a little."

"The mook they were hitting against, anybody would have scored eight runs."

Jared's part in this passion play was advocate for the defense. "York and Wakefield aren't just anybody," he said. "Trout's not a bad arm, and I think Newhouser—"

"Newhouser? He got out of the war for a heart murmur. Hell with Newhouser. You know what a heart murmur is? When a man gets scared shitless at his exam, that's what a heart murmur is."

This was getting a little close to home. Heart murmur, two kinked-up fingers, how different was it? "Trucks," Jared said. "I like the look of him."

His father ignored this. Once Marty Cleaves warmed to the topic of the Tigers' ineptitude, he had to get it all out of his system. "At least Jimmy Outlaw can say he's got flat feet. A man can't march with flat feet. Truth of it is, the team's been a goddamn mess since Greenberg went back in. Tebbetts, McCosky, Benton . . ." Marty ticked off the names of the Tigers who had enlisted since Pearl Harbor. "Christ, we've got nothing left."

"You're never happy unless you're miserable."

"I'm happy when Walter Briggs fields a major-league team,

Wakefield's a college kid. Fifty-two thousand dollars they gave him, and he's never swung at big-league pitching. Hell, he should be in the war, too."

Before yesterday's win, the Tigers had lost their two to the Athletics, dropping them to 9–9. Last night they'd gotten back on the right side of .500, and there was a doubleheader today. If they took both, they'd be in second place. Jared knew what was going to happen next.

"What the hell, let's go to the ball game," Marty said.

Jared walked to the back fence, where Emily was "helping" her grandmother clean spiderwebs out of the chain link. She was decked in spider silk from head to toe, and Grandma CeeCee—the great reader in the family—was saying something about fairies and Shakespeare. Jared wondered if something in the air around 1600, the Spanish Armada maybe, had actually brought fairies out the way that the beginning of the war had sprouted things like golems and the Tenfingers.

"Seen any fairies today?" he asked.

"Gramma says fairies come out at night," Emily said.

Jared nodded. "She's probably right. Mom, you mind watching the girl while Pop and I go to the ball game?"

His mother waved a hand. "Shoo," she said. "Do I mind. Go."

They did, and got to Briggs in time to watch the sad sacks who passed for major leaguers take infield practice. "Ted Williams would hit .500 against this bunch," said Marty Cleaves.

"And Greenberg would hit a hundred home runs."

"Well, hell, at least it's a ball game." They settled in and watched the Tigers miss cutoff men and throw to the wrong base, and lose both games of the doubleheader. Dizzy Trout, classified 4-F because he was hard of hearing and nearsighted, pitched the first game, and at least once missed a pickoff sign, which had the few thousand souls at Briggs Stadium falling all over each other to make blind jokes. After a while it got farcical. "This bunch is playing .500 ball," Dad said wonderingly at one point. "At least everyone else who watches baseball is suffering as bad as we are."

When they got back, Colleen had come over, and they decided to cook out. Seven or eight years before, in one of his periodic fits of initiative, Marty Cleaves had built a barbecue pit in the backyard. They fired it up and sat around in the long evening, watching the birds flit among the branches of the pines that lined the back of the lot. To the south, past the cemetery, the plume of smoke from the Rouge steelworks spread across the southern sky. Steelworkers made overtime like you wouldn't believe. Part of it was just the cost-plus contracts Ford had wrung out of the War Department, but if you'd ever been inside a foundry, you knew steelworkers earned every dollar they made.

The gate at the side of the house clinked and Walter Howes strolled into the backyard. He worked at the salt mine, too, and lived only three houses down from the elder Cleaveses. "I'll trade you a beer for a burger," he said, holding up a six-pack of Stroh's.

"Pull up some sod, there, Walt," Marty said.

Walt did, sitting in the grass, which for reasons of his lumbago he preferred to a chair. Jared couldn't figure this out, but Walt swore by it. When he had outfitted himself with a hamburger and popped the cap off of his first Stroh's, he sprawled out and said between bites, "Connor Flaherty's boy went to the Draft Marshal today."

Jared sat very still, looking out at the pall across the southern sky. All across Detroit, even on Sunday, the engines of the war churned the sky into a smoky soup. It made for beautiful sunsets and, when the weather was right, a lot of postnasal drip. He didn't want to talk about the Draft Marshal, but he also didn't want to look like he didn't want to talk about the Draft Marshal, because figuring out what exactly the Marshal did was one of the great armchair sports of wartime Detroit. Jared knew more about the topic than did the vast majority of his fellow Detroiters, but if he would ever have been inclined to blab, the past few days had set him straight. He looked at the veiled sun sinking down into the pines at the back of his father's yard, and he listened. Listening to people gossip, speculate, and come to completely erroneous conclusions about things Jared did every day was one of the few enjoyable side benefits of working for the OEI.

"Wonder if it's got anything to do with the thing," mused Marty Cleaves.

Walt shrugged. "Could. Draft Marshal takes a lot of boys."

But not all of them, Jared thought. "What thing?" he asked. A nice, neutral question.

"Oh, let's see . . . it was February. I remember because the niggers was just moving into the new housing project over by the smelter there on Fenelon. We was blasting out to one of the shallower parts of the vein," Walt said. "I wasn't there." He drove a truck between the blast sites and the giant crushers used to grind the salt boulders into pieces small enough to make efficient loads in the cargo elevators. He and the other drivers called themselves donkeys in honor of the animals that had done this work before trucks big enough were built. For the donkeys, it was a one-way trip down the elevator—or, in the mine's early years, a one-way trip down a shaft in a rope sling. They worked until they died, the only fatalities the mine had known after its first shafts were sunk in the late '90s. "Guess they found something wasn't supposed to be there, because they yelled for the foreman, and he yelled for a manager down from up top, and it wasn't an hour before we saw the Marshal and maybe a dozen of his boys. They took my truck back there, and then they cleared the whole mine out. Next day we went back to work, only that whole area was gated off and none of the men on that clearing crew showed up. The Marshal took every last one of 'em." Warren finished his burger and lit a cigarette. "That Draft Marshal gets what he wants."

"I seen one of those boys out in Ann Arbor," Dad said. "Maybe two weeks ago."

"Hell you did."

"Hell I didn't. I got a soft spot for the candy counter at Drake's there by the college, and if that wasn't Roy Halliday in line in front of me, I'm Gandhi."

Colleen and CeeCee burst out laughing at this. Emily joined in as soon as she figured out that someone had said something funny. "Grampa funny," she said, and laughed some more, big fake *ha-ha-ha*s that went on after everyone else had stopped.

"There ain't no candy counter in Detroit good enough for you, I guess," Walter said. "Where'd you get the gas coupons?"

"I save 'em just for that, take a drive on weekends. Before CeeCee and I go to the pictures."

Colleen had an odd look on her face. She glanced over at Jared and then asked, "What was he doing in Ann Arbor? Did the Marshal send him to college?"

Now it was Walter and Marty's turn to laugh. Apparently Roy Halliday wasn't college material. Jared could see the skin around Colleen's eyes tighten; she didn't like to be laughed at by men of Marty Cleaves' generation. He was willing to bet that she'd put the question that way so either Marty or Walter would get talking about what they thought the Marshal would do in this or that situation, but he couldn't figure out what had sparked her interest. Then she looked at him again, and he got it   she was probing to see if there was a connection between the cattle cars at Willow Run and her father-in-law's sighting of a recent OEI recruit in Ann Arbor. It had never occurred to Jared to do this. That's my girl, he thought. Looking out for me when I'm too scatterbrained to do it myself.

"I don't know," Marty said. "But he was there, and when I said hey he just looked at me and walked out. I ended up eating the sandwich they'd fixed for him."

What would one of the Marshal's men be doing in Ann Arbor?

Jared couldn't make sense of it. Didn't the Marshal put his men to work in one of the war theaters once they'd proved themselves? What was all the secrecy about if they were just going to Ann Arbor? Jared felt oddly disappointed by this revelation—he'd imagined the Marshal's service to be something daring and . . . well, esoteric. Maybe the Marshal really was drafting the foundry imps and just needed men to keep an eye on them. There'd been that goblin at the office. Jared started thinking about what Felton had said. Was he really just some kind of pawn in a pissing contest between the Marshal and Swerdlow? And if he was, how the hell had Swerdlow won?

Roy Halliday, Jared thought. It seemed useful to know the name. He turned it over in his mind as the sky darkened and Dad kept pace with Walt's strenuous drinking regimen. Conversation turned to other topics: the troubles over the Sojourner Truth houses, the war, the various profiteering schemes cooked up by Detroit captains of industry. All things they'd chewed over before, and took pleasure in because of their familiarity and constancy. The long summer evening finally reached darkness sometime around nine, and when Emily fell apart after an hour spent chasing fireflies Colleen and Jared took her home.

On Monday the mood on the Frankenline was subdued. Nobody hassled the Jeweler, nobody cracked wise about Moises, everyone kept his repertoire of ethnic jokes and insults in his pocket. Early that morning word had gotten around that the SS had declared the Warsaw Ghetto *Judenfrei*. The molders worked in silence, and the word from the day shift was that Moises hadn't come out of the Tabernacle all day. Around nine the sorting line sat idle because nobody could find the union crane operator who was the only guy allowed to run the scoop bucket. Outside, a full carload of clay sat dripping on the tracks.

"You ever wonder where the rest of the magic is?" Jem said.

"Here we are working on golems, and there's imps in the foundry, but where's the rest of it? Genies and dragons and such."

"There's the Tenfingers over to the Dearborn line," Felton said.

"Right, okay, but they're just imps, too. All's they do is count."

This wasn't entirely accurate. The Tenfingers separated piles of washers, nuts, rivets, hose clamps—anything small and lying around in quantity—into piles of ten, and stole what was left. Nobody had yet figured out where the stuff went, and it had just about driven Ford's inventory-control people out of their minds before they'd instituted a strict drawdown of all fasteners and similar items at the end of every shift. It had proved cheaper to hire men to count everything and return extra parts to one of the parts cages than to suffer the Tenfingers' continual depredations. Guys on the assembly lines saw the Tenfingers once in a while and described them as pale and stooped, wearing glasses, with long fingers and expressions of deep worry. Once in a while they caught one and killed it, but Tenfingers never fought back, and pretty soon the killing had lost its luster. Now, with the new drawdowns in place, they shuffled around more or less undisturbed. Word was they were starting to disappear.

Jared had never seen one, but he had a theory about them, which he shared now with Jem. "You know how ghosts are supposed to be what's left behind when someone dies bad?" he said. "The Tenfingers, I bet they're the same thing, only they're this remnant of every Ford accountant who ever had a heart attack from working too hard."

"Inventory managers," Felton said. "Accountants would be over across Schaefer Road counting pennies."

"Okay, inventory managers. Same thing."

"No, it's not. But it ain't worth arguing about." Felton picked up a shovel and walked over to the empty car. Jem and Jared stood around kicking pebbles into the canal until they figured out that Felton hadn't just picked up the shovel to avoid the discussion. He was really working. "Dang," Jem said. "That Felton is one mysterious nigger."

"Come on, Jem," Jared said.

"I guess we can't let him shovel out that whole car himself," Jem said, picking up a shovel of his own. Jared followed. "I heard there was frost giants destroyed an airfield up in the UP last winter," Jem said after they'd climbed up into the car.

Felton paused in the act of scraping clay out of a corner. "Where'd you hear that?" His tone of voice left Jared with the impression that Felton had heard the same thing. He picked up an amazing amount of news from the Negro soldiers he knew in Europe, most of which never survived to come out of Winchell's mouth stateside. Jared found it a little disconcerting what officers would say to each other when nobody else was around but colored mess workers or truck drivers. The Negro units seemed to know more about what the golems were up to than anyone else; Felton was of the opinion that the army stowed the golems back with the support units, which were more likely to be colored.

"One of my neighbors was an airman, got shot down and half burned up over England last year," Jem said. "So he's home now. He heard from buddies of his up to K. I. Sawyer that frost giants wrecked the field."

"So did Thor show up and kill 'em, or are they on their way down here?"

"Goddamn, Felton. We're in a war. Can't you take anything serious?" Jem was starting to get himself worked up, but then he froze. "Hear that one, J? Boom!"

Jared kept shoveling. "I asked my old man about that. He said they aren't working anywhere near here right now. They're out under Melvindale. So shut up and push your wheelbarrow."

"I don't think a frost giant would come down here now," Jem said with a great show of consideration. "Being it's May and all. They'd melt like Frosty the Snowman, wouldn't they?"

"They aren't made out of frost," Felton countered. "They're just giants who live way up in the north."

Jem waved away the distinction. "So they'd have some kind of heatstroke around here. I ain't worried about no frost giants."

The car was almost clean, and Jared left Felton to hose it out. He went back inside just as a golem came out of Moises' office. It looked around Building G just long enough to get its bearings, and then it walked out the door to the waiting train car on the next track. Jared watched it all the way into the car; every time one of the golems worked perfectly now, he was awash in relief. Moises came out onto the floor and stretched his neck. Damn awful day to be him, Jared thought, and walked up, trying to make it seem casual. The rabbi looked bad, he thought. Not that Moises had ever looked like he was ready to swim the English Channel, but his beard was tangled, his eyes were watery, and there was a tremor in his hands. This is a guy working himself to death, Jared thought. And the news from Warsaw can't be helping.

"Sorry, Moises," he said.

Moises didn't look at him. "Eh," he said.

"Yeah," Jared said. A question popped into his head, and since he'd been taught from an early age that changing the subject was as good a way as any to ignore a terrible truth, he said, "Is there anybody else doing this?"

Moises looked up at the catwalk. When he saw that nobody was around except the regular shift crew smoking butts while they waited for the screener to start up, he shrugged. "I have hear, yes. Is terrible times now, but good times for making."

Jared thought this over. Something Moises had said provoked a dim, embryonic idea in his head, but he wasn't sure where it was coming from, and Moises' fractured English didn't help any. Making.

"Say," he said. "Whatever happened to all those first golems?"

About two weeks after the Frankenline had started running, the first shipment of golems made from good old Michigan clay had boarded trains and gone off to join the war. Then whoever had planned Building G got a bucket of cold water in the face: the golems wouldn't get on the boat to go to Europe. For several days government and military planners burned up the phone lines to every rabbi in the eastern United States, and then they figured out that it was because the golems were made of American clay. That idled the project for three weeks, and nearly put the kibosh on the whole thing until some bright bulb somewhere proposed that they use the American golems for border protection. So the Frankenline kept on making American golems for a month until the shipments of European clay started to show up, but none of them had ever heard what happened to them.

Moises shrugged. "G-Two come and take them."

G-2. That was military intelligence. "They hunting spies or what?"

Another shrug. "I don't know. G-Two just take them. I see one here, one there."

"Here? In the plant?"

"In Detroit. Once down by the bridge, then I see one just two days ago in Eastern Market."

Eastern Market, Jared thought. Why would a golem be in Eastern Market, and what would G-2 want with a million farmers and street vendors and fortune-tellers? The flow of European imported goods into Detroit had been pretty much choked off for two years. What would G-2 . . .

Smuggling, Jared thought. That has to be it. G-2's worried about some kind of contraband. Spies, or something, encrypted messages; if there was a time and place in Detroit where you could slip a message to someone unnoticed, it was Saturday morning at the Eastern Market. So G-2 wants a golem watching out, and if they've got a golem watching out, the OEI has to be involved. Jared put it together. Swerdlow was full of shit; OEI didn't have anything to do with the FBI. The military guys hated the FBI because of Hoover's grandstanding, and they didn't like the OSS much, either, because Wild Bill Donovan was a little too eager to get his fingers in military pies. OEI and G-2 must be working together, Jared thought, and his frustration at being turned down by the Marshal— or submarined by Swerdlow—redoubled. What he wouldn't give to be in on the whole game. He got a tingle on the back of his neck just thinking about it.

"What did you mean by *making*?" he asked Moises.

The rabbi spread his arms. "Look. All magic that works, is making. Machines only are magic now."

The scoop bucket crane started up with a roar. Someone had finally tracked down the operator; time to get back to the line.

Swerdlow appeared on the catwalk about ninety seconds before the midnight whistle. "Cleaves!" he snapped. Jared went up the stairs and Swerdlow said, "What's going on at Willow Run?"

"I told you, Mr. Swerdlow. Colleen said nobody knows and everyone's just full of hot air."

"You need to tell me what happens to those cattle, Cleaves."

"Mr. Swerdlow. If you told me what this was all about I might be able to do you more good. I can't just bull around asking everyone I know why there's trainloads of beef cattle going to Willow Run." Jared was gambling, but he was damned if he was going to live out the war wondering every minute when Swerdlow would show up and want just one more bit of information. Get it all out in the open, he thought. Find out why Swerdlow wanted to keep you out of the Marshal's hands, and why the Marshal let him.

Swerdlow eyeballed him for a long time, long enough that Jared reached the conclusion that the gamble hadn't worked. Then Swerdlow said, "Could be you're right, kid. Let me sleep on it and we'll sort it out tomorrow. Stop in my office at two o'clock."

He's nervous about something, Jared was thinking as he changed in the locker room. Bad enough to have management on your ass, but Jared judged that someone was on Swerdlow's ass, too, and Swerdlow was making sure that there was someone else for the shit to roll downhill onto. That was enough to worry about for one day, but when Jared walked out of Building G and out to the parking lot at the western edge of the Rouge complex, he saw someone leaning against his car. Right away he figured it was one of the tire plant vigilantes, and he felt fine about it. If they wanted a fight, they'd found him in the right frame of mind. Special Service, Black Hand, sadistic Lithuanian vets; Jared was ready for it all.

"You Jared Cleaves?" the guy said when Jared was about thirty feet from the car.

"How'd you know this was my car?"

The man stuck out his hand. He wasn't on the Rouge payroll, that much you could tell by looking at him. Sharp suit, new hat, gold watch catching the streetlight, all of it decorating a body that moved with a kind of grace you didn't see from men who made their livings wrestling machines. "Easy, friend. I'm John Dash. We should talk."

"Who says?"

"Swerdlow's not giving you the whole story. I might, if you'll shake my hand."

Jared hesitated. No reason not to shake the man's hand, he thought, even though as he did his mind teemed with images of FBI or G-2 operatives clicking away at miniature infrared cameras. He swore to himself that the first time anyone flashed a badge at him, he was going to roll over on Swerdlow quicker than a dog wanting a belly scratch.

"Let's take a ride," Dash said. He walked around to the passenger door and got in. Jared started the car and pulled out onto Miller Road. When they stopped for the light at Michigan Avenue, Jared said, "Which way do you want to go?"

"You need to get home?"

Jared shrugged. "Not right away."

"Let's go down by the river. Get a beer."

The waterfront side of Jefferson just east of downtown was a thicket of bars. It was nearly one by the time they got there, but places in this part of town didn't get much flak over keeping the taps flowing late. A hand-carved sign hanging off a three-story dock-side warehouse said JOE SENT ME. It was quiet enough inside that Jared didn't particularly want to have a private conversation there, but Dash didn't seem bothered. He wasn't raising his voice, but he made no real effort to stay quiet, either.

When the beers arrived, Jared got to the point. "So how much trouble did I get myself into, coming down here?"

Dash shrugged. "Nobody wants trouble. Cigarette?" He dropped a pack of Pall Malls on the bar. Jared took one. "Only way there's trouble is if Swerdlow wants it. Right now he's made some for you."

"You going to ask me about Willow Run, too?" Jared said. "I'll save you the trouble. There's a new wing on the factory. Cattle cars go in, nobody knows what comes out. The guys who work there don't talk to anyone else. The girls who work with my wife are guessing it's some kind of chemistry project, what's the thing—"

"Chemurgical Society," Dash said.

"Right."

"Yeah, that's not it."

"Okay, what is it?"

Another shrug. "It's not the Chemurgical Society, I can tell you for sure. Ford's about given up on that. Could be just about any-thing else."

Somehow Jared's beer was already gone, and Dash had barely touched his. Something about this set off a warning bell in Jared's mind, but he couldn't pin it down. What the hell, he thought. In for a penny, in for a pound. If I get drunk I'll just complain about all the things I don't know. No harm in that. He waved for another. "So

Swerdlow's not giving me the whole story," he said. "What's he holding back?"

"Don't know if he's holding back or not," Dash said. "Could be he's just working from bad information. Either way, he's not giving you the whole deal."

"You going to?"

Dash traced a nickel through rings of condensation on the bar. "Depends on how the conversation goes."

"Conversation's not going to go far at all if you don't stop dancing around," Jared said.

Dash picked up his beer and took a long swallow. He looked Jared in the eye as he tipped the bottle to his mouth again. Jared bit down on whatever it was he'd been going to add. "Okay," Dash said. "When Swerdlow called the OEI, he didn't have to fight very hard."

He pushed the smokes toward Jared. "Go ahead. Light up and think about it."

Jared didn't need to think about it, but he took another. Seemed like everyone in Detroit could get cigarettes when he couldn't. "So you're telling me the Marshal didn't really want me."

"The Marshal wanted Swerdlow to tip his hand," Dash said. "Come on. You work sifting clay. What would the Marshal want you for? No offense."

"My old man says the Marshal took a bunch of guys out of the salt mine a while ago," Jared said. "They so much more suited than me?"

"You're taking this personally, Jared, and it's not personal. It's not about you or your fingers. The Marshal was waiting to see what he could do to make Swerdlow take a stand. That's all. Now, why would he want to do that?"

"The Marshal or Swerdlow?"

"Well, let's talk about Swerdlow. Why were you in such a hurry to tell me about Willow Run?"

"I figured that's what this is about."

"Because that's what Swerdlow wanted to know."

It wasn't a question, but Jared had the feeling that Dash was fishing, seeing if he would disagree. He ran through a quick mental calculus, not wanting to bring Colleen into this but not sure how he could avoid it, and concluded that if Dash knew everything he seemed to know, he'd already taken the trouble to figure out that Jared was married and had a little girl.

"He wanted me to ask my wife about it, yeah," Jared said.

"And you told Swerdlow what you told me."

"Yeah."

"Swerdlow tell you why he wanted to know?"

"No, what he told me was that he'd get both me and Colleen fired if I didn't do it. That was good enough for me."

Dash was nodding. "Yeah, I understand." He paused in mid-nod to drain his beer, and held up two fingers until the bartender looked their way. "Thing is, though," he went on when the beers had arrived, "I don't know if G-Two will see it the same way."

Taste of the smoke, drink of the beer. Steady, Jared told himself. "If you wanted to threaten me," he said, "you could have done it back in the parking lot."

"Easy," Dash said. "I'm buying the beer here. If all I'd wanted was to threaten you, I wouldn't have spent the money."

"Whose money are you spending?"

"Good question," Dash said. "Got a guess?"

Jared did, but he wasn't sure whether he should lay all of his cards on the table just yet. On the other hand, he was powerfully aware that Dash was in complete control of their interaction, that Dash knew a lot more about him than he knew about Dash, and Jared wanted to shade the balance a little more back in his own direction. If he was wrong, at least he'd know. Maybe. If Dash's reaction gave anything away.

"There's smoke coming out of your ears," Dash said.

Jared let him wait. Then he said, "It strikes me that if the Marshal was looking for Swerdlow to tip his hand, he might follow up once it happened."

"You think I'm OEI?" Dash grinned. "That's a good guess. It's wrong, but it shows you're in the right frame of mind."

He's lying, Jared thought. Pure intuition, but he felt it strongly, almost physically. "Okay," he said. "Who, then?"

"That's not on the agenda tonight."

"Dash, my frame of mind tells me you're bullshitting. If the Marshal was waiting for Swerdlow to make a move, he had to know that there was somebody Swerdlow would make a move for." Jared pointed at himself. "So who is Swerdlow talking to, and how did it get back to the OEI?"

Dash rapped his knuckles on the bar. "That, Jared old buddy, is what I need you to find out. You got butts? Here." He flicked the Pall Malls the rest of the way toward Jared. "When you know something, stop back over here. I like this place. Think I might make a habit of it. And if you want to know a little more about Swerdlow, check out what he does on Tuesdays." Leaving three dollars on the bar, Dash walked out.

Hell of a tip for four beers, Jared thought. He took a bite out of it by ordering another, and when that was gone he finished the full bottle Dash had left, just on general principles. By then it was after two, and Emily was going to be getting up awful early in the morning. Jared got up and drove home. Halfway there, on a deserted stretch of West Jefferson, a cop pulled him over long enough to make a crack about marines dying on Guadalcanal while goldbricks wasted gas and wore out their tires, then waved him on. Screw you, Jared thought. I'm working for the Marshal. This Dash guy, he's a test. Counterespionage is an indirect business. When he got home, he was riding a thrill, feeling like the setback at the Guardian Building had been a promotion in disguise.

* * *

Colleen sleeps on her side, legs drawn partially up and crossed at the ankles. One arm reaches out into the space where Jared should have been two hours ago. The other is crooked under her, the hand curled at her chin as if she's whispering a secret to someone who isn't there. To him. The night is cool, and fog has curled up from the sidewalks and backyards of southwest Detroit, become quietly incandescent in a full moon that is just beginning its long fall toward dawn. The glow permeates the bedroom and picks out the planes and curves of Colleen's body under a sheet whose drawn wrinkles recall the photographs Jared has seen of ravines fanning away down Southern California hillsides. He has the confusing sensation that he is in the air, and she on the ground. He flies above the body of his wife. To reach her he must leap, and he fears to cross the distance between sky and ground. She shifts in her sleep, makes a soft sound as she exhales and settles again. Six years, Jared thinks. Six years, and a child, and all the while letting little things go because they were grains of sand not worth fighting about, and now when they've become poisonous little pearls he finds that it's too late to do anything about them. The time to speak has passed, except both of them are able to say that something has gone wrong, they should have acted years ago. It wasn't so long ago that his love for her was the one thing in his life that saw him through everything else; now it is ravaged and confused, and every memory stings. The second part of this truth is that when the draft board turned him down eighteen months ago, Jared drew that shame disappointment into himself and would not let her salve the wound.

He holds his hand up so that it covers her. When he spreads the fingers, the last two move together. He's done this a million times before, but he reaches his left hand out and pulls his right pinkie away from the ring finger. When he lets it go, it springs softly back. He repeats the action, surprised all over again that part of his body is on strike and not coming back. Memories of using all ten of his fingers: counting to ten in the back of his father's car, playing this-little-piggy with CeeCee's invented verses that covered both hands and feet. All of them suffused with the estranging clarity of memories recorded by a mind that had not yet learned to think in shades of gray.

One of these days, he thinks, I'll get used to it.

Tonight, though, he will dream of the Dwarf. Jared pulls off his shirt and drapes it over the rocking chair in the corner where Colleen used to rock Emily to sleep. Only two years old and already there are so many used-tos. The goggling openmouthed joy of six months old has become the blazing movie-star smile of her third year. Jared watches the world seep into his daughter, watches her begin to take for granted things that used to knock her loopy with outrageous delight, and it kills him. How does he forgive her for reminding him that he has already lived out the time when he could be innocent and filled with wonder?

He bends to take off his shoes, remembers that he's already left them by the front door. He's still wearing his socks, though, so while he's in the neighborhood he takes them off. Then off come the pants and the only thing left to do is go to bed. Colleen pulls her arm out of the way. Jared lies on his back, waiting for her to reach out again, but she does not. He drifts off into a dream of the Dwarf.

Pontiac almost starved them out. His braves burned the farms surrounding Fort Detroit, sparing the French and reserving all of their brutality for the English. When a relief party tries to get through coming up from Lake Erie, the Ottawas burn some of the canoes and force the rest ashore on the other side of the river. On the near bank, out of rifle range but within sight of the fort, they spend a few days in leisurely torture of survivors. Frantically the fort's commander, Henry Gladwin, sends messengers, who return empty-handed while Pontiac lets it be known that he plans to remove the English from the north bank of the narrows between Lac St. Clair and the small ocean to the south.

Finally Amherst can spare some attention for the beleaguered western outpost. He sends soldiers overland from the East, James Dalyell leading the column and Rogers' Rangers loping alongside. Dalyell raises spirits in Fort Detroit, but it's Rogers everyone looks to. He knows the Indians, respects them a little too much for Amherst's taste, and can fight them the way no Englishman ever has. It's high summer, July 28, and if they don't do something about Pontiac soon, they won't be able to feed themselves when winter comes. In the aftermath of the failed supply effort, and with crow-picked bodies still hanging from stakes five hundred yards away, tempers are high. Scouts report that Pontiac is camped a few miles northeast, on the other side of Parent's Creek. Inside Fort Detroit, Dalyell and Rogers put their heads together with Gladwin. They draw up a plan for a breakout and punitive expedition. If they show teeth, Pontiac will turn tail; none of them doubt this, and they are certain that Pontiac doesn't know of their presence. A quick march, a predawn surprise. Burning lodges. It all sounds simple.

As they're making last-minute adjustments, just after midnight on July 31, the crack of a rifle sounds from the stockade wall, and the officers rush out. The sentry has spilled his powder trying to re-load with shaking hands, and he is raving about a devil in the forest. Gladwin himself, condescending to interact with the rank and file, slaps the sentry sharply across the face. Tears spring to the sentry's eyes, but he snaps to attention.

A savage in the woods, provoking you, Gladwin snaps. And now your powder is wet. Hold yourself together.

Yes, sir.

And then Dalyell sees—on the very walls of Fort Pontchartrain, dancing from point to point on the log walls—a capering figure, impossibly naked, its skin dully red in the torchlight, hair and beard flying. No Indian, Dalyell thinks. There are no beards like that among them. The figure wouldn't stand to the sternum of any of the assembled soldiers. Its eyes burn too brightly for reflected torchlight. It slaps its penis against its thigh, and when at this indignity someone fires a shot, it turns a backflip along the wall. Then it is gone.

Shot the bugger, someone says. Dalyell isn't so sure.

They leave two hours later, more than two hundred men, Rogers and his murderously hearty band among them. There is a trail to Parent's Creek, packed earth through empty fields and past burned houses. They move into the forest, the only sounds whining mosquitoes and the angry mutter of soldiers egging each other on about what they'll do to the Indians who have come so close to strangling Detroit in its crib. One of them hopes for another crack at the Dwarf, which seems to have escaped; they found neither blood nor footprints outside the wall. Little bastard got away once, and they couldn't pick up his trail, but they're not worried.

The scout comes back with news that the footbridge over Parent's Creek is intact and unguarded. It's nearly light. The soldiers pause to load their rifles, and then they march the last half mile to the creek. It's a beautiful shallow valley in the dawn, the forest becoming green again as night falls away and the smooth brown water stark between brushy banks. At the troops' approach to the bridge, a fox slips away into the trees. There goes their scout, one of the soldiers jokes. An officer silences him with a glare.

Twenty of them are across the bridge when a shattering volley cuts down every man still on it. The sound is like the sky-splitting crackle in the instant before a lightning strike, and the British troops already across the creek instinctively drop to one knee and fire at the first motion they see. The rear guard fans out to provide covering fire for them, and a second volley tears through them as they move. The lead group tries to get back across the footbridge, but sprawled bodies slow their crossing. In the powder smoke and screaming chaos, the English fire blindly, but the Indians are invisible.

Until they are everywhere. The dawn fills with whoops and screams as Indians materialize from every direction. They are behind the rear guard, then among them with knives and tomahawks; they come up from the shores of the creek into the lead group. The English turn their rifles into clubs, and those who have them draw swords, but there are too many already down, on the path and the bridge and in the creek. Dalyell calls a charge in the direction of Pontiac's camp, and one of the Ottawas drops from a tree to cut him down. The orderly column of soldiers disintegrates into a scramble of pairs of men grappling in the brush. Partners in this terrible dance switch, groups of three or four form and swirl apart; blackly gleaming blood mottles the pale earth of the trail and patters on the water from the weathered timbers of the footbridge. Sometime later, those British who could get away have, and the only sound is the ragged groaning of the wounded, cut off with the thud of tomahawks. Then it is over, and Parent's Creek has become Bloody Run.

The survivors straggling back to Fort Pontchartain will swear that the Red Dwarf was there.

CHAPTER 5

Saturday morning Colleen and Emily went to her parents' house. Jared fiddled around the yard for a while—moving a bird feeder, tightening up the gate in the fence at the side of the house so it swung true again, other little things he'd been meaning to get to since the end of the previous fall. Now it was May, and he no longer had the excuse of the weather. When the miscellaneous stuff was out of the way, Jared popped the hood on the coupe and had a look. Lately the Hop-Frog hadn't been hopping. Should probably just buy another one, Jared thought. We've got the money. But what with the war, nobody was making cars, and he didn't want to buy used.

So they'd have to nurse the old coupe along. Jared pulled the plugs and set them in a can of gasoline while he changed the oil and checked the filters. WWJ said that the newly formed Tenth Fleet would scrub the North Atlantic of U-boats, and that there was heavy fighting on Attu. The Luftwaffe bombed Malta, and the Nazis and Russians were gearing up for what looked like the decisive round of action on the Eastern Front. (WWJ said nothing about the rumors jumping around the Frankenline: the Germans were cooking up some kind of monstrous magic in Nuremberg, Himmler's SS was digging into the mountain beneath Wewelsburg Castle, a thousand witches conjured on Walpurgisnacht were being organized into a Hexenwaffe that could elude radar . . . an opposing stream of chatter held that all of these projects had failed.) In Asia the Chinese had launched a counteroffensive along the Yangtze River. Closer to home the Kelsey-Hayes wildcat strike was over, but the DeSoto bomber plant was out; first-quarter bomber production was lagging well behind schedule, although Willow Run looked to finally be on its feet. (Jared snorted at this; the plant hadn't picked up the nickname *Will It Run?* for nothing.) Ava Gardner and Mickey Rooney were divorced, ending one of the more puzzling showbiz marriages Jared could remember. After being rained out on Thursday, the Tigers won in thirteen innings, Hal Newhouser's first victory of the season. Newhouser struck out five times, but the Detroits took the game when with two outs in the thirteenth Boston's Tony Lupien dropped a Joe Hoover fly ball for a two-base error, and Roger Cramer singled him home.

After Jared had cleaned the plugs and screwed them back in, the Hop-Frog still labored before finally wheezing to life, and he shut it off again. "Shit," he said to the steering wheel. His dad showed up wanting to go to the ball game, but they ended up pulling the fuel pump and the lines, cleaning it all carefully, and turning her over again. Chug chug chug chug chug before she caught. "Shit," Jared said again. By this time it was after noon, but they pulled the starter to have a look, then swapped the battery from Dad's old Fordor Deluxe into the Hop-Frog. None of it made a difference.

"I hate to say it," Dad said, "but this car is haunted."

"Hell it is."

"I'll give old Arno Litmanen a call." Dad went into the house, and about fifteen minutes later Arno showed up. He was a weather-beaten old Finn who'd followed his sons down from the copper country in the UP. They liked Detroit and he didn't, but he stayed with them anyway, saying all the time that if he couldn't get back to

Finland to die, he was damn sure going to get back to Ishpeming. To which his boys said, Sure, Pa. When you go, we'll lash you to the roof of the car like a deer and drive you back ourselves.

Arno was a noita in addition to being a cantankerous old bastard. Jared had seen him stop blood, and Jared's dad told stories about when his own dad, Skeeter Cleaves, had gone hell raising with Arno back in the '80s when they were boys. Grandpa Skeeter said that Arno Litmanen could control the wind enough to make a tree fall against its cut.

"So whad blace is dis'ere zbrite?" Arno asked after he'd spent a good half hour looking over everything Jared and his dad had already looked over.

"I thought you were the noita," Dad said.

Arno didn't look at him. "Eh, boy?" he said to Jared. He had the blackest eyes Jared had ever seen, like someone had poured dirty oil into his eye sockets. "Where dis demon?"

"I told you, she just starts hard. I don't think there is any damn demon, but he don't listen to me." Jared waved a hand at his father.

"Oh no, he dere sure enough." With a wink Arno leaned into the engine compartment and pulled out a little bundle of bones tied together with baling wire. A single black feather stuck out from the middle of the bones.

Jared took it from the old noita, who was baring his teeth in a silent laugh. "Where the hell'd you get this? It wasn't in there a minute ago."

"Whad I come for, is to see, eh?" Arno slapped the car's fender. "Some Indian or colored god a hex on your car. You know a Indian or colored god you a grudge?"

"I sure don't," Jared said.

His dad came over to have a look at the charm. "How's bird bones make a car start hard?" he asked.

Arno shrugged. "Ask who pud it dere."

"Well, Plenty Coup's been gone for a while now, and I don't

know any Indians at the plant," Jared said, "and the only Negro I know is Felton. Magic isn't his style."

"Well, it's somebody's style," Dad said. "You best think about it." He and Arno went into the house to see if there were any other hexes or charms there. Jared set the bones on the roof of the coupe, shut the hood, and picked up his tools. What the hell was someone hexing his car for? He started it up just to make sure, and damn if it didn't catch the minute he touched the starter.

He was still sitting there when Dad and Arno came out to report that the house was hex-free. This news didn't cheer Jared as much as it probably should have; he kept thinking of what John Dash had said about Swerdlow holding back on him. He went to work, and watched three straight golems fall on their faces as soon as they walked out of the Tabernacle while only two made it out to the rail siding. "I best update my résumé," Felton said wryly.

"You and Moises both," Jared said.

During the last hour before the dinner whistle, Jared wrestled over whether he should—or could—ask Felton about the charm. If it was a charm. He didn't want to do it because he knew he'd only be doing it because Felton was colored, but when it came right down to it he couldn't help himself. Felton was predictably annoyed. "I look like a nigger with a bone in my nose?" he said. "Ask the boys at the foundry."

"Come on, Felton, I didn't mean anything by it. That's just what Arno said."

"Well, maybe he's right." Felton was still pissed. He took his lunch and walked off down the railroad tracks around the head of the canal slip. Jared didn't follow him; Felton was touchy about this kind of stuff, but he'd cool off. Wouldn't do any good to keep badgering him about it.

So what the hell, Jared thought. The foundry.

The steelworkers were all enjoying the evening at the edge of a slag heap. There was a dice game going on, and a bottle making the rounds. When Jared got close to the group, the bottle disappeared, and Jared stood there feeling like the turd in the punchbowl while two dozen colored men eyeballed him. "Um, look," he said. "Don't let me interrupt, you know? I was looking for—" He caught sight of the guy with the piebald arm, the one who had flushed the imp. "Say, man," he said. "Can I ask you a question?"

"Free country."

"Well, can . . . it's kind of private."

"You was down here with Felton before."

"Yeah," Jared said.

Taking his time, the steelworker lit a cigarette and shook out the match. He tilted his head away from the group, and the rest of his body followed. Jared went after him until they'd reached the other side of the slag. When they stopped, Jared couldn't figure out how to begin. "Uh, my name's Jared," was what in the end came out of his mouth. He extended a hand.

"Ellery."

Jared felt ridges of scar under his thumb as he shook Ellery's hand. "Pleased to meet you," he said. This is what manners are for, he thought. Gives you something to say when you've got no idea what to say.

"Likewise," Ellery said. "We gonna talk about the weather now?"

"No, I got this thing—here. The other day when you got rid of that imp, you said something about a houngan. Was that just talk, or do you know one for real?"

Ellery didn't answer right away. "Okay, man, look," Jared said. "I'm not just asking. Look at this." He showed Ellery the bundle of bones. "Someone put this in my car. You know anyone can tell me what it is?"

"Bundle of bones is what it is."

"Come on. Help me out here."

Ellery looked a little closer, but he made no move to take the charm. "What kind of bones are they?"

"I don't know. Does it matter?" Jared peered at the bones, remembered smells of Marty Cleaves' garage cutting through the infernal stink of the foundry. Most of them were an inch or two long. Some curled like ribs and others looked like leg bones or something, and then there was that marvelous skull . . . "I don't even know if they all come from the same animal."

"Any kind of animal missing around your house?"

"We don't have any."

"Where'd you find it?"

"In my car."

Ellery raised an eyebrow at this. "You find it yourself?"

"No, and I'd been all through that damn wreck trying to figure out what was wrong with it. This old noita my dad knows found it right away."

"What's a noita?"

"Finnish shaman. Was like it was invisible or something until he went looking for it."

"Hm." Ellery took a grimy handkerchief from his back pocket and covered one palm with it. "Give it here."

Jared dropped the bundle in Ellery's hand. Ellery hefted it and handed it right back. "Bird bones," he said. "You know what it did?"

"Well, something made my car start hard as hell."

"It start all right now?" Jared nodded. "Then that's what it was doing." Ellery started walking back toward the dice game. "I'll talk to the Piston Doctor," he said as he went. "See if he feels like helping a ofay with car trouble."

Ofay? Jared was wondering as he headed back to Building G. Piston Doctor? Again this seemed like something he should ask Felton about, and again he knew that he would in all likelihood screw things up by asking in the wrong way. Then he saw Swerdlow com ing around the slag heap, and forgetting all about Felton he thought, *Oh shit.* Swerdlow saw him, too, and came at him like an eagle stooping out of the sky. "So I didn't make myself clear before?"

"No, Mr. Swerdlow. It's not like that. I just haven't found out anything else so I didn't have anything to tell you."

"I didn't keep you out of the war to hear what you don't got," Swerdlow growled. "You got to come through."

"Why don't you ask someone who works there?"

"Not what I want to hear. Find a way, Cleaves. I want you in my office twice a week from now on." Jared started to protest. "Can it. There's a war on, and you work for a government project, and I decide whether you keep working on it or I cut you loose to pump gas over on Miller Road."

The threat bounced right off Jared—he'd heard it before, and figured he could manage Swerdlow's bluster, especially given what he'd learned from John Dash. What struck him was the flat assertion, right out in the open between Building G and the tire plant, that Swerdlow had Jared doing extracurricular work. *Keep your mouth shut, that's the way to learn,* his father had always said. The old man was never able to follow his own advice, but once in a while Jared kept it in mind. Swerdlow was worried. There was no way he would speak openly about this unless someone was bird-dogging him for results.

It was time to follow up on what Dash had said about Swerdlow's Tuesday nights. There wasn't any way to stay out of it anymore, and if through action Jared could contribute to the war effort—that was his duty. Jared seized on that idea and held it. Maybe he wasn't in the Pacific, and maybe he wasn't working for the Marshal; that didn't mean he couldn't do something more important than break up clots of clay. Anyone could do that. Jared started to feel as if he'd been thrust into a backstage drama, by luck or fate. Didn't matter. He had a chance to make a difference. He could prove to himself—

and to Colleen's parents—that he wasn't just a fake cripple who should be at the front.

"Snap out of it, kid," Swerdlow said. "Tell me about cattle cars."

"Tell me about bird bones in the engine of my car."

Swerdlow looked up. "Bird bones? Speak English."

"Somebody put a hex on my car," Jared said. "Know anything about it?"

"Let's walk." Swerdlow lit his cigar as they picked their way along the edge of the pits. "A hex on your car? What's that got to do with anything?" he asked.

"I don't know. You're the one who got me doing something shady."

"Whoa, there. Think of it more like being deputized," Swerdlow said.

"I get a star and everything?"

"Cleaves, I'm starting to get sick of your lip. No more talk about magic, and no more goddamn complaining. You tell me something soon, or we're going to have a serious problem." Swerdlow's eyes darted around as he spoke. Grime settled into the sweaty creases of his jowls. Something was eating him alive, and Jared planned to find out what. That wasn't going to happen right now, though, and break time was a-wasting; he headed back to Building G in time to eat half a sandwich before the whistle blew. The golems were four for four in making it to the rail siding that night. Jared felt a little better about his employment prospects, but the mystery of the bird bones nagged at him. He looked across the line at Felton, who was teasing a long line of barbed wire out of a head-sized gob of clay. An Indian or a colored, Arno had said. And Jared had answered that magic wasn't Felton's style, which you could tell by looking at him. If ever there was a guy more planted in the real world, Jared didn't know him (although since Jared's benchmark for this was his father, he had to acknowledge that he probably wasn't setting the bar very high). *Stolid,* that was the word Colleen's mother would apply to Felton. Or maybe *impassive*. Not a guy who would know anything about bird-bone hexes.

Jared had big plans for Sunday, especially since next Sunday was the thirtieth, when they would all sortie out to Lincoln Township so Jared could suffer the disapproval of his mother-in-law. The forty-eight-hour workweek made for good money, but it also made for feverishly packed Sundays that often as not were more tiring than a night on the Frankenline. On this day Jared was supposed to cut the grass, fix the screen door that wasn't hanging right because the mounting screws were pulling out of the frame, finally level the patio bricks after Emily tripped and skinned the hell out of her chin, and wash the Hop-Frog, all the while listening to the Tigers whip the Red Sox in the doubleheader. So many games had been rained out early in the season, it looked like there would be nothing but doubleheaders all the way to September, which was fine with Jared. Before all that, though, there was the visit to Marty and CeeCee's, during which Jared got shanghaied into changing a flat tire on his father's rusting '32 Fordor Deluxe because the old man had developed a case of situational arthritis. All the while he was thinking about the damn charm. He stopped in the middle of changing the Fordor's tire and sat cross-legged on the garage floor, picking through the bones one by one. The skull captivated him. So small, but it held the mind of an animal that knew how to migrate, build a nest, do a mating dance, all without ever being told. Feeling lacquered over by civilization, Jared lamented the loss of instinct. If he'd been a bird, he'd have known better than to get involved with the OEI. Probably he'd have known to avoid John Dash, too. As it was, he was tumultuous with ambition and shame—two things the bird whose mortal remains found their way into the Hop-Frog's engine compartment had never felt—with the result that he'd gotten himself into a pickle.

Marty caught him like that, head bent over the little pile of bones in his palm. "What the hell is wrong with you, boy?" Marty said. "You didn't throw that away yet?"

Folding the handkerchief around the bones, Jared said, "I'm still trying to figure out who put it there."

"Who cares?" Marty said. He produced a pipe and lit it, filling the garage with eye-watering Borkum Riff fumes.

"Thought you quit that," Jared said.

"It's war, kid. People are indulging their vices," Marty Cleaves said. "Plus it helps with the arthritis."

Jared put the bones back in his pocket and finished changing the tire. When he inflated it, he could hear the slow leak from the spare. Marty commented that somebody should patch it, and Jared nodded as he wiped his hands on a rag from the bucket under the workbench. "Yeah," he said, "somebody should." Then he went through the house into the backyard, needing Emily; but the backyard was empty. The Cleaves women had taken off somewhere, which they were prone to do when Jared and his father hid out in the garage. What I should do, Jared thought, is go back inside and patch the goddamn tire. What he did was walk back through the house, out the front door, and home.

.

Jared's next-door neighbor on the side away from Mrs. Pelletier is one Herschel Fontenot, who at forty-four years old has been three times married and three times divorced. Every time Jared thinks things are tough between him and Colleen, he reminds himself that at least he's not Herschel, who has adolescent and adult offspring appearing on his front stoop with what must be maddening frequency. The kids show up, often as not while Herschel's at work somewhere in the sub-basements of the Rotunda and often as not toting offspring of their own. Herschel seems like a decent guy to Jared, but it makes him a little nervous to think of all those younger

Fontenots running around the world. If they take after their father, pretty soon the whole of Detroit will be overrun by vaguely confused people with weak chins and a congenital inability to finish what they start. Herschel Fontenot's house looks like a time-lapse cutaway of household projects in progress: roof partially redone, half the soffits and fascia boards new and the other half rotting off their nails, south and west walls scraped and the south wall partly painted, a giant pit dug in the backyard for a brick barbecue that never came to pass. And then there are the marriages, the half-assedness of which is attested to by the continuous stream of progeny.

Since Colleen has spirited Emily away for the foreseeable future, Jared thinks as he walks up the sidewalk to his house, he has three options. He can go get some sand and level out the patio bricks that subsided over the winter; he can go see the Piston Doctor; or he can take advantage of the fact that Herschel Fontenot is sweeping his sidewalk and ask the man to help him take care of the beer in the fridge.

The day is hot. The Piston Doctor is distant and probably hostile.

"Hey, Herschel," Jared calls. "When you're done there, let's crack us a couple."

The push broom springs from Herschel's hands as if he's accidentally turned it into a snake. "Can do," Herschel says. Two minutes later they're parked on folding chairs in the backyard with a six-pack of Stroh's between them.

Herschel takes a pull. "Timely hospitality," he says. "I was about wore out."

"Yeah, I saw where you'd swept up almost half your walk there, and I thought, there's a man who works too hard."

The beers go up and down. Two more caps come off. "Where's your girls?" Herschel wants to know.

"Out with my mother. And speaking of it, I haven't seen one of yours drop by lately."

"They come, they go." Herschel shrugs. "All's they ever want is money, anyway. 'Cept my daughter Luanne. She's Daddy's girl."

Jared doesn't know which one Luanne is. "As many as you have, I'm surprised you can keep a roof over your head."

"Ain't that the truth. There's eleven, and five grandbabies already." Herschel shakes his head. "Don't know what I was thinking." He looks over the mouth of his bottle with an expression that tells Jared he knew exactly what he was thinking at the time. They laugh, but at the same time Jared is thinking of Colleen in the bed next to him, never quite touching.

"So what do you do for the Old Man?" he asks, to change the reel in his head.

Herschel lights a cigarette, then offers the pack to Jared. "Clerk in Special Projects," he says as Jared is lighting up.

He'll be a Tenfingers by 1950, Jared thinks. He already has the look: stooped, balding, worry lines chiseled into his face. "Mostly what I do is track R & D from overseas," Herschel goes on. "Mostly classified." Ford has plants all over Europe, and in fact makes money building munitions for both Axis and Allied armed forces. Just last week a group of bombers with engines made in the Rouge flattened a Ford-owned ball-bearing works in Germany. Jared figures two or three more Tenfingers will be born trying to balance the ledgers on that one.

"So Special Projects," he says. "Like Building G?"

Herschel tilts his head back and closes his eyes. "I know you work there," he says, "but we shouldn't talk about it."

"Yeah, we shouldn't." Jared is about to let it drop, but can't quite. "So are the Nazis mixing up werewolves over there?"

Herschel frowns, then gives up the struggle. "What I hear is that there's strange doings in the Carpathians, all right. Don't know about werewolves specifically."

"Damn," Jared says. Nazi werewolves.

"Tell you what I think, is that anything going on is, you know, related to the place," Herschel says.

"How's that?"

"Well, most of what we got going on here has to do with technological know-how, factory stuff. That's American."

This makes a strange kind of sense to Jared. He ran into Joe Dudek, Arlene's ex, a couple of months ago while picking up ration stamps, and Joe claimed that the airdrome he'd worked at had a genie that whipped up sandstorms when the Germans were coming to strafe the place. That was the kind of thing you'd expect in Tunisia, which as far as Jared could tell from newsreels looked a lot like Arizona. Probably a genie under every rock. But America was so overlaid and crisscrossed with different races and peoples that the only thing left to stand out was the great American imperative to build. The fact that Jared believed in Joe Dudek's genie story didn't prevent him from asking where the genie was when Joe got his finger shot off, however, which provoked a sour expression and a profane statement about the general trustworthiness of all things African and particularly Arab. Jared took a bitter pleasure from seeing Arlene's ex-husband reveal himself to be a knee-jerk bigot; it made him feel better about the torch he was obviously carrying for the newly again Miss Bannister.

"So what's German? What's Japanese?" he asks Herschel, who answers after popping his third beer.

"Well, your Germans, they've got all the Norse myth and such to work from, all the Volsung hooey." Seeing Jared's blank look, Herschel warms to the topic. "Hell, you think Hitler listens to Wagner all the time because he loves music? He's about the most unmusical son of a bitch that ever lived. He hears the *Nibelungenlied*"— Herschel lets the word roll off his tongue with a wink that says *ain't I smart*—"and he's thinking about magic swords and dragon's blood. Waiting for an old one-eyed man in a hat to show up and piss destiny all over him, looking for a giant wolf chained to a rock somewhere. But the only things seem to work for them are the real crazy chaos, you know, archetypes. Frost giants and such. It's like they answer a call, but don't always do what the Nazis think they will. Frost giants are a good example. Sure, they're raising hell up north once in a while, but they didn't show up at all when they were supposed to over at Stalingrad. At all. Truth of it is, none of this hocus-pocus, ours or theirs, is working nearly like it did at the beginning of the war. It's all wearing out. You want my opinion—" Herschel clamps his mouth shut when they hear the front door bang open. Emily's footsteps thumpthumpthump toward the back door, and Colleen calls Jared's name. "Well," Herschel says. "Family's home. Reckon I'll shove off. Thanks for the suds."

"Let's do it again," Jared says after him, although he badly wants to hear what Herschel might say about the Japanese, never mind about the Frankenline and by extension the employment prospects of one Jared Cleaves. He stands up and stretches as Emily turns the latch on the screen door and charges out onto the grass to meet him. Jared sweeps her up and settles her on his hip, bracing himself for what he assumes will be Colleen's anger that he's sitting around drinking on a Sunday afternoon.

Turns out he's wrong about that, as about so much else lately where his wife is concerned. She thinks it's funny that he's hanging around with Herschel. "Did any of his kids stop by to sponge?" she asks. "I'd have figured that a Fontenot could smell the beer all the way out to Jackson."

Jared's grinning at her both at the joke and at the fact that she's making a joke. Weird place, this world, he thinks again. And then: women. And then: well, maybe it's just Colleen. Couldn't every woman be like her, or all of us men would be so in love we'd go crazy.

* * *

That night Jared stayed up for an hour or so after the girls went to bed. Pleased at the solitude but also restless, he took a walk, passing his parents' house and heading on to the cemetery, where he wound through the moonlit headstones, listening to the sound of his footsteps change from the crunch of gravel to the soft scuff of manicured grass. For a minute he started to think about his conversation with Herschel, but he shut it down; Herschel hadn't said anything that Jared wasn't already seeing on the line every night. If the OEI mothballed the Frankenline, Jared figured he'd proved himself; they'd find something else for him to do. And if they didn't, he could always find another job. Anyone who wanted to work in Detroit was working.

Never did get the lawn mowed, he thought as he turned back toward home. Patio bricks leveled, either. Oh well; it's going to be a long summer. When he came in the front door, all of the lights were out. Colleen must have gotten up. He crawled into bed after a long restorative moment in the doorway of Emily's bedroom. All of this is for you, baby girl, he thought. Everything I do. Colleen scooted back against him when he came in, and in his exhaustion Jared was swept up in a fierce thankful gladness. It had been a long time since they had a drowsing late-night conversation. Longer still since they'd made love, and Jared let himself hope for even that. "Hey," he said.

"Mm. Glad you came home."

The feel of her back against his belly at once aroused Jared and made him sleepy. "I took a walk," he breathed into the back of her neck. "Forgot to tell you. The car's fixed."

"Mm. 'S wrong?"

"My dad says someone hexed it."

"Huh."

"Me and him and Arno Litmanen fixed it."

"Arno Litmanen?"

"Dad called him." Jared ran a hand down from his wife's shoulder to her elbow, feeling the smooth, solid muscles of her arm. He let the hand fall from her elbow onto her hip and trek a little farther down her thigh.

She covered his hand with hers and kept it where it was. "Love," she said.

Ah well, he thought. He'd never really expected it to work anyway.

At some point in the night, Jared woke up with a suddenness that left him surprised he was in bed. He looked around, taking in the darkness and the shape of his wife under the sheet, and thought: where was I just now? The dregs of whatever dream he'd been having leaked slowly away, leaving an aftertaste that put him in mind of the smell of wild roses. A return to sleep was impossible; he got up and went out into the kitchen, got a glass of water, and went out into the backyard. The night breeze swept away the last sensation of the dream, and Jared inhaled it deeply, feeling the clean bite of it in his lungs. Those roses, he thought, and put part of it together.

When he was seven, the year of the cash crisis in Detroit, his father had gotten up one morning after a long night at the bowling alley and decided that they were all going to take a vacation in Maine. "Clear our heads," he said, meaning his own head. As far as Jared could tell, he and his mother already had pretty clear heads. It was July, and they put new tires on the Model T and took a car ferry across the river and into the flat, empty expanse of Ontario, stopping at Niagara Falls long enough to get wet and grin at each other on a boat trip under the Canadian falls, after which Marty Cleaves pronounced himself aggravated that nobody had gone over in a barrel while they were there to see it. Tracking along the northern shore of Lake Ontario, they crossed the St. Lawrence and wove through the White Mountains, which left young Jared slack-jawed. His father, who had seen both the Rocky Mountains and the Pyrenees, called them unworthy of the word *mountain* until CeeCee slapped him on the arm and cut her eyes at Jared. Marty Cleaves looked over his shoulder and saw his boy gazing awestruck out the window, and with rare sensitivity he tacked right into the wind of the last words out of his mouth. "This here is a fine range of mountains," he said. "Some of them are named for presidents. Ha— wonder if that pinstriped bastard Hoover will rename one of them after himself."

They wound down into Fryeburg, Maine, and out of the mountains into a landscape of hills and lakes that to Jared looked like someone had taken Michigan, shaken it, and not smoothed out the wrinkles. "I hear this Portland is quite a town," Marty Cleaves said. "You know they invented canned food there?" They rolled past Sebago Lake, Jared this time able to share in his father's sentiment that as lakes went, it was pretty minor-league when you had Huron and Michigan for comparison. You could see across it the whole time, practically.

The ocean, though . . .

Sharp as the first sight of his daughter, Jared remembered the ocean: the strange wash of the air in and out of his lungs, the thicket of fishing boats rocking in the bay, the lobster buoys like pins pushed into a map, the freckling of islands with a sliver of open sea beyond—and the wild roses that grew along the shore.

A prickle of unease rolled up Jared's spine, and he didn't know why. Those two weeks on the road were the happiest he'd ever seen his parents together, and he was old enough now to know how a long vacation tended to wear on people. The time seemed charmed, and he hated to think that he was dreaming of it, as if proximity of those memories to his dreams of the Dwarf would poison the happiness he'd felt on that July afternoon he'd spent collecting shells and watching the gulls wheel over the docks. He'd seen a seal, at first mistaking it for a swimming dog, and his father had built sand castles with him, complete with moats filled with sea wrack and crab claws they agreed were monsters. Jared had cried when they left the ocean and drove inland, up into the wild interior of Maine, domain of logging trucks and hardscrabble farms. There was a small foundry in the woods outside a dot of a town called Brownsville Junction, where Jared saw molten iron for the first time, and beyond it a trail that crossed a river and snaked along the rising edge of a granite canyon called Gulf Hagas. The water was low at that time of year, but Jared felt like a mountain man as he sloshed across with his shoes held above the water and his father cursing the misfortune of having forgotten to bring his fishing pole. They picnicked on a granite outcrop thrust out over a pool that churned between a low waterfall and a fierce rapids where the entire flow of the river blasted between vertical walls not twelve feet apart. Marty Cleaves pointed out scars on the rock walls and speculated that the walls had been blasted, probably to ease passage for the logs coming down on their way to the mills in Millinocket and Bangor. Fresh off reading a book of illustrated stories about Paul Bunyan and Babe the blue ox, Jared imagined logs on the water, so thick you could walk on them from shore to shore, and envisioned lumberjacks, legs braced wide apart as with peaveys and force of will they broke logjams at the narrows below the pool.

"Say," Marty Cleaves said. "Did you know that's what *Detroit* means in French? 'The narrows.' "

Twenty-two years later, in his backyard a thousand miles from Gulf Hagas and unimaginably farther from sleep, Jared Cleaves felt the prickle in his spine return. It settled between his shoulder blades, and he tried without success to shiver it away. His dreams of the Dwarf, a clockwork cycle he trusted nearly as much as his belief in sunrise, had long ago instilled in him the nervous conviction that he had to pay attention to his dreams, and he gnawed at the possibility that he had dreamed of Maine. He'd never said the word *narrows* out loud; why did he remember his father responding to it?

"I'll bet Paul Bunyan dragged his peavey on the ground and

made this canyon," he remembered saying, and his mother and father had laughed.

"I'll bet you're right," Marty Cleaves had said. "Those do look like peavey marks on those rocks."

An awful weariness settled over Jared as the eastern sky began to lighten and the angry glow of a pour at the Rouge washed away the stars in the south. Paul Bunyan would give the Nazis hell, he thought, imagining Babe the blue ox charging a German formation, flicking Panzer tanks aside with great sweeps of his horns. The OEI was probably scouring the woods for them.

He heard a noise in the kitchen and turned to see the tiny shadow of Emily feeling her way along the edge of the table. "Daddy?" she said softly. "Daddy?"

This had never happened before. Emily woke up in the night like any other two-year-old, but she always made a beeline for the bedroom if she climbed out of her crib. Jared was overcome by the conviction that she'd woken up specifically to come looking for him, and he wanted to cry. "I'm here, baby girl," he said, easing the screen door open so he didn't startle her.

"Daddy." She raised her arms and he picked her up, feeling her sigh and relax back into sleep, her head on his shoulder and the warm density of her against his chest. We'll go camping in Maine, he thought. The three of us, and Colleen and I will be happy again. How easy it was to have this kind of faith with your little girl breathing softly into the hollow of your throat.

CHAPTER 6

All night Tuesday, Jared was distracted by jitters about what he would see at the end of his shift. Was Swerdlow meeting with the OEI? Nazis? Was it a quiet war among the auto titans, some kind of double cross brewing among the Gasoline Aristocracy? No way to tell, but Jared's mind swirled with possibilities. He was a one-man spy-novel factory.

Jem and Felton let him know it, too. He was missing obvious contaminants in the clay, and they hollered at him all night. Some of his mistakes got past them, too, to the point that first Ferenc and then Moises himself had to come over and dress Jared down. Which just made him mad and distracted at the same time.

Finally at eleven thirty Jem blew a gasket. "Jared, goddammit," he yelled. In his hand was an entire M1 clip. "How the hell do you miss this? Jesus. Get out of here. I'll clock your ass out myself."

Jared didn't need to hear it twice. He got the hell out of Building G. Problem was, then he had to spend nearly an hour and a half sitting in his car waiting for Swerdlow. After the first twenty minutes of watching the night condense on his windows, Jared threw the door open and took a walk, just to be moving. He wandered all the way around the generating station and the oxygen plant out to the southwestern corner of the Rouge complex. Looking back across the groaning tumult of fire and steel, he was suddenly proud to be part of it. Even a miniscule, peripheral part. There was something about seeing this might of millions of dollars and thousands of men and tons of steel and coal and rubber turned to the manufacturing of war. It gave him a thrill of tingling, atavistic pleasure that he would never confide in anyone who had not stood where he had stood and seen what he had seen. In this quiet corner, it all seemed perfectly realized — the systole and diastole of the Industrial Revolution, set free of platitudes about improving the lot of mankind. Freed to do what it was meant to do, which was through the act of creation to destroy. How could you watch the fierce glow of a pour or hear the tectonic rumble of a thousand tons of coal hitting the bottoms of the pits and not know that in this kind of power was perfect right? This, the Rouge, was the molten heart of a new world.

The immensity of it mesmerized him. Rooted to the patch of asphalt beneath his feet, Jared felt himself open up, felt the sensations of the Rouge pouring into him. He stayed that way for a long time, drinking in this feeling of pure passive communion—until with a jerk he remembered Swerdlow. Shit. What time was it? His watch said quarter after midnight. Jared tore himself loose from the spot and walked fast back to the main parking lot. Swerdlow's satiny '39 Continental was still there, and Jared relaxed even as he chided himself for woolgathering. He sure as hell didn't want to wait another week to see what Swerdlow's Tuesday after-hours itinerary was. He got back behind the wheel of the Hop-Frog and fidgeted for nearly half an hour before at last Swerdlow walked his windmilling fat man's walk out from the overpass landing and got into his Lincoln.

Jared felt like the Shadow as he followed the Lincoln along Miller Road until Swerdlow turned onto Michigan, heading downtown. Traffic was light enough that he hung back in case Swerdlow was as suspicious as Jared himself had been feeling lately. The Continental was easy to pick out even a couple of blocks ahead. It swung north onto Twelfth Street, and Jared had a bad feeling. What was Swerdlow heading into a Jewish neighborhood for? He couldn't be meeting Moises. Could he?

That wave of anxiety faded as first Swerdlow and then Jared passed the four-story brick building at the corner of Clairmount, where Moises spent the five or six hours a day he wasn't at the plant. About a mile farther on Swerdlow eased into the parking lot of a bowling alley. Jared parked across the street and waited about five minutes before following. There were two sets of front doors, one inside the other, and Jared peered through the small circular window in one of the interior doors. If he pressed the side of his face against its edge and only used one eye, he could see everything to the left. No Swerdlow. In the other direction his view was blocked by the shoe-rental counter. He gave it a good look anyway, feeling the thrum of rolling balls in his ear.

Just at the edge of his straining field of vision was a golem.

Jared stood back from the door and blinked, fetching up against the same feeling he'd had when he saw the Dwarf, which was that maybe he hadn't seen the Dwarf—and maybe he wasn't looking at a golem. The window was dirty, he was looking through it practically sideways, and the figure was three-quarters facing away from him. Nah, he thought. And he hadn't seen Swerdlow anyway, so it was time to shake these stupid jitters and go in.

About half of the lanes were active, with maybe 90 percent of the bowlers men off the night shift at one of the plants. The air was blued by smoke, and over the clatter of pins rose the aggressive laughter of men out late with few women around. In the far corner to Jared's right, a line of men hunched on bar stools. Two waitresses worked the twenty active lanes, and a jukebox Jared couldn't see was playing Glenn Miller. It took a minute for him to figure out that the guy at the far end of the bar was Swerdlow.

Man, would I make a lousy secret agent, Jared thought, and stepped back to where Swerdlow would have to have an owl's neck to spot him. Swerdlow was leaning on the corner of the bar in an intense conversation with a man whose back was to Jared. This second guy was dressed better than just about anyone else in the place; even from a hundred feet away, Jared could see that he was wearing a custom sharkskin suit and shoes polished to a gleam. His hat was two shades darker than the suit's charcoal gray and sat just a little back on his head. From the look of things, he was listening more than talking. Every so often he inclined his head or lifted one hand and let it drop, leaving a curlicue of smoke from his cigarette. Swerdlow leaned toward him, gesturing sharply with both hands at once. Trying to make a point, Jared thought, and had an instinct that Mr. Sharkskin wasn't listening the way Swerdlow hoped he would.

He'd been standing inside the door for too long. People were starting to notice. Jared flagged down one of the waitresses and ordered a Stroh's. He remembered the Pall Malls that Dash had given him. There were still five or six; he'd been rationing them. Now he lit one and shifted over to the left of the doorway, sitting at one of the row of low circular tables behind the step that set the lane areas off from the main part of the floor. The waitress took a while to bring his beer, and Jared killed the time spinning his ashtray around on the table and idly keeping up with the game closest to him. Four guys, speaking what sounded like Polish, all of them about five foot six and built like they spent their days pulling engines. They drank like fish, but it didn't seem to affect their games. All of them were better bowlers than Jared had ever been.

His beer came, and with it a little flash of inspiration. "Say, miss," Jared said. "You see that guy all the way at the end of the bar?"

She looked over her shoulder. "Which end?"

"Down at the right. He still talking to the guy in the suit?"

"Yeah."

"Ever see either of them in here before?"

Now she looked back at him, eyes slitted. "Who wants to know?"

He put five dollars on her tray. "Bring me another?"

The bill disappeared, and the waitress hesitated just long enough over making change that Jared stepped in. "Keep it."

Good thing Colleen works, he thought as she walked away. While he waited for her to come back, Jared swiveled around in his chair so he could see Swerdlow and Sharky without getting a crick in his neck. Only their heads and shoulders were visible above the rental counter. The conversation was still at a slow simmer; only difference was, Swerdlow had taken off his hat. No wonder; it was hot as hell. Sharky didn't seem bothered by it, though. Near as Jared could tell, he hadn't even shifted his weight on the stool.

Finally the waitress came back, and just as she bent to set his fresh beer down, Jared saw the golem again. It was at the far end of the bar from Swerdlow, still as a frog, looking down the length of the bar. All golems looked a little off, not quite human, with some quality that made you notice them in a crowd even though afterward you'd say that there was nothing remarkable about them. At least this was Jared's take on it, but looking around the bowling alley he saw that nobody was even giving the golem a second look.

"Those two are here every Tuesday," the waitress said.

Jared had to switch gears. Seeing the golem had blown his questions about Swerdlow right out of his mind. "What?"

"Tuesday," the waitress said. "As in today."

"Right. Okay, yeah. Thanks."

"I don't know the fat guy's name," she went on, "but the other guy says his name is Billy. A big joke for him—I think it's more like Wilhelm, if you know what I mean." She had warmed to the task of spying, and a light of plain meanness glittered in her eyes.

Jared nodded. "Is that so."

This revelation put him in mind of an Ernie Pyle column he'd read a couple of days ago, about German prisoners in Tunisia, how many of them had spent time in the States. Had they gone home out of a sense of duty? Had they just been visiting back home from their new lives in Chicago or New York, and been swept up?

And how many of them had stayed to become a fifth column? The FBI, taking credit for work Jared had heard the stateside golems actually did, said it had cleaned up all the German spy rings last year, but it couldn't be true. The German-American Bund hadn't gone anywhere, they were just keeping quiet. Their meetings were probably the only events in America more filled with undercover G-men than the average UAW local get-together.

The waitress was looking at him sideways again. "You a cop?"

Jared winked at her. "Let's leave that be, okay?"

"You got it, sport." She winked right back, a professional tic of the eyelid, and then she was taking evasive action to avoid the Poles' hands while she laid a fresh round on their table and emptied the heaping ashtrays.

The golem sipped mechanically at its beer. Jared had never seen one of them drink or eat before. He'd never seen one outside Building G, except for a few times when he thought he'd caught a glimpse of one in a newsreel from Italy or the Balkans. Each time, there in the manufactured dream-space of the movie theater, Jared had wanted to poke whoever was next to him and say *Hey. That guy, there. I made him.* The same feeling came over him now, a hunger for acknowledgment, validation of his clandestine part in the war effort. The Poles over there, who spent their working lives hauling engine blocks or axles, welding or stamping or riveting—Jared could say to them *I am one of you—but look, over there. That's what I made.*

He realized he'd been staring at the golem and forced himself to look away. On the lanes, two adjacent bowlers left two adjacent seven–ten splits. Can't be, Jared thought again. A golem in a bowling alley watching Swerdlow, who is talking to a German. If that's what Sharky was. Who knew whether the waitress could tell a German accent from any other? The way she'd said *A big joke,* though . . . like he was one of those immigrant Germans who made all of the jokes first so everyone would accept them. You saw it all the time.

Jared hadn't noticed Swerdlow getting up until he was nearly to the door, less than twenty feet from Jared's table. Jared froze and looked away, the back of his neck crawling until he heard the door open and close with a jingle from the cluster of little bells tied to the spring on its top panel. He looked and saw that Swerdlow was really gone. When he checked the bar again, Sharkskin Billy was still planted on his stool. The golem got up and walked toward the door. As it came closer, Jared's uncertainty evaporated. A golem for sure. I made you, he thought. Helped, anyway. As if it had heard the thought, the golem locked eyes with Jared as it passed. Its face was empty of expression, its eyes as dead as a fish on ice. The door jingled shut behind it.

Jared fought an urge to head out after it. Was it going after Swerdlow, or had it just seen what it needed to see when Swerdlow chatted up Sharkskin Billy? Holy smokes, Jared thought. It might be going to kill Swerdlow. I should be so lucky.

Then he was ashamed of himself. Swerdlow was an asshole, but Jared wasn't in a position to want him dead. Fired, sure. Jailed, maybe. Not dead.

Sharkskin Billy sat. So did Jared, for a while, as pins clattered and men roared and women dodged among them. Too many questions, and right then all of them seemed to have only bad answers.

A golem right here in Detroit, and not fresh off the Frankenline. God. All of a sudden the OEI didn't seem so intimidating; something was going on here that they didn't know about. Truth was, Jared didn't know enough about it, either, but right then he had his second little flare of inspiration. Answers weren't that far away.

* * *

There's been a graffiti war going on at the Rouge for about a year now. Ford cleaning crews go through half a million gallons of paint every year keeping the place as shiny as a factory can be, so it's not easy to get any kind of continuity, but whoever's fighting figures out the cleaners' schedule almost immediately every time management changes it. Graffiti follow in the cleaning crews' wake like camp whores after an army on the march. Some racial, some personal insults. There are various strains of probably seditious cartoons about the Old Man and FDR and Hitler. Someone's even taking on the Draft Marshal; every day for a week there's a new pornographic limerick about the Marshal in the bathroom between Building G and the attached scrapyard.

The point of the whole enterprise, if it can be understood collectively, is to inscribe the presence of the worker on the endless steel body of the Rouge. Ford hires men to trawl through the complex and record the latest acts of defacement; they file reports, and crews follow them to paint over the graffiti in white blocks that stand out from the sooty grime on the rest of the wall. For a while, some bright boy got the idea to space his graffiti out so that in erasing it the cleaners were painting Morse code messages on the walls: the first, and most audacious, spelled out FUCK YOU FORD on the interior wall next to a row of drill presses in a building Jared has never entered. He's only heard about it. For two days, until the painters got around to repainting the whole wall, the pressmen and -women had a bounce in their steps. Anomalous good cheer inevitably attracted attention from Special Service, which listened in until they figured out what was going on, and after that all graffiti, no matter how big or small, were painted over in whatever size of square was necessary to cover them exactly.

Guys who have been in street gangs leave their signs everywhere in grease pencil or lumber crayon. There are several poets, including a haiku artist whose every new offering is instantly surrounded by virulent anti-Japanese sentiment. Jared has been paying more attention to the whole situation lately because graffiti about Moises has begun to appear. The Old Man's well-known attitudes about Jews make for a congenial atmosphere, and caricatures of Moises quickly spread and incorporate more general anti-Jewish tags. The two thousand or so Jews who work at the Rouge aren't amused; they arrange a system of watches, and when they catch a Lithuanian welder in the act, six of them work him over with ax handles and tire chains in the parking lot the next night. Every one of them is fired; the Lithuanian is back at work a month later, when he gets out of the hospital and is strong enough to hold his torch again. That little strain of wall commentary stops for a while, but before long it's back, this time focused exclusively on Moises. The Lithuanian starts carrying a gun to work. Another group of Jews confronts him and he says, "Ey, God, I look that dumb?" When he shows them the gun, they disperse, but not before warning him that he's not the only guy in Detroit with a gun.

Jared hears about this last from Ferenc. "We got to start keeping an eye on the *rebbe*," Ferenc says. "Somebody stir something up." This concern coincides with a drop in production on the Frankenline. Increasingly often, the golems don't come to life, and sometimes when they do they just wander around the Rouge complex while one of the molders tries to coax them onto the waiting train. Sixteen golems is their daily quota; over the last month or so, they've been lucky to hit thirteen even when no external problems come up. The molders' theory is that Moises is worried about an attempt on his life; they mutter darkly about Nazi plots. Even without the Nazis, all it would take is one particularly unhinged anti-Semite, and there's no shortage of those in Detroit. Ford's *Dearborn Independent* might be gone, but Father Coughlin's only been off the air for a year or so. You've got your Lithuanians, your Poles, your Russians, and that's not even counting the Germans who since the war aren't so vocal about their membership in the Bund. It's got to be weighing on Moises. He's an old man, and has lived through more than any of them care to imagine.

So a detail accompanies Moises home at night and waits in the morning for him to come out of his apartment over a market on Twelfth Street. This is how Jared found out where Moises lives, because one day Felton got sensitive about being excluded from the protection and demanded that the Frankenline's *goyim* be added to the rotation. The molders grumbled about this, but Moises wouldn't forbid it, so twice in the past couple of months Jared has seen the old rabbi home. He's begged off the morning detail because of Emily.

Moises lived on the top floor of the building, at the back. He had one room with a curtained-off toilet, slept on a Murphy bed, and made his meals on a hot plate when he didn't eat at the all-night counter downstairs. If he wasn't at home, Jared figured he'd be at the counter.

He was home, though, and glowering through the inch-wide crack between his door and its frame. "Go home, Jared," he said.

"Moises, I got to talk to you."

"Go home."

"I need some help."

"What? Trouble with wife? Talk to priest."

Well, there was that. But Jared shook his head. "I saw a golem tonight," he said. "At a bowling alley. Watching Swerdlow."

The door opened a little wider, just enough for Moises to fit part of his face into the gap and sniff. "Beer," he said with that little extra bit of disgust that only old people from Eastern Europe could express.

"I'm not drunk, Moises. I had two beers. They wouldn't let me sit otherwise."

This was only half true, if that, but Moises seemed to go along with it. "Sit at bowling alley? Where Swerdlow was?"

"Yeah. Let me in. I need you to help me out."

The rabbi sighed. He shut the door to slide off the chain, then opened it again and shuffled across the room toward a tall pitcher of water on the shelf below a window that gave out onto the fire escape. "Sit," he said, and poured two glasses. He was wearing a bathrobe threadbare to the point of translucency at elbows and rump, and under it a wife-beater undershirt and boxer shorts that hung most of the way to his knees. Jared settled himself onto a couch with no legs and made room for Moises to sit next to him.

"Three hours only I sleep," Moises said. "Every night, three hours." He sipped his water. "Sixteen, eighteen hours I make the golems. You show up when I am about to sleep."

"Sorry," Jared said.

"So if I don't sleep, tell me what I am awake to hear."

Jared sipped the water and wished it was beer. "You said you'd seen golems around."

Moises nodded.

"Eastern Market, was that what you said?"

"There, and other places."

"Are they watching you, Moises?"

A laugh like dry leaves shook the wattle under the rabbi's chin. "I don't know," he said. "Sometimes I hope so. Sometimes not."

"Why not?"

"If they watch me, I am in danger. Golems only watch for good reason."

Jared let this sink in and confirm his suspicions. "I saw one earlier tonight."

Moises shifted around to face him. "Where did you see this?"

"The bowling alley up the road." Jared hesitated, but he couldn't see any reason not to give Moises the whole situation as he understood it. "Watching Swerdlow."

"You said this already."

I did, didn't I, Jared thought. Twenty-eight and already my memory's going.

Moises rubbed his eyes. "You have cigarettes?"

Only a couple, Jared thought. But he set the crumpled pack of Pall Malls on the couch cushion between them. Moises took one. Jared lit it, then lit one for himself.

"What are you doing at bowling alley so late?" Moises asked.

Well, now, Jared thought. "Moises, can we talk about golems?"

"Okay. What you want to know about golems?"

Jared had spent the whole drive over figuring out exactly how he wanted to phrase this. "The ones that won't go overseas. Do they look out for any threat against Americans, or are they only protecting Jews?"

Moises thought about this for a while, smoking his cigarette down until the coal was between his fingers. He gave no sign that the heat bothered him. All that working with golems must have turned his fingers to clay. When Moises had finished the smoke, he crushed it on his coffee table and said, "Is good question. In Europe, the golem looks out for Jews. Here, who knows? America is different."

"But if it's watching Swerdlow, it must think he's a threat, right?"

"Yes, I think so. The mind of the golem is hard to read. Maybe they know America fights Germany and so protect America because Nazis kill us. Maybe not. Is hard to know how literal they feel."

"Swerdlow was talking to a guy at the bowling alley. The waitress said he was German."

"Many Germans in Detroit. Germans everywhere. America is melting pot, right?"

"Sure, yeah."

Jared sat for a while. Something rattled in the alley behind Moises' building, and the rabbi cracked a smile when Jared jumped. "Hearing Nazis everywhere now," Moises chuckled.

"Seems like you'd have more to worry about than I would," Jared said.

"No. I did not die in pogrom when I was a boy. I did not die when Russians came in Great War. I did not die in cattle car, or oven, or out in forest. Every day I have now is extra. If they come for me now, I have made six thousand golems. What other man can say this?"

"That's some attitude," Jared said. "Don't you want to live?"

"Some things I would not want to live to see. Enough. You know about golems now. Tell me why on Tuesday two in the morning you are not home with your wife."

This was why he had really come, Jared realized. Or if it hadn't been, it was now. "We're not getting along too well," he admitted. "But didn't you just tell me when I got here that you didn't want to talk about this?"

"No more talk about golems, and you didn't leave," Moises said, with one of those expressive Eastern European shrugs.

"All right. She—since Emily was born, things have been different."

"How old is your daughter?"

"Two. She was two in April."

"And things are different how?"

"We don't . . ." Jared trailed off. How did you talk about this stuff? Especially when you were talking to an eighty-year-old Jew you'd never really spoken to before tonight. "I feel like we aren't man and wife anymore."

"Ah. Sex," Moises said.

"No, not that. Well, that's not all of it. I mean, I knew that would happen after the baby. You hear that from everyone when they hear you've got a baby on the way. But two years . . . does it ever change? I don't know what happened."

"Maybe is something else. Sometimes the child changes you to

THE NARROWS — 135

gether, sometimes not. You tell me. Do you have trouble because of your Emily?"

"I don't know," Jared sighed.

"Your wife. She is home with the girl?"

"No, she works out at Willow Run stripping engines."

Moises was nodding before Jared had finished the sentence. "Ah," he said.

"No, it's not that she's working. I ain't that kind of man. Even if I was, there's a war. We've got to do our part."

"Jared," Moises said. "You sound like poster."

"It's true. What, you want me to say I'd feel different if there wasn't a war? I might. Hell yes, I might. But there is, and I can't do anything about it, and I'm proud of her. She—" He cut himself off.

Moises wouldn't let it lie. "She what?"

Were they just two guys bullshitting about women? Where was the line that you crossed from jawing to confidence? Jared couldn't see it, and couldn't stop himself from saying what he needed to say. "She does more than I do."

Moises shook Jared's last cigarette from the pack, took his sweet time lighting it and savoring the first few drags. He set the cigarette down on the edge of the coffee table and held up both of his hands, palms toward Jared. "Show me," he said.

"Show you what?"

"Look," Moises said. He twitched his hands from side to side, and Jared found himself looking. The rabbi's hands were tiny, with thin fingers. His knuckles were swollen, and the index and pinkie fingers curved in toward the middle of his hands. Moises flexed each of his fingers, one by one, letting Jared see how each moved in its individual way, with its own limitations, its own path from straight to curved and back to straight—or as close to straight as he could manage. "With these I create golems, but to sign my name is pain. To turn doorknob, button trousers. But I make golems. What do you do with your hands?"

"I was supposed to be a soldier," Jared said.

Moises stood and slapped him in the face. "Never. No man was ever meant to be soldier. You are father. Husband. Worker."

"I dig clay, Moises," Jared said when he got his mind around the fact that he'd just been slapped by an eighty-year-old rabbi. "Even Colleen does a real job. A monkey could do what I do."

"Jared Cleaves. America needs engines. America needs golems. Your wife does one, you do the other. Stop this pity." Moises hit him again, just on general principles, apparently, then tapped himself on the chest. "You poison everything you touch when in here you believe you have failed. Stop. Your wife, your daughter. Why do you do this to them?"

Tears prickled at the corners of Jared's eyes. He couldn't form a response, and rubbed his hands over his face until he could get himself under control. "It ain't like that, Moises," he said. "You don't understand."

"Yes," Moises said.

"No," Jared said. He noticed the cigarette, burned down over the edge of Moises' coffee table, still smoldering. Waste. Everywhere he looked, waste. "You don't understand," he said again, and stumbled out the door.

CHAPTER 7

Four hours of sleep and bad dreams didn't make for a great morning. Without meaning to, Jared annoyed Colleen—who was angry to begin with because he'd been out until after three—and reduced Emily to tears by getting her orange juice in the green cup instead of the purple one. Colleen pointed out that Emily had asked for the purple cup, adding, "But I can see why you picked that one. You're pretty green yourself."

Jared kept his mouth shut. Then he didn't. "I'm tired, Colleen. I had to do something after work."

"I can tell."

"No," he said. "You can't. You sit there thinking you've got it all figured out, and you have no idea."

"Okay." She cocked a hip and folded her arms. "Tell me."

Jared froze. Tell her? This was the last thing he'd expected her to say. "Uh," he said.

"Go ahead and get your story straight. I'll wait."

"No, that's not it, come on, honey." Jared backed and filled, watching his wife's face harden and knowing that by her lights he deserved it. He wouldn't tell her about Swerdlow talking to Germans while a golem watched; either she wouldn't believe it or she'd insist on doing something, getting involved, and for the life of him Jared didn't know which would be worse.

"My juice all gone," Emily complained. It seemed like an opening, and Jared took it—but when he'd refilled Emily's cup, he saw that Colleen had abandoned the conversation and with it any chance he had to explain himself. Or unburden himself. The situation— situations—were wearing on him. He couldn't see anything clearly, even in his own kitchen, where he was using his two-year-old daughter to get him out of a predicament with his wife.

As soon as the horn honked out front and the Three Eens went to work, Jared packed Emily up and took her over to his parents' house. If he was going to be a lousy husband for the day, at least he'd avoid being a bad dad on top of it. What the hell, he could cut the grass or something. Be by himself for a while; somehow that never seemed to happen, and although Jared wasn't a solitary man by nature, everyone needed a little time to be his own company. As he pulled into his parents' driveway, he was doing the math again, even though he knew he couldn't make the figures come out any different than they had the last hundred times. If Colleen quit her job, they could make it, barely. Maybe. If nobody got sick; she had hospitalization through Ford, but the Frankenline didn't come with benefits.

So why don't you quit, dumb-ass? You don't make as much as she does, and she's got the hospitalization, and what the hell do you do, anyway?

The Marshal picked me. Twice.

He sure didn't want you near him when you went down there.

Spying's an indirect business. He picked me by not picking me, let me know that he had his eye on me. He wouldn't let me leave.

You're kidding yourself.

Damn problem you had conversing with yourself was that you always came out on the losing side.

Emily bounced on his lap, knowing where they were and boiling to get started on her day. "We drive to Grammy and Grampy's house!" she announced.

"Yes we did, baby girl." Jared opened the door and Emily shot off across the yard, then stopped dead at a new bush planted along the sidewalk. She dropped into her Crouch of Intense Scrutiny. "Emily look," she said.

When Jared caught up to her, she stood. "This bush new, Daddy."

"Is that so," Jared said.

"Yes!" She beamed up at him. "What kind of bush, Daddy?"

Jared didn't know. Rhododendron? Azalea? He had a dim idea that either would be blooming by now. "It's a fairy bush, I think."

Emily's eyes got wide, and she looked back at the bush. "Where the fairies?"

"I don't think they've bloomed yet, honey."

"When they bloom?"

"Let's ask Grandma."

"Okay!" Emily scooted up to the front door and again came to a screeching halt, this time because the door opened and a man who wasn't Grampa Marty came out. Emily stood, head craned back and one hand reflexively reaching behind her—for him, Jared understood, and suffered a stab of pointless but inevitable guilt that he hadn't been there to take that reaching hand in his own. The man on his parents' front stoop was tall, six-one or -two, with a sharp haircut that said *fed* and a black suit that bolstered the impression.

"Hey, kiddo," he said. "You must be Emily."

Emily stepped down off the porch, never taking her eyes off him. She backed into Jared, and he rested one hand on her head while smoothing her hair with the other.

"And you would be Jared Cleaves?" the probable fed asked.

"I would. Who are you?"

"Grant Meadows. OEI. I was just talking to your father."

"About what? Don't tell me the Draft Marshal's after my old man."

Meadows smiled. It looked genuine. "Hardly. Just between you and me, he has enough salt miners to last him three wars." He stepped off the porch and handed Jared a card. "Come on down when you've got the tyke settled in."

Jared didn't take the card. "Last time somebody told me to go down there, I showed up and they wouldn't let me in the door."

"There's a story there," Meadows said. He tucked the card in Jared's shirt pocket and walked to the street, adding over his shoulder, "Come on down if you want to hear it."

Inside, Jared turned Emily loose on CeeCee before adjourning to the garage. He lit a cigarette he'd found on the Hop-Frog's floorboards. "Still can't believe you aren't smarter than that," his father said.

"Makes you think I'm any smarter than you were at twenty-eight?"

"All right, let it be." Marty Cleaves thought for a minute. "You got another?"

That was the old man, right there. Jared laughed. "No, this is it." He held the smoke out for his dad, who took it and drew on it with pleasure that seemed exaggerated.

"So what's the OEI want from you, Pop?"

His dad took a little extra time with the cigarette before handing it back. "He's asking about the Dwarf."

"He what? How did he know?"

Dad shrugged.

"Come on, Pop, you must have told somebody. Who was it?"

"You remember everything you ever said to everyone? I don't. I had nightmares for a while. Told your mother. She wouldn't have spilled it, though. Only thing I can figure is I flapped my gums a little one night down at the bowling alley. Too many beers, what the hell. It happens. Didn't hurt anybody."

"No, I guess not. But now I have to go talk to him."

Marty went to his workbench and fiddled with the assortment of washers and screws scattered across its surface. Jared waited him out as he stacked the washers and tossed the screws one by one into a coffee can. It was no use trying to rush Marty Cleaves when he was fiddling. Usually it was no use waiting him out, either, but you at least gave yourself a chance that way. When Marty Cleaves fiddled, he was looking for an excuse to not say something he knew he should say, and if Jared knew one thing about his father, it was that the location and utilization of excuses was Marty Cleaves' great God-given talent. So Jared waited without much hope that his patience would be rewarded.

Marty Cleaves' other great talent was confounding expectations, though. "I believe this all has something to do with your mother," he said.

"This?" Jared repeated. "You mean the Dwarf has something to do with Mom?"

Marty looked imploringly at the garage rafters. Now he was back on comfortable ground, wondering what he'd ever done to deserve such cretinous offspring. "Now what the hell would your mother have to do with the Dwarf?" he asked. "Huh? I mean the OEI, genius son of mine. They know something about your mother."

"Okay," Jared said slowly. "You going to tell me, or should I start guessing?"

Washers rattled in Marty's hand as if he was getting ready to throw them like dice. "I don't know," he said. "She won't tell me." He rattled washers, and Jared waited. After enough rattles to put Jared in mind of Dolores Del Rio and maracas, Marty slapped the washers down on the workbench and said, "Back where your mother comes from in Arkansas, word was that *her* mother was some kind of wise woman."

"Granny Magruder was a witch," Jared said, just to clarify things.

"I didn't say she was. I said that's what people said."

Evasion was another Marty Cleaves specialty. "She's been dead for years, Pop. How would the OEI know?"

"They know what they want to know, is what I figure."

"But Mom won't tell you if it's true."

"Topic of anything like witchcraft comes up," said Marty Cleaves, "and I mean anything like herbs or birthing, any of that woman stuff that your Bible-thumpinest Elmer Gantry wetbrain might think is witchy, your mother won't say any more than a mouse. 'I don't truck with any of that,' she'll say. It's about the only time you hear the hillbilly in her anymore."

Jared was smiling at his father's impression. "You do a pretty good Mom," he said.

"Years of study," said Marty Cleaves. "You got another smoke?"

"I better go talk to whatsisname. Meadows."

"Yeah. You better." Marty sighed. "Keep your mother out of it. I did. It's a good thing you brought the baby over, or CeeCee'd have hid out in the garden all day."

"All right, Pop. I'll see you later." Jared went back into the house to tell Emily she was staying with Grandpa Marty and Grandma CeeCee for the day. She was wrapped up in some project with her grandmother and didn't even really notice when he left.

The same sergeant sat in the same cloud of smoke at the OEI office. "Morning," Jared said. "Marshal change his mind yet?"

"Funny." The sergeant looked up at a huge raven perched in the transom over the interior door. "Petey. You remember this guy."

"Sure do," the raven croaked. "Marshal said no thanks."

"Hear that, kid? The Marshal says no thanks. Hit the bricks."

"Grant Meadows asked me to come down. He can tell me to leave." Jared flashed Meadows' card.

With no change in expression, the sergeant said, "Petey. Tell Meadows he's got company."

The raven carefully turned itself around and flapped away into the recesses of the building.

"I thought ravens were supposed to be German or something," Jared said. The year before, a semi-organized campaign had nearly exterminated crows in parts of the United States before an ornithologist published an article in *Life* explaining that crows and ravens weren't the same, and adding that American ravens, since they'd probably never been to Germany, didn't need to be killed. There were still a damn sight fewer crows around than there used to be.

"Petey says he's an Indian shaman," the sergeant said. "I ain't never seen him change shape, though."

"So maybe he's just a talking raven."

"Could be. Ain't for me to worry about." The sergeant lit a fresh smoke from the end of the last, provoking a twitch of jealousy in Jared's tobacco-starved brain.

"You let me bum one of those?" he asked.

"I give you most of a pack last time, didn't I?"

"All right, don't put yourself out." Criminy, Jared thought. Guy burns through more butts in an hour than I've had in the last week, and he can't spare one.

The interior door opened and Grant Meadows stuck his head out. "Jared. Come on back."

They walked down a hallway that doglegged every forty feet or so, giving Jared the impression that it had been designed for defense against an infantry assault. Just when he'd completely lost his sense of direction, Meadows opened a door and nodded Jared through. The room they entered was a rough square about ten feet on a side, with bricked-in windows on one wall. Meadows' desk faced out from between the former windows. Two of the other walls featured built-in bookcases bending under the weight of more books than Jared had ever seen outside of a library. In one corner leather chairs bookended a coffee table. Meadows pointed to one of the chairs and went to his desk. Jared sat. The chairs were a hell of a lot nicer than he'd expected to see in a government office—but the OEI had a different set of rules. Could be Meadows was higher up on the food chain than Jared had guessed; or could be that since Jared's only real experience with offices was Swerdlow's little dungeon in the corner of Dearborn Assembly, he'd developed skewed ideas of what standards were applicable.

Meadows had a radio on his desk, playing the new Glenn Miller song, "That Old Black Magic." Jared considered making an ironic observation, and thought better of it. Meadows checked his watch and tuned the set to WWJ. "You don't mind, do you?"

Harry Heilmann's voice and the sounds of the ballpark made Jared more comfortable. "Not a bit," he said.

"Good. I find I think better with a ball game on." Meadows took a legal pad from his desk and settled into the chair opposite Jared. He uncapped a fountain pen with his teeth and wrote for a minute. "Just catching up on what your father and I talked about," he said around the cap.

"He said you asked him about the Dwarf."

"I did. Now I'd like to ask you some of the same questions."

"Don't you trust what he told you?"

Meadows took the cap out of his mouth and set it on the table. "It's standard practice when gathering information to ask more than one person—ideally before they've talked to each other, but that wasn't possible in your case, and in any event I doubt either you or your father will be changing your stories after twenty-four years. People remember things differently. I trust what your father told me as much as I'd trust a memory that distant coming from anyone else, but I'd still like to get your take. Okay? Nothing underhanded. I'm not out to catch anyone in a lie, if that's what you're worried about."

"Why are you interested in the Dwarf?"

"That should be obvious. Do you really not know, or are you fishing to see what I'll say?"

"I want to hear what you'll say."

"Candor. Good. Okay, I want to know about the Dwarf because it's widely believed that he, or it —"

"He," Jared said. "Not much doubt about that."

Meadows chuckled. "That's what your father said." Making a note on his pad, he went on. "All right, he appears when some disaster is about to befall the city. I believe you wrote a school essay on this once, so you know what I'm talking about. Cadillac and all that."

"How did you know I wrote an essay?"

"Edging toward classified information there, Jared. Let's just say the OEI is in the business of knowing things like that." While he talked, Meadows kept his pen moving. Jared had a powerful urge to get a look at what he was writing. Classified information, he thought. Wonder if Meadows would say the same thing if I asked about Mom. "Okay," Meadows said. "So why don't you tell me about the first time you saw the Dwarf?"

Jared paused to organize his thoughts and figure out how far back he should go to get the story set up right. "Well," he said. "My dad used to be a roadman for Ford . . ."

* * *

When he'd finished, Meadows had maybe half a dozen pages of notes. Now come the real questions, Jared thought. Wonder how much difference there is between what I just told him and what he got from Dad.

Meadows flipped through his notes and paused over something. "He actually stood on the hood of the car and waved his tackle at you?"

"I told you we knew he was a he," Jared said.

Meadows shook his head. "Man. I'm glad I didn't have to see that."

"Damn right," Jared said, and they both laughed.

"And that's when you injured your fingers."

Jared shifted his right hand into his lap, caught himself doing it, and with a flash of anger put it back on the arm of the chair. "Yeah," he said.

"Which is why you're here instead of in Tunisia."

Jared bit down on his first response. "I hear Tunisia's a picnic compared to Guadalcanal," he said, trying to smile and not quite succeeding.

"You'd be right about that," Meadows said. "Listen, I'm not trying to piss you off. What I'm interested in is the Dwarf. It—he—didn't do anything to you?"

"Tell you the truth, I'm not even sure I really saw him," Jared said.

Meadows sat back in his chair. "Jared. Now is not the time to revise your history."

"My hand got cut when my dad hit the brakes," Jared said. "I told you that."

"I know you did." Meadows capped his pen and tore off his notes from the pad. "Okay. We're going to need to follow up after I go over this with some other people in the office, but for right now I just have one other question."

"Okay, shoot," Jared said.

There was a sharp tap at the door. "That'll be Petey to show you out," Meadows said. He got up and let the raven in. It flapped up to the back of Jared's chair and stood there eyeballing him.

"You really a shaman?" Jared asked. He was thinking about the charm old Litmanen had taken out of the Hop-Frog, and whether it wouldn't be better to ask an Indian about it instead of bothering the steelworkers who didn't want him around anyway.

"Sure as hell am," Petey said.

"Huh," Jared said.

"About that last question." Meadows was still at the door. Jared got up and Petey climbed onto his shoulder.

"Don't you shit on me," Jared warned.

"Jesus Christ," Petey croaked.

Laughing, Meadows said, "Petey's housebroken, don't worry. Listen, though, before you go: do you ever dream about the Dwarf?"

Only last night, in the latest installment of Jared's constant cycle through the stories he read and told himself while writing his ninth-grade essay. The War of 1812 this time, when General Hull saw the Dwarf and was so shaken by it that when the British came up the river he surrendered the city without firing a shot. This is the only dream Jared can ever remember having that bores him. The fact that he can't skip over it, move ahead to 1863 or play Bloody Run again, cements in Jared a disconsolate certainty that boredom is somehow his lot. A job any chimpanzee could do, a marriage slowly hardening into puzzled and resentful misunderstanding, and the same god-damn dreams over and over and over. Maybe this was the disaster the Dwarf had meant for him, a slow-motion descent into misery without ever knowing exactly what he could have done to avoid it.

Not that he told Grant Meadows all that. *Sure,* he'd said. *I dream about it. Something like that happens to you when you're a kid, you dream about it.* Meadows had just taken it all in and said they should talk regularly, like once a week. Wednesdays were good. Jared agreed— one more appointment on his covert weekly calendar—and went back out to bake in the silence of the Hop-Frog. Swerdlow, John Dash, now Meadows. Everyone wanted reports. He wished he had a radio in the car, something to take his mind off the glassed-in still- ness. He picked at a small bud of scar tissue at the base of his thumb, souvenir of the fishhook from the night the Frankenline had turned out its first golem. Jesus, he thought. I need Colleen to help me sort all this out. Yes. This was the right thing to do. Just thinking about it made him feel better. It was an idea with some momentum behind it. An idea to build on. Plus Colleen would love having him come to her with a problem he admittedly couldn't solve. Wasn't every- one like that? Made anyone feel good to be told they were indis- pensable.

He plotted angles of approach all the way to work, kept plot- ting as he put on his coveralls and punched in, and then forgot all about it when Felton said, "Hey, J, you hear? Edsel died."

The one thing guaranteed to take a Rouge worker's mind off the war, worries about whether missed quotas would get the Franken- line shut down, the indifferent sadism of the nonunion foremen, racial animosity, and the plain deadening monotony of working the line was gossip about what was happening in the Rotunda. Espe- cially among the men of Building G, who had all been inside the Ro- tunda back before Pearl Harbor, the building across Schaefer Road had a kind of power. Did the Old Man have it in for Charlie Sorensen after Sorensen's design of Willow Run had gotten him on the cover of *Time*? Was Harry Bennett still tied up with the Black Hand—and were the Hand using the money they got from black- market parts salon to support Mussolini? Why had the Old Man kept on belittling Edsel even after letting him become president of the company? The Rotunda was like some medieval castle, full of intrigue and betrayal, and now that Edsel was dead—of cancer, or ulcers, or simple heartbreak after fifty years of his father's incomprehension and cruelty—the power vacuum would ratchet up Rotunda machinations to Shakespearean intensity.

"This is Bennett's chance," Jem said. "The Old Man's gonna be eighty in a month, and he ain't all there. Harry Bennett's gonna take over."

"Don't see it," countered Felton. "Ford's always been a family company, and that won't change now, 'specially with the war. I won't be surprised if they go without a top dog for a while until they can get Hank the Deuce out of the navy."

Jem scoffed at this. "Hell, the Deuce ain't any older than Jared. Long as Sorensen and Bennett are there to keep everyone fighting with each other, the Old Man'll just sit back and see who comes out on top. Then he'll make a call. Hell, maybe he'll put Mrs. Ford in charge."

They all laughed at this even though they knew Clara Ford was more than capable of getting smart men to work for her. She'd surely put the screws to the Old Man and Bennett when the UAW was fighting its way into the Rouge. Rumor had it that the Old Man wanted to hold out even after the labor-relations board and the War Production Office said Ford had to have an election at the Rouge—but Clara had told him flat-out that if he didn't let the men organize, she would leave him.

"I think old Charlie Sorensen would do a good job," Jared said.

Felton shook his head. "Could be, but he ain't family. Plus Bennett hates him and the Old Man thinks he's gotten too big for his britches, last couple of years. After he got his cover on *Time*."

"Damn, but it's a shame," Jem said. "Edsel put together some fine-looking cars."

They all agreed about this. The Lincoln Continental, now, that was a set of wheels a man could take pride in. "And he was sure as hell the most decent out of all of 'em," Felton said.

"Country at war don't need Lincolns and decency," Jared put in. "We need to get things done. You two have gone all moony-eyed. Which man is going to beat Hitler and the Japs? That's who I want to see in the job."

The argument went on until the magnetic detector went on the fritz again, and then they all stood around waiting for the electricians to show up while Swerdlow screamed at them from the catwalk. At one point, a little before midnight, Moises ran out of gurneys; when the last golem emerged from the Tabernacle and walked out to the rail siding—without mishap, they all noted with some relief—he came out to see what was happening. He saw the electricians and threw up his hands.

"Machines," he growled. "This is a job for men. Jared, Felton, screen this clay."

"We did," Jared said. "You're the one who's so worried about one little bit of steel."

There was about ten feet of conveyor belt on the other side of the detector that still had clay on it. Moises pointed at it. "Is enough for a golem. Did magnet check?"

Everyone looked at someone else. "It shut down soon as the fail-safe triggered," Felton said. He was closest to the detector, and had somehow become responsible for keeping an eye on it. When it went out, the line shut down automatically. The clay sitting on the other end had almost certainly been screened.

"Fail-safe stops line . . . ?" Moises snapped his fingers to get the rest of the message across.

Now everybody was looking at Felton. He clearly didn't like it. "Ask them," he said, pointing at the electricians. "It's supposed to stop right away, but for all I know that part's broken, too."

"Uh-uh," one of the electricians said. "Tell the rabbi to go do a bar mitzvah. We're trying to work here."

"Bah," Moises said. Grinding his teeth, he disappeared into his office and slammed the door. About an hour later, after the detector was fixed and the Frankenline was just done processing the rest of the day's clay, all hell broke loose.

CHAPTER 8

Jared woke up in darkness, trying to figure out how his Bloody Run dream had transmuted into him leading a line of golems through a cave with rocks coming down everywhere, all of them carrying armloads of gold like a bunch of medieval dragonslayers. He blamed Meadows; if the OEI hadn't stuck their noses in, Jared's dream circuitry wouldn't have gotten crossed up. Next time he went to Meadows' office, he'd let him know. This was for the birds, when an office full of spies could get a guy's dreams screwed up.

What the hell, though. Dreams were supposed to be all mixed around, weren't they? So why had Jared's dreams about the Dwarf always been exactly the same? Wasn't any reason to get worked up about it.

"Jared?" Colleen's voice.

"Yeah, honey." He started to sit up and reach for the bedside lamp, but a spike of pain in his forehead laid him right back down on the bed. He reached to his other side, looking for Colleen, and found only empty space. "What'm I doing on this side?" he mumbled. "Head's killing me."

"I bet it is." From the right, where he'd been looking for the lamp, Colleen took his hand in both of hers. "You were in an accident at work. You're in the hospital."

Things started to fall back into place. "Holy Jesus," Jared said. "That—"

Colleen put a hand over his mouth. "Shush. You're not supposed to talk about it. Your boss just put 'equipment failure' on the report."

Lucidity came and went, leaving Jared wondering what he had said in his delirium. She wasn't supposed to know about the golems. Nobody was. Had he said something when the nurses were around, or the orderlies? Worry made him nauseated, or maybe it was just his headache. He wanted her to know without it being him who told her. Just to share it with her.

"How are the other guys?" Jared tried to dredge up details of what had happened, but all he got were stuttering images, moments: Moises yelling, the door to the Tabernacle flying out into the room, the golem coming out looking all wrong—a feral kind of light in its eyes instead of the usual drowned blankness, a spastic excitement in its motions instead of the shuffling progress to the train siding they'd always seen before. The men on the Frankenline bolting for the doors, equipment flying everywhere . . . and lights-out. How much of this was remembered from last night, and how much rearranged and plugged in from the berserk golem from the Frankenline's first night? Two accidents on a line wasn't unheard-of, but Jared felt torn loose from his moorings in the world; drifting, he reached for something to anchor him again. The thought that brought him back to earth was an unwelcome intuition that this would be it for the golem project. Missing quotas, security hassles . . . how long would the OEI put up with it?

Colleen was starting to say she hadn't heard about anyone else, but Jared jumped in. "Wait a minute, what time is it?"

"Almost six in the morning."

154 —

ALEXANDER C. IRVINE

"So it's light? Colleen, is something wrong with my eyes?" The bottom fell out of Jared's stomach. He couldn't be blind. His mind bent under the weight of all the things he'd never see again. Emily.

"Your eyes are fine, honey. There's a bandage over them because you've got a whole string of stitches across your forehead." She paused. "You're squishing my hand."

"Oh." He relaxed a little. "So I can see."

"Pretty sure," she said, teasing him a little. He almost snapped at her, but caught himself. She must have been worried sick. Both of them could use a little humor.

"So what hit me?" he asked.

"I haven't seen you. You were bandaged up by the time I got Emily over to your mother's house and made it here. Want me to get a doctor?"

Jared tried to sit up again, more slowly this time. It still hurt, but he could do it. "Yeah," he said. "Let's get out of here."

"We'll let the doctor decide that. Be back in a minute." Colleen pecked him on the cheek, and the door to his room opened and closed. A few minutes later she came back. "Honey, the doctor's here."

"Morning, Mr. Cleaves. I'm Dr. Begala." The doctor stifled a yawn. "Excuse me. End of a long shift."

"I know how that is," Jared said.

"Yes, you Ford boys have kept me busy tonight. You have a headache?"

"It's not too bad," Jared said. Which it wasn't, compared with a knife in the eye.

"Good. I'm going to take your bandages off so I can examine your stitches, and along the way we'll get your eyes warmed up again. Mrs. Cleaves, would you mind getting the lights?" There was a click. "Thank you," Dr. Begala said. Jared felt the doctor's hands on his head, peeling off some tape and then unwinding what seemed like a mile of gauze, or whatever they'd wrapped him in. He started to sense light in the room.

"Thought the lights were off," he said.

"It's a sunny morning," Dr. Begala said. "Even through the curtains. Keep your eyes closed until I tell you. Let's give them some time to adjust."

The last of the bandages lifted away, and Jared's head started to itch. As he scratched, Dr. Begala prodded gently at his forehead. Jared flinched. "That'll be sore for a while," Begala said. "See this, Mrs. Cleaves? Look like links of a chain to you?"

"I can see it," Colleen said.

"I used to see marks like that quite a bit when the unions were trying to get in," Begala said, "but it's been a while now. You run afoul of Special Service, son?"

"No, I was on the line," Jared said. The idea of strikebreaking golems struck him as funny, but he kept it to himself. One of the molders had once whispered about organizing the golems into a union, and the next day he hadn't shown up for work. "I'm not sure what happened."

"Okay. Try to open your eyes. They're swollen, but everything should be in working order."

Jared blinked, squinted, rolled his eyes around in their sockets. Eventually he got them open and found the dimness in the room tolerable. Dr. Begala stood off to his left at the side of the bed, and Colleen was right in front of him at the foot. His head started to hurt more, and before he could stop himself he grimaced.

"Does the light bother you?" Dr. Begala asked.

"Just my head. Feel like I went fifteen with Joe Louis."

"Hm. I'm going to check you for concussion again. Open your eyes as widely as you can."

Jared did, determined not to let on how much it pained him. "All right, good," Begala said. He held up a finger. "Now follow my finger without moving your head." He moved his finger up and down, side to side, going a little farther each time. "Okay," he said. "You're going to have a hell of a headache for a few days, but I think you're all right."

"Good. I'm ready to go home."

Begala nodded. "I'll send a nurse to check you out." He walked toward the door.

"Hey, Doc," Jared said. "You treat a hillbilly named Jem or a colored fellow by the name of Felton tonight?"

"Don't think I saw anybody named Jem. Is that for Jeremiah?" Jared didn't know. "Well, I don't think I saw him. I did treat a Negro named Felton Devereaux, but unlike you he walked from the ambulance into the emergency room. I put six or eight stitches in his mouth and another few in his head. Is he a coworker?" Jared nodded. "I imagine he'll be back at work tonight. You, on the other hand, should put your feet up for at least a day. See to that, will you, Mrs. Cleaves?" Begala smiled and closed the door behind him.

Colleen sat on the bed. "I've already called in for today. Emily can stay at your parents', and we'll just take it easy."

"That sounds good," Jared said. It was Thursday, though. He was supposed to talk to Swerdlow after his shift, and Jared had a feeling that Swerdlow wouldn't see a few stitches and a headache as reason enough to miss their rendezvous. He'd have to figure something out. After he took a good long nap.

A nurse came in to sign Jared out and put a fresh mile of tape around his head. This time she left his eyes clear. "How many stitches did I get?" he asked her.

She paused to count. "Well, they're in three sections. Thirteen, and five, and seven. Probably spells something in Morse code," she added with a wink. When she was done, she asked if Jared could walk, and since he could, she accompanied them as far as the elevator and then went on her way with a cheery admonition to Colleen that she should keep her husband out of trouble.

"Well, how do you like that," Colleen said in the elevator. "As if you'd been in a brawl or something."

"Oh, she was just joking."

"Flirting, more like." Colleen put her arm through his.

"Flirting with me by talking to you? That's a new one," Jared joked, but he didn't press it because he liked the way she was leaning into him. It had been a while since he'd felt like he meant something to her, and if twenty-five stitches was all it took, then what the hell. Being able to tell the story about being brained by a rampaging golem more than made up for it even without the gentle weight of her pressing into his side.

"You don't know anything about women, do you?" she said with a half smile and a shake of her head.

Jared's first instinct was to enumerate all of the things he did in fact know about women, but some dim kernel of self-preservation still survived in the lower parts of his brain, and he kept his mouth shut instead. Which was what Colleen had wanted in the first place. He liked this sensation of marital normality, of knowing when to give your wife the small victory when you could have pushed things. She did it for him, he knew, even if he didn't notice it most of the time.

And he couldn't really tell the berserk-golem story anyway, since the Frankenline didn't officially exist. Briefly Jared wondered if some journalist out there was looking into it. He imagined some bright bulb noticing that some of the soldiers in the newsreels from Attu didn't look quite right—although the truth was that he worked with golems every day and still couldn't swear for certain that he'd ever seen one in a newsreel. But now that the Allies were gearing up to invade Sicily, the next step would be the Italian boot, and then the golems would start playing a much more prominent role. Sooner or later somebody would track down Building G. Jared worked in a place that almost nobody knew about, doing things that nobody would believe if he told them. It was an odd sort of privilege, but one that took at least as much as it gave; he saw the outrageous and magical every night, and no one would ever know. Even Colleen would probably write off whatever he'd babbled last night to Jared having his bell rung. That might be something to ask Grant Meadows about, Jared mused as he stood, swaying just a little, outside the front door of Henry Ford Hospital waiting for Colleen to bring the car around. When she did, he didn't notice right away because she was driving his dad's Fordor Deluxe instead of the Hop-Frog. She got out and called to him, and he shuffled over and poured himself into the passenger seat. He was asleep by the time they'd gotten to the first traffic light.

Colleen came in around one to ask him how he was feeling and if he wanted lunch. While he was still blinking sleep out of his head, Emily sidled around her mother and came to stand at the bedside. For the first time since she'd gotten big enough to climb onto the bed, she didn't, instead gazing wide-eyed and solemn at the thick bandage encircling her father's head.

"Daddy?" she said.

"Yes, honey."

"You okay, Daddy?"

"I'm okay." It was pretty much true. His head hurt, but not any worse than a bad hangover. "I thought you were at your grandma's."

"You, you, you have a boo-boo on your head?"

"It's okay, baby girl. The doctor fixed it up."

She thought about this. Jared tossed back the blanket and put his feet on the floor, bracketing her. "Daddy's hungry," he said. "You want to come eat?"

"Pick up me," Emily commanded, sticking out her arms.

"Honey, Daddy might not be able to pick you up right now," Colleen said, but Jared was already catching her under the arms and standing to carry her out into the kitchen. She laid her head on his shoulder.

"I got her, babe, it's okay," he said, even though lifting her thirty pounds set the blood pounding painfully in his head. "What's for lunch?"

Jared hadn't eaten in something like eighteen hours, and the crack on the head had made him even hungrier. He put away three egg-salad sandwiches and a pickle, and then split an apple with Emily, who barraged him with questions about his head. Between answers, he tried to carry on a conversation with Colleen; it wasn't often that they got to have a casual lunch all together, and stitches or no stitches he was going to make the most of it. "Oh," she said after bringing him his third sandwich. "I thought of you yesterday, asking me about that new building. They just went in and built a big stack there. I don't know what line they're putting in, but something's making an awful lot of smoke, and it doesn't smell like they're burning cows. Our production's finally revving up to where it's supposed to be, so I thought it was a new parts line or something. But there was some kind of accident yesterday around noon. We heard the sirens, and Arlene—you know how nosy she is—went to see what happened since we were all at lunch anyway. She was twenty minutes late coming back, and all she could tell us was that there were four or five men badly hurt, and soldiers everywhere. Men in suits, too. They wouldn't let Arlene get close enough to see anything. So I don't know if that earns you your twenty dollars or not, but I thought I'd mention it."

"Huh," Jared said. He was mulling what she'd said, and he had his own conclusions about the men in suits—Grant Meadows featuring prominently—but the mention of Arlene's name had swirled together in his concussed brain with the flirtatious nurse, and Jared Cleaves found himself wanting to talk to Arlene Bannister more than he wanted to be in his kitchen.

She wasn't a war widow exactly, although she called herself one. The previous fall, right before the American retreat from the Sbeitla Valley, her ex-husband, Joe, been patching a little hole in the rudder of a Flying Fortress when a Stuka dive-bomber came down out of the sun. Joe had just jumped off the Fortress' tail when a shell pinged off the plane's fuselage and passed between the middle and ring fingers of his left hand. He'd run thirty yards to the nearest trench and hit the bottom face-first before he realized that something was wrong with his hand, and after the bombing he'd gone back out and found his ring finger lying there under the tail of the plane he'd been working on. There was a perfect half-moon carved out of his middle finger, exposing unbroken bone, but the impact of the shell on his wedding ring had pinched the ring finger off clean as a whistle. Joe Dudek was a superstitious man, and when he got back to Detroit the first thing he did was divorce Arlene, reasoning that his wound would have been less severe if he hadn't been wearing a ring and therefore that his maiming was a message from the gods that he'd been mistaken to marry. Upon hearing this story Jared had concluded that Joe Dudek was one dumb Polack, primarily because the former Arlene Dudek was one honey of a woman.

"What you say to Daddy, Mama?" Emily asked.

She was decorated from head to toe in egg salad, eggs having been plentiful lately, and Colleen went to work on her with a washcloth. "Just talking about work, baby girl."

"What you say about work?"

"Just telling Daddy about work. Grown-up stuff."

"No," Emily said, pushing away the washcloth. She climbed down out of her booster seat and ran out of the kitchen, coming back a minute later with the belt of Colleen's bathrobe wrapped around her head. "Emily have boo-boo like Daddy," she announced.

The sight of her banished thoughts of Arlene Bannister from his head. "Oh no," Jared said, scooping her up and holding her upside down. "Here we go to the doctor!"

Twenty minutes later, after playing out the doctor scenario, doing damage control when Jared's refusal to actually put stitches in

Emily's head drove her to screaming fury, and finally putting her down for a nap, Jared came back out into the kitchen. He glanced at the clock over the table; it was five after two.

"How's your head?" Colleen was drying the dishes.

"Not too bad. I took some aspirin."

"Good." She paused. "I'm sorry you got hit in the head with a chain, but it's good to have you around."

"Yeah, this is nice," Jared said, meaning it and feeling guilty about his covert Arlene thoughts. "I'll have to get hit in the head more often."

"You feel up to a picnic? Something quiet. We could just go over to Belle Isle, let Emily run around a little after she wakes up."

I should have seen this coming, Jared thought. He went to Colleen and kissed her on the cheek. "I should go in," he said. "I don't get sick time."

She turned to face him. "You don't have to go in. We've got money in the bank. And you have a dent in your head, and your daughter and your wife would like to spend some time with you."

Jared felt the moment come and go, the brief opening when he might have leveled with her about Swerdlow and John Dash and Sharkskin Billy, the OEI and whatever the hell else he'd gotten tangled up in. A year ago I would have already done it, he thought, and close on the heels of that thought came the demoralizing realization that they spent too much time apart to really know each other anymore. He wondered again what he'd said during the night, hearing Moises' voice say *loose lips*, and that echo bottled up whatever confession he'd been about to make. Colleen saw in his face that he was about to tell her something, and then that he'd chosen not to; she wiped her hands on the dish towel, folded it on the edge of the sink, and said, "Never mind." Without looking him in the eye, she added, "I'll give you a ride. Go ask Mrs. Pelletier if she can keep an eye on Emily for a minute."

When she dropped him off at the front gate off Miller Road,

Jared stood watching his wife drive away and wanting to have the last hour to do all over again. Sometimes you've already failed by the time you figure out that you need to make a decision, he thought. I could walk home right now and start packing up a picnic, and it wouldn't change anything. Wouldn't fix what I did, even though I'm still not sure what I did.

"Dumb shit," he said out loud, and started walking toward Building G.

Somebody had cleaned up the rogue golem's mess, and the Franken-line was humming along like nothing had ever happened. "Hey there, Red Badge of Courage," Jem said as Jared took up his position on the line.

"Shut up." Jared attacked the clay, hoping nobody else would say anything. Goddamn golem, he thought. If it hadn't busted my head, Colleen wouldn't have taken the day off work and I wouldn't have made a monkey out of myself. I hope somebody stuck it in a god-damn kiln and then went to work on it with a chisel.

This train of thought further befouled his already bilious mood, because now he wanted to know what had happened to the golem but he didn't want to ask. Fuming, he destroyed lumps of clay and flung metal into the scrap bins—or near them, since in his fury his accuracy suffered. Eventually Jem said, "I hope you don't think we're picking all that up for you."

Jared put down his trowel so he wouldn't stick it in Jem's eye. He put both hands on the conveyor-belt railing and just stood still, thinking Okay. Okay. Okay.

"If you two are going to fight, let's stop the line so we can all go outside and watch," Felton said. He had a line of stitches on his lip like half a mustache, but didn't look any the worse for wear.

"I ain't said a thing about a fight," Jem said. "Jared's the one spoiling over there."

"Hillbilly got a point there," Felton said. "What's got into you?"

"Don't you call me a hillbilly, nigger." Now Jem was ready to fight.

Felton looked at him. "All right, I won't. But you call me a nigger again, I'll stop the line myself and you and me'll settle things." When Jem didn't respond, Felton turned his attention back to Jared. "Come on. Spit it out."

Jared took a deep breath and picked up his trowel. "Nothing. Colleen and I are bickering, that's all. Forget it."

"Aw, man, woman trouble," Jem said. All of his aggression evaporated just like that, instantly replaced by sympathy. "Ain't that the worst?"

"Let's all settle down and stop throwing metal everywhere," Felton said. "We got golems to make."

What with all the hostility, they'd let about forty feet of clay go by unsifted, and when the molders saw it they blew up and stopped the line themselves. Moises heard the ruckus and came out; then he blew up, too, red-faced and spitting, how could they do this after what happened yesterday? Most of his fury was directed at Jared, so when Swerdlow came in to see why the line was stopped he found a tableau of enraged rabbi, sullen molders, sulking clod-busters, and in the middle of it all Jared Cleaves about to boil over with shame and frustration. "Goddammit!" Swerdlow shouted. "Are we going to make any goddamn golems tonight, or should we just invite Hitler into the White House right goddamn now?"

The tension in the room broke, or more accurately refocused itself on Swerdlow, as the unsifted clay was sent back up the belt and the molders stood around smoking and grousing about Americans. Swerdlow hooked a thumb at Jared. "Outside."

When they'd gotten maybe a hundred yards down the siding, Swerdlow stopped. "Trying to get yourself fired, that it? Think you can get shut of me that easy, kid? You're in deeper than that."

"You got me in," Jared said.

"Goddamn right I did, and you don't get out just by fucking up enough that the crazy kike fires you. Not that he could. I'm the only man can fire you from this, Cleaves."

Jared was half intending to take a swing at Swerdlow when he turned around, just to be done with it all, but something in the look of the man stopped him and made the impulse seem mean and small. Look at him, Jared thought. A homely bald fat man, not even the solid heavy kind of fat but loose and wobbly, always sweating. He must always feel like he's about to flow down into his shoes and disappear. One more life swallowed up by the Rouge. Then the moment of charity passed, and the image seemed funny. Swerdlow turned into a little puddle of shit. Perfect. A little coal of anticipation sparked to life inside him, and Jared reminded himself that he was working for the Marshal. He was the OEI's man, he was on the case. "Right now I don't care who fires me, or if somebody does," he said. "But if it's you, just to make sure we understand each other, I'll find somebody who's interested in your meetings with your sharkskin Kraut. You two talking about soccer, maybe?"

Fear flashed across Swerdlow's face. "Who told you about that?" he hissed.

"Little birdie," Jared said. He grinned, enjoying the sensation of having something on Swerdlow—of acting instead of reacting all the time. "You still want to fire me?"

Swerdlow recovered himself. "You need to watch yourself, Cleaves. Maybe you know something, maybe you're just passing a message. But you tangle with me, brother, you'll be sorry."

"Same to you. But just so we don't get at each other's throat quite yet, here's a little something on Willow Run. You hear about the accident out there?"

" 'Course I did. It was in the paper."

"Yeah. Well, the *Free Press* didn't get the good part. Guess who showed up to take the wounded men away?" Jared waited, hoping to learn something by Swerdlow's guess, but Swerdlow wasn't giving him anything. "Soldiers. Keeping everyone back from a factory accident."

"Big deal," Swerdlow said. "Probably something classified on that line. Happens all the time."

"Sure it does, but it's not every time that the OEI shows up to keep everyone on the same page."

Swerdlow frowned as he worked this over in his head. "Okay," he said after a while. "Go on back. We'll talk on Tuesday."

"We'll talk when I have something to tell you," Jared said. "Meanwhile, why don't you think about telling me what goes on with your Kraut buddy?" Again he waited, and again Swerdlow kept his mouth shut. Which was a kind of small victory, Jared thought as he walked back to Building G. If he could find out what was really going on at Willow Run, that would be serious leverage.

He was starting to enjoy the game. Man, this cloak-and-dagger stuff could be fun. Shouldn't enjoy it too much, though, he cautioned himself. Who knew what John Dash wanted, or the OEI, or Swerdlow? Any one of them could go through some private calculus and decide that Jared Cleaves was a pawn with a little too much ambition to be a king. That wasn't true, although Jared was having fun watching Swerdlow get jumpy. Best defense is a good offense, Jared thought. If I'm going to end up under a lightbulb somewhere, I'm for damn sure not going to be the only one.

That stubborn exhilaration—the conviction that beneath the rust of circumstance was the shining steel of destiny—didn't leave during the rest of his shift, and when Jared got out to the Hop-Frog, he was on the horns of a dilemma. Colleen was more than likely still resentful that he'd decided to go to work instead of spending the day with her and Emily—and she had good reason. Truth was, for all of his frustration at the way things were between them, Jared knew he wasn't keeping up his end of the bargain, either. It wasn't intentional, but the distance between them made it a little too easy to quit on the kinds of little gestures and actions that nourish a marriage. Like taking a chance to have a picnic instead of going to work, or—dammit, he reminded himself, you still haven't gotten her flowers or anything—a little tin of candy left on the dashboard of the car. But there was Swerdlow, and Dash, and the weird little charm stuck in the Hop-Frog's engine, and what kind of man was he if he didn't take action when all of this might be threatening his family? Jared weighed this conflict while cars streamed out of the Rouge's endless parking lots and the buildings that only ran two shifts went dark. The light of a pour blazed up from the foundry. I still might lose my job over this, he thought. It's not much of a job, but it's mine. I was chosen for it. And if Swerdlow's talking to Germans, I'd be a traitor not to find out everything I can.

Swerdlow was running scared. He'd be on his way to the bowling alley right now. Jared knew what he was going to do, but he chewed it over a little more anyway. Moises came shuffling out of the darkness, silhouetted against the dying glow of the pour. He climbed into a waiting car about fifty yards from Jared, a nearly new Buick, which flicked on its headlights and drove away. The rumors that swirled around Moises bubbled back up in Jared's mind—who was giving him a ride? What had happened to the arrangement with the molders?

Jared started the Hop-Frog and followed the Buick into Detroit and out Twelfth Street. When it pulled over in front of Moises' building, Jared drove past, slowing to get a look at the driver. It was the Jeweler, and as his tension drained away Jared felt a little sheepish. The Jeweler had the extra dough—maybe his wife worked, too—and he'd bought a nice car on time. It made sense. Three minutes later he was in the bowling-alley parking lot sorting through various theories.

There was an argument in the parking lot among four or five men, and right as Jared was about to unlatch the door and go looking for Sharkskin Billy, two of the guys went at it, staggering and grappling like hockey players with fistfuls of each other's shirts, throwing wild punches without much visible effect until one of them actually tore the other guy's shirt clean off. His opponent took advantage of the sudden freedom to swing from the heels, a long looping right that settled things. Jared heard the flat splat of the punch landing through the Hop-Frog's closed window. The torn shirt went fluttering in a long arc as the challenger took a step back, flailing for balance. He hit the ground on his left side, got to hands and knees, and then flopped face-first onto the ground. There ensued the typical postfight exchange of recriminations and placatory hand waving, and then two of the guys picked up their cross-eyed buddy and dumped him into a car. As they drove off, the winner of the fight picked up his shirt and held it out at arm's length. I can read your mind, Jared thought. Right about now you're figuring out that your woman can't bring that shirt back from the dead, and you're also working out how you're going to avoid having her peel the skin off your ass because you came home from the lanes with your knuckles skinned and a brand-new dishrag.

He opened the door and got out. The shirtless pugilist looked at him. "Now ain't this a bitch," he said.

"You landed a good one, though," Jared said.

The guy shook his head. "Asshole. He's my cousin. I ain't bowling with him no more." With that he stalked across the parking lot, shirt flipped over one shoulder, to a broken-down Pierce-Arrow.

Jared paused between doorways to repeat his neck-craning reconnaissance from a few days before. There was that waitress again, and the same knot of Poles in front of the table where he'd sat. Jared felt like a regular even though he'd only set foot in the place once. Swerdlow and Sharkskin Billy were probably at the end of the bar, and the golem was likely watching from its station at the other end. The golem—could he talk to it? He'd never heard one speak, didn't know if they could. Didn't know what he'd ask it.

The outside door opened and hit him in the ass. "Jesus, buddy, you gonna stand there all night?"

Jared pushed through the inner door and hid out at the shoe-rental counter, peering toward the bar. There was Swerdlow, and there was Sharkskin Billy—and there was the golem. Jared had the feeling that he'd traveled back in time; everything was identical except that damn Glenn Miller song, playing even here. Moises was probably sitting in his ratty bathrobe with a glass of water. Jared considered walking up to Swerdlow and asking to be introduced. Maybe it was time to really start acting from a position of strength. Trouble was, he didn't know if he was in a position of strength, and if Sharkskin Billy was really some kind of spy, a wrong move on Jared's part could land him in the river. Swerdlow could be right, Jared thought. I might be way out of my depth here.

Okay; it was enough to know that the bowling-alley rendezvous was still happening. Jared went back outside, an excited bounce in his step, feeling like a forward observer safely back in friendly territory. Then he saw John Dash leaning on the fender of the Hop-Frog, smoking a cigarette and looking off into the night sky.

Everything really is the same, Jared thought. What next? When he got close to the car, he said, "What, there's no other fenders in Detroit you can lean on?"

"Join a bowling league, Jared?" Dash wasn't smiling.

"Call it reconnaissance," Jared said. "Who's the guy in the sharkskin suit?"

Dash glanced over Jared's shoulder. "He's in there, huh? Figures. What happened to your head?"

"Accident at work."

"Dangerous work, making golems."

Jared wasn't about to bite on that, and from Dash's sudden grin he could tell Dash knew it. "So what brings you out here?" Jared asked him.

"Looking for you."

"Well, you found me. Thought I was supposed to look for you."

"You were. Then you started acting like a secret agent. Not getting ideas, are you, Jared?"

"I've got an idea that I want to know what you want from me."

"Right now I want to know what you're doing coming out of a bowling alley where your boss is meeting with probably a German spy."

"If this other fellow is a German spy, how come you haven't turned him in?"

Dash smiled again. "How come I haven't turned *you* in? Already you've done enough to be very interesting to the FBI."

Just bluster, Jared thought; all the same a cold knot settled just under his sternum when he thought of his parents, Colleen and Emily, God forbid *Colleen's* parents, reading in the paper that he'd been taken in for FBI questioning. "Here we go again," he said. "Soon as I stop rolling over for you, you come out with the threats. All right. Why *haven't* you turned me in? If you're just trying to sucker me into doing something I can get arrested for, you've done it. Come on, you put me onto Swerdlow's trail, now you're warning me off. What gives?"

"I want to know what Swerdlow talks about with his buddy in there."

"Should I tell him who's asking?"

"Please don't. That would move things along rather faster than I'd prefer."

"Suit yourself," Jared said. "I'll try to explain that to the golem in there."

Dash blinked. "The what?"

"You heard me. Now stop getting my fender dirty. Time for me to go home."

Easing himself off the car, Dash looked at Jared with what Jared took to be new interest. Good, Jared thought. Now you know I've got something you don't. He got into the car and drove home, all the way wondering what he could do with this knowledge, whether it would save him or make him enough of a hot potato that everyone couldn't get rid of him fast enough. He killed the Hop-Frog's lights before turning into the driveway, and went through the house like he was sneaking past sleeping cobras—which was more or less how he felt. When he slipped into bed next to Colleen, he could tell she was awake. Not wanting to make the first move because he knew it would be wrong, Jared lay staring at the ceiling until after a while she said, "I thought you were coming home."

"I was," he said. "I wanted to. There's—" How to do this? he wondered. "The thing with Willow Run. There's no twenty dollars."

Admitting to this made him feel a little better, hopeful even, as if now that he'd started the confession Colleen would help him finish it. Please, he thought. We could do this together. Except she'd had nothing to do with it beyond answering a question he shouldn't have asked in the first place.

"Why'd you want to know, then?" she asked.

"Swerdlow made me. He wants to know."

Colleen rolled over to face him and propped herself up on one elbow. "Why didn't he just ask someone at Willow Run?"

"I—" The truth caught in Jared's throat. Not the truth that Swerdlow had made him a pawn in some spy game, and that Jared's involvement had drawn other interested parties the way a bowl of beer draws slugs, but the truth that Jared was enjoying the game and had started playing it himself out of what now, late at night in his own bed with his wife, seemed to be plain dumb bravado. Plus wounded pride. If he'd had tin snips in the bedroom, he'd have cut off his two damaged fingers as a pledge of faith . . . and tomorrow afternoon, when he was back at work with John Dash flickering at the edges of his vision, he'd have gone back on the pledge, because the real unsayable truth was that now Jared had to see how the game would play out.

THE NARROWS — 171

"He's gotten me into the middle of something," Jared said. "He says if I don't find out about Willow Run, he'll fire me."

"You could quit," Colleen said carefully. "We could manage on . . . until you found something else."

And just like that Jared was trapped between pride and common sense. "I don't think it would work," he said, which was true but at the same time a lie because he knew he couldn't tell her why it was true, and that made him a liar about his reasons if nothing else.

Colleen knew it, too. "Why not?" she asked, more gently than she had to. "Is something else going on?"

"I met some people because Swerdlow wanted me to," Jared said. Another half-truth. "He says I might be in trouble."

She reached across the space between them and smoothed his hair. Jared closed his eyes, soaking in the feeling of her palm on his forehead, brushing lightly over the stitches. "I want you to listen to me, Jared," she said. "I love you, and I won't ask anything more about this. But if you are putting our daughter in danger because you can't come to grips with not being in the army, I'm going to leave you. I won't want to, but I'm not going to live with my husband tearing this family apart because he'd rather be seven thousand miles away. You hear me?"

"I hear you," Jared said. He didn't open his eyes.

"I mean did you hear all of it? Including the part about loving you?"

"I heard that, too." He wanted to say something else, but the fearless honesty of his wife had made it impossible for him to lie, and he couldn't trust himself to tell the truth. After much, much too long, when it was too late to do any good, he opened his eyes in the darkness and said, "Don't leave me, Colleen. Please don't leave me."

CHAPTER 9

He hadn't meant to sleep; it seemed more right to lie staring at the ceiling in a futile effort to pinpoint the exact moment when things had really started to go wrong. Jared knew that moment didn't exist; distance had accreted around his marriage through a thousand forgotten instances of withheld affection and bitten-off angry words. Still, he thought he should have looked for it, made it up if necessary, to give this terrible void a point of origin tangible to his mind.

Instead Emily wrestled the bedroom door open in the morning and climbed up onto the bed. "Um, Daddy, Mama, Mama, Mama," she said. Colleen and Jared had only recently figured out that this wasn't a stutter. When Emily wanted to talk, often the impulse started her mouth moving before she knew what she wanted to say. As a result, many conversations with her began with five or six repetitions of *I* or *you* or *Mama* before galloping away when she hit on a topic. Jared looked at the clock: a little before seven.

"Mama what?" he asked.

"Mama said wake up."

"Okay. I'm up." Hoisting Emily onto his hip, Jared walked out into the kitchen in his underwear. Colleen was sitting with the newspaper. "Hey," he said. "Aren't you going to be late?"

She folded the paper, but not before Jared noticed that she'd been reading box scores. Colleen pretended not to like sports, but Jared knew that deep down inside her beat the heart of a baseball fan. "Thought you could use a little extra sleep," she said. "But I need the car. Can you take the streetcar to work?"

"Yeah, I guess." Jared was puzzled. Had he dreamed the conversation during which she'd outlined the scenarios that would make her leave him? And now she'd let him sleep in? He decided not to think too hard about it. "You need keys?" Colleen was always losing her keys.

She waved a key ring at him. "Nope. I've got 'em." As she passed him on the way to the door, she gave him a kiss on the cheek and said, "You believe that Newhouser?" He stood there stunned while she walked out the door. He couldn't remember the last time she'd kissed him. Or the last time she'd talked about baseball. The world was a strange place this morning, and he liked it.

After he'd fried himself a couple of eggs and taken a shower— alternately freezing and scalding as Emily played with the bathroom faucet—he walked her over to the cemetery. People walked their dogs there, and she liked to pet the dogs and pepper their owners with questions about what kind of dogs they were. It was getting time to add a dog to the Cleaves household, Jared thought. Every kid should have a dog.

If he'd had the car, he'd have taken Emily to the pound then and there. Colleen would be okay with it, he thought. They'd talked about it before, and Jared found himself newly of the opinion that the time had come. Some kind of mutt, bright-eyed and ready to run around with a little kid. It would make a nice change from spending his working hours making golems designed to kill people, even if those people were Nazis.

Emily was hugging a golden retriever and humming in its ear.

The dog endured her affection with good humor, panting and occasionally turning its head to lick her face. Its owner, a middle-aged woman wearing clothes a little too young for her, smiled down at Emily, and Jared, unable to help himself, smiled at both of them. All three, if you counted the dog.

"You want a dog, baby girl?" Jared asked.

"Yeah!" she shouted.

"Well, we'll get you one."

She let go of the retriever and ran over to grab on to his leg. "We go now get dog!"

"Probably tomorrow. Mama has the car, remember?"

"Tomorrow we get dog!"

"You bet, honey," Jared said. To himself he thought, huh. How do we get this one past Mama?

Problem for another time. Right now his little girl was happy, and he was happy, and for some reason his wife was being nicer to him than she had to. Good enough. "Okay, little miss," he said. "Time to go to Grandma and Grandpa's."

Marty Cleaves was sitting out on the front porch reading the paper when Jared pulled up. Emily yanked on the door handle and scrambled off his lap to run up to her grandfather, destroying the paper in the process. There was a light breeze, and *Free Press* pages soon decorated the hedge. Emily chased them around and threw them up in the air; when Jared went to stop her, his father called out, "Let her be. It'll give me something to do."

"Suit yourself." Jared sat on the porch and watched his daughter's newsprint rampage.

"So you talk to the OEI?"

"Yeah."

"What'd you tell them?"

"Same thing you did, unless you decided to lie."

"No, I didn't. No reason. I think they're watching the house now. Afraid the Dwarf will show up for coffee or something."

"I got the impression that they're more interested in figuring out whether the Dwarf is working for the Nazis."

Marty Cleaves looked up at the sky and arranged his features into his characteristic why-am-I-surrounded-by-imbeciles look. "Now how the hell would the Dwarf be working for the Nazis if it's been around for three hundred years?"

"That's what I said. Emily, come here, honey. That's enough."

Emily arrived smudged with newsprint. "Looks like a situation for Grandma," Dad said. "CeeCee! Why don't you come out here and see your granddaughter!"

CeeCee came out, took one look at Emily, and said, "Men. Emily Eloise, you come here this minute."

"Grammy!" Emily fell into her grandmother's arms.

"Hose that little girl off in the backyard," Jared said.

"I'll hose you off," CeeCee said. "You just watch yourself."

She and Emily went inside. Emily's voice carried like an air-raid siren, especially when she was happy, and for a few minutes Jared just sat in companionable silence with his father, listening to his daughter, thinking about his wife.

"What do you think about those Tigers?" Marty said.

"Well, they won more than they lost so far." By one game, and it was only good for fourth place, but they were only two out of first. This was one of those take-what-you-can-get years. Jared figured his dad was starved for baseball; the Tigers were on the road for two weeks and hadn't left on a good note, splitting a doubleheader with the hapless Red Sox.

"Newhouser yesterday against the Yankees," his dad said. "Blindfold and cigarette time."

"But they won." Jared flashed on Colleen reading box scores. Everything's going to be all right, he thought. For the Tigers and for us. "And we got Trout tonight, he's doing okay. Then off to Fenway."

"You wait. Time they come back, we'll be dead last."

"Come on."

"Three at Fenway, Shibe and Griffith after that. Four at Shibe, five at Griffith. Five." Marty Cleaves shook his head in disgust at the Tigers' future ineptitude. "Dead last. You watch. Fourteen-game trip, be lucky if we go four and ten."

"Nah." Jared stood up. "Well, Pop. Much as I love your sunny outlook, it's time for work. Take care of my baby girl."

"Watch out for that Dwarf," his father said.

The Rouge that night was full of strange specters. The Tenfingers were out in force, moving in groups anywhere there was something to be counted. On one of the lines where they'd once done finish work, the crews who now assembled jeep chassis there amused themselves by throwing their tools up at the long loops and whorls of ectoplasmic goo that draped the rafters. Some of the tools stuck, and the goo wrapped around them and arranged itself into artful patterns. Everyone was singing sardonic and profane variations of "That Old Black Magic," which was all of a sudden on the airwaves as much as Winchell. Elsewhere in the plant, one-ton trucks came off the line looking like monstrous Lincoln Continentals. Felton's theory, met with derision for its obviousness, was that they'd all come out of the woodwork because of Edsel's death. He pointed out that the groups of Tenfingers, which they'd stopped the Franken-line to go observe, had the look of a funeral procession, which was true, but Jem justifiably noted that the Tenfingers always looked kind of funereal.

Nobody got much work done except Moises, who gave not a damn about Edsel Ford and cared even less who would run the company now. He ran ahead of the line and emerged glowering from the Tabernacle to monitor their progress. "Look at him," Jem said. "Good thing he can't barely speak English."

Felton was just coming back in from his latest excursion, this one to look at one of the giant spectral Continentals that was driving around the parking lots off Miller Road. "You'd think he'd know enough to cuss us out just from listening to Swerdlow," he said.

"He can too speak English," Jared said, and too late realized that he should have kept his mouth shut.

"What, you talked over the state of the world with him? Go out for some bagels?" Jem needled him. Jared dithered, uncertain how to extract himself from this line of conversation, and then was rescued by the appearance of Ellery in the loading-bay doorway. Jared saw him and put down his tools. Ellery disappeared through the door again, and Jared followed. "Well, don't you exert yourself," Jem said after him.

Outside, Ellery waited next to a freight car they hadn't yet gotten around to hosing out. "Piston Doctor said come on by," he said. He held out a folded piece of paper. As Jared took it, he went on. "Don't come at night, and bring the bones."

Jared started to unfold the paper, and Ellery raised one of his scarred hands. "Play it smart, now."

"All right." Jared pocketed the paper. "Thanks."

Ellery was already walking away. "Welcome. I'll call it in later."

Saturday morning Jared popped out of bed early, fed Colleen a line of hooey about taking Emily to feed the ducks at the cemetery pond, and headed for the city dog pound. Emily fidgeted on his lap, once pulling herself upright by holding on to the steering wheel until she started bouncing up and down and slipped to plant one tiny foot squarely on Jared's testicles. He managed not to crash the Hop-Frog, but after that she was exiled to the passenger seat. The pound was the most depressing place in Detroit, was Jared's opinion. All those doomed animals, there through no fault of their own, looking through the chain link with their vulnerable canine optimism. Three times in his life Jared had been in a dog pound, and all three times he'd needed weeks afterward to get rid of the conviction that he should buy a huge farm out in the middle of nowhere and take every dog with him. This morning was no different. Jared had to keep reminding himself that they were there for *a* puppy, that he was only one man and could take only one dog. The others would just have to fend for themselves. But God, the choosing was a miserable burden; spending half an hour in a city pound was enough to make a guy—even a guy who worked on a classified project and drove himself crazy wanting more people to know what he did and how important it was—seriously consider the proposition that many things in life were better kept secret. Would the world be happier if only a select cabal knew what was going to happen to most of these moist-nosed and eager canines? Jared didn't know about the world, but he was pretty sure he himself would sleep better at night if he didn't have to think about the fact that most of the dogs who licked his fingers through their cages were going to be smoke in a city incinerator come Monday.

Emily, of course, had no such knowledge to interfere with her enjoyment. She laughed and laughed at the touch of each dog's nose or tongue, running from cage to cage as if the whole place existed solely for her pleasure. Jared wished he were two again. Once they'd taken a turn through the whole place, the selection process whittled itself down to either a litter of seven or eight black-and-brown mutts who boiled up to the front of their cage in a single mass of furiously wagging tails and lapping tongues or a single quiet prick-eared yellow dog, maybe three or four months old, who sat watching people go by with a calm interest that struck Jared as almost heroic. He went and found a slope-shouldered and whiskey-breathed attendant, who said they called the yellow puppy Claude. Was he always like that? He was. "Fine little dog," the attendant said. "I don't want to prejudice your selection nono, but today's his third day."

Claude. Goofy name for a dog, Jared thought. "Let's have a look at him," he said.

The attendant opened the cage, and Claude stood up and trotted over to them. He glanced up at the attendant, then briefly at Jared, before sniffing at Emily's face and licking her nose. He was about big enough to look her in the eye.

"How big you figure he'll get?" Jared asked, relying on the attendant's experience.

"Dunno. I only ever see 'em three days at a time."

"Kind of dog you think he is?"

"Mutt. Who knows?"

The attendant's indifference frosted Jared, but it made sense. How could you stay there day after day if you let yourself get attached? He squatted to talk to Emily. "This doggy's name is Claude. You like him?"

"Yeah!" She already had her fists buried in the ruff around Claude's neck, and was giggling as she halfheartedly tried to fend off his energetic licking.

Jared stood again. "Okay. What do I have to sign?"

"You did what?" Colleen said.

Over her shoulder Jared could see the other two Eens chatting gaily over coffee and muffins, ostentatiously ignoring the marital strife inside the front door. "That Old Black Magic" was playing on the radio, and for the first time in his life Jared wished he was hearing "Don't Sit Under the Apple Tree," a song he hated—or, for that matter, any other song recorded in the history of mankind. Anything but goddamn Glenn Miller.

"We talked about this," he said. "Remember?"

"I remember we talked about it, yes. I don't remember that we came to a decision."

"Look at him," Jared said, pointing out to the car, where Claude was leaving nose prints all over the passenger window. "He's a good little guy."

"Jared—"

"Emily's crazy about him."

If looks could kill. "Of course Emily's crazy about him. She's a two-year-old."

"What you say, Mama?" Emily piped up.

"We're talking about your doggy, sweet pea," Jared said. He was going to get murdered for it, that comment, but deep down inside he knew that Colleen liked dogs. By tomorrow she'd be feeding him bacon even as she kept Jared over the coals for not clearing it with her ahead of time. This is a fun game, he thought. Makes her happy to pretend she's more indignant than she really is, makes me happy to play at getting away with something, makes Emily happy to have a dog. Everybody wins. Of such little games were marriages made.

He looked back up at Colleen. "Let's introduce him to the girls. How about it?"

She tried to make a show of holding out, but Jared knew all that remained was formalities. "We'll try it," she said.

"That's my girl." Jared stood and headed for the car, calling over his shoulder, "Wait'll you see the collar I got him."

The collar hung like a yoke on Claude's skinny neck, leather with a double row of metal studs. "I figured with a name like Claude, he needs to look tough," Jared said.

"So the other dogs in the neighborhood won't make fun of him?" Arlene said, and let out her brassy-dame laugh. She practiced at it, the way she practiced smoking cigarettes exactly the way Katharine Hepburn smoked, and asking nosy questions the way your mother-in-law did. Jared liked Arlene—more than liked her, if he was honest about it—but he often wondered what she was like when she wasn't trying to be Arlene. It was like having a movie star around, only one who was neither famous nor rich and who worked stripping damaged bomber engines in Ypsilanti, Michigan. What Arlene was, was a woman living life under the unspoken assumption that someone after her death would write a mesmerizing biography of her. Colleen thought she was ridiculous but enjoyed her company. Jared was guiltily smitten with her, and had the impression for reasons unclear to him that she would welcome an overture. Maybe just because it would add a bit of scandal to her biography.

Nadine, as sensible and levelheaded as Arlene was flamboyant, said, "You could always call him something else."

"I tried that on the way home," Jared said. "Emily about broke all the car windows screaming. Believe his name is going to be Claude."

"Cod!" Emily agreed. She held Jared's hand, as if she knew that Claude's fate was as yet uncertain and was determined to stand with her father against her mother's skepticism. Or maybe Jared was making that up. Still, it felt good to have her at his side, her little fingers hooked into his and her eyes tracking her doggy—who, while the humans discussed his fate, was making the rounds of the kitchen and living room. He snuffled under the table for crumbs, worked his thin snout under the front of the stove, and stuck his entire head under the living room couch, where Emily tended to stow bits of breakfast cereal and fruit. "Look at him," Jared said. "You'll never need to vacuum again." This earned him another half-smiling dagger of a glance from Colleen; by the time they looked back to the newest member of the family, he was curled up at the side of the chair next to the console Philco. With a deep sigh, he dropped his chin onto his paws and fell asleep.

"There's a dog knows he's home," Arlene observed.

"We'll see," Colleen said. "How old is he?"

Jared shrugged. "Have to take him to the vet to find out, I think. He hasn't got much tackle, so he's probably not six months yet."

"Dear Lord, Jared," Nadine said.

"What? It's the best way to tell."

"No it isn't," Nadine said. "Look at his teeth."

"He's sleeping."

"Well, when he wakes up look at his teeth. If his big teeth are in, he's probably six months or more. 'Specially his size."

"His size don't mean a thing unless you know what breeds he is," Arlene put in.

"Those prick ears say husky," Nadine said.

"Or German shepherd," Jared said. The sudden profusion of opinions had him wondering if they were all channeling his father.

"Be just like you to get a German dog in the middle of a war," Arlene said. "But I don't think he's either. Look at his color. Doesn't he look like a corgi?"

"Not long enough," Jared said. "Plus look at his legs."

"Could be his mother," Arlene said.

"Or father," Colleen said.

"I doubt that," Arlene said with a laugh. "How's a corgi going to get to a dog with legs that long? Jump?"

All three women laughed at this, and Emily joined in with her *ha-ha-ha-ha* that meant she had no idea what was funny but was nonetheless happy that everyone else thought something was. "You women," Jared said. "Look what you're teaching my daughter."

CHAPTER 10

The thirtieth of May dawned cloudy, but cleared up just as Jared piled into the Hop-Frog and began what he had come to think of as the Dead Man's Drive out the Ford freeway to Michigan Avenue and then out along Whittaker Road to the fell lair of the Stuart in-laws. Despite a good-faith effort, Jared had failed to acquire one of his father's signal traits, the ability to avoid without conscience obligations that interfered with a man's God-given right to drink beer and tinker around the house on a Sunday afternoon, or any other time for that matter. This failure galled him today during the forty-five minutes it took to reach the elder Stuarts' sixty-year-old farmhouse and its twenty acres of artfully neglected fields and woods.

Colleen considered her husband's failure to get along with her mother a character flaw on his part, although she never shied away from the fact that Deirdre Stuart was a know-it-all snob. Her rationale, as near as he could peg it, was that if she could get along with Marty Cleaves, Jared had a duty to make nice with her mother. He had to admit this was persuasive. Considered objectively, Marty Cleaves was exasperating to a degree Deirdre Stuart could not approach because Marty Cleaves simply didn't give a shit what people thought, whereas Deirdre Stuart emphatically did. It was easier to excuse snobbery than self-absorption, in Jared's book; but he also knew that the first time Colleen's mom gave him a vocabulary lesson, his reaction would not be objective.

Look at it this way, he thought as they pulled into the driveway. At least Colleen isn't anything like her mom. This was Jared's standard self-admonition whenever he was about to interact with Deirdre Stuart. It was by no means an unambiguous consolation, though, because it always started him thinking on Marty Cleaves' long-maintained proposition that all women were doomed to become their mothers, and that the ones who were most unlike their mothers when young made up for it with a vengeance after they turned forty. On the topic of sons taking after their fathers, however, Marty Cleaves was atypically silent.

Jared got out of the Hop-Frog feeling somewhat less doomed than usual because they had Claude with them. Stroke of genius, getting a dog, he congratulated himself. One of two things will happen: either Deirdre will love him, and spend all kinds of time fawning over him that she might be using to get my goat, or she'll hate him and I can apologize right out the door and spend the day in the woods. My secret weapon. The last piece of my armor, buckled on before I enter the dragon's lair.

Theo came out onto the porch to meet them. Emily ran to him shouting, "Gampa Feo!" He scooped her up and set her on his hip, and Jared had a flash of himself at Theo's age, the weight of a grandchild balanced against his side. Like riding a bike, he thought. Must be you never forget it. Theo Stuart was the picture of the southern Michigan country gentry, trim and fit in his khaki pants and short-sleeved madras shirt, his steel-colored hair showing no signs of receding. He wasn't a rich man, but he was comfortable. As Jared's father said, *Theo Stuart doesn't work on his own car.* Jared might have added that when Theo poured his morning coffee, he looked out the window at his land from a house he owned free and clear. He went into the print shop he owned whenever he felt like it, and spent the day building ships in a bottle when he felt like it.

Face it, Jared told himself. You don't like coming out here because you want this to be your future instead of the Cleaves' bungalow in southwest Detroit. It shamed him, but it was true. Jared wanted everything the Stuarts had except their reactionary politics and patronizing attitude toward guys like him. He wanted the butcher-block table in the kitchen, the rocking chairs on the wrap around porch, the deer and pheasant and foxes in the fields behind the barn. He wanted the ease of waking up in the morning with nothing to prove.

Emily wriggled out of Theo's arms to greet Gamma Deeda, who was coming out with a tray of lemonade. Striking woman, Deirdre Stuart; looks were the one thing she had in common with her daughter, the same dark hair, the same air of confidence in the carriage of the shoulders and the way they looked you in the eye. "Emily Eloise," she said. "Just look at you."

"Look at me, Gamma Deeda!" Emily agreed.

"You must be stiff from the drive," Deirdre said. "Let's relax over some lemonade. Theo squeezed it this morning."

Fresh lemons? This might be worth a vocabulary lesson, Jared thought. Swerdlow would have a stroke if he thought a goldbrick like me was drinking fresh lemonade. He was chuckling to himself as Colleen went up on the porch to take the tray from her mother. Claude bounded out of the car and scouted around the front yard, disappearing into the hydrangeas to the left of the porch stairs.

"New addition," Theo commented. He and Jared shook hands and they tracked Claude's progress through the shrubbery.

"Emily was dying for a dog," Jared said. "I like 'em, too. Every kid should have a dog."

"Tell her that," Theo said with a wink and a nearly imperceptible nod toward his wife.

Uh-oh, Jared thought. "She doesn't like dogs?"

"She likes them all right, as long as they don't come into the house."

Touchdown, Jared thought.

Theo saw the thought cross Jared's mind. He cracked a smile and glanced at his watch. "Tigers are on at one, I think. Double-header today, right?"

"You believe they're only a game out?" Jared said. "My old man lies awake trying to figure it out."

"How is Marty?" Theo asked. Claude wormed his way out from under a bush and climbed the stairs to the porch.

"He's Marty Cleaves," Jared said as they all settled on the porch. "Never happy unless he's miserable."

"Oh my goodness," Deirdre said. "What is this?"

She was looking at Claude as if he were an expressive dangling modifier, or a sentence fragment that she found alluring despite all of her better instincts. Claude looked up at her, bright-eyed and panting. "Cod!" Emily exclaimed.

"Isn't he cute?" Deirdre said. Jared boggled. "Emily Eloise," Deirdre went on. "Is this your doggy?"

"Cod my doggy!" Emily said. She grabbed him around the neck, and Claude slathered her face with affection. Jared couldn't figure out how he should feel about this; was it good because he'd done something Deirdre could approve of, or bad because she might let Claude in the house and therefore eliminate his escape route to the barn and Harry Hellmann's call of the Fenway doubleheader?

"Cod?" Deirdre repeated with a sidelong glance at her daughter.

"His name is Claude," Colleen explained. "Jared brought him home yesterday," she added with an edge that, if Jared was any judge, wasn't quite as sharp as she'd meant it to be. Ha, he thought. I win. Who can withstand the charm of Claude?

Deirdre toggled into hustling-hostess mode. "Well," she said. "He'll need a bowl of water. Theo." Theo winked at Jared again and went into the house. Deirdre was considering something. When she spoke, it was to address Claude directly. "Even pert little yellow dogs such as yourself do not enter my house, Mr. Claude. Is that clear?"

Claude wagged his tail and licked Emily some more. Jared started to wonder if by whimsically adopting Claude he hadn't fulfilled some expectation on Deirdre's part. He could imagine her categorizing him as just the sort of person who would get a dog without consulting his wife, who would know better. It was true as far as it went; he was that kind of person. But he could see that Colleen liked Claude, and Emily was crazy for him, so there was Jared's vindication, whatever Deirdre Stuart thought.

Theo came back out with a serving bowl half filled with water. "There you go, fella," he said, setting it down where Claude would notice it. Claude immediately started drinking. "Look at him go," Theo said. "Good-looking little guy, isn't he, Dee?"

An ally, Jared thought. Everybody likes Claude.

"Of course he is, Theo," Deirdre said. "He's a puppy. Have you ever seen an unattractive puppy?"

She had a point there. Jared hastened to keep the conversation moving in the right direction. "He's already housebroken," he said, lying through his teeth—although fact was, in the past thirty hours Claude had only messed in the house once, and he did seem to have a dim intuition that he was supposed to do his business outside. Jared attributed this to innate intelligence, although Claude's previous owner might well have begun the housebreaking process.

"I doubt that," Deirdre said.

"Pretty much, he is," Jared said.

" 'Pretty much,' " Deirdre echoed. "Is there an ugly much? Such an odd expression. The colloquial use of language is a great mystery."

"This look like a classroom, Dee?" Theo said. "It's just something people say." He scratched Claude's ears, then looked up at

Jared. "What the hell kind of collar is this? Did you mean to get a bulldog?"

"His name's Claude," Jared said. "I figured he needed a leg up."

"Claude's a perfectly good name," Deirdre said. "It means 'lame,' you know. From the Latin."

"You don't say," Jared said, nodding and at the same time mobilizing his inner reserves against Deirdre's congenital need to be tendentious. No, sir, he thought. Today I refuse to be baited. "I thought it was French," he said with an ostentatious show of cheery inquisitiveness. "Like *Detroit* means 'the narrows.' "

"Certainly it's from the Latin. And De*troit*"—she gave it an extravagant French pronunciation—"is more properly 'straits.' "

"Okay," Jared said, giving not a shit in the world. "Straits." Now that's out of the way, he thought. She's happy because she's gotten to correct me; I'm happy because Claude got into her house. On balance, I win. He was riding a wave of good feeling from Claude's reception that even a Deirdre Stuart classroom moment could not ruin. Like sunlight, he felt the pressure of Colleen looking at him; he cut his eyes in her direction and didn't quite suppress a grin.

They sipped lemonade and watched Claude and Emily run up and down the porch. Jared watched Deirdre for clues about how things would proceed, and saw her finish her glass and set it down as if she'd gotten a cue. "Well," she said. "I've got a cold ham inside, and some deviled eggs. How about some sandwiches, and then we'll take our two- and four-legged youngsters for a little walk in the fields?"

Deviled eggs were one of Jared's favorite nonsexual pleasures, along with cigarettes and Emily and a clean line drive into the right-centerfield gap. "That sounds fine," he said, and picked up the lemonade tray to collect the glasses. "I'm about hungry enough to eat the shell off an egg."

"Let us all hope it doesn't come to that," Deirdre said with a magnificently tolerant smile, and they all went inside. Theo held the door, and Jared noted with unadulterated glee that he stood aside for Claude to enter after all of the humans had gone ahead.

Jared had figured that everything was going better than it had any right to, and when he got into the kitchen he discovered he'd been right. There, stuck to the door of one of the new Frigidaires that had an electric freezer, was the cover of yesterday's *Saturday Evening Post*. EDGAR SNOW REPORTS ON GERMAN ATROCITIES was the top article teaser, but that wasn't the point; the cover illustration, immediately recognizable as a Rockwell, showed a muscular red-headed woman, sleeves rolled up over powerful forearms and goggles pushed back on her head, munching on a sandwich with a rivet gun in her lap and one booted foot casually grinding a copy of *Mein Kampf* into the floor.

That's my wife, Jared thought—and almost immediately added, *Not me.*

Deirdre was already taking the cover and showing it around. "Our daughter," she said. "A regular Rosie the Riveter."

"I strip engines, Mother," Colleen said, and Jared loved her for her willingness to split hairs in front of her mother when his honor was at stake. "I've never held a rivet gun in my life."

"Don't denigrate yourself, darling," Deirdre said. She looked at Jared and held his eyes while she said, "You don't know how proud you make your father and me."

A thick silence filled the kitchen.

"Of course everyone does his or her part," Deirdre said, and opened the Frigidaire to retrieve the ham.

Over the sandwiches and deviled eggs, which Jared now begrudged their deliciousness, conversation inevitably turned to wartime industry. Theo, who had been easing himself out of the print shop by 1941, found himself drawn back into the business by the flood of contracts from the defense industry. "We're doing training manuals, schematics, the whole shebang," Theo said. "License to print money, is what it is. And the best thing is, I already had men trained to take over for me, so all I do is show up a couple of times a week to make sure we're getting jobs out on time." He shook his head as if unable to believe his good fortune. "I've even done some classified work, but I don't want to take too much on; you wouldn't believe the red tape."

Sure I would, Jared thought.

"Do you know, I heard the most extraordinary thing," Deirdre said. She dabbed a bread crumb from the corner of her mouth before continuing. "Henry Ford, of all people, has secret projects at River Rouge."

Again Jared felt Colleen's gaze like midsummer heat on his face. "Is that so," he said.

"It certainly is. You know I'm treasurer of the Saint Paul's Soldiers and Sailors Aid group." Jared did. "Well, the other day an army officer spoke to us, and I'm revealing this in strictest confidence—" She paused to make eye contact with everyone, imparting the seriousness with which she regarded the secrecy of what she was about to reveal. "—and said that there is an entire sector of the River Rouge factory devoted to the rebuilding of soldiers from the parts of dead men."

"They've got the scientists working overtime on that one," Theo said.

"The parts of dead men," Deirdre said again. "It's like that Frankenstein movie. I would scarcely be able to believe it had I not heard it from this man, who knows whereof he speaks, I can assure you."

Jared was mortally certain that if he looked at his wife, she would be boring holes in him with her eyes. You bet I said something I shouldn't have after the golem clocked me, he thought. She knows. He nearly killed himself holding back a comment about Frankenstein

Meets the Wolf Man; oh, the Herschel Fontenot–inspired embellishments he could have added about Nazi werewolves swarming out of the Carpathians. In his head he spun out a conversation with Herschel, who would likely keel over dead of laughter if he knew the kind of deluded moonshine people spread because they had no idea what really went on inside Building G. At the same time, it was killing him that he couldn't set Deirdre and Theo straight. *This is what I do,* he wanted to tell them. *Colleen is on the cover of The Saturday Evening Post,* but in our invisible little corner of the Rouge we're winning the war.

When the golems make it to the train siding, that is.

"Isn't that something," he said, and felt the heat on his cheek abate. *You know, don't you, Colleen?* he thought. *You know, and you haven't even told me.* That was strength Jared didn't know if he had. He was filled with admiration for his wife.

"Krauts are going to piss themselves when they see that," Theo said. "I was in France in '18, but I sure as hell wouldn't have fought Frankenstein."

"You don't sign up for that," Jared agreed.

"Can you imagine," Deirdre said. She was positively aflame with the idea, leaning forward in her Adirondack chair, eyes sparkling and one hand unconsciously holding the remains of her sandwich on her lap. "Can you imagine the knowledge, the skill, the . . ." She waved a hand in a rolling motion, conjuring both the word she was looking for and the supreme difficulty of locating that exact word. "The *puissance* involved in discovering something of this nature? It is a victory over death, loaned—not given, loaned—in the service of war." Deirdre fell back, catching her sandwich as it slid off her right thigh. "War is a horrific thing, but perhaps some good can come of it."

Jared thought of Moises, destroying himself every day on the Frankenline, and he doubted her.

"Well, the tide's turned in the Pacific, that's for sure," Theo said. "We can thank our Colleen for that. Keep those bombers in the air, my girl. That plant finally running like Ford said it would?"

Tell them about the cattle cars, Jared thought. He willed her to say something other than what he knew she would say, but when she simply shrugged and said, "We're all doing our part, Daddy," he didn't blame her. How could he? It was true. Still, it ate at him knowing that her part was celebrated on the cover of *The Saturday Evening Post* while everyone except the other guys on the Franken-line, and Swerdlow and the OEI, thought he spent his days doing work fit for a trained monkey.

All the air had bled out of the day. Claude was snoozing, his paws hanging over the top step. I need to get out of here, Jared thought.

Theo saved him. "Jared," he said. "Let's let the girls visit. I need a hand moving some old lumber out in the barn. Claude can come along if you can wake him up."

Out in the barn, Theo fired up a radio and leaned against the rear wheel of a tractor that probably hadn't been started since he'd bought the place. Harry Heilmann was catching up on the news from other games; Bill Nicholson of the Cubs had hit two home runs, the first round-trippers the team had managed all season. "You ever hear of that?" Theo said, shaking his head. "A team goes to the end of May without a home run? This wartime baseball is three-card monte, I'll tell you what."

"Bill Nicholson," Jared said. He didn't follow the National League, but the Cubs were only two and a half seasons removed from a World Series loss. It was a long fall from that to six weeks without a home run. "My old man says hockey's in better shape."

"That's because hockey's a sport for liquored-up Frog lumber-jacks," Theo said. "You can't get into the army, even in Canada, if you're a dipsomaniac missing a bunch of teeth."

I'd like to see you say that to Mud Bruneteau, Jared thought. He called Claude, who was rooting around in one of the empty horse stalls and felt no need to answer his master's voice. Jared went into the stall and found the puppy digging through a pile of rotted straw. Smells of horseshit, dusty wood, bat guano: the barn's olfactory gumbo. *Don't take any wooden nickels,* a long-dead rumrunner said in Jared's mind. On the radio, the second game of the doubleheader was just getting under way; the Tigers had won the first behind Trucks, but were resorting to Stubby Overmire to pitch the second. Harry Heilmann was talking about John McHale, who had made his major-league debut in Friday's loss to the Yankees.

"Theo," he said from the stall. "Your shop ever do any work for the OEI?"

"The who?" Theo said. "I deal with so many goddamn acronyms in the government, not even Deirdre could keep them straight."

Claude perked up at something in Theo's tone. Taking advantage of the break in his infatuation with the straw, Jared shooed the puppy back toward the front of the barn. "OEI," Jared repeated. "They're some kind of secret outfit. I heard they're doing something strange out to Willow Run."

"Only thing strange about Willow Run is that it's finally making airplanes. You're too young to remember this, but Ford made himself a reputation in 1918 as a man who couldn't build boats because they weren't cars. Same thing almost happened at Willow Run; you can thank Charlie Sorensen that Colleen still has a job."

Jared replayed that last bit, combing it for insinuations that the Cleaveses would be destitute without Colleen's job. His sensitivity to slights of every sort increased the closer he got to the Stuart household, and it was damn near unbearable now. "I hear Sorensen's on his way out," he said.

"That so?" Theo looked at Jared as if trying to figure out whether this tidbit was reliable.

"That's the word around the plant. The Old Man didn't like how much credit Sorensen got for Willow Run."

Now Theo looked calculating, like he was incorporating this possibility into a decision about his stock portfolio. "Hm," he said after a while. The Tigers submitted meekly to Lou Lucier, and the Red Sox came to bat against Overmire, a rookie with all of five starts this year whose most recent result had been a loss to these same illustrious Sox last Sunday. Harry Heilmann congratulated the army for taking complete control of Attu after repelling yesterday's desperate Japanese assault on Chichagof Harbor. Jared wondered how it had taken so long for the army to kick the Japs off a piece of American territory (and why the Japs had wanted it anyway); he wondered if any golems had been involved from those first late-1940 batches of Washtenaw County clay; he had a bad feeling about the Tigers' prospects; he questioned what strange alignment of stars had resulted in him getting a dog into Fortress Stuart and *still* coming out on the short end of the interaction with Deirdre. That old Deirdre Stuart black magic, he thought.

"Anyway," Theo said. "I don't remember any jobs coming through for the OEI. What's it stand for?"

Jared shrugged. "Not sure."

Theo squatted to rag Claude around a little, letting the puppy gnaw on his knuckles. Soon as he got good and wired, Claude took off running around the barn, kicking up swirls of dust that caught the light coming in through the hayloft window. A flutter of wings came from the rafters, putting Jared in mind of the unseen observers in the Rouge's ceiling beams . . . and before that, the rustle from a barn on Munger Road, not so far from here, back in the 1919 he remembered as the foundational dream of his life. Colleen said there were birds in Willow Run, too, roosting in the girders over the course of the plant's namesake creek—now directed at ridiculous expense through a subfloor culvert built to mimic its original course. Birds, Jared thought, brushing his hands across the bundle in his pants pocket.

* * *

Emily slept all the way home, then ran around in the yard with Claude while Jared washed the dust of Washtenaw County off the Hop-Frog. Colleen came out to observe his chamois technique. "My mother's a little hard to take sometimes," she said.

Jared was dumbfounded, and immediately chagrined that her understanding was so unexpected. She hadn't apologized for her mother in years, but why should she? He didn't apologize for Marty Cleaves. Marty Cleaves was a phenomenon of nature.

"Nah," Jared said. "I'm used to her. Plus I think she was disarmed by Claude."

"Even though she made the crack about his name?"

"That right there is my clue," he said, wringing out the chamois with a flourish.

After a pause, she said, "You're not very much like your father, you know that?"

He stopped in the middle of working the chamois over the Hop-Frog's hood. He wanted to look at her, but didn't trust himself not to cry. "How's that?" he asked, keeping his voice absolutely level.

"Marty Cleaves only worries about other people when their feelings reflect badly on him," Colleen said. "Jared Cleaves always worries about how what he does affects everyone else."

"Interesting," he said. "What's your take on Deirdre Stuart?"

"Do you know, she was a crossword-puzzle champion?" Colleen said, her inflection eerily like her mother's. This always happened after they'd been out to Fortress Stuart, and it always gave Jared the heebiest of jeebies; fortunately removal from Whittaker Road and its environs gradually returned Colleen's voice to normal. "Put that together with marriage to Theo Stuart, and you become a snob out of self-defense."

"Crossword puzzles?"

"She quit last year when *The New York Times* started running one," Colleen said. Claude ran past, tongue flapping and Emily in hot pursuit. "If the stodgy old *New York Times* was going to run a crossword, she said, the whole thing wouldn't be fun anymore. But she started doing them back in the '20s when it was a fad. She won contests. I think she still has the first book of them she got when I was a little girl."

Mrs. Pelletier came around the wall of hedges and shrubbery that hid her yard from the street. "Is that a puppy?" she asked.

Emily peeled away from chasing Claude and charged over to Mrs. Pelletier. "Cod my doggy!" she shouted, pointing at where Claude had been when she left off the chase.

"Jared Cleaves," Mrs. Pelletier said. "You did not name that handsome little fellow after a fish."

"Claude," Jared said. "You have to sort of assume the *L*'s when Emily talks."

"Oh, don't I know it," agreed Mrs. Pelletier.

The dog in question had his paws up on the chain-link gate that led to the backyard. Jared went over and let him through so he could tear up the flower beds that neither he nor Colleen had put much work into this year. Emily ran to watch through the gate, coming back with chain-link lines all over her face. "You look like a waffle, baby girl," Jared said.

"Waffoo!" Emily said.

The next two days were good. Amiable breakfasts, fun with Emily, no disasters at work. Tuesday the news spread that Henry Ford himself, eighty years old and so far gone in some unspecified dementia that he never appeared in public without someone physically supporting him, was the once and future president of the Ford Motor Company, which everyone knew meant that Harry Bennett's long-aborning coup was at last complete. "Look out now," Felton said on the line that night. "See if Bennett don't start selling golems out the back door to the Black Hand."

"Would that work?" Jem asked. "They're Italian. Only Jewish mob around here was the Purple Gang, is what I heard, and they're all dead."

"He'll sell 'em to Rothstein, then, or Atlantic City. You wait. Pretty soon every casino bouncer in the country'll have EMET scribbled on his forehead."

Bennett's underworld ties formed the basis of the night's conversation. It was all bullshit, was Jared's opinion. At least probably. Even Harry Bennett, whose balls clanked when he walked down the street, wouldn't go up against the OEI. That's what he had all the suits in the Rotunda for. And the Old Man, with two strokes ravaging his brain and his only legitimate son dead, wasn't a strong enough figurehead for Bennett to hide behind if the Office of War Mobilization came gunning for him.

Rattle rattle rattle of Ferenc hooking gurneys up to the track, again and again. Jared reached the end of his shift with no memory of the previous nine hours. He skipped his appointment at Swerdlow's office. Let that son of a bitch stew a little. He went home, had himself a leisurely smoke in the backyard listening to the trains clacking down the Michigan Central tracks, and crawled into bed. Colleen was dreaming. She murmured deep in her throat, and Jared stroked her hair to settle her. "Mm," she said, and snuggled back into him. The next thing he knew, he had a raging hard-on. Got to shoot to score, he thought, and pressed into her. He thought his heart would explode in his chest when she pressed back.

CHAPTER 11

He wakes up on top of the world, a new man. Nothing, absolutely nothing, like getting your ashes hauled to change your outlook. Even pouring rationed coffee that's mostly chicory seems fine. Even the news that something like half a million coal miners are on strike in Appalachia, which threatens steel production at among other places the Rouge, can't put a dent in Jared Cleaves' invincible sense of well-being. Even the fact that the Tigers lost a doubleheader to the sad-sack Red Sox on Sunday and then split with the Athletics Monday doesn't get to Jared because they won on Tuesday and are now seventeen up, sixteen down, only two games out—and who can expect better than that with Greenberg and every other able-bodied man in the service? There's an omen in there somewhere, if Jared cares to tease it out. "See what happens when you come home from work?" Colleen says, winking as she reaches around him to get a spatula from the big vase next to the stove.

"Honey, you have clarified my thinking." Jared gives her a grin. The coffee burns the hell out of his mouth, but he doesn't care. After two years, over the last three days he suddenly feels like he's married again. Emily grins through a mask of dried egg yolk, and

Claude comes out from under the table to nip at Jared's shorts. Rockwell could paint this moment, if he was in the habit of painting adult men in their underwear.

Strength restored, Jared steels himself to go see the Piston Doctor, mostly because in the flush of his postcoital optimism he's convinced himself that he'll learn something that he can use against Swerdlow—or maybe just keep Swerdlow from using against him. This will also give him an excuse for not keeping his appointment with Meadows, who will likely be in a bad humor about it. There's a moment of panic when Jared can't find the slip of paper Ellery gave him; then it turns up in the little clay bowl where he keeps his spare change, underneath some old books of matches and the receipt from Colleen having something dry-cleaned. What she's dry-cleaning, he doesn't know, but he takes the Piston Doctor's address along when he drops Emily off at Mrs. Pelletier's, not going to his parents' because he doesn't want his father asking questions. Then he's on the Fort Street streetcar, riding all the way into Cadillac Square and then walking through the hot morning, wishing he'd taken the car but knowing that given current circumstances it's better for his car not to be seen in the vicinity of a Negro shaman. On the way he reads the paper. The invasion of Sicily is supposed to happen any minute; Mexicans are rioting in Los Angeles; Iffy the Dopester is inflamed by the prospect of mediocrity. Jared tosses the paper in a trash can and walks down East Lafayette to Brush, and then just around the corner is the number.

The Piston Doctor is maybe sixty years old, with a belly like a wrecking ball straining the front of his bib overalls. He wears no shirt, and moves with the imposing grace of a man who carries prodigious muscle under his fat. His hair stands nappy and uncombed out from his head, putting Jared in mind of Buckwheat, only a much older Buckwheat gone to seed and conversant with the principles of Caribbean black magic. Or so Jared imagines. The Piston Doctor's English is thick with some island accent, and his ears are pierced with piston rings that glint in the lamplight when he turns his head to point out where he wants Jared to sit. His front four teeth are missing, both top and bottom; the others are bright yellow, matching the sclera of his eyes. A real live witch doctor, three blocks off Woodward Avenue. For some reason Jared is put in mind of the guy arrested maybe ten years ago for the murder of Benny Evangelist. That guy was some kind of witch doctor, too, or so the papers had said at the time.

"Ellery said you need to see me," the Piston Doctor says before Jared can get his mouth working.

"Yeah. Um, he said you might know something about . . ." Jared is already pulling the bird-bone charm out of his pocket. The Piston Doctor puts his finger to his lips and won't look at Jared until he's pulled all of the drapes closed. White chintz. A radio somewhere is tuned to WWJ, and the air is heavy with the spicy odor of something cooking in the kitchen. All in all, a pretty ordinary place, until you start to notice the little figurines made out of car parts that clutter every horizontal surface. There's a squadron of lug-nut warriors on the mantel, waving dipstick spears and shields made from what look like magnetos. On the coffee table crouches some kind of turtle monster made of sprockets and an oil pan, with a spark plug for a head.

"Can you make these things move?" Jared asks.

"You come here for a show or to see why your car won't start?"

"All right, then," Jared says, and with a grin the Piston Doctor waves a hand. The turtle monster gets up, a tiny blue electrical arc flaring from its nose, and walks to the other end of the coffee table, making room for Jared to set down the bundle of bones. Then pieces start to fall off it, and the oil pan clanks to the tabletop and lies inert. A sprocket wobbles on the edge of the table, then tumbles to the floor. The Piston Doctor's face is set in lines of sorrow.

"All of it goes away," he says softly.

The remains of the turtle critter put Jared in mind of the aftermath of a tank battle. He wants to tell the Piston Doctor about the golems, but doesn't dare. "Maybe," he says.

The Piston Doctor unwraps the bundle and pokes at the bones with a finger that's missing its first joint. "Turtle bite that off?" Jared jokes.

The look he gets in return is as serious as stomach cancer. "You don't want to know."

Jared shuts up while the Piston Doctor sorts the bones out. He picks up the tiny skull and pricks his thumb with the beak. A bead of blood rises, and he dabs it on the cloth wrapping.

"An Indian made this."

"An Indian? Why's an Indian not want my car to start?"

"What Indians do you know?"

"None. Well, old Plenty Coup, but his house burned down a couple of weeks ago and he's not around anymore."

"Hm." The Piston Doctor leans back and sticks his hands under the bib of his overalls, resting them on the mass of his belly. "Those are the bones of one bird. A blackbird. You have blackbirds around your house?"

"I guess so. Who doesn't?" Jared is thinking of Mrs. Pelletier's bird feeders. Every bird in Michigan probably passes through her yard twice a week. They've ignored his own feeder so far this year, though, which is why he moved it a couple of weeks ago.

"Look," the Piston Doctor says. "Nobody don't care about whether your car starts or not. Point of this here was so you'd look for it. Now you looked for it. What you supposed to do now?"

"You're the witch doctor."

"I am the Piston Doctor. This is not my area. I tell you, though, somebody put this in your car so you'd find them. It is a signal."

"So I should look for an Indian." Jared thinks this over. "I think

Plenty Coup's house had already burned down when the car started giving me trouble."

"Maybe it isn't him," the Piston Doctor says with a shrug. "There's plenty of Indians in Detroit. Go talk to the window washers, the guys who paint the bridge." He takes his hands off his belly and stands, clearly done with Jared. "You find the guy, stop by and tell me what happened. Feel like I should keep up on what the competition is doing, you know?"

Pretty good day, all in all. Even coming home and stepping in dog shit by the front door doesn't put much of a dent in Jared's good humor. The Frankenline was typically mind-numbing, but that wasn't anything new. Jared steps back outside to find a stick, and then sits on the front stoop scraping the sole of his shoe. He wipes the stick on the underside of the evergreen bush growing to the left of the door, and as he's looking that way his gaze falls on the burned-out remains of Plenty Coup's house. Hm, he thinks.

Next thing he knows, he's standing on the sidewalk in front of the fallen-in house. The firemen hadn't stuck around once it was clear that there was no body in the house, and the cops lost interest after a cursory canvass of the neighborhood. A couple of times Jared spotted people combing the ruin for whatever might be salvaged. At some point, probably after the war, the lot would be bulldozed, and if Plenty Coup had family they might sell it to a GI home from the Pacific. Or who knows, maybe the old Indian would show up as mysteriously as he had gone. Jared can't figure out why he's having this urge to poke around the wreckage, but having it he definitely is. He walks up to the concrete stoop, where snaking patterns of soot tell the story of fire and water. Part of the front wall is still standing, and most of the wall to his left. The roof has completely fallen in, and the big spruce tree between the house and the little store on the corner is half burned. Jared wonders if it will live, or if a city forester will come and take it down.

The back of his neck prickles as a chill breeze seems to blow out of the house. It's a nice cool night, but there's something spooky about the draft coming from the jumble of charred timbers and the tar slurry of melted shingles. Piston Doctor's got me jumping at shadows, Jared thinks, but he changes his mind about looking around. Too dark to find anything anyway. As he walks back home, he looks over his shoulder, and when he comes in the front door he steps in Claude's little memento again.

He's in a steel cage with bodies pressed so tightly it's a struggle to draw breath, and when he does inhale the stink of shit chokes him. Days-old urine burns his eyes. Dreaming, Jared thinks *train car* and tries to tell himself that in the dream, but it's not getting through; in the dream is only fear and heat and flesh next to flesh next to flesh as if they have all become one mass of muscle and bone, rolling eyes and minds so far gone in terror that if there were room they would destroy each other in panic.

The sensation falls away and he is alone. Still caged, but without fear. Expectant. Clanging echo of steel on steel, the scream of friction, voices of men and beasts. He spirals back into the mass, feels it surge into space, divide once again into individuals each of whose noses register one thing and one thing only.

Fire.

It is dark, and they surge back toward their confinement. Their flesh finds only steel, he is eater and prey, the exhalation of fire and the air drawn in to feed it. Alchemy of transformation, flesh into food into flesh, and the hunger abates.

The fire overwhelms them. He grows stronger.

* * *

Jared, honey, you're dreaming.

There was just about nothing in the world Jared hated more than going to the movies by himself, but after a night of poorly remembered but unpleasant dreams he had woken up bearing a grudge against whatever inscrutable fate had put him in the position of having strange Indian magic perpetrated on his car—not to mention all of the various Swerdlow-related fuckery that was taking a belt sander to his sense of well-being. He'd been such a miserable son of a bitch all morning, and he was so mistrustful of his own ability to make it to work if he didn't find some way to remove himself from all human society, that he foisted Emily off on Mrs. Pelletier and headed for the Lafayette Theater. The alternative was downing boilermakers at ten in the morning, and he clung to enough self-respect to avoid that. So far. Something had shifted in the night, eroding the good feeling that had carried him since Sunday the way the rush of waves on a beach sent the sand streaming away around your feet, tickling a little in farewell, leaving two tenuous links to the earth where the weight of your body pressed down. It was a wonder what the Piston Doctor and dimly remembered dreams of fire could do to a good mood.

The Lafayette was still showing *Frankenstein Meets the Wolf Man*, which had been out for at least three weeks. Could have been worse, Jared thought. Could have been nothing but war movies. If he had to see another war movie, especially one with Robert Taylor, he was going to snap. He bought popcorn and Vernor's Ginger Ale, feeling diffusely resentful of the red carpet and painted woodwork along the balcony. Movie theaters. If ever there were places to be avoided when you were on your own, here was one. What was the point of all this show, this fakey opulence, this faded architectural showbiz dream, if you couldn't share it with someone?

Goddamn Piston Doctor, he thought. Goddamn Swerdlow. Goddamn Dash. Goddamn puppy. Claude was like one of Herschel Fontenot's kids, only around all the time and a quadruped; you knew you should send him away but he was so damn charming you liked having him around and from this liking contrived to ignore the fact that you knew he would cheat and betray you. Already the house bore numerous unmistakable signs of Claude's presence even apart from the smear on the rug that remained after Jared scrubbed the shit off. At this moment Jared was wearing a pair of boots with part of one sole chewed away. That little prick-eared bastard had suckered them all, watching so placidly from his cage and then curling up by the chair like he'd lived there all his life. Truth was that Claude was a prankster. To Emily he could do no wrong, but he savaged without compunction the possessions of the adult Cleaveses, and when you went looking for him with murder in your heart he was invariably sprawled on the rug innocently gnawing one of the eight zillion rawhide chews and old knotted rags they'd spread around the house. Crafty little critter. Jared admired him.

Mrs. Pelletier adored Claude, of course, and took him into her house with extravagant promises of food and affection. It figured. She gushed over what a darling little puppy Claude was, so well behaved for such a young dog. Might come in handy if Colleen followed through on her threats to exile him if she wasn't going to be allowed to kill him herself.

Noon on a Thursday, there were about twenty people in the theater. Jared settled himself in the first row of the balcony and rested his feet directly on the brass plaque reading PLEASE DO NOT PUT YOUR FEET ON THE RAILING. He was vaguely hoping that some bored punk would make a remark about him sitting in nigger heaven, just so he could have the satisfaction of scraping his knuckles up on someone's head. But no such luck; there were at least two other white people in the balcony, along with four or five colored. Ordinarily—although Jared didn't consider himself any apostle of racial harmony—he would have derived an inarticulate sense of that's-niceness from this show of integration. Today it just made him want to hit someone because it was one factor depriving him of the opportunity to hit someone. It was that kind of day.

On the topic of racial integration Marty Cleaves had issued a pithy verdict back in February, when the Sojourner Truth conflict was at a boil. Detroit was a nice town before the hillbillies and southern coloreds showed up, he said. The hillbillies show up thinking they've brought Tennessee with them, and the coloreds come up here and think they're white because the Underground Railroad came through here eighty years ago. Between the two of 'em, someone's going to burn this town to the ground.

Jared was thinking about this as he walked back out into daylight, and the movie stayed on his mind while he was at work that night, or rather he thought about the newsreel. Pantelleria, then Sicily. Would he be in Tunisia waiting for the word to move out if he hadn't seen the Dwarf? Or would he be scraping jungle rot from between his toes while waiting to see which malarial Pacific speck was next on MacArthur's agenda?

Could be you'd be fish food, he told himself.

He was annoyed that the newsreel hadn't mentioned the golems, not that they ever did. What the hell had they made six thousand golems for, if nobody was going to show them? They couldn't all be on secret missions; Europe would be neck-deep in golem commandos, and some journalist with more nose for story than sense of wartime security would have written about it. As it was, they'd only seen actual footage of the Aleutians and last year's roundup of Nazi spies in Florida, and even those reels hadn't made clear that there were golems involved. People didn't know just to look at them, especially on film. They had to be told. Fuck secret projects, Jared fulminated silently. Doesn't a guy like me deserve some recognition? Maybe all the golems were just standing around in England waiting for the invasion of Europe that was supposed to happen in the next year, or maybe in the fall if Italy folded up quicker than expected and Hitler had to give the Russians some breathing room. Not that the Reds were giving him any choice, especially since the frost giants had proved every bit as reliable as Stubby Overmire's fastball; the worst fate Jared could imagine for himself wasn't as bad as getting his ass shot off in minus-forty Stalingrad.

Break clay, hose out train cars, smoke break, ignore Swerdlow, tell Jem to shut up. Repeat until whistle. Clean tools, change clothes, go home. Jared fell into bed thinking about golems and werewolves, and reproaching himself for not doing more to follow up on what the Piston Doctor told him. None of it felt real. He didn't feel real. He was broken somehow, unable to put his finger on what was wrong, unable to say something was wrong because then he'd have to explain what. He wondered where Plenty Coup had gotten to, and fell asleep angry and afraid.

In a dream Jared is counting the scars on the back of his right hand. One long line over the knuckle at the base of his pinkie, and another paralleling it above the ring knuckle; both stop in about the same place, halfway up the back of his hand, and both date from the day after he saw the Dwarf, when a surgeon straightened out the bones and tried to repair the nerve damage. There are others, from fights or slips when he was helping his father rebuild the shed behind their old house, one pretty good gouge from getting spiked by a kid named Mickey Hussein when he was playing second base in a sandlot game over off Seven Mile Road, although what he was doing up there in Chaldean Town he can't now remember. That one, Mickey, was the only kid in the game with spikes, and his toe spike had come right through the heel of Jared's glove as Jared went to tag him. There's a little curlicue at the base of his palm to this day. This night.

He looks up from the counting and sees the Dwarf watching him. Smoke comes from his eyes and he pulls on his scrotum with one hand, elongating the flesh like taffy. *Why'd you do this?* Jared wants to know. The Dwarf starts to sing a song: *Do your balls hang low, do they wobble to and fro, can you tie 'em in a knot, can you tie 'em in a bow . . .*

Another voice enters the dream: the Piston Doctor saying, *Boy, you got problems.*

I thought it was ears, Jared says.

The Dwarf laughs and ties his earlobes and scrotum into one big knot, then does a series of back handsprings until he's out of sight. The Piston Doctor is still there, and now he has Petey the raven on his shoulder. *Some dream,* Petey says. *You do this much?*

What, dream?

Dream like this.

Jared has to admit that he doesn't, not much. Petey thinks this over. *You might yet,* he says.

This makes the Piston Doctor laugh. *You should have seen his mother,* the Piston Doctor wheezes. *And you think this boy can dream?*

Sure I can dream, Jared says. *That's what I'm doing.*

He's a little chafed by the Piston Doctor, coming into his dream and lipping off. Jared isn't a prophetic dreamer, no real clairvoyance or anything; he doesn't know for example that two days ago the first Allied caravan since 1941 crossed the Mediterranean, because that won't be in the paper until tomorrow—and he doesn't know that something is gathering on the Brockenberg, and he doesn't know that tomorrow the Tigers will go down in flames to the Athletics, although this last he suspects.

What he knows is that he's about had it with people coming into his dreams just to insult him. *Go to hell, Piston Doctor,* he says

Tough guy when you're sleeping, aren't you, the Piston Doctor says.
Been to Plenty Coup's house lately?
What?
The Dwarf laughs.
And hey, what about my mother?
The Piston Doctor tells him.

CeeCee Cleaves had been born Cecelia Ruth Magruder in 1892, somewhere near the Arkansas-Missouri border. Her father, Phelps Magruder, worked a small farm and lumbered in the winters; her mother, Arcadia Eloise Magruder—née Lounsberry—took in sewing when she wasn't working the farm or steering the house through the ravages of her four older boys. She also dabbled in a little Ozark magic, mostly telling local girls how to ascertain who their husbands would be. Cadie Magruder taught her daughter what she knew, but the girl proved comically unsuited to follow in her mother's footsteps.

Even when it came to the question of her own matrimonial destiny, CeeCee managed to embarrass herself so abjectly that she remained convinced all her life that her last attempt at magic was what convinced her father to send her north to Chicago. Following the time-honored formula bequeathed her by her mother, who passed in 1914, CeeCee went into the woods during a full moon, turned in nine complete circles while repeating her favorite Bible verse, *A bundle of myrrh is my well-beloved unto me; he shall lie all night between my breasts*—one of the salacious bits from the Song of Songs, but not too salacious, and anyway wasn't she looking for a husband?—and then picked up the first stone her foot encountered. Stuck to its underside was a long, curling reddish blond hair.

Michael Cleaves. He was the only boy in the county near her age who had that hair. She thought of it then, waving thick and shiny over his forehead and down over his collar. Her hands—and not just her hands—tingled at the imagined sensation of twirling it around her fingers. He was twenty years old, just as she was, lean and graceful as a panther but quick to laugh and lacking any malice toward man or beast.

Why didn't I do this years ago? she wondered. Nearly all of her friends, at least those who had any spark of sight, had gone to the woods before they were fifteen. CeeCee, wary of doing something wrong and ruining her only chance to know, had waited, and it was fear of becoming an old maid that had driven her out there that night. She went home actually dancing along the moonlit path, and fell into bed with a smile, and dreamed of Michael Cleaves.

The next day she was down at the dry-goods buying a needle when she heard that Michael Cleaves had drowned in Whistler Creek.

She tried everything. She boiled an egg, filled the scooped-out yolk cavity with salt, and ate the egg before going to bed. The man who brought her water in her dreams was dead Michael Cleaves, and she woke up trembling out of fear that the water in the gourd had come from his poor drowned lungs. She wrote the names of six tolerable boys on slips of paper, blushing as she wrestled over whether to include Martin Cleaves, Michael's older brother. In the end she did, and slipped all six scraps of paper under her pillow. When she awoke in the middle of the night, as she'd known she would, she removed one of the slips and drowsily let it fall to the plank floor. CeeCee fell asleep calmer than she'd been in days, knowing that Michael Cleaves could not plague her now—and then rose at dawn to find that she had unwittingly dropped two slips to the floor, those of Michael Bonebreak and Martin Cleaves.

After this calamity she believed herself truly haunted, and nearly swore off any kind of conjuration. But one last sign might be

available to her, and on April 30—this would have been in 1912—
she wet a handkerchief and hung it out in the cornfield between her
house and Whistler Creek. May Day morning found her flanked by
her mother and little brother Joel, waiting for the sun to rise high
enough that she could read the initials that would be apparent in the
wrinkles of the handkerchief. As she and her mother stood thunder-
struck, Joel, with the pride of a boy who has only recently mastered
his letters—and in a place not overly concerned with literacy—
said, "That there's an *M,* and right next to it a *C.* Who's MC,
CeeCee? Who is he?"

Clearly it was time for drastic action. Five hours later, against
her mother's fearful admonitions, CeeCee walked out to the well at
the side of the house, the mirror from her parents' bedroom under
one arm and her father's watch in her other hand. He was clearing
rocks from the back field, and only wore his watch to church and fu-
nerals anyway, on both occasions so he could count the minutes
until he was free again. At precisely noon she angled the mirror so
the sun's rays skimmed off its surface and fell straight down into the
well. She believed to the end of her days that the light fell slowly,
gliding over each mossy stone in the shaft of the well as CeeCee
Magruder, now that she was committed to this foolhardy course of
action, unwillingly cataloged every mishap that might befall the
maid so daring as to bring sunlight into contact with this water that
seeped up from the lightless underworld. She might see nothing but
bands of light fading into the depths, in which case she was destined
to die an old maid; she might see only her own face, pale and life-
less, signifying her death before May Day next. That had happened
to a girl her mother had known thirty years ago, over to Rolla, Mis-
souri. And worse: what if she saw poor dead Michael Cleaves?
Wasn't that just another sign that she would never marry—or were
the grannies right when they murmured through the gaps in their
teeth that scrying was the Devil's work? Was she to be bride to a
dead man?

What have you let yourself in for, girl? CeeCee thought, and the light fell onto the surface of the black water, and what she was thinking as the face of Michael Cleaves rose up to meet her gaze was *I had to know.*

There was no question of her staying on in Eureka Springs after that. CeeCee Magruder was marked, both by her misadventures in divination and by the stubborn specter of Michael Cleaves. A cousin had gone north in 1909, first to Chicago and then to work on the Detroit & Ironton Railroad. By the end of summer 1912 CeeCee found herself in Melvindale, Michigan, feeling the nights turn cold and longing for the familiar silence of Ozark dawns as her sleep fractured under the assault of automobile engines and train whistles and the brawls that erupted nightly in the gin mills along Dix Avenue near the railyard where her cousin Del turned wrenches. Del didn't look strong enough even to lift some of the tools he used, but that didn't stop him getting in fights, from which he always emerged marked up but swearing the other guy was headed for the hospital. One night when Del's wife was visiting her people over in Jackson or somewhere, he showed up on the front stoop slumped in the arms of a grinning younger man who woke CeeCee up out of a sound sleep by standing in front of the house shouting, "Which is the goddamn house of Delbert Magruder?"

CeeCee struggled into her robe and came out of the mildewy room at the back of the house where she slept. When she opened the front door, there was Del, head lolling and one eye swollen shut, and before she could stop herself she said, "Lord Almighty, what's happened to him?"

The man holding Del up grinned at her. "He's just drunk, is all."

"But his eye . . ."

"Oh, he don't even notice it none. He gets up in the morning, he'll be telling you all about how the other man's in traction or some such. Don't you believe him."

CeeCee straightened up. "He's my cousin. I will so believe him."

"Well, you do that," the man said. "I'm just saying, is all."

"You can go say it to someone else." CeeCee stepped out of the house and took Del's weight.

"Want me to help you get him lying down?" the man said.

Not for a million dollars was CeeCee Magruder going to let this man in her house. "Thank you, no," she said. "I'll manage."

"All right, then. You don't have to thank me."

This stopped her in the doorway. She leaned Del into the jamb and kept her hip against him in case he started to list. Over her shoulder she said, "Thank you for bringing him home."

"You're welcome."

He was still standing there, making CeeCee uncomfortable enough to speak again. "Who did that to his eye?"

"What, you mean the guy in the hospital?"

That grin. "Please. Who was it?"

"Why, it was me. Thought you'd figured that out already."

"You—"

He waved both his hands as if shooing a fly. "Wasn't nothing. We got to joking at each other." Peeling his lower lip down to expose an inch-long cut, he added, "Del got one in, too. It's all even. Tell him I'll see him tomorrow night."

Speechless, she watched him start to walk back down the street. Then he stopped and said, "You're his cousin, right? From Tennessee?"

"Arkansas."

"What's your name?"

She told him, and then it was only polite to ask his, and somehow she wasn't at all surprised to find that his name was Marty Cleaves.

* * *

The discovery that she hadn't been entirely wrong—that she hadn't been so maladroit a backwoods diviner as everyone in Eureka Springs had thought—made the Detroit winter almost bearable. She began to see Marty Cleaves with increasing frequency, and by some process she was never to understand, all of the confusion and torment surrounding her memories of Michael Cleaves combined with the guilt she'd felt about writing Martin Cleaves' name on a slip of paper in her darkening bedroom the previous spring, and the strange alloy of memory and loneliness at some point became love. It didn't hurt that this Marty Cleaves had a ready grin and just enough dickens to keep her interested without making her worry that it would ever turn mean. He was a Ford roadman, so sometimes he wasn't around all that much, but CeeCee was well imprinted with her mother's dictum that a marriage functioned more smoothly if punctuated by periods of absence.

Not a fairy tale, then, but a happy match, and CeeCee was forced to revise her opinion of Detroit. If this place had bred a man who gave her as much joy and laughter as Martin Cleaves, then the sooty, frigid winters and stifling summers could be forgiven. She became pregnant in October 1913, and like every other married couple that includes no tyrants they instigated a lively round of arguments about naming the baby. CeeCee was partial to Alice for a girl and Jared for a boy; her husband was willing to go along with Jared—although he preferred Ned—but he swore he'd tear out his tongue before calling any offspring of his Alice. Truth was, he couldn't think of a girl's name that sat right with him, so he was fighting a rear-guard action and hoping for inspiration.

Martin's parents, who lived in Ypsilanti, had opinions of their own. Skeeter Cleaves, a mechanic who owned a shop in Depot Town, figured that Clarice was a fine name for a young girl, and also, what was the word . . .

"Alliterative," Mabel Cleaves finished for him. She was a teacher at the high school and could be counted on to fill in the gaps in her husband's ready vocabulary. "It's alliterative, and it's horrible."

The four of them were drinking hot cocoa on the porch of the elder Cleaveses' Queen Anne home on Pearl Street, walking distance from Cleaves Engine and Spring as well as Ypsilanti High School. It was an unseasonably warm December afternoon, a Sunday, and they'd all just come from church, after which CeeCee had sworn that if she didn't get some air she would expire on the spot. So out there on the porch, swaddled in every blanket Mabel Cleaves could excavate from the monstrous cedar chest in the attic, CeeCee was watching a man drive a Model T past the house when her mother-in-law said, "Why not Michael? A boy could do worse than carry his father's name."

The look that passed between Mabel and Skeeter told CeeCee that this sentiment had some history behind it. It occurred to Skeeter right then that he should stir up a new batch of cocoa, and as he went inside, CeeCee said, "Michael?" The name did not appear on their marriage certificate.

Uncharacteristic sheepishness lengthened the lines of her husband's already angular face. "My Christian name's Michael," he said, and was already adding "but I don't go by it" as his wife started to say something and then fell over in a dead faint.

When she regained her senses, Mrs. Cleaves was chattering about how being in the family way was the absolute devil on a woman's nerves, with frequent asides about the betrayal of a son who couldn't use the perfectly good name his parents had given him. CeeCee let them all think that she'd swooned because of the baby in her belly, and she said not a word about her husband's decision to use what apparently was his contentious middle name instead of his mother's preferred moniker. Never, as long as she was married to Michael Martin Cleaves, did she mention her adventures in conjuring back home in Eureka Springs. Neither did she attempt anything witchy during her pregnancy or when Jared Carlyle Cleaves entered the world in July 1914, or afterward; but she nurtured within herself a small spark of satisfaction that, after all, she'd been right.

The Piston Doctor and the Dwarf both laugh. So does Jared. It's a good story. He especially likes the way they're lying to him about Mabel Cleaves sharing Deirdre Stuart's principal character flaw. When he wakes up, before dawn, he has an aching hard-on and no recollection of the dream beyond a gauzy image of the Dwarf waving its balls around like Dick Wakefield in the on-deck circle.

CHAPTER 12

The papers were full of news about what they were calling the Zoot Suit Riots in California, with much breathless speculation about whether fifth columnists had infiltrated the local Mexican population and started the disturbance to interfere with war production. Jared remembered Mount Clemens, twenty-four years ago, watching the brightly dressed column of musicians parade in front of the courthouse where Henry Ford was on trial. It's a big country, he thought. Here I am in Detroit, where I thought we had people from all over the world, and I don't think I've ever spoken to a Mexican. We got French, Irish, colored, Italian, Ukrainian, Polish, Hungarian, German, Chaldean, Jewish, Finns, Chinese, Indians . . .

He got lucky on the streetcar, finding both the *Free Press* and the *Times,* which meant that he could find out both what really happened and what William Randolph Hearst thought about it. As a rule, Jared didn't read the *Times* because he'd been taught to mistrust Hearst, who would hang union leaders for treason if he could get away with it. Times were strange, though; even FDR had resorted to similar threats to break the rubber strike down in Akron, and there were all kinds of conspiratorial mutterings about why the coal strike a couple of weeks back had ended so quickly.

In front of the OEI office, a line of men with dogs stretched around the corner. Jared found out that they were there because the OEI had put out the word that they were looking for dogs that demonstrated unusual abilities. "Rusty here can sniff out land mines," boasted the guy Jared asked.

"How'd you teach him that?"

"Took three dogs, but I got my technique refined. Tell you what, he's the real McCoy."

"I mean, how did you get the mines?"

The man snorted. "Shit, anybody can make a mine."

Jared went inside. Before the desk sergeant could unbolt his mouth from around his cigarette, Jared said, "You got the whole kennel club outside."

"War is hell," the sergeant said. "Meadows has been looking for you."

"Couldn't have been looking too hard," Jared said. "I've been where I always am."

"Can you find his office?"

"Sure." The sergeant jerked a thumb over his shoulder, and Jared wound his way through the labyrinth to Meadows' door. He knocked and stuck his head in, catching Meadows in the middle of digging something out from behind one of his filing cabinets.

"Where the hell have you been?" Meadows wanted to know.

"Hard to keep a schedule when you're running down Kraut spies," Jared said.

"Oh, really? Is that what you're doing?"

"I don't know. I was hoping you'd tell me."

Jared could see Meadows making an effort to simmer down. "Okay," Meadows said. "It's been a circus around here." He shook his head, eyes downcast, and laughed bitterly. "Place is going to the dogs, if you'll forgive the expression."

"What, you're not a dog person?"

Meadows didn't seem to think this was funny. He tried to smile out of politeness. "I've got to be careful how much I tell you. I'm sure you can appreciate that."

Jared didn't say that he was being careful, too. Going to the dogs, he thought, and remembered the Piston Doctor's oil-pan turtle, and the vacant golems destroyed on the shop floor, and Herschel Fontenot saying things weren't working like they should. That sounded like going to the dogs, all right. Tough times in the OEI.

"I don't know exactly what's going on between the Marshal and your boss at River Rouge," Meadows went on, "but I do know that when the Marshal tapped you back in 1940, he believed you—and everyone else on the golem project—had some kind of sensitivity that would help things along. Create a critical mass, if you're familiar with that term." Jared wasn't, but he didn't say so. "Then in May," Meadows went on, "the Marshal was getting leery about Swerdlow and made a second move for you, to see what Swerdlow would do. The question we have is how all this is related to the Dwarf. Does Swerdlow know that you've seen the Dwarf?"

"I never told him," Jared said.

"Are you telling me that he doesn't know because you never told him, or he might know but not from you? The difference is important here."

This was where Jared was supposed to play dumb. Spying is an indirect business, he reminded himself. "I don't think he knows. He's never said anything about it. Near as I can tell, he picked me out because my wife works at Willow Run and he wanted to know what was going on there."

Meadows thought this over. "Willow Run," he repeated.

"That's right. There's a new building out there, and Swerdlow leaned on me to get my wife to find out what it was for."

"Why wouldn't he tap someone who worked there directly?"

"Don't know."

"Well, it makes sense if he's trying to keep something to himself," Meadows mused. Jared started to wonder just how much of the conversation was genuine, and how much was Meadows pretending to air out questions whose answers he already knew so he could see what Jared would say.

"If I knew what was in that building," Jared said, "I might be able to work Swerdlow a little better."

"Maybe, but you're not going to hear it from me."

Jared shrugged. "All right. It's your call."

Meadows made some notes. "What do you think is there?" he asked when he'd finished.

"Something the OEI's doing, that's for sure."

"What makes you think that?"

"I heard some things," Jared said. "Mostly from the women who work with my wife."

"Let's stop beating around the bush here. What have you heard?"

"That when there was an accident there a couple of weeks ago, OEI showed up and took over the evacuation."

"Who said it was OEI?"

"Nobody said it out loud. I put it together from what people told me and some things I saw Swerdlow do."

"And you're pretty confident that we're involved out there?"

"Pretty much."

"Okay. You're right. Let me tell you a little about OEI. Just like the Germans are working on rockets and we're getting better radar, both sides in this war are flat-out trying to develop other resources. It's OEI's job to oversee efforts on this side and to gather intelligence on what the Germans and Japanese are up to—and let me tell you, they're up to quite a bit. Things haven't been going well for us or them, near as we can tell, which is why we have a line of dogs out on the sidewalk." Meadows winced as he said this, the same way he'd winced when Jared brought up the Japanese internments a few

THE NARROWS — 221

weeks ago. "I can't go into details, but now that you know our mandate you'll understand why we're interested in you and the Dwarf."

"What, you want to use the Dwarf?"

"Ideally, yes. But everything we know about it makes that seem unlikely. Our primary interest right now is in discovering what your encounter with the Dwarf means for the city."

"Who else has seen it?"

"You're the only one we know of. Frankly, this has us a little worried, since typically the Dwarf has appeared to someone immediately before that person suffers a major misfortune that affects the city. But you're twenty-four years out from your encounter, and during those twenty-four years Detroit has come a long way. So our working hypothesis is that given the fact that you're now working in an OEI-related project, the Dwarf's interest in you means that your project will go wrong. Possibly very wrong."

"I don't see the connection," Jared said. "You think in 1919, the Dwarf knew I'd be making golems?"

"Could be," Meadows said. "Time doesn't work for beings like the Dwarf the same way it does for you and me."

"You know what happened with me and the Dwarf," Jared said. "He jumped on the hood of my father's car, and when my father hit the brakes my hand banged into the dashboard and broke a whiskey bottle. You can all relax."

Meadows leaned forward. "Don't take this the wrong way, Jared, but did that really happen? I don't doubt that you saw the Dwarf, but are you sure you aren't arranging events in retrospect so they fit some other idea you have about your childhood?"

Where the hell was this coming from? "What did my dad tell you?" Jared demanded.

"Easy. He told us the same thing you did. Still, it's been twenty-four years, which is a lot of time for people to agree on the version of a story that suits them. Look. You're misunderstanding the nature of the Dwarf. He doesn't signal personal misfortune, even though some of his appearances cause it. The Dwarf sets in motion chains of events that have until now played out to cause serious damage to the city of Detroit. We have no reason to believe that this time will be any different, even if the time frame is more elongated than usual. Be very careful, Jared. We don't know what you're going to do, so we have to be vigilant in managing the consequences of your possible actions."

"Why don't you just send me to Oklahoma or someplace? Then I couldn't do anything to Detroit."

"Those kinds of measures have been considered," Meadows said. His tone gave Jared a chill. "For now, though, we're hoping for another contact between you and the Dwarf because a number of us in the OEI would very much like to put it to work. You know where the Nain Rouge originally comes from, don't you?"

"Sure. Normandy, in France."

Meadows looked hard at Jared for a long moment after he'd spoken. "You learned that in school, I'm assuming."

"This old French Canadian who used to run a speakeasy, he knew my dad. He told me."

"You ever hear Swerdlow talk about Normandy?"

Jared snorted. "Swerdlow couldn't find France on a map."

"How about the people he's talking to?"

"Couldn't tell you. Is there something I should know?"

"There's something you shouldn't know. I'm just making sure you don't know it. The minute you hear anything about Normandy, or France at all, in a conversation involving Swerdlow, you come directly to me."

"All right. But I think you're barking up the wrong tree. Swerdlow's only interested in Willow Run."

"That may be. We're not worried about only Swerdlow, though."

Taking a minute to process, Jared leaned back in the chair and looked at the ceiling. It was stamped tin, with little bunches of grapes all over it. "So what are the Germans and Japs up to?" he asked. "I mean, that you guys are interested in."

"Well, I'm not giving anything away telling you about the frost giants, I'm sure. The Nazis are working on a number of things. The problem for them is that because—and pardon me if I get a little academic here, I did my graduate work in this area—because their culture is so centered on death and chaos, those are the only forces they have any skill at harnessing, and this turns out to be a double-edged sword. It's awfully hard to harness chaos; more often than not, you just end up unleashing it without any real idea of whether it'll work for or against you. The frost giants, for example, were supposed to come down on Stalingrad last winter. Instead they've fanned out across the northern parts of the world, and while they've done some serious damage to Allied facilities, we're also hearing that they've worked over the Nazis pretty well, too."

This pretty much squared with what Herschel Fontenot had said. Meadows went on. "The Dwarf, by the way, is the same kind of chaotic figure. In fact there's a figure out of Norse myth that's kind of like the Nain Rouge. Ever hear of the Alfar?"

"Nope."

"There are a bunch of different ones. Some of them are supposed to be dwarfs that cause disease and misfortune, et cetera. Also one of them maybe suckered Sigmund into killing the dragon."

Sigmund? Jared thought. What dragon? He didn't want to look ignorant in front of Meadows, so he let it go.

"That's just one more reason why we're keeping an eye on it," Meadows said. "On him. And on you. How's your personal life?"

"What?"

"Friendships, marriage, job. How are they going?"

"None of your business."

"Oh, but it is. It may well be that growing chaos in your life is a signal that the Dwarf's planned—let's just go ahead and call it disaster—is coming closer. You've noticed that this city has been pretty tense lately, what with the Sojourner Truth problems, housing shortages, and so on. I don't want to press this too hard, but if things really go south for you, we need to hear about it. Okay?"

Jared didn't like the way this was going. What happened between him and Colleen was their own business. Still, he'd come this far. "I guess," he said. "If you're sure it means something."

"We're not sure, but we need to gather all the information we can. And we need to be able to count on you."

"You can."

"Glad to hear it. Could be you're our trump card, not that you need that kind of pressure." Meadows glanced at his watch. "You should be getting to work, I think."

Trump card. Jared liked the sound of that. "Yeah. Hey, you never told me what the Japs are doing."

"Ever hear of a tengu?"

"Nope."

"Old mountain spirits that can change into birds. We're pretty sure that some of them are scouting around here to get numbers on war production." Meadows winked at Jared. "If you see an old Japanese man turn into a bird, give us a call."

"You're pulling my leg."

"Only sort of. They're out there."

"I thought all the Japs were in camps."

Meadows grimaced. "I don't want to talk about that. And in any case it's not certain that a tengu in human form has to be Japanese."

"You sure Petey isn't one of them?"

"Ha. Wouldn't that be a kick in the teeth. No, Petey is, as near as we can tell, a regular old Iroquois shaman. He used to work on the high steel, building bridges and so on, but decided he liked being a bird full time. Speaking of, do you need him to get you out, or can you find your own way?"

"I think I can do it this time."

"Good. Take care of yourself, Jared."

"Will do." They shook hands, and Jared wandered out onto Woodward and drove to work seeing Japanese spies on every telephone wire. Hell of a way to see the world, he thought. On the other hand, it wasn't any more paranoid than thinking that Detroit was going to go up in flames because his marriage was rocky.

It didn't hit him until dinner break, when he was sitting out by the turning basin on a slag heap that the collectors had missed. Tengu. Bird. Bird bones. "God damn," he said softly. That's what the charm was supposed to tell him. Plenty Coup was a tengu. The Japs were watching him.

But why? Did they know about the Dwarf? They wouldn't care about the golems.

Felton and Jem were looking at him. "What?" they said.

"Nothing." He held up his sandwich. "One more Spam sandwich and I'm gonna kick a blind man."

"Now, that's a short fuse," Jem said. "You need to get laid more often."

Of all the things Jem could have said right then, that was the one guaranteed to send Jared into a blind rage. It had only been three days, but already he felt like he'd been celibate for a year again, mostly because Colleen had displayed not the slightest interest in a repeat engagement. Jared was mystified, frustrated, and horny, and he took it out on Jem. They rolled around on the asphalt by the slag heap trading wild punches until Felton and the Jeweler separated them. "Get your goddamn hands off me," Jared growled at the Jeweler, who shoved him away from Jem and stayed between them. Felton had Jem's arms behind him and was talking into his ear; Jem relaxed a little, and Jared did, too. He licked a trickle of blood from his lip. Around them, a loose ring of bored workers from the lines near Building G had gathered to see if there would be an encore.

"All right," Jared said. "Short fuse. I didn't mean anything."

Jem prodded at the bridge of his nose. "Sure," he said with a shrug. "We've all of us had a hair trigger lately."

"Two of you went and ruined my dinner," Felton said. "Violence kills my appetite, guaranteed."

"What do you have?" Jem asked.

"Spam sandwich."

This cracked Jem up. "Maybe Jared'll want to finish it for you," he said.

Felton looked at Jared, who held up both hands, palms out. "Both of you, I swear to God," Felton said. He threw his sandwich in the canal and walked off around the corner of Building G. The onlookers wandered away. Jared tested his lip again. The bleeding had already stopped. Another night on the line.

He had to do something with the aggression, though, and since he couldn't in good conscience beat the hell out of Jem after apologizing to him, he instead went and staked out the Bel-Mark Lanes after work. The parking lot was jammed with the Friday crowd, and Jared ended up parking way the hell away and gone back by Moises' apartment, which struck him as a bad idea right about the time he'd walked back up to the bowling alley. He didn't feel like walking all the way back and finding another spot, so he concentrated on his plan for the night, which was to see if Swerdlow and Sharkskin Billy met on nights other than Tuesdays, and if so to follow Billy after the meeting. First order of business was to locate the subject, as the cop radio shows might have said, so he went in and bellied right up to the bar, wedging himself in between a knob-knuckled Pole in overalls and a tired-looking Jewish guy in a rumpled suit with a bunch of straight pins stuck through the right lapel. A line rat and a tailor. Peering around the Pole's meaty shoulders, Jared saw the golem standing off in the shadows between the Wurlitzer and a utility closet door. When he looked the other way, Sharkskin Billy was in his usual spot at the end of the bar—but Swerdlow wasn't.

This was interesting. It had the feel of opportunity knocking, particularly considering that even in Swerdlow's absence, the golem was there. Billy had to have noticed it by now, unless he was more than usually oblivious. Might be an interesting conversation there. Jared rehearsed telling Billy that he was under golem surveillance, enjoying the imagined look of fearful panic this information might provoke; then he discarded the idea, figuring it wasn't a good plan to have too much scripted beforehand. Best, probably, just to introduce himself and see where things went from there.

Which is what he did, tapping Billy on the shoulder and saying, "Evening. We haven't met, but I think we know each other. Jared Cleaves."

Billy swiveled his stool around. He displayed a perfect set of teeth and immaculate manners, extending his hand and saying, "Jared. Billy Miller. Swerdlow's told me quite a bit about you. I'd buy you a drink if you didn't already have one."

"You can get the next," Jared said, and drained off half of his beer. He wiped his mouth and said, "So what does old Swerdlow say about me?"

"Oh, he's very bullish on you. Thinks you might be the answer to our problem."

"That so? Around me, Swerdlow's pretty tight-lipped about what that problem might be."

"And he should be. Loose lips and all that." Billy saluted Jared with his drink, something amber and clinking with ice. He polished it off and said, "Let's talk somewhere else. You drove here?"

"Car's a little way back."

"I'll give you a ride."

Billy's car was a dark green Airfoil DeSoto that made the Hop-Frog look like a go-cart. They settled in a booth at the back of an Irish bar in Corktown, a one-hop throw from Briggs Stadium. Jared had walked by this place maybe three dozen times on his way to or from Tigers games, but this was his first time on the inside, and he didn't much care for it. A little too much nostalgia for the Auld Sod, which if it had been so great what were all the Irish doing here, was his way of thinking, and he was Irish on his mother's side. Billy came back from the bar with a bottle of Bushmills and two glasses. He poured them each three or four fingers and sat back to sip his. "It's not Stroh's, I know, but when in Cork . . ." Billy said with a mocking grin.

Looking around the bar, Jared wondered why Billy had brought him here. There were four guys clustered in the elbow of the bar, their clothes freckled with pinhole burns that said welder. In a booth at the front sat two down-and-out-looking hillbillies, one of them sliding his empty glass back and forth across the table between his cupped palms. They looked like brothers. Six men. It was one o'clock in the morning, but it was also Friday. Detroit in wartime: there were places where people couldn't convince themselves that they might as well have a good time while the world blew up around them. Well, not around them, exactly; far as Jared knew there hadn't been any squadrons of Junkers bombing Wayne County. The war was a long way off.

Except not really, if Plenty Coup had been some kind of were-bird Japanese spy. And not if the man sitting across this cigarette-scarred booth was another kind of spy.

"So, Billy," Jared said. "You German?"

"Loaded question, friend. You mean German or German?"

"I mean, why does Swerdlow lean all over me and then check in with you at the Bel-Mark to pass along what I say? Why are you so interested in Willow Run? I didn't know better, I'd think you had something up your sleeve."

"Or I'm trying to find out before someone else."

"Why?"

"Because the someone else is German."

"Which doesn't mean you're not."

Billy sipped his whiskey. "Jared. This is dangerous ground. If you're asking me am I a spy, I will say no. And then if I am, I will catch you looking the other way some night and the knife I'm right now resting on your left knee will cut your throat. You've got a wife, a daughter; you want to take that chance?"

The pressure of the knife point on his knee brought a vibrant clarity to Jared's thinking. He had all the answer he needed, didn't he? The question now was how to get to Dash, and how to convince Colleen that she and Emily needed to clear out of the house for a while. "I didn't want to get into this," he told Billy. "All I wanted was to enlist. They wouldn't let me, and then Swerdlow decided he'd found his patsy. I figured that much out now, but what I don't get is what's in this for Swerdlow."

The knife pressed a little harder on Jared's kneecap. Just a re-minder, he thought. A peacock spreading his tail. If Billy really wanted to take me out, he wouldn't have shown it.

"Swerdlow has his own set of problems," Billy said. "All you need to know is that I'm not going to leave him alone, and he's not going to leave you alone, until we know what's happening out at Willow Run."

"You know OEI's interested in this, right?"

The knife fell away. "What have you told them?"

"Nothing. They're following me around because I saw the Nain Rouge when I was a kid. They staged a big tug-of-war over me, suckered Swerdlow into making a stink to keep me out of the Mar-shal's hands. Not a smart play, if you ask me. Swerdlow might as well have put a sign on me that read 'Here's the guy I'm hoping will get me out of trouble with these guys who might or might not be Nazi spies.' "

Billy took this in. "What's the Nain Rouge?"

"Means 'red dwarf' in French."

"I know."

"You know French?"

Billy smiled and sipped at his Bushmills. "I'm full of surprises."

The whiskey burned Jared's throat, summoning a memory of the bottle in his five-year-old hands. "I could use a few less surprises," he said.

"Tell me about this Dwarf."

"The idea is that he appears when a disaster is about to happen. I saw him when I was five."

"And no disaster?"

Jared shrugged. "Not yet. OEI isn't convinced the clock's run out, though." He paused. "Listen, I'm not going to get arrested for talking to you, am I?"

"Has Swerdlow?"

"You didn't answer my question."

"That's because it's another version of are-you-German, and I'd hate to have our conversation degenerate just when we might be about to do each other some good."

"Billy. The only good I want you to do me is leave me alone and tell Swerdlow the same. My wife strips engines at Willow Run. She doesn't have any idea what's going on out there. I even asked the OEI when they were interviewing me about the Dwarf, and the guy laughed in my face. For all I know, they're hiding Paul Bunyan and Babe the ox out there. I can't help you guys, and I wish you'd leave me alone." To his shame and surprise, Jared found that his eyes had filled with tears. "Just leave me alone."

"I wish I could," Billy said, with what sounded like real sympathy in his voice. "But I only have so many assets here. The sooner I get what I want, the sooner you can go about forgetting that you ever saw me. Until then, keep on passing the good word to Swerdlow."

Jared got up. He was walking to the door when Billy called out. "Oh, and about John Dash? You stay away from him, you'll be doing yourself a big favor."

During the hour's walk back to where he'd left the car at Twelfth and Clairmount, Jared would have sworn that things could not have gotten any worse. Then he saw the golem leaning against a newspaper box near the Hop-Frog, and came damn close to puking up the little whiskey he'd drunk. He slowed down, keeping some distance between the golem and himself. "What do you want?" he asked it.

It didn't answer. Figured. He didn't really think they could talk. It did stand up, though, and station itself between him and the car. Jared's stomach did an adrenaline flip, and he made a sharp left turn through the door to Moises' apartment building. He ran up the stairs, the skin on the back of his neck electric with the awful anticipation of the golem's iron hands closing on him. It was like being scared to death by *Suspense* or *Lights Out;* he loved it. This was living. This was what he was meant to do.

Moises answered the door before Jared could knock three times. "Here you are again," he said. "Three in the morning, here is Jared Cleaves."

"There's a golem out front of your building. I think it doesn't want me around," Jared said. He looked over his shoulder, still shedding the remnants of his expectation of murder. Moises stepped back from the door and Jared went in, sitting where he'd sat last time. Sure enough, Moises was wearing the same bathrobe with the same wife-beater under it and the same thicket of gray hair curling up to the base of his neck. Scatterbrained from the night's events, Jared considered whether there was some sort of hair-density requirement in rabbi school. Did you have to be able to grow a beard down to your sternum?

"I think you don't worry about golem," Moises said when he'd returned with his glass of water.

"I think I do," Jared answered, the words leaving his mouth at the exact instant he parsed what Moises really meant. "Oh. You mean I don't need to."

"Yah. Golems know who is okay."

"I hope so," Jared said. "You think it'll let me go to my car?"

Moises shrugged. "Are you okay?"

Well, there was the situation with the two guys who might be Nazi spies, Jared thought. Easy for a golem to misunderstand. "Yeah," he said. "I'm okay. I don't know if they know I'm okay, though."

"You want I should tell it?"

What Jared wanted was for Moises to tell the golem to go find Sharkskin Billy, but he wasn't sure how Moises would take an attempt to suborn murder—not to mention the necessary prequel that Jared had been in contact with an espionage ring. He yawned, suddenly crushed under the combined weight of fatigue and the disappearance of his adrenaline rush; when he rubbed at his eyes, he could feel a tremble in his fingertips. "I don't know," he said. "I don't know."

"You should go home to your wife," Moises said.

"I don't know if she wants me." Jared sighed.

"She does," Moises said. "Only she doesn't want what you do."

Jared spread his arms and fell back into the chair. "What am I doing? I got myself into a situation here, and all I'm trying to do is get out."

Moises' gaze, pitiless and rheumy, carved right through that little fiction. "What is it with war," he wondered out loud, "that makes men want it so?"

"I don't want the war."

"Lie," Moises said.

"I don't. I'm glad I'm not up to my ass in mud somewhere ducking bullets. What pisses me off is—"

"That you did not choose," Moises finished for him. He waited for Jared to contradict him, then went on. "I did not choose, either."

"What, you'd rather be shooting it out with the SS in Warsaw?"

Moises planted his elbows on his knees and pointed at Jared. "Tell me something, Jared Cleaves. Do you believe in God?"

"Sure, I guess."

"Bah. You guess. If you guess, you don't believe. My life I have given to God, and what do I hear when I get to America? Frost giants. What do I see? Ghosts and imps. What do I fight for, if not God? And what is fighting for God if anyone who believes in a different God . . . if everything else is true?" The old rabbi's tone had modulated from challenging to pleading. He held his hands out as if Jared might place something in his hands to restore his faith, and if it had been possible Jared would have done it just to see that expression leave Moises' face. "The golem is a gift from God," Moises said. "What is this gift if other gods give other gifts? I have made golems from anger; now I am no longer angry. Now I am without hope. This is a war for machines and men."

Jared started to object there, but Moises ran over him. "How many bombers does Willow Run make this week?"

"I think about sixty," Jared said.

"So this is two hundred fifty bombers per month. How many other factories make bombers? Five? Six?"

"Yeah, five or six."

"So this is at least a thousand bombers per month."

"No it isn't. The other plants can't make but one a day."

Moises amputated this quibble with a shake of his head. "If there are no strikes and the machines do their work, I make perhaps three hundred golems per month. I can make no more, and no one else can do this. Henry Ford has promised a bomber an hour. If he does this, he will make more bombers himself than I can make golems, and there are five other factories. Which will win this war, Jared Cleaves?"

"But you can't make bombers. I can't make bombers. We're doing our part." Jared stood up. "That's what I wanted to say before. I don't want the war, hell no, but I want to do my part."

"You do your part. I do mine. The golems drown on their way to England, to Tunisia."

This was a chance to get Moises' expert opinion on the question of what happened to golems if their ships were sunk, but Jared suffered an attack of tact and passed up the opportunity. "So you make more. That's what we do. When we win this war, you'll see Eisenhower and MacArthur in the newspapers, but it'll be Detroit that does the job. It'll be our planes and our tanks and our jeeps—our people. You and me."

"Our people," Moises repeated. He was slumping back into his chair. "Heavy words. You tell me people will win this war, this means golems will not. This is not a war of belief; it is a war of machines. And people—our people? I have no people anymore." Moises' eyes closed, and he rested his head on the back of the chair. "Go home, Jared Cleaves. The golem will not harm you."

Unwilling to let the conversation end there, Jared stood in Moises' room wringing his brain for something to say—but how could he contest what Moises said when it was so obviously and horribly true? "All right, Moises," Jared said. "I'll see you tomorrow. Today." Uselessly he added, "Get some sleep, okay? I'm sorry I bothered you."

No response. Moises could have been asleep already—Jared had a morbid urge to place a palm over the rabbi's open mouth, just to see if he was breathing. Something told him he'd intruded enough for one night, though; he shut the door softly behind him and plodded down the stairs and out into the humid night. The golem was still there, leaning on the Hop-Frog's door. When it saw him, it pushed itself away from the car and met him halfway.

"Hey," Jared said. "I made you."

The golem placed a hand flat on Jared's chest. There was judgment in its gaze; he was being weighed because he had gone with Sharkskin Billy. Justifications presented themselves, but Jared didn't speak. If he were a golem, he would mistrust words, and surely the golem would know that he and Moises had spoken? His eyes hurt, and a tic started up in his left eyelid.

"He's okay," Jared said. "Just tired, is all. Believe me, I don't want anything bad to happen to him."

The golem took its hand away and stepped back, nodding toward the Hop-Frog. It melted into the shadows alongside Moises' building, and Jared stepped around the car. Twelfth Street was empty except for a single car making a left turn from a side street. Jared watched it approach, saw the driver's window roll down, all in slow motion as his exhausted brain tried to calculate the threat. The car was a Packard, not Billy's DeSoto—but cars were easy to find in Detroit. Jared couldn't think, couldn't even make his legs run. He stood there and awaited whatever was going to happen.

"Hey, Jared," John Dash said, leaning out the window and braking to a stop. "I was wondering if you were at the bowling alley. Feel like a nightcap?"

"Nah, I need to get some sleep," Jared said. "My daughter gets up early."

"You see you-know-who tonight?"

"Yeah, he was up at the lanes. I didn't talk to him." Billy's warning to stay away from Dash rang in Jared's memory; he was jittery with fatigue and paranoia, wanting only to go home, or maybe to Mexico. "There's a guy from work I owed five bucks. Stopped by to pay up, and now I'm headed home. Rain check?"

"You bet," Dash said. "You second-shift guys are real night owls." He said it with a smile that gleamed in the backwash from the Packard's headlights.

Jared laughed, hoping it didn't sound as nervous as he felt. "Some of us. I haven't gotten a good night's sleep in a month. No sense rolling around and keeping the wife up." Had Dash seen the golem? he wondered. Would he recognize one?

Dash started the Packard rolling south again. "Rain check it is," he said, and drove off with a wave. Jared got in the Hop-Frog, stepped on the starter, and made a U-turn as calmly as he could. Ahead of him, Dash's taillights glowed as the Packard made another left turn and disappeared into the night. Jared felt like there was a bull's-eye on the back of his neck. Where was Billy? Had he seen Dash drive by? Had he seen Jared duck into Moises' building? Neither of them would know Moises lived there . . . would they? A fresh set of uncertainties churned in Jared's head. He worked them over as long as he could, got nowhere except more confused, and gave up. You could only dodge so many bullets in one night; no sense inventing more.

CHAPTER 13

He was expecting to wake up with a head full of cotton wool, but Emily took care of that by planting one of her little knees squarely on Jared's testicles when she came to get him out of bed. So instead of cotton wool, he had the kind of glaring wakefulness you only got when your initial sensation of the day was a flattened scrotum. He rolled over onto his stomach, which Emily took as her cue to ride him like a horsey, and to take his mind off the molten lead in the pit of his stomach Jared played along with it, neighing and rearing all the way out into the kitchen, where he fell over sideways with a last theatrical whinny. Emily ran to the table to get her juice, and Jared said, "Argh."

"Have a good time last night?" Colleen asked with an arched eyebrow.

"Not in the slightest. When the war's over, I'll tell you everything, baby, but if I spilled now I'd have to kill the both of us."

She brought him a cup of coffee despite the rank odor of bullshit in the air, and he sipped at it while his balls quit hurting. My little girl, he thought. Good for at least one ball crushing a month. The *Free Press* said that the Tigers had won four in a row, which was scarcely to be believed, and that Allied bombing was doing a number on Pantelleria, and that Hitler was still stuck in the Russian mud. Good news all around. "Say," Jared said after a couple of minutes reading the paper. He fingered the stitches on his forehead. "How about you take this zipper out?"

"Can't wait until Monday?"

True, he did have an appointment at Henry Ford on Monday, but how hard could removing stitches be? Colleen knew how to sew. "It's been ten days, right? That's what the doc said."

Colleen did the deed while he sat in a chair in the backyard, where the light was better than anywhere inside. Emily watched with her typical intense concentration. "What are you doing, Mama?" she asked over and over again, each syllable given the same emphasis as if she'd memorized the phrase whole, which if Jared stopped to think about it seemed pretty likely. Twenty-five stitches, less than ten minutes, and then Jared felt a little less freakish than he had for the past week and a half. Emily wanted to play with the little knotted pieces of thread, and they let her because the choice was between Emily angry because she couldn't play with the thread and Emily frustrated when she lost the thread. It was easier to distract her when she had lost something; you could almost always substitute something else. Which is what they did when she started complaining that she couldn't find Daddy's stitches; the yard, after all, was full of fascinating things like dewy spiderwebs. Colleen went off to work with Nadine and Arlene, the Three Eens zooming down Mr. Ford's highway in one of Mr. Ford's cars to one of Mr. Ford's factories. It was enough to make you want to move to Nevada, out in the desert somewhere, where nobody owned anything, or at least Mr. Ford didn't own anything. Unless he had a piece of a silver mine or a saguaro cactus concession, which he probably did, Mr. Ford having a demonstrated tendency to buy anything that piqued his in-

It was a day to get the hell out of Detroit, at least for a little while. Jared thought about calling in sick to work—what were they going to do, fire him just when they thought they'd figured out the Dwarf situation?—but decided against it. He'd go to work, but the war could get along for a day without him worrying about it. What to do with Claude, though. You couldn't very well leave a six-month-old puppy, if he was even that old, loose in the house. And Jared wasn't a betting man, but he would have wagered that a staked-out Claude would be a noisy Claude, and a noisy Claude would bring hellfire and perdition down from Mrs. Pelletier. Unless, he thought . . .

"Of course I'll watch this adorable little creature," Mrs. Pelletier said, more to Claude than to Jared. "You just watch out, though. I might not want to give him back."

"Emily'll kidnap him back if she has to," Jared told her with a grin. He left Claude playing tug-of-war with a delighted Warren Pelletier, and Mrs. Pelletier peeling the skin from some cold fried chicken so she could teach the puppy to stand on his hind legs. Claude would probably be a trained circus performer by the time Colleen got home from work. Jared packed sandwiches, a bottle of milk, and Emily into the Hop-Frog and headed north until the city thinned out into farms and small towns. It was nine thirty in the morning and he didn't have to be at work until three; by ten he planned to be sitting by a river somewhere watching his daughter splash around and letting the sun on his face recharge his reservoir of faith in the innate goodness of humankind.

As it turned out, the day went even better than that. Jared happened upon a little lake somewhere near Mount Clemens, and on the lakeshore was a camp store that had a couple of canoes for rent, along with fishing tackle, and Jared spent one of the finest hours in his memory floating around in the lake watching Emily fish with a stick onto which he'd tied a few feet of line and a hook. It was hot and sunny, but the breeze over the lake left Jared supersaturated with the coolness of the water and a deep, wordless pleasure at doing nothing. He paddled the canoe to a bank of lily pads filling a notch in the lakeshore and cast a few times along its edge. It was too hot for the fish to be interested in anything more than heading for the bottom, but that was okay; he watched dragonflies and water striders, he watched his bobber, he watched his daughter, who pulled her line in every thirty seconds or so just in case a fish had managed to hook itself without her noticing. All the while she kept up a running commentary on the lily pads and the bugs and the brightness of the sun on the water and all of the fish that she pretended to catch. At the end of the hour Jared had eaten so many pretend fish that his pretend gut was about to bust. Emily was getting restless by this time, so he paddled back along the shore to the dock behind the camp store, Emily hanging her head over the side the whole way so she could trail her hand in the water and watch the long-dead worm at the end of her line. When he steered the canoe along the side of the dock, Emily reached out to touch the splintery gray wood. "Careful you don't get a splinter, baby girl," Jared said, and as the words left his mouth Emily's stick fishing pole jumped over the side.

When Emily was surprised in a good way, her mouth opened so wide it put Jared in mind of a boa constrictor about to swallow a tapir. Jared leaned forward, reaching to catch the stick before it could hit the water under the dock and be gone. He'd just gotten it between finger and thumb when Emily, her boa-constrictor face already transformed into speechless delight, leaned, too. They hit the water at about the same time. Over Jared's head, he heard the clunk of the canoe's opposite gunwale banging into the dock; he had Emily's stick in his left hand, and without consciously telling himself to he had caught her arm with his right. They popped up in the darkness under the capsized canoe. Emily coughed. "You okay, baby girl?" Jared said. She clung to him and he could feel her head nodding against his chest. Then she coughed again.

"Okay," he said. "We're going to go under the water again, just for a second."

"Don't want to."

"I know. But when we come up I'll show you the fish you caught. Okay?"

"Okay."

"Hold your breath." He didn't know if she knew how to hold her breath, but before she could ask any questions he ducked under the chest-deep water, bounced one quick step to the right, and came up into sunlight. "There we go," he said.

Already forgetting that she'd been scared, Emily leaned back to look around for her fish, blinking water out of her eyes. As she shifted her weight, Jared noticed that she'd grabbed hold of his chest hair. "Ow, yow," he said, prying her hand loose. She laughed and threw herself backward—a trick she'd just picked up in the last month or so, and next time she'd think twice about it; arching her back, she dunked her head under the surface of the water she'd forgotten was there. She came up wide-eyed and gasping, and Jared had to laugh. "Okay, little fishy," he said. "Let's not do that again, okay?"

"Okay," she said, wiping the water from her eyes.

He splashed ashore, leaving the canoe until he'd gotten his daughter on dry land. As he set her down, he remembered that he was still holding her fishing pole. "Look, Emily," he said, squatting in the shallows. "You caught a fish."

A juvenile bluegill, maybe four inches long, flipped and thrashed at the end of the line. Jared caught it and smoothed down its spiny dorsal fin, holding it so she could get a better look. She reached out and touched the side of its head just as it flared its gills. "What's that, Daddy?"

"Those are its gills, honey. That's how it breathes the water."

"Oh." She thought about this, and he loved her so fiercely that his breath caught. "Can we eat it?"

"No, this one's too small."

"I want eat it."

"Next time we'll catch one that's bigger, okay? We have to let this one go so it can grow up." Carefully—more carefully, to tell the truth, than he had with the fishhook stuck through his own thumb on the Frankenline—he worked the hook out of the little bluegill's jaw. "You want to touch it again? Then we have to let it go."

She did, running a finger along the top of its head.

"Okay, bye, fishy," Jared said, and set the bluegill down in the water.

"Bye, fishy," Emily echoed. She waved as it darted away under the dock.

Jared pulled the canoe ashore and then went back to pick the rod he'd rented out of the weeds. Emily sat on the beach and watched the whole show. He borrowed a towel in the store and dried her off as best he could, then himself. He'd lost his shirt when the canoe flipped, but he didn't feel like searching the lake bottom for it. Back in the Hop-Frog, Emily said, "Where your shirt, Daddy?"

"In the lake, honey."

"I take my shirt off, too!" She tried, and got tangled in the wet cotton, and then came the blowup Jared had known was inevitable. He worked her arms out of the sleeves, pulled the shirt over her head, and settled her in the backseat.

"There," he said with a grin. "Now both of us don't have shirts."

"Both of us!" she said. By the time he was back to a paved road, she was sprawled asleep in the backseat. On the way back to the main highway, the overhanging tree branches shook loose a memory: trees leaning over the road, twenty-four years before, flashing into the old Model T's headlights—and then the Dwarf. He shook it off, but not before an unsettling image had worked itself into his mind, of the Dwarf watching him, watching Emily, from the trees surrounding the lake. Jared glanced over his shoulder at his daughter. Was he wrong the way his father had been wrong? Had the Dwarf chosen her, and appeared to him just to set him on the course that would lead to her birth?

Jared smacked himself in the head. Shut up, he thought. That's crazy. A day like this, and you try to turn it into some kind of *Dark Destiny* episode. He laughed at himself, and Emily said something in her sleep. To be in a bad mood on a day like this, you had to be some kind of wacko.

He handed Emily off to Mrs. Pelletier and an exhausted Claude at two thirty and was slamming his locker when the shift-change whistle blew. Nine hours of busting clay and jawing with Felton and Jem followed, indistinguishable from any other Saturday on the Frankenline except for the lack of minor catastrophes and animosity, and Jared fell into bed a little before one, thinking as he dropped off to sleep next to Colleen that he hadn't wasted a single second that day on Swerdlow or Dash or tengus or any of it.

All day Sunday Emily wanted to go to the lake again, but they didn't have the gas stamps to do it, and the Hop-Frog's tires were bald as a slice of baloney. No tire stamps, either. Try explaining that to a two-year-old who wants to catch a fish, Jared thought as he mowed the jungle that had sprouted up in his backyard. See how far you get. On Monday fishing was still Emily's fondest desire, so to distract her Jared walked her and Claude over to CeeCee and Grampa Marty's, waited until Emily was thoroughly engrossed in picking bugs off the tomato plants and Marty had threatened to sell Claude to the Indians—his standard figure of speech for the removal of any annoyance that had a metabolism—and then caught the streetcar downtown to get Meadows' take on Plenty Coup being a tengu. Jared wasn't completely certain he wanted to broach the topic, but if there were Jap spies in Detroit and he didn't tell the OEI, what the hell kind of patriot was he?

The sergeant at the OEI office squinted at Jared. "You again."

"Meadows here?"

"Just a sec." He turned to Petey, who was asleep on the transom. "Petey." The bird, or shaman, or whatever, squawked and looked around. "The grand high muckety-muck here wants to see Meadows."

Petey cocked his head and looked at Jared. "Meadows went to lunch," it said.

Lunch at ten o'clock in the morning? The sergeant tossed a memo pad to Jared. "Leave him a note."

Jared tossed it back. "I'll stop by a little later."

"I'm going to lunch, too," Petey said. He flapped down and landed on Jared's shoulder. "Buy me a hot dog. Awk."

Well, this doesn't happen every day, Jared thought. "Sure," he said, and walked back out onto Woodward with Petey on his shoulder. He went to the White Tower lunch counter on West Larned.

"What the hell are you doing?" the cook said when they came in.

Jared sat down near the door. "I'll have hash and eggs, over easy. He'll have a hot dog."

"With the works," Petey added.

The cook raised an eyebrow. "He always do that?"

"Don't know," Jared said. "I never ordered him a hot dog before."

"One hash and eggs, one victory sausage," the cook said, with a now-I've-seen-everything shake of his head. "You want coffee?"

"Sure."

"The bird want coffee?"

"Ask him."

"You want coffee, bird?"

"Dog soup for me," Petey croaked.

"I'll be goddamned," the cook said.

Snatches of conversation—Tigers lost both games to the Sens yesterday, most of the striking coal miners were back to work—drifted from the five or six other people in the White Tower. One of them, a fiftyish fleabag blond woman sipping coffee so adulterated with creamer that it looked like a milk shake, called out, "Better put down papers."

"Hey, Cook," Petey said. "The old lady pissed herself again."

This brought guffaws from most of the diners, but the cook started laughing so hard that he had to set down his spatula and wipe his eyes with a corner of his apron, which given that article's state of filth put the cook in serious danger of some kind of corneal jungle rot. He wheezed and coughed, then bent to light a cigarette on the burner under the grill. "That there is the funniest thing I've heard in weeks. You should get that bird on Jack Benny."

The woman, meanwhile, had gone rigid with furious dignity. Jared pitied her a little, watching as she sipped her barfly's coffee with a daintiness that bespoke a militantly Emily Post–smitten mother. When the cook set a glass of water in front of Jared, Petey hopped down onto the counter and dipped his beak in.

"Keep the bird on the stools, willya?" the cook said.

"I don't think he can reach the glass from a stool."

"Well, then he's not drinking. I got health codes to live up to."

"Fat chance of that," the woman said.

"With you around, anyway," the cook said. "Lighten up, Mabel. It ain't every day we get a talking bird in here."

"I'll call the inspectors myself," Mabel snapped. "Filthy bird. Talks English, all right; does it talk German, too?"

Everybody quieted down at this. Jared remembered the crow exterminations.

"Hey, pal," the cook said. "Maybe you can get this order to go."

"Come on. This bird works for the OEI."

Now the White Tower was dead quiet. Petey broke the silence. "Thanks a lot. Awk."

"I'm going to scramble those eggs," the cook said. "Over easy don't travel real well."

* * *

They ended up on a bench in Cadillac Square, Jared eating his hash and eggs out of a carton and tearing pieces from the hot dog to feed to Petey. He realized what he must look like: a bum with a tame bird. "Had to go and open your big mouth," Petey croaked after swallowing the last of his hot dog.

The bird was right, but Jared wasn't in any mood to be chastised. "You rather they nailed your wings to the wall?"

Petey flapped up and around him in a circle, landing again on the bench to Jared's left. "I can take care of myself," he said.

"Wish you'd changed back into a man," Jared said. "Now, there's a showstopper."

Petey ruffled his feathers. "Been two years. Not sure I can anymore. Anyway."

Jared forked up the last bits of egg, took a bite of toast, and set the carton aside. "So what do you want from me other than a hot dog?"

"Awful suspicious," Petey said.

"What, the OEI doesn't feed you?"

Stalking back and forth on the bench, Petey grumbled to himself. "Marshal's watching you," he said after a while.

"I know that."

"Marshal's not your friend."

"I'm starting to think I don't have any friends."

Petey whistled. "Sure you do. Who took care of your tengu?"

It took Jared a moment to catch up, and when he did he was speechless. Petey bounced up and down on the bench, one bright black eye trained on Jared. "Plenty Coup," Jared said softly.

"Goddamn right."

"Why didn't you just tell me?"

A sound came from Petey's throat that Jared belatedly identified as laughter. "Awk awk awk. Marshal's not my friend, either."

"Does the OEI know about Plenty Coup?"

Petey bobbed his head up and down. "Don't know I told you, though."

It didn't make sense. Jared dug the heels of his hands into his eye sockets and pressed until the headache subsided. He'd been getting them a lot since the berserk golem kayoed him with the chain, and he'd irrationally hoped that getting the stitches out would fix the problem. What I get for believing in symbols, he thought through the pain.

"Marshal wants what the Marshal wants," Petey said. "Right now what he wants is you. Awk."

"Well, he's had me for two and a half years. About time for him to decide what to do with me, isn't it?"

"Wants you out where you don't know too much to do him any good."

"What the hell's that supposed to mean?"

Petey preened at one of his wings. "You and me," he said when he was done grooming himself. "Take a trip on Sunday."

Jared sifted through a hundred possible questions. "Okay," he said. "Where should I pick you up?"

"I'll come," Petey said. Then he spread his wings and flapped away.

Wednesday night the Jeweler didn't show up. To a man the molders refused to take up his job, their resolve surviving even the combined browbeating of Moises and Swerdlow until Swerdlow picked out one of them at random and said, "You. What's your name?"

"Hristo."

"Hristo, you don't start making me some golem dicks, you're going to hit Miller Road. And by the time you get there, I'll be on the phone with the feds talking about a certain Czech who's obstructing the war effort."

A flush spread over Hristo's face. One of his hands clenched. "Is not my job," he said. He was an older man, deep into his forties, with a rooster tail of salt-and-pepper hair and the build of a man bred to carry blocks of stone for medieval estates.

"It's your job now, or you can start walking." Swerdlow checked his watch. "It's three twenty-six. I'm gonna go take a leak. Probably I'll be back at three twenty-eight, and either there will be Hristo making golem dicks or Hristo's footprints leading away from here to wherever it is malingering Slav morons go when they're too god-damn stupid to play with mud."

When he was gone, the molders consulted with each other while Jared, Jem, and Felton stood around feeling grateful that the Frankenline was a cost-plus contract. If they were over at the Briggs body plant, they wouldn't be getting paid for this time—which complicated Jared's allegiance to the Tigers somewhat, since Briggs owned the club and had sunk a pile of money into old Navin Field before renaming it Briggs Stadium. Jared didn't feel right about pay-ing to see a ball game when his money flowed uphill to a man who might keep his workers on the line twelve hours and only pay them for two. Jem didn't care about baseball, and Felton had somewhere along the line picked up an allegiance to the Birmingham Black Barons of the Negro Leagues, so this particular ethical conundrum usually appeared as part of Marty Cleaves' ongoing lament about the miserable quality of wartime baseball. Jared's father was neutral on the topic of unions, but he had no love for Walter Briggs—or, for that matter, for Henry Ford, whose decision to cashier all of his roadmen when he'd blanketed the country in Ford dealerships still rankled Marty. So in the end what usually happened when Jared groused about putting money in Walter Briggs' pocket was that his father shrugged and said, "They're all of 'em bastards. Money's got to go somewhere, and a man's got to watch a ball game." Then they could get back to ridiculing Newhouser's heart murmur.

* * *

"You know they have talking birds over at the OEI?" Jared asked Felton while they were waiting for the molders' powwow to break up.

"Do tell."

"Either a crow or a raven. Wanted me to buy him a hot dog last time I was there."

"Last time?" Felton eyed Jared. "You over there regular?"

"More than I want to."

"So the Marshal got you after all," Felton said.

"Looks that way."

"Don't say I didn't warn you," Felton said, and it occurred to Jared, maybe only a month after it should have, that Felton might have been having some of his own conversations with the OEI. With Meadows, even. Felton saw him chewing this over, and looked like he might have more to add to the conversation, but Swerdlow bulled through the catwalk door and they all scattered to their stations. "Have a meeting of the local?" Swerdlow called out. "I don't see any dicks on those golems."

Hristo, his head bent down to his chest, was carefully molding genitalia. When he'd finished the first package, he held it up without looking at Swerdlow, and then pressed it into the crotch of the golem closest to him. "That's the way, fellas," Swerdlow said, and slammed the door behind him. At the end of the night, everybody chipped in and Hristo walked out with ten bucks, if not his dignity. He didn't show up the next day, but the Jeweler did, and on Friday a one-eyed Pole had taken Hristo's place.

The Draft Marshal showed up that night, just as a train was pulling in with clay. His motorcade blocked the tracks, so everyone had to stand around practicing their various methods of appearing infirm while he surveyed them. "Who is this new man?" the Marshal asked Swerdlow.

"How the hell do I know?" Swerdlow grumbled. "Another Polack the Cossacks missed."

"Did you ask him what happened to his eye?"

Swerdlow threw up his hands and stomped out of the building.

"You there," the Marshal said, pointing at the Pole, who pointed at himself. "Yes, you. What's your name?"

Another molder whispered to the Pole, who nodded and said, "Casimir."

"A king's name. What happened to your eye, Casimir?"

More murmuring among the molders. Casimir spoke briefly to his translator, who looked up to the Marshal and said, "Blasting in Wieliczka salt mine."

"Would that be the one with the delightful shrines?" the Marshal said. He rested his bulk on the catwalk railing. His two adjutants stepped away in case the railing collapsed. "A salt mine. Come with me." He beckoned to Casimir, who stood dumbly, not understanding until the Marshal's order was translated. Then he nodded. The Marshal left without another word, Casimir following, and they all got back to work.

Jem elbowed him. "Boom, J. Something's down there. I told you."

"Shut up." Jared spent the rest of his shift wondering what exactly was going on down in the mine where his father worked. Sometime during the last month, he'd lost his ability to believe in coincidence. What was it, Sunday, when he and his dad had gabbed about using salt to clear ice off the roads? Was the OEI cooking up some kind of supersalt for winter operations in Europe this year? Jesus. Could be anything. Or could be nothing, but nothing had been nothing lately, not when the old man across the street was a shape-changing Japanese spy killed by another talking bird and turned into a little bundle of mojo next to the Hop-Frog's engine block. This was the kind of thing that made it hard not to see patterns in the pigeon shit on the sidewalk. And then there was Roy

Halliday, he thought. The Marshal took him, what, three weeks ago? More? He'd have to ask his father.

First thing, though, was to talk to John Dash. Mulling it over, Jared decided he didn't want to go meet Dash alone. He wasn't sure what was going on between Dash and Sharkskin Billy, but if Billy was going to start waving a knife around, it was time to play things a little cooler. "Boys," he said. "Feel like a couple?"

"I'm in," Jem said. He wasn't twenty-one until September, but if there was a bar in Detroit checking ID since the war began, Jared didn't know of it. He looked at Felton.

"Where'd you have in mind?" Felton asked.

There was the problem. Raking through his memories of the bar where he'd gone with Dash, Jared thought he remembered black faces. "I know a place," he said, with more certainty than he felt, but what the hell; if there was trouble, they'd go somewhere else, and Dash would know to follow them.

The eagle shit on Friday, went the saying, and the Friday-night crowd at Joe Sent Me was a-jingle with the eagle's leavings even though the day's overcast had turned into a steady rain. The juke was pumping out Tommy Dorsey, the floor was awash in spilled beer, and Jared had to turn sideways to wedge himself up against the bar and get drinks for the three of them. Jem and Felton were off in a corner under a framed newspaper photo of a bloodied Reuther and Frankensteen, taken right after the Battle of the Overpass six years ago. Jared wondered at the symbolism of this—celebration or commemoration? No way to tell, but the crowd sure had the look of men who were reaping the benefits of Reuther's courage: steel-toed boots, stained clothes, and stained knuckles. By the time he'd delivered the drinks, Jared had decided not to worry about it.

"See the Black Legion anywhere?" he said as he handed Felton a beer.

Felton cracked a smile—if the crowd was by no means a meeting of the Urban League, there was still a fair bit of pepper mixed into the salt—but Jem took offense. "Don't go bad-mouthing the Legion," he said. "They got me this job."

"How many niggers they pull out of the line in front of you?" Felton wanted to know. His smile was gone.

"I ain't gonna hear this, Felton," Jem said. "You can complain about colored folks getting the short end all you want, and I don't deny it, but you try being a hillbilly coming up here. It ain't no easier."

"All right," Jared cut in. "I shouldn't have brought it up. We all got a job, let's toast that."

They did, but Jem couldn't leave it alone. "You try coming up here with everything you own in your back pocket, city people wouldn't piss on you if you was on fire, see if you don't need a little help from the Legion. All they ever did was get people work."

"Is that why the National Guard was out at Sojourner Truth this spring?" Felton asked. "Seems to me it was Legion boys with baseball bats in those pickets."

Jared leaned forward so he was between them. "Fellas, I didn't come out here to fight over Sojourner Truth again. That's all settled. The Legion's a sore spot with both of you, okay, but they're not here and we are. How about we just have a beer and bitch about Swerdlow?"

He looked back and forth between them, wondering just when everybody had gotten so damn thin skinned. Two and a half years they'd worked on the Frankenline in relative harmony, and now the last couple of weeks Jem and Felton had been bickering nonstop. It felt like something was coming to a head between them— between southern whites and southern blacks all over Detroit, was the truth—and Jared hated to see it happen, but he was getting sick and tired of mediating all the time. He had his own problems.

"Swerdlow," Jem said. "I hate that fat son of a bitch."

Okay. That was a start. Jared relaxed a little, looking back over the crowd, and there was John Dash, tilting his head toward the back of the bar. "Don't go anywhere, fellas," Jared said, following Dash through a swinging door that led to a storage room, which in turn led through another door to a stubby pier. They stood under a wooden awning, listening to the rain and the soft lap of the river against the pilings under their feet.

"So what have you been up to?" Dash asked. "If I didn't know better, I'd think you brought some Building G muscle along because you didn't trust me."

Jared laughed, mostly because this was the second time in a month someone had mistaken Felton for some kind of goon, and Felton was about the least goon-like of all the workers in the Rouge. "They're busy refighting the Civil War," he said. "You could stick a knife in me and leave me out here and they wouldn't notice until I didn't show up for work tomorrow."

It might have been true, but Jared played it up because he wanted to diffuse any tension that might arise when he brought up Sharkskin Billy.

"You worried I'm going to stick a knife in you?" Dash asked. When Jared didn't answer right away, he lifted an eyebrow. "What's going on?"

Right, Jared thought. You just happened to be driving down Twelfth Street at three thirty in the morning the other night, and now you want to hear what story I'm going to tell. Okay. "Well, I talked to Swerdlow's buddy Billy, and he didn't exactly spell it out for me, but I got the distinct impression that he was some kind of spy for a guy name of Schickelgruber. So I'm starting to put some things together here, but here's one thing I don't get. You're keeping an eye on everything, you wanted me to let you know what Swerdlow and Billy were up to. Why?"

There it was. Here I go gambling again, Jared thought. He pictured Jem and Felton looking around for him, asking if anybody had seen where he'd gone. Maybe they would come out onto this splintery pier and find him with a knife in his liver—or maybe he'd already be floating down the river. One of them would go and tell Colleen, probably Felton because he was a grown man instead of a kid with a grudge against the world, and Emily would grow up with the story of her father being murdered at the back step of a waterfront dive. And I did this on purpose, Jared thought, incredulous at himself. Why the hell didn't I tell Swerdlow to piss up a rope? Two million people in swollen wartime Detroit, not one of them can't find work if he wants it.

Something that wanted Jared to believe it was a flash of intuition danced just beyond the range of his ability to articulate it. It felt like the first time he'd ever confronted algebra, as if he were fighting his way through a membrane in his head, and on the other side was a brand-new way of thinking about the world.

He never had gotten the hang of algebra.

Dash was watching him. Jared thought he might comment on Jared's woolgathering, but all he said was, "It's interesting, isn't it? What're they up to?"

"Don't run me around. Why do you want to know?"

"What did Billy do to you, Jared? You're acting scared."

"You're goddamn right I'm scared. I have my boss tied up with a guy who I think is a Nazi spy, and either one of them could point the finger at me. And if they did, the only guy I could go to would be you, and for all I know you're a fucking Kraut spy, too. Plus my wife said she'd walk out on me if she thought my daughter was in danger, and I'll tell you what, the whole thing makes me wish I'd just put a bullet in Swerdlow's head a month ago."

"Billy wouldn't have liked that too much."

"At least I'd've known right away."

"Did he threaten you?"

"Yeah." Embarrassed at both his fear of Billy and the way he wanted to lap up Dash's protectiveness, Jared left it at that.

"You want me to do something about it?"

The question hung there. The drone of airplane engines drifted down from the sky. Out on the river, a freighter moved ghostlike through the rain, the lights on its superstructure haloed and glittering. "Who are you, Dash? Is that your real name?"

"Nope. And it doesn't matter what my real name is. For our purposes, John Dash is the guy you need to deal with."

"Why do I need to deal with you?"

"Well, let's see. You've got a spy threatening you; your boss might fire you; you're tied up with the OEI and you don't know what they want from you. That's a lot for anyone to have on his plate. Maybe I can help."

"What's the trade?"

"First you make a decision. Yes or no."

What kind of debt did you assume when you asked someone to kill for you? "You still haven't told me who you are."

"I'm a free agent where you're concerned, Jared. I'm not on Billy's team, and I don't work for the Marshal. Can't say much more than that." Dash finished his beer and flipped the bottle into the river. Reflected light from windows along the riverfront caught in the ripples from the splash. "Tell you what. Lie low over the weekend, spend time with your family, come talk to me on Monday. How's that sound?"

"All right," Jared said. "Hey, what do you know about salt?"

"Salt?" Dash frowned. "You mean table salt?"

"Rock salt."

"I don't know a thing about salt. Should I?"

"Beats me."

Dash shrugged and walked off along the side of the building, fading into the rain. When Jared went back inside, Jem and Felton were gone. He drove home and lay in bed, mind churning, and fell asleep to dream about 1805.

* * *

A blacksmith beats the curve into a horseshoe. From the corner of his eye he sees motion in the window of his smithy, and turns to see the Dwarf. He drops the unfinished shoe, which leaves a blackened rune in the plank floor. Smoke from the Dwarf's burning gaze pools against his ceiling—then it is gone, and he dumps a bucket of water over the length of iron charring his floor. Leaning out the window, he sees black handprints on the frame, and a single long black hair curls over the sill. As soon as he notices it, the hair vanishes in a tiny puff of smoke.

He walks out into the street, looking left and right, mouth open to call his wife away from her mending. The smith knows—Jared knows—what happened to Cadillac and Dalyell; he's seen the ghosts of Dalyell's men while hunting along the banks of Bloody Run. I haven't challenged the Dwarf, he thinks; it has no cause to bear me a grudge.

There's a stir down around the corner. Shouts, a single rifle shot. Jared groans in his sleep, and somewhere in 1805 Detroit a baker's assistant knocks ashes out of the bowl of his pipe. The ashes fall to the hay-strewn floor of the stable where he has gone for a quiet smoke; a thin haze of flour settles around his feet. He gets up and returns to work, and behind him an ember begins to feed.

By the end of June 11, 1805, every building in Detroit has burned except a stone warehouse at the edge of the river, and those hours pass in front of Jared's dreaming mind like a movie, a newsreel. There are the golems, muscling buckets up from the river. He watches the fire leap and slither from roof to roof, watches sparks swirl up from lost buildings and shower down behind the bucket brigades, who, limned by fire in the fall of evening, put Jared in mind of steelworkers backlit by a foundry pour. Somewhere cattle are screaming. The fire, it never stopped burning, he thinks. Every spark is the eye of the Dwarf watching over the city he must destroy again and again. In his bed, 138 years exactly after the fire, he sweats as if he is passing futile buckets up the line and watching the water flash into steam.

He is feeling for the bedside clock before he's fully awake. The feel of it floods him with relief; at some point along the journey from asleep to awake, Jared has convinced himself that he's falling into 1805, that when he wakes up it will be to witness a sooty dawn with the handle of a bucket cutting into the palm of his hand. But no, he's got his alarm clock in his hand, solid and round, the crack across its face rasping along the pad of his thumb. June 12 now, he thinks. He's never dreamed on an anniversary before, and he's never felt during a dream that he was about to be enveloped in a real moment, dragged away from his tangled sheets in 1943 to face the uncertain future of a smoking ruin and Indians in the forest who re-member Pontiac. Incorrigibly the certainty arises within him that in the dream world he's left behind, a real ruin smokes and awaits the coming of Judge Augustus Brevoort Woodward, who laid out a new city over the carbonized remnant of the old.

What's happening to me? he wonders.

"Hmm?" Colleen stirs. At the foot of the bed Claude snuffles in his sleep.

Jared sets the alarm clock back on the nightstand. "Nothing, honey." He lies back, slides his arm under the back of her neck. She rolls into him, and he drifts as light returns to the sky here in the troubled Asshole of Democracy that is his home.

Emily climbs up onto the bed at six thirty sharp, burbling about a spider in her room. She's not scared of it, in fact wants Jared to catch it so she can get a better look. He gets a jelly jar from the kitchen and finds a loose envelope in the stack of bills on the kitchen table, and they go spider hunting. It isn't where Emily saw it, and for a kid who is usually all sunshine in the mornings she doesn't have much of a sense of humor about this event. "I bet there's a whole bunch of spiders outside on the patio," Jared says. "Let's catch one of those and you can look at it."

This ploy almost doesn't work because Emily is halfway through a story about a conversation she was having with the spider, and the idea of leaving their interaction unfinished is the worst thing she's ever heard of. "Well, honey," Jared says. "Why don't we go ask one of his friends where we can find him?"

She hasn't thought of this. Her face knits up in comically fierce concentration. "Okay," she says, and runs for the side door, Claude right behind like a prick-eared yellow shadow. Jared follows, still in his boxer shorts, and has a sleep-dopey intuition that Mrs. Pelletier will disapprove. There they are, though, out on the still-uneven bricks of the patio, peering among the peonies and greenery for the spiders that must be there. Claude takes the opportunity to water some of the weeds Jared hasn't pulled. One yellow-and-black-striped specimen looks promising, but Jared can't figure out a good way to get it without wrecking the fine dewy geometry of its web, an action Emily vehemently prohibits. So they search the ground, poke at the stems of unidentified weeds, and at last imprison a big brown muscular-looking spider in the jar. It's an athletic little critter, racing around the interior of the jar's rim until it slips and falls to the bottom, and then trying again. Jared takes it inside and looks for something more substantial to put over the mouth of the jar—aha, the checkbook. The exhibit goes on the kitchen table, close enough to Emily's booster seat that she can get a good look but not quite close enough for her to reach out and tip the jar over—this last precaution not occurring to Jared until Colleen threatens that the spider safari will end badly if the spider escapes and she happens to kill it with Emily in the room.

Daughter transfixed and wife skeptical but acquiescent, Jared escapes to the bathroom to take a leak. It's one for the ages, makes him wish he had a stopwatch so he could brag about it later. Often

Emily stands outside the bathroom door talking to him while he's doing his business, and he contemplates catching a spider first thing every morning so he can drain his bladder in peace. It'd be tougher during the winter, since Colleen is a sworn enemy of every invertebrate that enters the house, but Jared indulges himself in a fanciful listing of what he would be willing to do in return for Colleen's permission to keep a spider or two around. Fix the drip under the kitchen sink. Level the patio bricks. Stop baiting his mother-in-law. Well, no. Well, maybe.

Empty at last, Jared opens the door so Emily—who has remembered that she's congenitally incapable of leaving him alone while he's in the bathroom—can affix herself to his legs. He walks her into the bedroom and finds a pair of pants that aren't too caked with clay. The laundry pile in the corner of the bedroom tends to look like a sculpture of the aftermath of an artillery barrage by the end of the week, and the room smells like a cave. He detaches his daughter, struggles into a pair of petrified Levi's, sticks her back on, and walks back out into the kitchen, grinning down at her like a fool while she hangs on to his front pockets and bounces up and down on the tops of his feet.

"So a couple of the guys from the line are going fishing tomorrow," he says to Colleen when they're out in the kitchen, and immediately realizes he's made a terrible mistake. One, he's lied—but what the hell is he supposed to do, tell her he's headed off on a clandestine mission with a talking bird? The real problem is that he's told a lie that will inflame his daughter with a desire to accompany him on an outing that obviously has to be solo. What a heel.

"I think that's great," Colleen says, which makes him feel even heelier, or more heelish. "I always worry that you don't have friends."

"Fishing!" Emily crows, bouncing up and down. "We go fishing!"

"This is grown-up fishing, baby girl," Jared says. "We'll go fishing some other time."

"We go fishing!"

"Yes, we will, but not tomorrow."

Colleen scoops Emily up and sets her back in front of the spider. "You haven't told this spider about meeting his friend," she says. Emily looks like she might contest this blatant effort to distract her, but she is two, and she was in fact talking to this spider's friend twenty minutes ago. Almost at once she's babbling away at this new spider, whose name is CeeCee. Claude pays close attention to them both, the end of his tail flipping back and forth whenever the spider does another lap around the jar.

Grateful for her intervention, Jared still wants to have the last word on the topic of his social life. "I have friends," he says.

"No, you don't. You have lots of acquaintances, but who are your friends? Really."

Come to think of it, that's a pretty good question, but Jared has no desire whatsoever to devote any thought to it. He can tell Colleen's about to get wound up on the topic; diversionary countermeasures are called for. "I see my folks, I see the guys at work. A guy doesn't have to be Arlene Bannister to be happy."

Just as he's hoped, the mention of Arlene sets Colleen off on another train of thought. Jared has surmised that Colleen knows of the undercurrent of attraction between her husband and the second of the Three Eens. "Funny you should bring her up," Colleen says, a little danger in her voice, and Jared reconsiders the wisdom of his diversion.

"She collects friends like people collect stamps," Jared says. "I don't mean that she's not a real friend to you, I'm just saying that it's important to her to be able to say she's got a ton of friends. I'm not like that."

There is suspicion in Colleen's gaze. Jared shrugs, as if to say *Hey, it is what it is,* and she decides not to pursue it. "So who are these guys you're fishing with?" she asks.

"Jem and Felton," Jared says, because he can't think of anyone else, and his father long ago drummed into him the importance of keeping a lie internally consistent.

"Where are you going?"

"Don't know," Jared says, truthfully. "Someplace Jem knows."

"Okay. If you're taking the car, how about you drop us off at your parents'?"

"You got it, babe." Jared gives her a kiss, smelling the last little bit of sleep wafting from her body. In that instant of absorption, Emily knocks over the jar containing CeeCee the spider.

CHAPTER 14

Jared heads to the ball game with his father that hazy afternoon. "You hear Pantelleria surrendered?" Jared asks his dad.

"What's Pantelleria?"

Marty Cleaves doesn't read the papers except for Ernie Pyle, who is still in Tunisia.

"It's the island we needed to get out of the way so we can invade Sicily. Once we get Sicily, it's right across the Strait of Messina to the boot. Then straight on to Berlin."

"Ah," says Marty Cleaves. "Who's pitching?"

Jared looks at the program. "Hal White."

The Tigers have lost five in a row. There is hope after yesterday's rainout, which gave the team's ragged arms a day of rest and set up a Sunday doubleheader in which the Tigers will have Trucks and Bridges on the mound, but only a fool gets too optimistic after a five-game losing streak. In the pages of the *Free Press,* Iffy the Dopester has made the transition from avuncular cynicism to outright disgust. He compares Stubby Overmire unfavorably to his grandniece Ophelia. That guy has the best job in Detroit, Jared thinks. He can say anything he wants, and he doesn't even have to put his name to it. Unlike Jared Cleaves, who can't say what he wants to say and doesn't get to put his name on the work he does every day.

"So the Marshal yanked a guy from our line yesterday," he says. "I think it was because he worked in a salt mine before."

"That so?"

"What's going on down there, Pop?"

"All I do is drive a truck, kid. They don't consult with me."

"But you were talking about Roy Halliday a while ago, and now there's this Polack the Marshal took. . . . Seems weird, doesn't it?"

"OEI want you to ask around about this?"

"Pop, I'm in some trouble. If there's something going on down there, I'd appreciate you telling me."

His father looks at him. "What kind of trouble? Are we talking about the Dwarf?"

"It's always the Dwarf. I'm . . . I've been having dreams."

This earns him a stranger look. "What kind of dreams?"

"For a long time I've dreamed about the Dwarf. Lately it's been different, though. More intense, and there's . . ." Jared looked around at the sparsely populated bleachers. ". . . golems in these dreams about the Dwarf."

Marty Cleaves has probably never heard the word *golem* in his life, but he can put two and two together. "Golems are the things you build."

Jared's chest unknots. What is it they say about confession? "Yeah, and now they're in these dreams I've always had. Last night they weren't, but I was dreaming about the Dwarf, and . . . you know how they say that if you die in a dream, you really die? I had that kind of feeling about the dream I had last night. Not dying, but like the dream was absorbing me. Like part of me was splitting off and staying there."

"What's this got to do with the OEI and my mine?"

"I don't know. Christ, I don't know." Jared is suddenly and des-

perately glad that he is with his father. Marty Cleaves hasn't been a
great dad, but he's always been there when Jared really needs him,
and now at twenty-eight years of age Jared needs his father like he
never has. "Dad," he says, and clenches his jaw, fighting not to cry.

"Hey, kid." His father puts a hand on his shoulder. "Hey. Easy.
Come on, tell the old man."

Jared does. A to Z, marital troubles and German spies and the
OEI and all the rest of it. As the words leave his mouth he understands how absurd it all is, and he hasn't even mentioned the possibility that really frightens him. Finished for the moment, he stands
up. On the field, the Tigers aren't looking terrible for a change.
Jared walks up the rows of seats to the closest spectator. "Say, man.
Got a cigarette?" Lucky burning in his mouth, he sits back down
with his father and waits for wisdom, Marty Cleaves style.

"I still don't get what this has to do with my mine," Marty says,
and Jared has to admit that he doesn't, either. "So what do you want
me to say? You're in trouble, all right. One thing I'll tell you: keep
that woman. You've got a little girl, and you need to keep that
woman. I did a lot of things wrong in my life, and I'm long past
when apologizing makes a difference, but I'll tell you what, I held
on to your mother. You're going to take a lesson from your father,
take that one."

"Yeah," Jared says. He's wrung out and shaky. "I know."

"Far as the rest of it goes . . . boy. Stay away from this Billy character, but don't get too close to Dash, either. Or Meadows. Any of
them. Seems to me like the only one you can trust far as you'd
throw a piano is the bird."

"Unless he's the tengu."

"Jared my boy, if he's the tengu, then you're just playing out the
string. Like this bunch of cripples." Marty waves down at the field;
Jared realizes he's paid not the slightest attention to the game.
What's the score?

"Pop," Jared says. "That's the problem. What if . . ."

He can't make himself say it, but rising to the occasion, Marty Cleaves says it for him. "What if the OEI, Meadows, even the bird, are gaming you? What if they know all about Dash and the other guy and you're bait? Is that it?"

That's part of it, Jared thinks. "They're in trouble, Pop. I'm a little worried that they're going to use the Dwarf to fake something that'll put them back center stage."

"They don't need to fake the Dwarf, boy," says Marty Cleaves. "I'd be more worried that the Dwarf is faking them."

"Jesus," Jared murmurs. This is a brand-new angle on the situation. Trust Marty Cleaves to come up with a perspective that makes a bad situation possibly worse.

"I got myself in a couple of tricky situations when I was running liquor during Prohibition," Marty says. "One time I thought the Purples were going to punch my ticket because they burned down that old place on Munger Road. You remember that place?" Jared nods. "They killed those boys out there, and left a gunsel waiting for me next time I stopped by. He asked me was I in on it, and this was one of the only times in my life I told the truth just because I couldn't think of a good lie. Saved my bacon, too. In on what, I asked him, and he looked at me for a long time, long enough that my balls crawled right up into my gut and I was wishing I'd written a will. Then he said, Okay, maybe you ought to try another line of work." Like the golem and me the other night, Jared's thinking. Maybe I ought to try another line of work, at least if Moises doesn't even believe that we're making any difference. "That's why I went back to the mine. I always said it was the Dwarf, but it was that afternoon. Sun kind of slanting down from the hayloft, and I'm in the barn with a gun pointed at me. Saw in the bathroom mirror that night that I still had a little smear of oil on my forehead from the gun barrel, where he'd pressed it in a little." Jared's father mimics the motion now, leaning forward with one arm crooked out in front of him. "Was right after that I took you and your mother to Maine, and I'll tell you what, we almost stayed there. Would have if your mother wasn't so attached to that idiot cousin of hers down in Melvindale. I was working at the mine by the next Wednesday. Shoot, and now you tell me that the goddamn Dwarf followed me even there."

"Did I say that?"

"Pay attention, boy. This is all the Dwarf's doing." Jared's father grips his shoulder, long fingers digging under Jared's collarbone, eyes aflame with the fervor of sudden enlightenment. "He's set you up. OEI's got nothing to do with that. That's what that night was about, why you hurt your fingers. It's all been waiting since 1919, believe you me."

"Come on, Pop."

"I'm serious. All these years," Marty Cleaves says in wonderment, "I thought the Dwarf was after me, and now I figure out it was you all along. What a lot of time I wasted."

Does realization always come too late to help? Jared wonders. "Not wasted," he says. "You took it on yourself. Now I'm a grown man, and it's time to face up to it."

Marty shakes his head. "Wish it had been like that. Truth is, the Dwarf's an excuse. Always was for me, and look, Cadillac made his own mess and blamed it on the Dwarf. Same with Hull, same with Dalyell, Christ, nobody with any sense would have tried to get the drop on Pontiac in his own goddamn woods. I can't believe Rogers went along with it. He should have known better."

He sees Jared grinning at him. "What?"

"You were paying attention when I wrote that essay."

"Hell yes, I was. What kind of a father ignores his son's schoolwork? What I was saying was okay, maybe they saw the Dwarf . . . no, all right, I've seen it so I'll believe they saw it, too. But just because you saw the Dwarf doesn't mean you can blame everything on it. There's one of your old man's mistakes you should know better than to repeat."

Mulling this over, Jared finds himself nodding. "Okay, Pop. I take the point."

"Don't just take the point. Act like you believe it." Jared's father jabs him in the chest. "Believe it. But right now you have to go to work."

It's the top of the seventh, Tigers actually threatening to win. Jared has to be on the Frankenline in half an hour. "All right, let's go," he says, but Marty Cleaves shakes his head.

"I'll catch the streetcar," he says. "Goddamn Dwarf's not going to make me miss this game. Not when the Tigers are ahead."

Jared and Felton took their dinner break on the roof of Building G. Colleen, with her typical resourcefulness, had cobbled together a pretty decent meat loaf that tasted like meat even though it was mostly bread and eggs, and he was enjoying the last of it while he took in the view of the diabolical engine that was Detroit. Cars, planes, ships; steam, smoke, fire. "If we win this war," he said, thinking of the conversation he'd had with Moises the week before, "Eisenhower will get all the credit, but we're the ones really doing the job. Right here." He spread his arms, taking in the whole of the city. "Detroit's going to win this war if it gets won at all."

"All this messing in spy shit's got you confused," Felton needled him. "Next thing, you'll be buying war bonds, plaster your house with posters in case Emily starts talking about troop movements."

"It doesn't bother you that you're not fighting?" Jared asked.

"Not a damn bit. I'm forty-two years old. War's for the young men. I can do more good making golems." Felton bit into his sandwich, talked to Jared as he chewed. "Is that why you're dancing around with all this cloak-and-dagger stuff? Because you're not waiting to hit the beach at Sicily?"

"I feel like I should serve."

"You got a two-year-old girl, that's who you need to serve."

"You have any kids, Felton?"

"No." Felton took another bite of his sandwich, and this time chewed and swallowed before answering. "I was married when I was younger, but my wife died. Cancer. We never had kids."

Jared hadn't anticipated this turn in the conversation, and—selfish but true—didn't find it particularly welcome in the midst of his ode on patriotism and the grimy magnificence of his home city. He fell silent and finished his sandwich. "Sorry," he said after a while.

"Yeah," Felton said. "It was a sorry thing."

"Forty-two, though. That's not too late."

"Too late to care," Felton said.

There was no answer to this. Jared held up an apple, yet more evidence of Colleen's mysterious puissance in the alchemy of food. "Want some?" When Felton nodded, he gripped the apple in both hands and with a sharp twist snapped it in half along the axis of its core.

"Pretty good trick," Felton said.

"My old man showed it to me when I was a kid. I practiced for years before my hands were strong enough to do it."

They munched down the apple, core and all, spitting the seeds out over the edge of the roof. "I'm serious, though," Jared said, wanting to pick up the previous line of conversation. "We're going to win because guys like you and me can pour more steel than the Japs and the Germans."

"Plus they can't get here to bomb the hell out of us like we're doing to them," Felton reminded him. "And I'd rather lose the war than pour steel. Damn, but that's miserable work. Even without the imps."

"You're crazy. Way the Japs treat the Chinese and Koreans, you think colored people would all work in banks if they won?"

Felton looked down and shook his head, as if he could not believe the idiocy of the people fate had conspired to present him. For a moment, Jared thought he was looking at Marty Cleaves in black-face, but that wasn't a comparison that did either man justice. "Foundry's a shitty place, is all I'm saying. You never heard of exaggerating for effect?"

"Not talking about losing the war, I didn't."

"Well, now you did. And the way this town is lately, I'm not sure how much I'm exaggerating."

Here we go again, headed into a conversation that I don't want to have, Jared thought. "You talking about Jem?"

"I'm talking about Jem and the half a million other cracker morons like him. Seems like everybody in Detroit's spoiling for a fight right now. I can't hardly walk to the store for bread without some damn fool wanting to fight the Civil War all over again."

Hearing this echo of the joke he'd made to Dash the other night made the hairs on Jared's arms stand up. He was sensitive to coincidence lately, for reasons that he couldn't articulate but vaguely suspected to result from talking to Meadows about the Dwarf. "People are touchy," he agreed. "It's hot, ration stamps are tighter than a virgin midget, and even if you got money there's nothing to spend it on but booze."

"There's that," Felton said with a nod. "Plus you got the Packard strike and the riots down south, now there was the Zoot Suit thing in LA. Tell you what, it feels like something's brewing here."

"What, a riot?"

"Don't know. Something. You get this many pissed-off people in one place, something's got to give."

They stood up to head back to the Frankenline. Jared picked tarry gravel from his pants. "Hope you're wrong," he said. "That's just what the Germans would want."

A golem shouldered past them as they walked back in through the bay doors, moving out into the dark to wait for the morning train. Jared saw Jem coming around the corner from wherever he'd gone to eat, and waited for him to catch up. His skin felt weirdly charged by the golem's passing. "Might as well be us," Felton commented.

Jem heard him. "Hell, no," he said. "We can talk, and I ain't never seen no golem girls."

"Jeweler gets sick again, you just might."

Laughing, they went back to work.

Sunday morning bright and early Jared caught a spider for Emily and they took it over to Marty and CeeCee's, Jared secretly gloating over the effect an arachnid guest would have on his mother, whose attitude toward creatures with more than four legs was even more antagonistic than Colleen's. "What in God's name are you doing?" she snapped when he came in the door with the jar.

"Ask your granddaughter," Jared said, calculating—correctly, as it turned out—that the spider's chances of survival wholly depended on Emily's backing. CeeCee turned to look at Emily, and Emily yanked the jar from Jared's hands and held it up so her grandmother could see the friend of the friend of the spider she'd talked to before in her room. CeeCee shot Jared a venomous look, but her heart wasn't in it; by the time Emily had set the spider up in their kitchen, the two generations of Cleaves women were deeply involved in what Emily and this spider—named CeeCee like the rest of them, which brought out a gruffness in Jared's mother that he recognized as her automatic response to a compliment she couldn't admit to appreciating—had planned for their trip to the moon. Victorious, Jared escaped back home, where Petey was perched on the fence. Jared wasn't sure what you said to a shaman bird in this situation, so he just sat in the car with the windows open until Petey flapped over and settled on the passenger seat.

"Where you been?" he croaked.

"Had to foist the girls off on my parents," Jared said. "Where are we going?"

"Take Grand River," Petey said. "Get out of town."

Jared drove and Petey directed, all the way out past where he'd taken Emily fishing, deep into the stands of regrown forest that ringed the city. The Hop-Frog's windows were down, and the breeze ruffled Petey's feathers. Jared enjoyed the smells of trees and earth and even manure. "Farmy," he said, thinking of the long-ago trip with his father to Mount Clemens. He felt now as he had then, along for a ride with no thought of control over what was to happen. You agree to take a trip with a talking bird, you pretty much give up any idea that you're in charge.

They hit Highway 59, and Petey told Jared to head west. Half an hour later they were in a little town called Howell, and Petey started giving Jared rights and lefts, the last of which ran them down a dead-end dirt road. Jared could smell water, and when he ran out of road there was a tiny cabin, painted a color Jared realized right then he'd always thought of as Hunting Camp Red, visible through the trees to the left. "This must be the place," he said. Petey hopped out the window and flew to the cabin's porch. When Jared got there, Petey was on a windowsill next to the door. He cocked his head at the doorknob, and Jared went inside. The cabin was a single room, not much bigger than an ambitious ice-fishing shack, with a chair, a propane stove, a table, and a couch that might have folded out into a bed. The plank floor was partially covered with oval rag rugs that put Jared in mind of a hunting trip he and his father had taken to a second cousin's cottage in Tustin, way up north. Old license plates hung from nails in the yellow-pine walls, along with a pair of ice tongs and various other rusted objects Jared couldn't identify but thought might be kitchen implements from the previous century. Interspersed among the bric-a-brac were several sets of antlers and what looked like a mummified pair of bear paws. The room smelled like old wood smoke. A fireplace centered the wall to the left of the door, facing the couch, and there were enough afghans on the chair to hide a grown man.

Petey perched on Jared's shoulder as Jared shut the door. "Question for you," he croaked.

"Okay."

"I said I had to peck out your eye, you let me?"

Jared flashed on Casimir the salt miner, plucked out of Building G, and also on something Herschel Fontenot had said: a one-eyed guy in a hat. He wasn't wearing a hat, but the question unsettled him anyway. "Hell, no, I wouldn't."

"Good," Petey said. "Have to kill you."

"You're a bird. You couldn't kill me."

"Awk. Kid yourself." Petey flapped over to the back of the armchair that faced the hearth. "Start a fire."

"Are you serious?"

"Fire."

"No, about killing me."

"You don't think I could?" Petey cocked his head.

"What do you weigh, a pound?"

Petey whistled. His one black eye bored into Jared. "Okay," Jared said. "Okay. I don't want to know." He peeled bark from a couple of the logs stacked next to the hearth, then took out his pocketknife and shaved some tinder from the logs themselves. There were matches on the mantel, over which a muzzle-loader and a bamboo fishing rod formed a large *X,* and the wood was well seasoned; the fire started on the first try. Smoke billowed out of the fireplace, and Jared worked the flue lever back and forth, but the chimney wouldn't draw.

"Leave it," Petey said.

Jared kept yanking on the lever. "We're going to choke to death."

"No," Petey said. "Need the smoke. Sit in the chair."

"What, are you going to peck my eye out now? Thought I answered that question."

"Sit," Petey squawked. Jared did. The smoke stung his eyes, and he closed them. "Good," Petey said. "Keep 'em closed. Hear me."

"I'm listening."

"Don't listen. Hear."

"What are we doing?"

"Awk," Petey screeched in his ear. "Don't listen. Don't talk. Hear."

Jared did, letting the hiss and crackle of the fire, the muted creak of the chair frame, the sound of his breath in his head thread their way into his mind. Something broke, silently

Petey is whispering, but what occupies Jared's mind is the way the smoke doesn't seem to bother him anymore. He draws it into his lungs and feels the walls of his mind collapse like wet plaster. You've done this before, Petey says, and through his surprise at the fact that Petey speaks in a human voice Jared tries to form a question. Sure you have, Petey says. Jared looks for him, but he isn't there, and Petey tells him to cut it out.

But is this—

Cut it out.

They're walking together through an unfamiliar landscape, following a creekbed that winds among steep hills. Limestone overhangs hide caves at every bend in the creek; the water is greenish but clear, with silvery fish darting above a pebbled bottom. Jared can feel Petey walking next to him, but when he looks there's nothing there but low-hanging branches, thick with the pale green buds of spring.

It's June—

Cut it out.

Jared looks for Petey again, doesn't see him, keeps walking along the narrow path, nodding in agreement to something his father said a long time ago: a moment made for hindsight.

Bad attitude, Petey says. You want to go home?

Kind of.

Under one of the overhangs, Jared sees himself sitting in the chair from the cabin. Petey leans close, beak right up against his ear. If you want to go home, Jared hears Petey say—and he can see the bird's beak moving—do it now. Wait for Billy or Dash to come for you.

Is that—

You want to talk or walk?

Jared walks, passing the vision of himself. The hills wind lower and he finds himself in a floodplain, roughly plowed and sown with corn. A teenage girl is tying a wet bit of cloth to a cornstalk, and when Petey starts to speak Jared shushes him. I know.

And he does know. He remembers exactly what the Piston Doctor told him in another dream, the memory coming bolt-necked and implacable as Frankenstein. My mother, Jared thinks. It's because of her—

Not just her, Petey says. Her and the Dwarf. Then Petey seems to reconsider. Unless it's because of her that the Dwarf came looking for you.

This is momentous news—and somewhere in the recesses of his mind Jared is linking it to Marty Cleaves' comment about the OEI and his mother—but at the moment he's too busy suppressing giggles to give it the attention it deserves. His dream of the Piston Doctor and the rubber-testicled Dwarf is fresh and present now, and he's laughing at the story as if he's never heard it before, which he sort of hasn't because this isn't a dream, not really—he's not asleep, he's probably asphyxiating from the plugged chimney in the cabin somewhere the other side of Pontiac with an ensorcelled crow—or raven—deciding whether or not to peck out one of his eyes. Jared loses the train of thought and settles for the comfortable pronouncement that This Is Different. There's his mother, and the uncle he's never met, and his grandmother who's been dead for how long, since about when he was born, and there goddammit is the Dwarf peering through the half-grown cornstalks at the whole scene while his mother goggles in disbelief at the magical verdict: she will marry Michael Cleaves who has drowned in the stream that flows past Jared's feet.

Petey says Don't—

—but Jared does. This is impossible, he thinks, and it shouldn't work but it does. Jared falls through the floor of the dream, Petey calling him back, but he's far gone in this moment tailor-made for hindsight, and in the dark, dark subbasements of his mind he finds a way.

Jesus Christ. Petey, what is this?

It's not a dream. These feelings, what are they, who is feeling them?

To stretch, to spread—impossible in this cave of steel and stone. The right angles where the walls and ceiling meet cut him; he flinches from them, and his fury grows. He feels the thrum of the strength in his body, increasing by the day, his bones creaking at the pace of their growth. He rears up, crashes his head into the unyielding ceiling, snaps at the steel beams; his teeth score them but they do not break. They will; he is nearly strong enough; but it may not happen in time, for he realizes that he is the target of an expectation that he wants to meet without knowing what it is.

A vast inherited wisdom has flowered in his mind, a chorus of his forebears' voices telling him what he is, whence he has come. He senses that they are . . . not lying, for that would require the intent to mislead. Mistaken. They are mistaken. Something about his circumstance differs from theirs in a manner incomprehensible to them. This angers him, and he snaps at the remains of the beasts that are his food. The spoiled taste of the meat is repellent. His ancestors battled heroes, incinerated cities, clawed spaces in the earth, and learned patience; but patience does not come naturally to him, not when his deep memories ring so jarringly against the unnatural geometry of this cave where he has come to self-awareness.

He lowers his head to sniff at the floor of artificial stone. The scent prickles in his nostrils, and he snorts out fire.

Time has become inexact during his confinement, but he knows that the humans have not come in many days, since he took three of them for a meal along with the beasts. Feeling their lives drain between his teeth, he had become conscious of the pride of his ancestors, and it filled him with a savage joy together with a compulsion to do it again. Feed, not on the beasts but on his captors.

(and here Jared knows something in his nerve endings, that he has wanted this feeling his entire life, this sensation of taking from an enemy the single thing the enemy is most loath to give, which is at once his pride and his life, at the moment when the two cannot be disentangled. This dormant ache, and the Dwarf, always the Dwarf—these have driven the twenty-eight years of his life—

Cut it out—)

Chaos has a scent, and he smells it now, borne upstream on the subterranean river of time. His ancestors' voices are greedy for the nourishment of disorder, and their call can no more be resisted than the first crack in the eggshell. He inhales, groans his desire, exults in the vibrations of the steel walls. What is coming he does not know; but he knows he must go to meet it. He gouges the floor and groans, then realizes what he has done and bends to see. Understanding glimmers briefly and is lost in the rush of desire to know what that scent is that torments him. What approaches, and why?

I am of this place and not of this place, he thinks. The notion shocks him, but it has the weight of truth; it settles into his apprehension of the world as if it has been waiting for him to give it voice. He has traveled a great distance, been born in a land distant and strange. What approaches is both invasion and rescue.

The dichotomy tantalizes and angers and frustrates him. His ancestors are puzzled. Their experience holds nothing like this. Mine, he thinks. This place is mine, and who would destroy it would destroy me.

As one, his ancestors—

(*my* ancestors, Jared thinks, rolling the word and the idea around in his head while Petey tries to shut him up, Jared testing the idea of *ancestor* that he's never considered—does he have ancestors? His grandparents came to Arkansas from Ireland via Brooklyn via Louisville via St. Louis, and all along the way there were Germans and Indians and Frenchmen and sure he can admit it every so often a Negro banging their way into the once-upon-a-time pure Hibernian line of his descent—but ancestors. They speak—

—and who speaks back but the Dwarf, who might be dangling by his scrotum from the I beams that angle high above the concrete floor and who might as well be ensconced in the spreading pale green boughs of the trees somewhere up above where Jared's mother is putting a hand to her mouth as her young brother says *That there's an* M, *and right next to it a* C, and that spells Jared's natal destiny)

He sniffs at the floor again, cocks his head to listen. Yes; there. There were spaces in the earth, and where there were not spaces there was the strength and the will to create them. Vibrations reach him: the dim ring of searching men, the boom of underground thunder.

Not up and out, then, not yet. But there is no time to wait. So: down. Into the tidal pull of the earth.

Flex. Feel the floor give a little, feel it crack. Begin to dig.

* * *

The sun was down when Jared returned to the chair in the cabin, with the fire burned down to embers and the air gray with wood smoke. He looked to his right, expecting Petey's bright black eye, and saw only the bamboo rod and its intersection with the oiled steel of the muzzle-loader's barrel. His legs would barely support him, but he got out the door and dragged in the sharp clean lakeside air, hearing the door bang shut behind him and resolving on the spot that he would die rather than enter that cabin again. Home, he thought. I have to get home. Somehow he did, making the turns back to Highway 59 and tracking his way down from Pontiac into the Sunday pause of the city. Along the way he reminded himself that he was fishing, yes, and elaborated on the lie until he thought it would withstand Colleen's scrutiny. He concocted various stories about Jem reeling in a trophy with every cast; discarded those and applied the same story to Felton; figured it might be better to have both of them fill their creels; then settled on general futility as the best way to go. Didn't catch anything—he rehearsed the story in his head—but that was how it happened sometimes, and that small un-truth was so vastly preferable to speaking about what he now knew, what he'd experienced, that he couldn't even muster the will to feel guilty about it. And sure enough, Colleen asked him, and he mur-mured into the back of her neck that the fish weren't biting, and she patted his thigh and went back to sleep.

Fucking Petey, he was thinking as he, too, slipped into sleep; is everyone in my life going to make me tell lies?

Of course he dreams of the Dwarf, only this time the Dwarf strad-dles a blackened roof beam in the remains of Plenty Coup's house while a crew of golems salvages copper pipes and cast-iron sinks and anything else that might be useful. A long line of them stretches away west toward the hulking silhouette of the Rouge, which in the dream lies at the other end of a long steel bridge across a marsh that stretches for miles, punctuated by dead trees thick with blackbirds.

Don't look over your shoulder, the Dwarf says.

Jared's right there with Satchel Paige's famous follow-up: something might be gaining on you.

On you, the Dwarf says.

If I wake up out of this dream and I'm sleepwalking down the street, I'm going to hunt your scorched ass down and tie your balls around your neck, Jared threatens.

I'll do it for you, the Dwarf says—and he does. Jared has to laugh.

So now you know, the Dwarf says. Jared looks past him, and across a foreshortened landscape sees Willow Run. Can't trust 'em as far as you can throw a piano, the Dwarf says. You should tell Meadows to kill it.

I don't know if it's still there, Jared says.

The Dwarf unknots its scrotum and lets it dangle below the beam. It's rocking back and forth on the roof beam like a kid on a teeter-totter. Yahoo! it yells, and then stops, piercing Jared with a glance like it's expecting him to say one particular thing. What that thing would be Jared has not the foggiest idea.

Is all this because of my mother? he asks. Or is it like the dragon, and you're some kind of thing I knew before I was born.

Who cares? the Dwarf says with a shrug.

But the Piston Doctor's story, it's true.

Sure it's true. What, you want to be a magician? Bet Meadows would love it. Then you could work for the Marshal. No more clay busting for you.

I do work for the Marshal, Jared says. The Dwarf snorts.

Is it ever over? Jared asks.

A passing golem, arms full of twisted copper piping, bites the Dwarf's scrotum as it passes. Whoo! the Dwarf yells. Fish are biting tonight! A crafty look comes over its face, and its voice drops to a conspiratorial whisper: wonder if the Cleaveses are.

Before he can think about it, Jared has grabbed up a broken two-by-four and whipped it straight at the Dwarf. The board nails the Dwarf just over its left eye, knocking it off the beam to land flat on its back in the charred debris. Cadillac, Jared is thinking. That was Cadillac's mistake.

The Dwarf sits up, a big dent in the side of its forehead. Dalyell's, too, it says. This is too easy. I need a new challenge. Remember what I said about our scaly friend, eh? It lisps deliberately on the word *scaly,* and Jared sees that its tongue is forked. He snaps awake with Colleen shaking him, saying *Jared, honey, you're having a nightmare.*

CHAPTER 15

All day he felt like the dream hadn't quite gone away, as if Petey and CeeCee had somehow conspired to make the boundary between sleeping and waking a little more permeable; his mother was an unwitting conspirator, sure, but if the last month had taught Jared anything, it was that even unwitting conspirators had plenty of chances to make themselves, well, witting. The sensation clung to his skin as he put on his coveralls before work, and he caught himself looking around for the Dwarf and examining his skin to see if he could actually pinpoint the pores that were leaking dream. Did anyone see the Dwarf twice? Jared flexed his hands as if his fingers were digging grooves in concrete, and he had an irrational conviction that the dragon at Willow Run, if he ever saw it—if it was real and not just a product of whatever Petey had done to him in the cabin, but no, he'd dreamed of the cattle before he'd known there was a dragon— would have two malformed digits on its front right claw. *Remember what I said about our scaly friend* . . . does it count that I threw the board in a dream? Jared wondered—and immediately realized that the only reason this worried him was that he'd subconsciously arrived at the conclusion that the real Dwarf was visiting his dreams for the purpose of provoking a confrontation. Maybe he always had been; maybe the Cadillac-Dalyell-blacksmith-Hull dream cycle was the Dwarf's own oneiric newsreel, played over and over for an audience of one. At that moment, as he took up his station on the Frankenline, Jared had no idea whether he'd even decided to write his high school paper on his own. Could be the Dwarf had pushed that as well.

It was a hell of a thing to realize at twenty-eight that you couldn't figure out whether you'd ever made a meaningful decision in your life. For one thing, it made you one miserable son of a bitch to your coworkers, which circumstance was becoming more frequent. Jared didn't even wait for Jem to start in with his boom shtick that night; as soon as he saw the kid, he said, "I'm letting you know ahead of time. First time you open your mouth about my dad, I'm breaking a shovel off in your ass."

Jem stood very still for as long as it took for Jared to shut his locker. Then he took a deep breath and said, "I thought you were pretty okay when I started here, but you know what? Not one real bad thing has ever happened to you, and still you walk around like you're the unluckiest bastard on the face of the earth. I'm about sick to death of your damn long face when you've got all the family in the world, and your baby girl."

Coming from a kid who had come up as hard as Jem had, the words felt like a spear stuck through Jared's lungs. Jem was staring at him, red-faced and eyes bright with unshed tears. Ashamed, Jared broke the eye contact and looked down at his hands. Simple as that, he thought. How did I get so far off the track? How is it that I go through my life every day and don't notice something that Jem picks out just from standing next to me at a conveyor belt covered with mud?

He tried to say something, but when he opened his mouth all he could think of was to tell Jem about the dreams. Jem wasn't the kind of guy you could confide in about dreams. Jared's head was stormy with all of the different ways he should apologize and explain and justify and defend, but before he could get words out of his mouth Jem was gone onto the floor. The only thing to do was clam up and wait for it all to blow over, which it hadn't by the time the shift ended and Jared found himself in the Hop-Frog heading east on West Jefferson toward Joe Sent Me. The eagle having shit three days ago, most people inclined to spend their money in bars already had; John Dash was the only paying customer in the place when Jared walked through the door. Seeing him put Jared in a powerful mood to go fishing with Emily, preferably in Montana, but he'd gotten himself into this and the only thing to do was get himself out before it was too late.

Dash was signaling to the bartender before Jared sat down, and he slid an unopened pack of Luckies in Jared's direction. "Good to see you," he said, and stuck out his hand. Their handshake felt less like a greeting than the consummation of a deal, and Jared wasn't sure what exactly he'd just agreed to. The dream was still thick on him; he had a hard time convincing himself that any of this was real—except Jem's dead-eye assassination of his self-pity. That was real, and that was why he was here. End this, he thought.

He opened the pack of cigarettes and turned one over in his fingers. "What do you figure you're buying with these?" he asked softly.

"It's just a pack of smokes, Jared. You don't ever seem to have any."

Here I am meeting with a guy who might be a spy, Jared thought, and we're talking about me being a cigarette mooch. "Spent all my money on war bonds," he said.

"Me, too." Dash grinned. "Best thing you can do. So how was work?"

"Not so good." Jared studied his right hand, half expecting to see the ring and pinkie fingers grow scales.

"Swerdlow giving you trouble?"

Jared shrugged. "Mostly I have other things on my mind." He took a deep breath and lit the cigarette. There was something almost sacramental about the touch of flame to tobacco, and the first draft of smoke had the taste of some kind of communion. *Dash offered, I accepted,* he thought. *Now I have to see the bargain through.*

"Can you get a message to Billy for me?"

Dash's left eyebrow lifted. "A message."

"Not that kind of message. I mean actual words."

Dash appeared to consider this as if the possibility of talking to Sharkskin Billy had never before occurred to him. "I told you before, Billy and I aren't on the same team."

"I know." Jared resisted the urge to spell it out.

"What's the message?"

"Tell him I have his answer."

"Why don't you just tell Swerdlow?" There was a slight smile on Dash's face. *He's teasing me,* Jared realized. *He knows what I want, and he's needling me some to see if I know where things stand.*

Jared played along with it. "I don't want to be bringing a knife to a gunfight," he said.

"You calling me a gun?" Now Dash was grinning again. "What is the answer, Jared?"

"You know what Billy's after?"

"I do. You told me, remember? You've told me plenty." Seeing how this disconcerted Jared, Dash reached over and clapped him on the shoulder. "Don't worry. I knew anyway. You're actually playing this pretty well."

"For an amateur," Jared said. "Pros like you and Billy, that's a different league."

"True enough. So what do they have over there at Willow Run, anyway?"

"You telling me you don't know?"

"I sure don't. Never looked into it, really. I've got other concerns."

"Other concerns," Jared echoed.

Dash shook a Lucky from the pack he'd given Jared and chased the first drag with the last of his beer. "They do involve you, in a sort of peripheral way. Some free advice: stay out of Paradise Valley over the next week or so."

"Why? What's going to happen?"

"Well, you saw what happened in Los Angeles and Beaumont, and . . . where was the other one?"

"I don't know." Summer of race riots. Felton's foreboding rang in Jared's ears.

"Beaumont," Dash said. "What a dump that place is."

"I've never been there."

"I have. Los Angeles, too. Just my luck. Take care, Jared." Dash left money on the bar, way too much for the beer they'd drunk. A bitter taste filled Jared's mouth, combination of the beer and smoke and the inescapable conclusion that he'd sold something of himself tonight.

If it kept Billy away from Colleen and Emily, though, it would be worth the trade; not that he wanted to have to explain that to the FBI. Fatherhood, Marty Cleaves had once told his son, was the gradual process of you acclimating yourself to all of the various options you had to take out on your soul in order to raise a family. Jared remembered the moment with the kind of luminosity peculiar to memories of events that you know right away are some kind of watershed, the kind of moment that you remember both for what happened and for how you knew you'd remember it later—Emily reaching for Mrs. Pelletier's lawn jockey flashed through his mind. Marty Cleaves had seemed to feel the same way; he cocked his head as if playing the sentence over in his mind, and then, after due consideration, said, *Not that I know everything about raising kids.*

Jared, thirteen at the time, hadn't heard anything so funny in as long as he could remember—and it was still funny now, sitting in a dumpy waterfront bar with the small spoils of his chat with Dash. Maybe I'll get lucky and the two of them will kill each other, he thought. Some plan. The alternative was to spill his guts to Meadows and throw himself on the mercy of the Marshal, if there was such a thing. No sir, he thought. My options are narrowing right down.

The brown water, the scars on the granite walls of Gulf Hagas. The brown water, the scars of industry on the shores of the Detroit River.

Time to shoot the rapids.

The thing about shooting the rapids, though, was that while you could choose to point yourself downstream, the way you got there—whether you got there at all—was up to the water. Tuesday afternoon the Draft Marshal pulled his train of Cadillac limousines up to Building G's bay doors and, without even waiting for Swerdlow to show up and fulminate, escorted Jared right off the Frankenline into the back of the lead car. He sat across from the Marshal and the Marshal's two flunkies, and nobody said a word all the way downtown. The limo pulled into a subterranean garage, the electric door opening to admit them and then closing again without any visible operator.

The Marshal and flunkies formed a flying wedge, leading Jared through a maze of hallways even more byzantine than the upper floor containing Meadows' office. Eventually one of the flunkies opened a door and held it for the Marshal and Jared. Meadows was waiting for them in a small conference room, and he didn't even wait for the two of them to sit down before ripping into Jared. "You dumb bastard," he said. "I try to give you a heads up so you'll stay out of the way, and what do you do but spill your guts to a goddamn

Abwehr spy. We've been working on rolling up his network for six fucking months, and now the whole operation might be up in smoke."

"I . . ." Jared sat heavily and put his head in his hands, rubbing at the bridge of his nose. "I didn't know you were counterespionage."

"That's your excuse?" Meadows said incredulously. "You blabbed because you didn't know our goddamn *jurisdiction?*"

Out of the corner of his eye, Jared noticed the Marshal silently quivering with suppressed laughter, his fat rippling like soil liquefied in an earthquake. "No, it was just the first thing I could think of to say."

"Well. Now that we've cleared that up, how about we address the topic at hand?"

"I wanted to protect my family," Jared said.

"By telling a German spy that you possess information that another German spy is looking for?" Meadows leaned theatrically back and spread his arms. "I can't wait to hear this."

"This guy threatened me."

"Which guy?"

"Both of them. Dash a while ago, just kind of offhand. He said that once I'd talked to him he could get me in trouble. And then Billy on Friday."

"What did he say?"

"He stuck me in the knee with a knife."

"So you went to Dash," the Marshal prompted.

"Yeah. We'd . . . we'd talked about it before."

"Talked about him killing this Billy?"

Jared nodded. Behind what he hoped was an earnest expression, he was grilling his memory, hoping for some certainty that he was telling the truth. Since the last dream with the Dwarf, in Plenty Coup's house, he hadn't been able to keep anything straight. The room wasn't doing him any good, either; painted a pitiless white, with two glaring bulbs hanging from a conduit in the ceiling, it had the feel of . . . well, it was a kind of interrogation room. But without the table it would be his imagination's knee-jerk image of a torture chamber. He wished there were a clock somewhere in sight.

"Did you ask him to?" Meadows asked.

"No, but he let me know that he might if I asked him."

Meadows leaned forward and spread his fingers on the table. "Jared. Why would Dash make this offer?"

"I don't know. You guys are the spooks."

"We are not spooks," the Marshal said. "Our charter mandates that we explore nontraditional means of warfare outside the purview of the other government research institutions."

Jared didn't want to ask him what *purview* meant, and couldn't anyway because Meadows had lost patience.

"Has it occurred to you that the whole time you've been in contact with Dash, he's been taking little steps to put you in his debt?" Meadows asked. "Telling you about Swerdlow's meetings at the bowling alley, then dropping little hints that he might take care of Billy for you, then this last meeting . . ." He let that hang, giving Jared the impression that he knew exactly what had happened in that discussion; Jared imagined an OEI imp hanging by its fingernails under the dripping boards of the pier behind Joe Sent Me. "You've been played, bo. Both Dash and Billy are using you, and unless I miss my guess they're both using you as cover for when they take their shot at each other."

Now Jared was completely lost and didn't even bother trying to hide it.

"Look," Meadows said. "I'll spell it out for you. The Abwehr— that's the outfit your buddy Dash works for—works for Admiral Wilhelm Canaris, who as Nazis go is not a terrible guy. Couple of months ago he even put a hit out on Hitler in Smolensk."

"You're shitting me." The thought of a German admiral taking a shot at Hitler didn't square at all with the way Jared understood the

Nazis—which, he reflected, might just mean he didn't understand them very well at all.

"I shit you not. Put a bomb on Schickelgruber's plane, but it didn't go off. He'll try again, if he lives long enough. Now, the reason he might not live long enough is that the SD, which is the spy arm of the SS, lies awake at night figuring out ways to monkey-wrench anything the Abwehr is up to. Himmler would kill Canaris in a New York minute if he thought he could get away with it. Billy, your other spy buddy, is Himmler's guy in Detroit. He wants to know about Willow Run because the SS also runs Hitler's version of this office, out of a castle up in the mountains, and earlier in the war our guys managed to liberate a certain object from a crypt under that castle." Meadows watched Jared carefully as he spoke, and Jared could feel the Marshal's cold appraising gaze as well. I'm in real trouble here, he thought. If they think I know too much about this, they're going to lock me up just to be on the safe side. Or worse.

Could he tell them about his little trip with Petey? There were ways to shade it, leave Petey out of the story. Maybe blame the whole thing on the Dwarf, which Meadows would buy because he was clearly convinced that Jared was some kind of weather vane where the Dwarf was concerned. And he was probably right about that, which meant that Jared should probably tell him about throwing a two-by-four at the Dwarf the other night. He felt himself sweating, and the contours of the table and chair, the faces of the other two men, grew distorted and indistinct as if Jared was beginning to dream. The prickling sensation he'd felt on his skin returned, and he looked at his hands expecting not scales this time but some visible evidence that he was slipping between sleeping and waking.

Meadows was still talking, and Jared made an effort to pick up the train of his speech. "Why don't you just take them out?" he said, playing for time.

"There are maybe a dozen SS spies in the country looking over industrial sites. We don't have a good handle on all of them, and if we don't nail the whole operation at once we'll lose the survivors. Spy hunting and stock speculation, Jared; timing is everything. We're flying solo on this, too, because we've got orders straight from the top not to let Hoover or anyone else in on what Billy and his pals are really after, not after the way Hoover nearly screwed up the . . . never mind. The point is that we have a duty to remove this network. All of it, at one stroke. And you, for whatever reason, are getting sand in our gears here."

"You know why," Jared said.

"Ah," the Marshal said, steepling his fingers on the brass-studded mound of his belly. "At last we come to the point."

Meadows had his notepad out again. "We're talking about the Dwarf?"

"We've always been talking about the Dwarf," Jared said. He stumbled over what to say next, and Meadows stepped in.

"You don't need to apologize for wanting to serve, Jared," he said. "But what you have to understand is that there are a good many situations in which a loose cannon who wants to serve does more harm than good."

Jared accepted the implied rebuke. It was true, and even if it wasn't he was in no position to argue motivation. The fact was, he'd compromised a counterespionage operation, or at least compli-cated it, and along the way consorted with the enemy. Down here in the basement of the OEI, his reasons didn't matter very much.

"Colleen," he blurted. "She said she'd leave me if she thought—"

"What does she know?" the Marshal cut in.

"Just that Swerdlow wanted me to look into Willow Run. I told her I didn't know why."

The Marshal and Meadows exchanged a glance.

"We're going to take that at face value for now," Meadows said. "Let's stay focused here. She said she'd leave you if what?"

"If she thought I'd put Emily in danger."

Meadows mulled this over. "That's why you went back to Dash, because you thought Billy might threaten your family?"

"Yeah."

"What did Dash say?"

"I just asked him to get a message to Billy."

"And what was the message?"

"I wanted him to tell Billy that I knew what he wanted to know."

Meadows capped his pen. The Marshal sat in his chair like a wax sculpture. "Jared," Meadows said, "that doesn't make any sense. You didn't need Dash to pass a message. Swerdlow's the one you needed off your back."

"But what if Billy decided to get rid of me after I told him?"

"What if Dash decided to take you someplace quiet and give you a blowtorch tan?" Meadows responded.

Jared had no answer for this. He swallowed, trying to wet his throat. Hadn't he gotten all of this worked out just a couple of days ago? Why couldn't he make it make sense now?

"I had to trust somebody," he said. "Billy or Dash. And Dash never pointed a knife at me."

"Okay," Meadows said.

"And I guess I wanted Dash behind me."

"I don't know about that," the Marshal said. Jared looked up and saw his jowls quaking; apparently the Marshal never laughed out loud.

"Like I said. I had to trust somebody. And if I had Dash tell Billy, maybe Billy would figure that Dash was protecting me. You said they don't get along, right? I thought, maybe if I got lucky, they'd just cancel each other out and I could—"

"Forget the whole thing," Meadows finished. As Jared nodded, Meadows went on. "Kind of closing the barn door after the horse is gone, but it's not the dumbest thing you could have done. But you know you it won't work, right? Because of the Dwarf."

"We need the Dwarf, Cleaves," the Marshal said.

"You can have it."

Nobody laughed.

"Remember what I asked you about your personal life?" Meadows said after a short silence. "We're still inclined to believe that when your life reaches a crisis point, the Dwarf will take some action. You're a kind of barometer for it."

"And it would appear that your crisis has arrived," the Marshal added. "Your wife may leave; you're in a difficult position with two German spies who want different things; your job is in danger; and if things go wrong for you here, we might have to remove you from circulation."

Meadows waited long enough for the blood to drain from Jared's face, then added, "For a while. Don't worry, Jared. We're not going to kill you. Not really the way we do things around here, and in any case you're our best chance at getting to the Dwarf."

"What do you want from the Dwarf?" Jared asked him.

"What do we want from it?" the Marshal repeated. "Mr. Cleaves. The Dwarf has destroyed this city once, and nearly accomplished the task on two other occasions. This is a resource of profound strength, and of a nature that it is our office's mandate to investigate. Imagine the Dwarf convinced to take an interest in Berlin. Or Tokyo."

A vision swept over Jared, of Tokyo in flames like Detroit in 1805. Or Berlin, the Rhineland sky lit by fire, the Dwarf leaping on the Brandenburg Gate, its capering shadow cast across the stones of the Alexanderplatz. In that instant he could smell the smoke, feel it sting his eyes. The dreams, he thought. Like a shorthand for a life I never lived but someone did, and someone else might. He felt again as if he'd never fully awakened after seeing the dragon, and even more so after pegging the Dwarf in the head with a two-by-four.

"Are you even here?" he mumbled.

A crease appeared between Meadows' eyebrows. "Jared," he said. "Are you all right?"

"Don't know," Jared said. "Since the last time . . . I'm having a hard time telling what's real."

"Last time what?"

"Last time I dreamed of the Dwarf."

"Which one was it? Cadillac again? Dalyell?"

"No. I was . . ." Jared kept it together enough to be careful. "A house across the street burned down a month ago. I was there, in the dream. Saw the Dwarf, saw some golems. I, ah . . . I threw a board at the Dwarf. Hit the little red bastard right in the head."

Meadows nodded slowly. "I see. And you think this means that something's about to happen?"

"You're the one who mentioned Cadillac and Dalyell."

"They didn't attack the Dwarf in a dream, Jared. That was real life."

"Nope," Jared said. "You're right. And if you have another explanation, I'm all ears."

He was done speaking. Unless he was about to implicate Petey, there was nothing left to tell. The Marshal and Meadows looked at him, then looked at each other, and as if an air current in the room had shifted Jared became conscious that they'd reached a decision. The extended pause was corrosive, leaving him an interminable space of time for second-guessing everything he'd done since the first time Swerdlow had asked him about the new building out at Willow Run; it gnawed at the last bit of his composure, and for one of the few times in Jared's life, panic brought real clarity. There was something he'd forgotten after all.

"I know what it is," he said. "In Willow Run." In the silence that followed, he added, "And I know it's gotten loose."

"How have you come into possession of this information?" the Marshal asked. Behind the question lay a proposition: answer correctly, and you go home. Man of few words, the Marshal, but you had to admire the way he made them count.

"It's more like the information has come into possession of me," Jared said.

"Another dream?" Meadows prompted.

"Yeah."

"Was the Dwarf involved?"

Jared shook his head. "This one was different."

They waited for him to elaborate, but didn't press when he kept his mouth shut. About the time Jared had resigned himself to finding out whether the OEI had its own jail, the Marshal said, "Mr. Meadows. Do you still hold the same opinion you did when we entered this room?"

"I haven't heard anything to change my mind, sir."

"Nor have I, as illuminating as this conversation has been. What you will do, Mr. Cleaves," the Marshal said, "is tell Swerdlow what you know."

"All of it?"

"Don't be stupid. Of course not all of it. But you will answer the question he asked of you regarding the activity at Willow Run. Do not leave him in any doubt, Mr. Cleaves."

Jared stood when the Marshal did, but Meadows remained in his chair. Confused, Jared took a step toward the door. He stopped when the Marshal shut it. "We're not quite done here, Jared," Meadows said. He looked down at his hands. "I hate this place sometimes. You saw us at our most ridiculous the other day when we had the kennel club meeting, but I feel like I should warn you that things might not have hit bottom."

This confession threw a wrench into Jared's relief at not being handcuffed and left to molder in a cell somewhere. It also felt like an opening, though, and Jared took it. "Are you guys digging in the salt mine?" he asked.

Meadows looked up at him. "Do us both a favor and tell me your father isn't snooping around," he said.

"Okay," Jared said. "My father isn't snooping around. Are you going to answer my question?"

"No, we're not digging in the salt mine," Meadows said. "Concentrate on your wife and your daughter. I think you know by now that Marty Cleaves can take care of himself."

His interlude at the OEI turned Jared into a plain idiot during the first half of Wednesday's shift. Felton and Jem were so disgusted with him that they wouldn't even talk to him by the time the dinner whistle blew, which was all right because Jared had lapsed into an uncommunicative daze an hour after putting on his coveralls. He spent most of his dinner break walking in curlicues among the slag heaps between the foundry and the canal slip, watching seagulls stake out their evening patches of poisoned water. *This is it*, he thought over and over. *This is the chance to get free of it all. Colleen already knows I'm not going to get twenty bucks out of it, and don't kid yourself, bo—the Marshal won't think for more than a tenth of a second about making you disappear. You aren't cut out for playing with the big boys, Cleaves.*

That was the realization he'd been looking for, even if he'd had it before and had just recently found another route to an old conclusion: that he was out of his league, and that coming through for the OEI meant he could get out of the game for good. Jared hunted Swerdlow down somewhere in a back corner of Dearborn Assembly, where Swerdlow was haranguing a morose gaggle of machinists about their collective inability to make replacement parts that fell within specs. "If these engines ever make it into airplanes, which I doubt," Swerdlow was screaming as Jared came up, "they'll go five minutes and stop for an hour just like this goddamn line!" He spun on Jared. "What do you want?"

"We need to talk," Jared said.

"Not now."

"Yeah, now." Jared started walking away. He'd committed himself to telling Swerdlow, but he still held out a dim hope that Swerdlow's sheer stubbornness would get in the way; it would be perfectly in character for that guy to make life hell trying to get a piece of information and then not listen when Jared finally dug it up. Or had it presented to him by a talking bird.

"Hold up, Cleaves," Swerdlow called out. He was panting from his exertions over the machinists when he caught up to Jared. "What is it?"

"Can't tell you on the floor."

They ended up under the giant scoop bucket hanging over the canal slip. Jared leaned against the scaffolding that supported the catwalk, and Swerdlow paced along the edge of the water, tapping each piling as he went back and forth like a duck in a carnival shooting gallery.

"The thing at Willow Run is a dragon," Jared said.

Swerdlow stopped, his hand resting against a piling. "A what?"

"A dragon."

"You're an asshole, Cleaves. This is important."

"Got yourself in a bind, Swerdlow? Got a little too cozy with Wilhelm from the bowling alley? What's he got on you?"

Swerdlow took a step toward Jared. "You keep your mouth shut, you son of a bitch. You've got no idea."

"I think I do. I talked to Billy, too. And I talked to some other people. You threaten a man's job, and his wife's job, he's going to take steps. I found out what you wanted to know. Now I'm out of it, and you can just belly up to this big old bowl of shit you served yourself." Jared closed the rest of the distance between him and Swerdlow; he was practically butted up against Swerdlow's shirtfront. "Fire me now. I'm a long way past caring. You afraid to tell Billy what he wants to know? Why? Figure that you could give a little something to him, bank some money that nobody would notice, hope that it didn't kill too many guys overseas? A dragon. What do you think Billy's going to do when you tell him? Think he'll just melt away, or will he maybe get a message to his boss holed up in his castle up in the mountains, and then there'll be an accident at Willow Run and everyone will just forget about it? I'll tell you something. The last month I've been in mortal fucking fear of putting a foot wrong because I was giving myself an ulcer worrying about what I'd do if you cut me loose from this job. Now I don't care because I just now figured out, dumb shit that I am, that you've been doing the same thing. Billy's SS, Swerdlow. The guy he works for, this is Heinrich goddamn Himmler. What do you think's going to happen when you've given Billy what he wants? I hope you have your bags packed before you meet him. Get your wife to the train station ahead of time, and don't tell anyone where you're going."

"Take it easy, Cleaves," Swerdlow said, suddenly all conciliation. Jared didn't buy it for a minute. "Hey, I get it that you're pissed, I would be, too, but this isn't what you think."

"Sure it is. It's exactly what I think. You talked yourself into believing something you knew wasn't true, and now . . . man, it's shit when you find out that you're a little lower on the food chain than you figured." Swerdlow had stopped talking; Jared couldn't. All of the rage and fear and self-loathing he'd felt was pouring out of him, and he couldn't stop it and didn't want to. "Buy the missus something nice, did you? Sock away a little something for after the war, a piece of land up north? You're a sucker. Right now you're thinking about running, but you can't run from these guys, not even if you try and bounce them off onto me. Somebody's probably watching us right now, or watching you, anyway. How much did he offer you?"

A sound like he was strangling came from Swerdlow's mouth; then he spoke. "Ten thousand."

"Not bad." It was more than the mortgage on Jared's house. Four years' worth of busting clay. "You see any of it yet?"

Swerdlow shook his head and wiped a hand over his bald head, smoothing down the few strands of hair that had come unstuck from the humid air. He inhaled, held the breath, sighed it out. "Cleaves. I, ah . . . thanks. I'm gonna take some steps now, and I won't even ask how you know all this. You gotta believe me, I only asked you because of your wife, I figured she'd know—"

"I don't want to hear it. Tell yourself whatever you need so you can sleep at night, but leave me out of it. I got what you wanted. Now you tell Billy, and you tell him for me that I'm done, too." Jared paused, and some of the anger started to drain out of him. "A dragon, can you believe it? I mean, I make golems every day. I see the Tenfingers, I've talked to a bird. But a dragon. That's different."

"Yeah," Swerdlow said. He was hoarse.

"If I'm you, I buy the train ticket now, I talk to Billy in a public place, and I disappear."

"Yeah. That's a good idea."

"But you know you have to tell him, right? No way to back out now."

A nod. "Yeah. I know." Swerdlow coughed. "Where do you think we should go?"

"Canada's only a bridge away. Ten grand is a lot of money. Last you a long time in Mexico."

"Loretta'd never go to Mexico. Maybe Arizona . . ." Swerdlow was lost in thought, and Jared realized that he'd only then learned that his wife's name was Loretta. What kind of woman was Loretta Swerdlow? A stay-at-home charity volunteer and Wednesday bridge player? A steely enforcer of ironed doilies and hushed voices? A catalog-thumbing social climber? For all Jared knew, Loretta Swerdlow might strip engines at Willow Run. Maybe that was how Swerdlow had tumbled to the idea of looking for him in the first place.

"Hey," Jared said. "Whatever you're doing, you should do it. Call your wife. Get packed. I know a lot more about this than I ever wanted to, and I'm telling you, watch your ass. Do what you need to do and then disappear." He surprised himself by sticking out his hand. "For a manager, you weren't a total sack of shit."

"You're the only clay-buster whose best part didn't run down his mama's leg," Swerdlow said, returning the shake.

"I'm taking a half day," Jared said.

Swerdlow nodded. "I'll write it up. Here's hoping we never see each other again."

"Amen," Jared said, and went straight to the Hop Frog without even changing out of his coveralls.

Colleen was up when he got home, reading a book in the living room, legs folded sideways under her like a schoolgirl. "What are you doing here?" she asked, taking in the coveralls and the poleaxed expression on her husband's face. "You didn't get fired, did you?"

He collapsed onto the couch next to her, and was grateful all out of proportion when she didn't complain about the upholstery. "I should be so lucky," he said. "Just talked to Swerdlow. Took half a day. Everyone needs half a day once in a while."

"He's all right with it? Even though we don't have the big secret?" She was joking with him, but behind it was real concern. Nothing is ever hidden as well as you think it is, Jared mused as he settled into her, feeling her arm come to rest around his shoulders. He turned her book so he could read the cover: *It Can't Happen Here.*

"Any good?" he asked. Claude padded down the hall and thrust his head under Jared's free hand. He'd started sleeping in Emily's room, and he was drowsy, resting his chin on Jared's thigh. Jared scratched his ears, and Claude thumped his tail lazily on the rug.

"Not really," she said. "Kind of a pretend future with fascists in charge. It passes the time." Colleen took in a slow breath, let it out. "It's hard when you're not around all the time."

"Yeah," he said after a pause. "I didn't want it this way."

With his head settled on her left breast, he could feel her nod and her intake of breath before she spoke. "I know." She raised her hand to stroke his hair. "Is this over?"

"Soon," he said.

For a while she didn't respond. Then she said, "Emily decided she wants to learn how to read."

"Wow," he said. "That's some little girl."

"Yeah," Colleen said.

"Pretty soon she'll be writing stories for the spiders."

He felt her laugh before he heard it, soft and weary and wondering. A parent's laugh, the kind that comes from realizing one more time that your child always has one more surprise in store. Jared raised his head and kissed his wife at the corner of her eye, feeling the brush of her lashes on his chin.

"I'm beat," he said.

"I'll be in pretty soon," she said.

"If it's real soon, I'll still be awake," he said. She cupped the back of his head and kissed him on the mouth, eyes open and searching his.

He stood and yawned. Claude looked at both of them, concluded that he'd gotten all the affection he was going to get, and wandered back down the hall to Emily's room.

"I'll be along," Colleen said. Jared snuck a peek over his shoulder and saw her sliding a bookmark into *It Can't Happen Here*.

CHAPTER 16

At about four thirty the next afternoon, while Jared was standing at the rail siding with a shovel in his hand, two Detroit cops came to arrest him for the murder of Carlton Swerdlow. "For what?" he said dumbly, part of him realizing that he'd just heard Swerdlow's given name for the first time. One of the cops cuffed him while the other asked him where he'd been the night before. Jared looked around at the Frankenline. Everyone had stopped working to gawk at him. Even Moises was standing in the doorway to the rebuilt Tabernacle. Not one of them, not even Jem or Felton, would look him in the eye. "Asleep," he said. "First night in weeks I haven't dreamed." Which struck him almost immediately as the wrong thing to say, although he couldn't articulate why.

"Anyone can place you there?" the cop who'd cuffed him asked. They were already walking him to the car. Jared was thinking of what he'd said to Swerdlow the night before, and it took him a moment too long to answer.

"My wife," he said. "I took a half day. Swerdlow signed off on it."

Which it turned out Swerdlow hadn't. Jared was booked into the city jail and put in a holding cell with seven other men, four of

302 — ALEXANDER C. IRVINE

whom were sleeping off what appeared to be truly epic benders. Jared hadn't smelled a similar concentration of urine since the last time he'd cleaned out the garbage can holding Emily's diapers, and this was worse because piss smelled much more virulent when it hadn't come from your daughter. The other three guys sat in a group on a lower bunk in the corner, muttering darkly about someone who had apparently turned them over to the Detroit PD. The evening passed with toxic farts from the unconscious and gruesome threats from the ambulatory. Around nine o'clock a uniformed cop came to take Jared to an interrogation room, which made clear to him how misguided he'd been in the basement of the OEI on Tuesday. The room he entered had a square wooden table with three chairs around it, an ashtray in the center of the table, and a drain in the floor that it seemed to Jared must exist for the sole purpose of draining the blood of suspects into the sewers of Detroit. He was a little surprised when nobody hit him during the first fifteen minutes of his interrogation. The two detectives, Eads and another guy whose last name was unpronounceable and who went by the name of Detective Kaz, went over where Jared had been after he'd left the Rouge. "Home," he said. "I went home about eight, and I was beat. Crawled into bed and got up like I always do when my little girl crawled into the bed at six thirty."

"Anybody see you leave?" Kaz asked.

"I talked to Swerdlow last thing. Told him I was taking a half day, and I took a half day. Walked into my house, my wife was reading a book and my puppy nibbled on my knuckles. When I went to bed she was still reading."

"What was she reading?" Eads this time.

"*It Can't Happen Here,* I think was the title."

"That any good?" Eads asked.

"I don't know," Jared said. "I'm not much of a reader."

"Sinclair Lewis is a pinko," Kaz said.

Jared didn't respond.

"You and Swerdlow talk about anything before you went home?" Kaz asked.

"I was looking for him because I wanted to ask him about taking the half day," Jared said. "At my dinner break, I tracked him down in Dearborn Assembly. He was giving a few machinists hell. I said I wanted to talk to him, and we went and talked."

Eads took his turn. "About?"

"The war. What does anyone talk about?"

Jared never saw the slap coming. The left side of his face lit up, and tears jumped from his eye. "Ahh, Jesus!" he said. "What was that for?"

Both of the detectives were looking at him with perfect equanimity. He wasn't even sure which one had hit him. "Just making sure we're all on the same track," Detective Kaz said. "It's easy to get off on dead ends."

"I told you. We shot the breeze. He seemed worried about something, but when you're a line rat you don't worry too much about what's on the manager's mind." Jared blinked the tears out of his eye, wiped at it with his left sleeve. "I told him I was taking a half day, and he said he'd write it up. Then I went home."

Eads' eyes were dead as a golem's. Jared didn't even want to think about the things he'd done in this room. "Your line isn't union, though. You don't get half days."

"We can if the foreman or a manager okays it. Swerdlow did."

"Except he didn't," Kaz said. "He put in his full shift, and there's no paper saying you get a half day."

"He said he was going to," Jared said.

This time the fist was closed, and Jared's head swam with the force of it. He lost track of time, and got back on top of it only when his forehead slumped into contact with the tabletop. "Guys. Officers. Uh, Detectives," he heard himself saying. "What?"

"You go out by the canal slip," Kaz said. "What did you talk about?"

304 — ALEXANDER C. IRVINE

The conversation, Jared reflected as he waited for his ears to stop ringing, would have been a lot easier if he had known what the detectives knew. He had the OEI up his sleeve, but he didn't want to play that card unless he knew he had nothing else. If they kept tuning up on him, though, he wasn't going to be able to remember what he had and what he didn't—which was probably the point.

"Jared," Eads said. "Look at me."

Jared raised his head. His left eye was already swelling shut.

"Kaz asked you a question," Eads said.

"I had to talk to him because I've got some trouble with my wife," Jared said. "Figured if I could spend a night with her, maybe things would ease up a bit. It's tough when you never see each other."

"Yeah," Kaz said. "My wife couldn't take it."

"Mine, either," Eads added.

"So hey, our sympathies, but we're a little skeptical that you just wanted to get marriage trouble off your chest," Kaz went on. "You didn't like Swerdlow much, did you, Jared?"

"No, I sure as hell didn't."

"Why not?"

"He was Special Service," Jared said. "And he's still a sadistic asshole. He can't hassle the union guys, so he drops most of his shit on our line because we're an open shop. You interview the rest of the guys on my line, you won't find any of them who liked him much. We get sick of him refighting the Battle of the Overpass on our line all the time."

"You said *get*," Kaz said.

"And *drops*. Swerdlow's past tense now," Eads said.

"Yeah." Jared rubbed at his eye. "Officers—"

"Detectives," Eads corrected him.

"Right. Detectives. I don't know what's going on here. I talked to Swerdlow last night, and now you tell me he's dead. What makes you think I did it?"

"What kind of car do you drive?" Kaz asked.

"A '35 Ford coupe, the five-window."

"Tag?"

"BP-5839."

"You drive it to work today?"

"Yeah."

"You happen to look in the backseat?" Eads asked.

Jared thought about it. "No. Don't think I did."

"Huh," Eads said. "Well, if you had, you might have noticed this." He tossed a photograph onto the table. Jared recognized the backseat of his car, and he recognized the shirt Emily had stripped off on their way back from fishing. When he saw the way the shirt was discolored, he got a cold lump of lead in the pit of his stomach.

"Recognize that shirt?" Kaz tapped the photograph with his pencil.

"Yeah. It's my daughter's." Jared tried to swallow the lump away. "We went fishing a while ago and tipped the canoe, so when we got back to the car I tossed her shirt on the floor back there. Guess I forgot to put it in the laundry."

The two detectives looked at each other. "I guess you did," Eads said mildly. He'd leaned back on his chair's back legs.

"I mean when we got back from fishing," Jared said.

Kaz was tapping the pencil point on his front teeth. "If we call your wife, what's she going to tell us?"

"About what?"

Eads' chair banged back to the floor, and Jared flinched. As soon as he realized they hadn't hit him again, he started to admire how well they had the whole thing choreographed.

"About where you were last night," Eads said. "What time did you go to bed?"

"About nine. A little after."

"She come with you?"

"She was reading. I told you that."

Eads was nodding while Kaz took notes. "Right, *It Can't Happen Here.* I'll ask her if it's any good. You bang her?"

"Detectives—"

He saw it coming this time, a cobra-quick right from Eads, but by the time he'd started to duck his bruised eye was bleeding and the ringing in his ears had returned. "I said were you fucking your wife last night?" Eads shouted.

"No," Jared said miserably. "No, we haven't . . . ah, much." Last night he hadn't even minded. The closeness had been enough. Now, absurdly, he was feeling diminished by the admission in front of these two knuckledraggers.

"You go out looking for tail?" Kaz prompted.

"No. I slept." He blotted at the trickle of blood with his sleeve. "What do you guys want from me? I went home early, I slept. I got up this morning, I spent the day playing with my daughter, I went to work."

"Sure Swerdlow didn't turn you down for your half day?" Kaz asked. "And then you left anyway and went looking for him later? That's the way it looks from here, Jared, and once we match all that blood in your backseat to Swerdlow, you're going up on murder one." He stopped taking notes and looked Jared in the eye. "You confess now, we can talk about something else, maybe manslaughter. Maybe Swerdlow had it coming, I don't know. When you're a cop, lots of people look like they had it coming. But you got a cheesecloth alibi and a whole shitpile of evidence against you. Might be time to make the best of a bad situation." He raised the pencil. "And the other thing is that we've got a witness who saw somebody in your car dumping Swerdlow's body in the creek that runs out of Elmwood Cemetery."

"Somebody could read the tag on my car in the middle of the night? In the middle of the cemetery?"

"You getting smart again?" Eads leaned forward and put his hands on the table.

"No," Jared said quickly. "I didn't do this, and I'm trying to figure out who would say I did."

"Okay, let's run with that," Kaz said. "Let's just say that somebody had you picked out as the perfect fall guy for the murder of Carlton Swerdlow. He waited until you had no alibi, he stole your car in the middle of the night, killed Swerdlow, got rid of the body, and then put the car back without you noticing. Who would that guy be? Any ideas?"

Billy. Who else? "The creek in Elmwood Cemetery," Jared said.

Eads smirked at him. "Yeah. Bloody Run. Funny, isn't it."

Both detectives saw the look on Jared's face. "Come on, Jared," Kaz said. "I'll give you the benefit of the doubt for about the next fifteen seconds. You know more about this than you're letting on. I'm betting Eads can get it out of you, but there's a war on and I don't feel like working over a guy in a wartime industry if I don't have to. Swerdlow in on some black-market parts? Yeah, we know all about that. Every couple of weeks our local sons of Sicily off somebody over a load of tires or a crate full of machine tools. That what we're talking about here?"

Jared shook his head.

"Okay, what is it?"

Wild-card time, Jared thought. Still he hesitated over the decision. He'd only have one chance. He could tell Kaz and Eads about Swerdlow's dealings with Billy, but that would lead to Dash and ultimately to the OEI. Better to get the intermediary steps out of the way.

"You guys make a phone call for me?" Jared asked.

Kaz's pencil came to attention over his notepad. "Who do you want us to call?"

"A guy named Grant Meadows. He works for the OEI."

The pencil smacked flat on the table. Kaz looked at Jared like he'd just then figured out who pissed in his cornflakes. "The OEI?" he said. "Did I hear that right?"

Jared nodded. "Yeah."

"For chrissake," Eads said. "We don't have time for this."

Kaz mulled things over while Jared broiled in the waves of hostility radiating from Eads. "Tell you what," Kaz said eventually. "We're going to go waste a goddamn lot of shoe leather right now interviewing solid citizens who don't know a thing about this, including your wife, who I'm sure will be thrilled to have a conversation like this in front of your little girl. Then we're going to come back and talk to you some more. Meantime why don't you reconsider who you want to call."

Eads went to the door and let in a uniformed cop. Kaz cuffed Jared again, and the uniform led him back to the holding cell. Before the interview room door shut behind him, Jared heard Kaz call out. "And, Jared? Anytime you feel like shortening up our wild-goose chase, let us know, okay? Eads and I would appreciate it. We're both out of shoe stamps."

He'd missed evening chow in the holding cell, and the guard wouldn't let him make a phone call. Jared bought a pack of cigarettes from a well-heeled fellow inmate at the extortionate price of two dollars, then made some of it back selling butts to new guys as they were ushered in throughout the night. Stress and lack of sleep had him sharply attuned to the flaking away of his capacity for rational thought; he could tell that he wasn't right in the head—Eads' exertions hadn't helped—but being able to diagnose the problem didn't get him any closer to fixing it. During the night he lapsed into spells when he thought one of his cellmates was a golem; then for a while he was convinced he'd seen the Dwarf in the corner; he felt like he must be about to break out in pustules, buboes, from the intensity of the dream-state bottled up in his waking consciousness. He tried to think about Billy, figure out what his game was, but he couldn't string two ideas together. Had Billy found out about the dragon?

Was the message Jared had given Dash enough to tell Billy what he needed to know? Work the problem, Jared told himself. If Billy can afford to get you out of the way, it means he knows what he needs to know. Something Meadows had said swam up in Jared's brain, a concern that the Germans might . . . God. He couldn't put it together. Was there going to be an attack?

Jesus Christ, did I tell them where to go?

Someone had a deck of cards, and to pass the time the prisoners played gin, but Jared couldn't keep track of the points and they kicked him out of the game. All the bunks were taken, and he tried to sleep in one corner, but snapped awake to find a hand in his pocket. Jared swung at the pickpocket, missing and grazing his knuckles on the wall; as he got to his feet, the guy was backing away with a half smile on his face. "Come on, bo. You know how it is."

Uniforms came, bringing new arrivals and springing other fortunate souls. Every time the key turned in the lock, Jared looked up hoping for Colleen.

At about seven Friday morning, breakfast arrived: scrambled eggs and toast with a paper cup of ersatz coffee. Jared picked at it, then traded the remainder for a second cup of coffee from one of his roommates who'd spent most of the night complaining about his ulcers. The coffee put him back on his game for a little while, but he'd faded back into semi-awareness by the time another uniform showed up to take him back to the same interview room. Kaz and Eads were already there, looking like they hadn't slept any more than he had.

"Leave 'em on," Kaz said to the uniform, who was looking for his handcuff key. "We won't be long."

Jared sat where they told him to sit, and a minute passed during which first Eads, then Kaz, would sigh and shake his head. "The damnedest thing, Jared," Kaz said after a while. "We went to your house to talk to your wife. She wasn't around the first time, before we found your car at the Rouge, and she wasn't around this time, either. Six o'clock in the morning, no answer at the door. What time does she leave for work?"

"About seven, usually. Or whenever her carpool shows up."

"Who drives?"

"Arlene Bannister, usually."

"Know her phone number?" Jared shook his head. "Okay. Bannister with two N's? We'll track her down, see if she knows where your wife's gone. Unless you have a guess."

"She's at work."

"Nope. Personnel at Willow Run says she never showed today."

She's left, was Jared's first thought—and then, much worse: Billy. "Oh no," he whispered.

Kaz leaned forward. "I didn't catch that."

"My wife's parents live outside Ypsilanti," Jared said. "If she—if she's not at the house, she's probably there."

"What's the name?"

"Theo and Deirdre Stuart. On Whittaker Road. I think it's Lincoln Township. Maybe Belleville."

"Think she's walked out on you?" Eads asked without a trace of pity.

Jared nodded. He couldn't see it any other way, at least not any other way that didn't involve Billy. "Yeah," he said numbly. "Looks like it."

"How much did she know about your beef with Swerdlow?" Kaz asked.

"Some. She's my wife. But I didn't have any more problem with Swerdlow than anybody else."

"Could be," Kaz said. "But his blood's not all over the backseat of anybody else's car."

"Call her for me," Jared said.

"Tell us where you killed Swerdlow," Kaz said.

"I didn't kill Swerdlow," Jared said. "But if you call my wife, I'll tell you something."

"We got all the stock tips we need," Eads said.

Fighting panic, Jared quit trying to negotiate. "Look," he said. "I know who stole my car."

Eads winked at his partner. "About goddamn time."

"Call my in-laws and I'll tell you."

Kaz sighed in frustration. "How about you tell us and I won't leave you alone in here with him?" he said, pointing his pencil at Eads.

"Do that, and I swear to God I'll lie my way right to the god-damn morgue," Jared said. "You get what I'm telling you? This guy might have done something to my wife. Bring in the Gestapo, you get nothing from me until you tell me she's okay."

Eads looked over at Kaz. "He's got spirit."

"You figure that's worth a phone call?"

Eads shrugged.

"Ah, what the hell. Go make the call. I'll keep our boy company."

Eads left, and Kaz doodled on his pad for a while. He seemed content to pass the waiting in silence, but Jared was about to go out of his mind. "Anybody see my car come back?" he asked when he couldn't stand it any longer.

Kaz shook his head. "Bunch of sound sleepers on your block." He looked up at Jared. "Feel like getting a head start on this before Eads comes back?"

"I need to know about my wife and my daughter," Jared said.

"Yeah, family," Kaz said. "Crazy the things a man will do for his family."

"It's not crazy at all," Jared said. "That's the whole point."

Neither of them had anything to say after that. Eads came back about ten minutes later. "Talked to your mother-in-law," he said. "She doesn't like you too much."

"Tell me about it," Jared said.

"According to her, your wife and daughter showed up there when you didn't come home last night. That enough for you?"

"Are they still there?"

Eads sat down. "We've been awful patient, don't you think? How about you show some gratitude?"

"Are they still there?"

"Kaz, how about you get a cup of coffee?" Eads said without taking his eyes off Jared.

"Come on, partner. Timing is everything."

A flush came and went on Eads' face. When he spoke, it sounded like he was biting off his own teeth. "They're still there. If it makes you feel better, your mother-in-law is hoping they'll stay."

"No surprise there," Jared said. "The guy who stole my car is named Billy. Last time I saw him he was driving a green Airfoil De-Soto. He hangs out at the Bel-Mark Lanes out Twelfth Street."

"You know all this how?" Kaz asked.

"Did you call the OEI yet?"

Eads tagged him a good one, flush on the ear. Jared went over sideways and out of the chair, banging his head on the linoleum floor. He knew he couldn't get up, and didn't try; right then he couldn't even see. Through the ear pressed to the floor, he was convinced he could hear the sound of something immense, digging. Oh, he thought. Here? Thanks, Mom.

"That's for not telling us before," Kaz said. "And no, we didn't call the fucking OEI."

Jared heard the door open. "Take him back," Eads said.

He fell back and forth through time, through dreaming and waking. He was in a jail cell in 1943 Detroit; he was on the banks of Bloody Run watching Pontiac bury a knife in Swerdlow's ribs; he was a crow watching Cadillac brandish his sword at the Dwarf; he was the dragon, wriggling through the earth a thousand feet from sunlight, the taste of salt burning in his mouth, he was the Piston Doctor, walking his balky figurines across his coffee table while outside fires burned in the sidewalk trash cans and long white shadows rose in the dusk. Through it all he cried out for Colleen, for Emily. Sporadically he would spasm awake, and the faces of his cellmates would regard him until he slipped away from them again. At some point they put him in a corner and ignored him. At some later point he began to notice that the holding cell was packed with bodies redolent of liquor and rage. The storm in his brain receded, so slowly he wasn't aware of any change until he became conscious of a true red alert being sounded in his bladder. He got up, and somebody said, "Holy sheepshit, the mummy walks." He found the seatless toilet and took a leak that put every previous emptying of his bladder to shame. Two-thirds of the way through, there were whistles, and when the last trickle had faded from the bowl, everyone—even the guard watching through the bars—broke into applause. "Damned if I ever saw anything like that," the guard said. "You ought to be in the circus, chum."

Jared tried to speak. His tongue and palate grated together like two pieces of stone. There was a pail of water near the door; he wet his whistle and said, "What day is it?"

His admirers agreed that it was Sunday.

Jesus, Jared thought. Between Eads and the golem, I missed a lot of this summer already. "What time?"

Afternoon sometime, was the consensus. The guard looked at his watch and said it was four o'clock, a little after.

Jared leaned against the bars. He was starting to sweat from the press of bodies. "My name's Jared Cleaves," he said to the guard. "Can you find either Detective Eads or Detective Kaz and tell them I need to see them?"

"Don't know if Eads or Kaz works Sunday," the guard said.

"They've got me in here on a murder," Jared said. "I didn't do it, and now I figured out who did. They'll want to hear this."

"That so," the guard said. He didn't move.

"Please," Jared said. He wasn't sure how long he'd be in himself, and an edge of desperation roughened his voice. "Just see if they're around."

The guard thought about it. "Okay," he finally said, and started to walk off shaking his head. "I never saw anybody piss like that."

Twenty minutes later, the guard came back to inform Jared that neither Kaz nor Eads was available. Jared took the news reasonably well given the fact that he thought the world might be disintegrating around him. "Okay," he said. "I want to make my phone call."

"What?"

"Listen, man, I've been in here since Thursday without being charged. I don't have the money to scare up a lawyer, but come on, isn't habeas corpus three days? And I haven't made a phone call."

"You really been here since Thursday?"

"Check your log."

The guard did, and came back. "I can't believe it," he said. "Thursday. You ain't heard from a lawyer?"

"I was sleeping off my interrogation."

"Mm. Well, look, it doesn't say you've made a call, but you wouldn't believe what it's been like around here. Seems like every hillbilly in Detroit has a bone to pick with a nigger, and the other way around. It was up to me, we'd send 'em all back to Kentucky or Africa. This used to be a nice town."

"Okay," Jared said. "Can I call someone?"

The guard cuffed him, led him to an unused office, and found a phone book in a drawer. Jared first looked up the OEI, and found no listing. Figured. He thought some more and looked up Grant Meadows. There were two men by that name, one in Detroit and one in Ferndale. "Heads or tails?" he said to the guard.

"What?"

"Never mind," he said to the guard, and dialed the Detroit number.

Someone picked up on the fourth ring. "Hello?"

"Grant Meadows? It's Jared Cleaves."

"Jared. Where are you? The Marshal's an unhappy man when he doesn't know where you are."

Relief washed over Jared. He could feel it in a loosening under his rib cage; he took a deep breath, feeling his lungs fill. "I'm in jail. Detroit cops think I killed Swerdlow."

"Billy killed Swerdlow."

"There's a couple of detectives down here who could stand to hear that. I asked them to call you three days ago."

"Fucking flatfeet. I'll get right on this, Jared. Sit tight."

"I'm not going anywhere," Jared said. "Listen, I think I know where the you-know-what is going to come up."

"I'm walking out the door."

Meadows hung up. Jared dropped the police phone back into its cradle. "Everything go okay?" the guard asked.

"We'll find out." Jared stood, and the guard led him back to the cell.

Waiting again, with what felt like a reasonably firm grasp on reality, Jared decided to confront the very real possibility that Colleen had left him. It didn't last long. He went through the standard progression of disbelief, heartfelt inner pledges to eliminate his various imperfections, baffled fury, and—all within a space of maybe ten minutes—a disgusted determination to think about something else. She couldn't really have left, he thought. I work hard; I'm a good father; I never cheated on her even with Arlene around nearly every day. What the hell is a guy supposed to do?

Hell of a question. Seemed like every time he asked it, and he'd

316 — ALEXANDER C. IRVINE

asked it a lot during the last couple of years, he'd come to a point
where the question had no real answer. What the hell were you supposed to do? What made sense. Or if love was involved, what
needed doing, whether it made any sense or not.

That was progress. If the dragon didn't come up and burn the
city down, and whatever the Germans had planned didn't work out
for them, and neither Sharkskin Billy nor John Dash managed to kill
Jared, he at least had an insight about love to work with. It was the
only environment in the world where the nonsensical could be ra-
tionalized in good faith. Why the hell else had Jared gotten em-
broiled in not one but two Nazi spy plots?

Now you're kidding yourself, he thought. You did it because
you couldn't help but do it. Had nothing to do with Colleen.

Well, it felt like it did, he thought in his own defense.

Ah, come off it. You wanted to be Sergeant York, and if you
couldn't do it on Guadalcanal, you figured you'd do it in Detroit.

That's not the only thing. What the hell, was I supposed to just
ignore all this? We're talking about Nazi spies, for crying out loud.

Sure, but you never just went to the FBI, did you?

I would have lost my job.

Big loss. You really have that much invested in breaking up clay?

It's my job.

Colleen's right. She makes enough to get you by while you find
something else.

Not now, smart guy. She didn't show up on Friday. See if she
ever works for Ford again.

Ford wants engines stripped, he'll hire people who know how
to strip engines.

Ah, shut up.

Jared ended this internal death spiral when he realized he was
hearing the two roles as they might be voiced by Jack Benny and
Rochester—and Rochester was right. He looked around the holding cell, saw that it was even more crowded than it had been when

he'd come back from calling Meadows, and started listening in on conversations. Southern accents all around, complaining about the local Negroes. Several of the more recent arrivals looked like Jared must have when he got there after Eads' ministrations; Jared wondered whether they'd been marked up by cops or the aggrieved colored population.

"Tell you what," one of his cellmates said, fingering a loose tooth. "I get out again, I'm getting some boys and going nigger hunting."

"Damn right," a few others said.

Stay home tonight, Felton, Jared thought. An hour or so later a uniform showed up and called his name.

Walking down the hall to be processed out, Jared said, "So who went my bail?"

The cop looked at his clipboard. "Says here the guy only gave his name as Petey."

"Is he out front?" Jared asked. What a charge it would be to see Petey's human form. "This guy an Indian?"

"Don't know. I just file the papers. Ask me, you're goddamn lucky to be walking out of here. If Eads and Kaz weren't out on riot duty, they'd have thought up something new to charge you with."

Riot duty? What was it like out there? "There's a riot?"

"Nobody's calling it that yet, but they will. Niggers are saying white folks threw a nigger baby off the Belle Isle Bridge, whites are saying a nigger raped a white woman in the park out there. All the sailors on the island are hunting coon out of season. Goddamn mess. We'll be lucky if we can keep it out on the island. This gets onto Woodward, we're going up in smoke."

They got to a barred window where a uniformed cop gave Jared back his wallet and keys. "Only reason you're leaving is because nobody can find Kaz or Eads, and Roosevelt hasn't suspended habeas corpus yet," said the cop on the other side of the window. "Don't take any vacations."

A dozen or so other cops filed past them in riot gear. Jared waited until they'd passed and then asked the cop, "You know where I can find Eads or Kaz?"

"Tonight?" snorted the cop. "Manning the Alamo, like the rest of us. If you knifed that guy, do us all a favor and get yourself killed tonight."

CHAPTER 17

Knifed, Jared was thinking as at shortly after ten o'clock he walked out of the lobby and almost ran into Grant Meadows, who was waiting for him just outside the door. Gunshots popped in the middle distance, and the air shivered with the wail of sirens. Jared wouldn't have recognized Meadows from ten feet away; he was unshaven and dressed in wrinkled khaki pants and a two-tone zip-front sweater. "You're not Petey," Jared said.

"Nobody's seen Petey in a week," Meadows said. "Unless you have. Let's walk."

A police car roared by, the barrel of a shotgun thrust out the passenger window. "The cops impounded my car," Jared said. "I need to get out to Ypsi."

"Your family is fine."

"They won't be if Billy goes out there."

Meadows stopped as they got to Woodward. Southbound traffic was backed up as far as they could see. Fires burned that way, and a steady stream of northbound cars ran red lights and blared their horns. Jared saw broken windows and one old Chrysler running on bare rims, the remains of its tires flapping along the pavement amid

320 - ALEXANDER C. IRVINE

bouncing sparks. "Trust me when I tell you, Jared, that Billy isn't going out there," Meadows said. "Billy's got something else on his mind tonight." He started to say something else, but his voice was lost as the riot reached them. A running figure shot out of an alley and slewed through the Woodward traffic. Jared just had time to register that it was a Negro before a mob burst onto the street in pursuit. Cars squealed to a halt in a barrage of horns, and bottles flew in long arcs to shatter on the pavement around the fleeing man. He got away, and the mob turned its rage onto the cars their arrival had stopped. Windows were shattering, the sound like cymbals all up and down Woodward Avenue, and as if they'd fallen from the sky people had suddenly jammed Woodward as far south as Jared could see. Fires bloomed left and right, and a shout went up from the mob as they dragged a colored motorist from his car. He disappeared behind a wall of bodies, and Jared saw the car tipped up on its side with a crunch that cut through the snarling exultation of the mob. The Woodward streetcar was frozen at the Gratiot intersection; rocks and bottles pelted its chassis, shattering windows, and three men were working at its rear door while inside, Negro passengers held on to the handles. Police whistles echoed, but Jared couldn't see any men in blue—and what would they do if they were here? he wondered. Gunshots split the night from somewhere to the east. In Paradise Valley. Stay home, Felton, Jared thought again.

Meadows dragged him out into the surge of bodies, first north and then south as one group or another carried them along; they angled across the current toward the west side of Woodward. Somewhere along the way, a flying bottle grazed Jared's scalp, and another hit him squarely on the point of his shoulder, numbing his right arm. He raised his left arm and found himself actually swimming one-armed through the heaving mass while Meadows hauled on his paralyzed hand. There was a small eddy off one corner of the stalled streetcar; trying to shake some feeling back into his arm, Jared leaned against the chassis and, looking over his shoulder, saw the impact of a man's head against the window. The glass starred and fell apart in the frame, showering Jared with fragments; the fight went on as he forced his way back into the mob, arriving on the western sidewalk feeling as if every square inch of his body surface had been beaten with iron bars. He leaned against a newspaper box, trying to catch his breath as fire caught in the seats of the streetcar and the mob retreated from it like oil from detergent. Two bodies lay in a clinch near the rear of the car. One black, one white, neither moving.

All the while Jared was thinking, *I know you're here, you son of a bitch.* He waited for the Dwarf to show itself.

"Jared," Meadows panted. "Where is it?"

Jared shook his head, still expecting to spot the Dwarf on the roof of a burning car, or dangling from a telephone pole. He looked over at Meadows and saw that the OEI man's face was turned up to the sky. Trying to follow what Meadows was looking at, Jared traced the line of buildings on the east side of Woodward, coming to rest on the extravagant pile of the Guardian Building. Meadows turned to look west, then glanced back over his shoulder at Jared. "Is that where—?"

Jared put it all together then, the horizon of his understanding expanding so violently that he staggered from psychological vertigo.

John Dash's voice in his head: *I have. Los Angeles, too. Just my luck.*

Billy curious about Willow Run.

Meadows grilling him about his dreams, and the Marshal's oily lust to enlist the Dwarf.

And Dash again: *You've already told me plenty.*

"No," Jared said, not because he didn't believe but because he needed the moment of denial to get his bearings. "You motherfucker," he said to Meadows. "You did this."

"This?" Meadows repeated. "You mean the riot? No, we didn't—"

"I mean the dragon, you son of a bitch!" Jared raged. "You let the goddamn dragon out through my old man's mine! Didn't you?"

Even in the midst of the immolation of downtown Detroit, Jared was turning heads. Meadows looked around, didn't like what he saw, and pulled Jared northward. "Listen," he panted as they went. "I protected you and your father as much as I could." They stopped at a bus shelter and stepped into it. Something banged on the roof. Meadows leaned against the wall and said, "You remember the day you showed up and all the dogs were outside?"

"Meadows—"

"That was when it all tipped over," Meadows went on. "That right there was when we went from sublime to ridiculous." Jared started to interject again, but Meadows ducked his head and held up one hand. "The Marshal knows it's all coming apart," he said. "We were going to use the dragon anyway, but once the dragon got interested in you, the Marshal . . . what he said was, *I think we should go for broke,* which if you've talked with the Marshal much you realize is not the way he usually talks."

"Go for broke," Jared repeated.

Meadows nodded, then flinched as something shattered on the street nearby. A strange lull had fallen inside the bus shelter, as if they were invisible there, on the other side of some membrane from the violence only yards away. It was a dreamlike kind of feeling, and Jared had a hunch he knew what it meant.

"The Dwarf's the real prize, is what you're saying," Jared said. "And all this . . . did you know what Dash was up to?"

Meadows kept nodding, his gaze cast down to the pavement between his feet. He's losing his handle, Jared thought. It's a bitch when your plans actually work. When you're basically a decent guy who gets vacuumed up into a game played by men with the scruples of vultures.

Jared Cleaves knew a little something about that.

"And it's okay with you, that a Nazi spy touches off all this," he said. He waved at the street, and as if summoned a crowd boiled out of an alley and overturned a Packard two lanes away. The crowd swirled around the bus station, and bodies rank with the smell of gasoline crowded around. Fearing that the mob's madness would infect him, Jared fought his way out onto the sidewalk, looking for some space to breathe. Meadows followed, shouting something that was lost in the tumult except a phrase—"to our advantage"— almost immediately torn away by a volley of gunshots from less than a block away. Instinctively Jared looked in that direction, and like he was staring into a kaleidoscope the carnage stretched away as far as he could see to the vanishing point of the waterfront. His field of vision narrowed down to a pinprick of guttering orange light, and he felt the mob's murderous ecstasy seeping into the borders of his mind as he spun on Meadows, the blindness gone as quickly as it had come.

Meadows bulled into him, and Jared shoved back, sending him stumbling against a phone booth. The OEI man got his balance and looked around, barely noticing Jared, his expression utterly beaten and lost.

"You think the Dwarf is some goddamn *moth*?" Jared screamed at him. "You think you can sucker it in by letting the dragon loose and then *sweet-talk* it into bouncing over to Tokyo, like you're doing it a *favor*? Jesus Christ, Meadows—"

The gas tank of the overturned Packard went up with a whoosh. Jared threw one arm up over his face and flinched away from the wave of heat, and in the last instant before his sleeve cut off his field of vision he saw Sharkskin Billy eeling his way through the mob. He pulled his arm back and looked again, but Billy was gone. Meadows saw that Jared was scanning the crowd; he opened his mouth and then someone immediately behind Jared grunted as if he'd been punched in the gut. At the same time Jared felt blood inside his shirt. He spun around and the first thing he saw was the knife in Billy's hand, blood on its edge gleaming black in the firelight. The knife described a shallow arc on its way to the pavement, where it skipped twice and was kicked into the street by someone running by. Billy hit the pavement himself a split second later, shoulder-first, hard enough to bounce his head on the curb. Only then did Jared see the golem that loomed behind Billy; open-mouthed he stood, absently aware of the blood now soaking the waistband of his pants, as the golem reared back, its trench coat flaring out, and drove its fist into Billy's head. The impact flattened Billy's skull like a water balloon in the instant before it bursts. Blood sprayed from his nostrils over the curb and his legs shot out stiff, the spasm lifting the lower half of his body completely off the ground before he fell limp, head and shoulders on the sidewalk next to a parking meter and legs splayed across a storm sewer.

The golem stood and looked Jared in the eye. The contact was electric; the sounds of the riot faded to a muted roar like the ocean heard in a seashell, and the smell of Billy's blood invaded Jared's nose. His heart pounded. The wound in his side burned. The knuckles of his two bad fingers ached as if he'd delivered the punch himself. He licked his lips and tasted salt. Jared knew that not all of these sensations were his. The golem pointed south, and when Jared tracked the motion he heard an engine start. The car sat untouched at the curb twenty yards away; it was an ancient black Model T, with a crank starter. No one had turned the crank. The passenger door opened. The smell of whiskey drifted to Jared the way the blood scent had when the golem caught his eye.

"Mother of God," he heard Meadows say behind him.

He must have been walking, but he wasn't aware of moving his legs. The streaming crowd parted around him as if he were a phone booth or a street sign; no one looked at him, and he could no longer hear their voices or their footsteps or the chorus of sirens that rose all over downtown and in Paradise Valley and on Belle Isle. When he was five or six, Jared had believed that each of his steps torqued the earth a little farther along in its rotation, and that belief returned to him now as he approached the car and got in. The Dwarf sat in the driver's seat on a liquor crate from which came the muted clink of full bottles. More glass crunched under Jared's boot soles as he settled his feet on the floorboards.

Raising itself off the crate, the Dwarf wedged open the lid and handed Jared a bottle. Jared uncorked it and took a long drink, feeling the burn in his sinuses. When he took the bottle away from his mouth, it shattered in his hand, whiskey soaking into his pants and trickling into his boots. He looked at the Dwarf, who was grinning the grin of Marty Cleaves.

"Bullshit," Jared said. "You're not my father."

The Dwarf shrugged and dropped the Model T into gear. Jared tossed the neck of the bottle onto the floorboards between his feet. Pathways revealed themselves among the wreckage left by the riot, and the Dwarf squealed the Model T's tires as it cornered onto Michigan Avenue.

So that's where we're going, Jared thought. He picked glass from his lap. "You think I'm going to fuck this up," he said.

The Dwarf shrugged again.

"You aren't doing me a favor, that's for sure."

The Dwarf scratched its balls and floored the accelerator; the Model T roared and leapt ahead. Every traffic light on Michigan changed as they blazed up to it; the rooming houses and gas stations and machine shops on either side of them were dark and insubstantial, tricks of the light. Jared thought he saw a shadow pass across the street, but when he leaned out the window to look at the sky there were no stars to cast a shadow. Traffic thinned out as they left the riot zone. The bars around Briggs Stadium were empty; Corktown had apparently either bunkered down or headed downtown to watch the show. Or jump in. They passed the bar where Jared had met Billy for the last time; he averted his eyes for fear of seeing himself inside. Jared's senses grew strangely liquid, and when he looked at the stadium again he was seeing the old Navin Field, before Walter Briggs had closed off Cherry Street and built the massive outfield upper decks. Jared could see through an open concourse, across the open expanse of the field and to the rows of seats along the third-base line. That old black magic, he thought.

"What's your hurry?" Jared asked the Dwarf. "You wanted all of this, right?"

The Dwarf wouldn't look at him. The Model T rocked on its springs as it wrenched the wheel to make the turn north onto Twelfth. Sparks shot from the Dwarf's beard, and it sweated tiny beads of running steel. Around them now were low brick buildings, their windows empty, punctuated by taller structures housing small factories. They passed churches, a small park. Ahead was the intersection of Twelfth and Clairmount, pulsing with the red of police lights. A dozen black-and-whites, and three vans, formed a skirmish line around a cluster of men standing calmly at the building's front door. No; not men. Golems. Jared snapped back into the now, the dream-time of riding with the Dwarf peeling away from him like a chrysalis. There were the golems of Detroit, joining a pitched battled with Detroit police on the pavement of Twelfth Street. Petrified by the spectacle, Jared watched, transfixed by the monstrous physical strength of the golems and their pitiless determination. What the hell was he working for, he wondered—an end to the war or a superhuman militia to cripple the poor flatfoot bastards, angry and frustrated at the chaos, who had orders to break up groups of men loitering on the street? Jared heard screaming, and wondered if Kaz or Eads was dying here. Gunfire crackled, not just the pop of handguns but the stutter of tommy guns and the ursine roar of shotguns. Some of the golems went down, falling in splatters of clay, and Jared watched with a detachment born of abject misery.

The Dwarf was bent over, its forehead against the steering wheel, heaving with laughter. It turned its head to look at Jared with tears streaming out of its eyes. Smoke clouded the cramped space inside the car. If I had the neck of that bottle still in my hand, Jared thought, I'd stick it right in your neck.

But Dash, fucking Dash, where was he?

Jared jerked the door open. The Dwarf sat upright and its mouth fell open. "That's right, you son of a bitch," Jared said as his feet hit the pavement. "This isn't over." He ran from the car and ducked around the side of Moises' building, hitting the sidewalk once when a shotgun boomed nearby and he heard the load of buckshot savage the air over his head. Scrambling to his feet and making the turn into the alley behind the building, Jared bulled straight into a golem. It caught him by the shirt and lifted him off the ground, then set him down on his feet in front of it.

"Let me go," Jared said. "You know why I'm here."

The golem hesitated, its indecision like a reprieve from execution, and Jared ran past it, his lungs burning. The fire escape at the back of Moises' building hung aslant; Jared leapt and caught the ladder at the second rung, rode it as it swung down and rolled around to plant his feet as it clanged onto the alley concrete. He got to Moises' back window and jammed his fingers into the gap between sash and sill just as he heard the gunshot inside. With a wail he heaved at the sash, shattering the window and reaching through to rip the shade down.

Moises lay sprawled across the couch. John Dash sat across from him, where Jared had sat during his visits, and Dash was setting a Browning automatic down on the coffee table about where Jared had set his glass of water a month ago.

328 — ALEXANDER C. IRVINE

"Jared," Dash said. He got up and gave Jared a hand through the broken window; numbed by sorrow and confusion, Jared let him. There was nothing for him to do here anymore. Always just a little too late, he thought. That's Jared Cleaves.

But why had the Dwarf looked so surprised?

"Careful there," Dash said as Jared got his balance and stepped the rest of the way into the room. Outside, the police shot the golems to pieces and the Dwarf drove Marty Cleaves' old bootlegging wagon along Oakwood Avenue. Inside, Moises was dead. Through the soles of his feet Jared felt the impact of bullets on the building, and he heard the groaning crunch of a car being overturned. "You're pretty good at this, friend," Dash said. "Circumstances being otherwise, we might have an interesting conversation."

Jared stopped at the side of the couch. "You never needed me to find out anything about Swerdlow," Jared said.

"Nope," Dash agreed. "Mostly I needed you to confirm what I thought about him"—he nodded toward Moises—"and to distract Billy. But I'll tell you the truth, I think you have a talent for this."

The Browning lay within arm's reach. To his left, a sound came from Moises, and Jared flinched, thinking the rabbi was alive.

"Just air leaking out," Dash said. "He's got an extra hole." He saw the look on Jared's face and held up a placating hand. "Sorry. I don't mean to be flip, I really don't. Let's not get crazy ideas, okay?"

"You know the dragon's out, right?" Jared said.

"No, I didn't know that. The dragon was more Billy's area, anyway. I guess that means he'll get a medal."

"If he does, it'll be posthumous," Jared said.

Dash's mouth quirked. "Is that so? Good for you. I should have spent more time cultivating you."

Cultivating: the word caught in Jared's mind. He didn't bother to correct Dash's impression that he'd killed Sharkskin Billy. He had been cultivated. And not just by Dash; Meadows and Swerd-low and Billy had done it, too, and now his wife had left him and his job lay dead on the couch and if Jem had been right before about Jared never experiencing a single really bad thing, that damn sure wasn't the case now. You couldn't even keep your mouth shut about Petey in the White Tower, Jared thought bitterly. What made you think you could play this game with guys like John Dash?

"You and Meadows have some interesting conversations about me?" he asked Dash.

"I've never spoken to Grant Meadows in my life," Dash said. "The only reason I know who you're talking about is because I listened in to the conversation you had with your little birdie in the park. If the OEI played you, Jared, they had their own reasons for doing it. Just like I had mine."

A crash came echoing up the stairwell beyond the open front door. "That'll be the golems," Dash said. He shut the door and shot its dead bolt. "Persistent, if not very clever, creations. Excuse me. Looks like I'm taking the back way."

Jared didn't move from his post at the arm of the couch, be-tween Dash and the broken window.

"Jared, please," Dash said. "I said you were doing well, and I meant it, but you're an amateur. Are you really going to try me? Here? I've spent a lot of energy in not killing you so far. Don't make it all wasted. I'm going out the back."

"Moises told me a little while ago that he didn't matter," Jared said. "He said that the war was going to be won by machines."

"He might be right. Have been right, I mean. That's what tonight's show is about. How many people are going to show up to work tomorrow?" Dash grinned. "Not you, that's for sure, although we didn't set all this up just to keep you home. Tell you what, why don't you just pretend this never happened? Plenty for you to do

330 — ALEXANDER C. IRVINE

just keeping your marriage together. That Colleen is some woman, and I hope you won't mind me saying that you have a beautiful daughter."

All the while, his grin challenging Jared.

"Okay," Jared said. He stepped to the right, against the bookcase with its row of spines lettered in Hebrew.

"There we are. Discretion is the better part, et cetera," Dash said. He walked past Jared and swung one leg out through the fire escape. "Hey," he said, pausing in the act of climbing out. "Are there golems out here?"

"There was one," Jared said. "Cops probably chased it off by now."

"Could be." Dash appeared to consider his options. "Espionage, Jared. It's all about decision making. Inventory control, if you will. That Henry Ford is a man worthy of admiration."

He ducked his head under the crooked windowsill, jammed there where Jared had left it, and as his head turned Jared picked up the gun. Dash stood on the landing of the fire escape, silhouetted through the broken glass, and Jared shot him in the back, the gun kicking upward as he pulled the trigger because he couldn't grip it properly. Whatever sound Dash made was lost in the roar of the gun; the impact of his body brought a groan from the rusted bolts holding the fire escape to the brick wall. Jared's ears rang, and his right hand ached from the Browning's recoil. He dropped the gun and sat on the back of Moises' couch, looking at his fingers. What do you know, he thought. The draft board was right. I had to do that more than once or twice, I wouldn't be able to hit the ocean from the beach.

Dash didn't move, and Jared looked at Moises' body, head tipped back over the other arm of the couch, mouth open as it had been the last time Jared had walked out of this room. I was worried that he was dead then, Jared thought, but I didn't go back to make sure. He pressed two fingers under the rabbi's jaw, and felt no pulse. What did you say?

"Sorry, Moises," Jared said. "I don't know the words."

He looked up at a motion in the doorway. A golem stood there, its left arm amputated below the elbow and holes punched in its face. Expressionless, it regarded him, and Jared made no effort to excuse himself. He was done with that. He'd killed John Dash, and nothing was any different.

Other golems crowded behind the first, and the room filled with them. Jared wondered what had happened to the police. He'd find out soon enough. The golems surrounded the couch; one of them moved Jared out of their circle with a gentleness only possible in a being of unimaginable strength. He was put in mind of the night, not so many days before, when he'd come back in from dinner and stepped out of the way of a golem emerging from Building G. That was what he'd felt then, a strength so vast it could not be bothered with his own presence. He felt it again now. "I," he said, and didn't know what he had meant to follow.

A sound filled the air although nobody spoke. The golems lifted the body of their creator from the cushions of the couch, and blood borne by gravity pattered onto the stained fabric. Moises' body rode on the shoulders of his creations; they carried him out the front door and out of sight, leaving Jared alone with the body of the man he'd known as John Dash cooling on the fire escape. From far away he heard the crack of guns.

I will go, he thought, with a formality that surprised him. The way I came. He went to the window and swung one leg out so he could plant a foot on the fire escape next to Dash's body; having shot John Dash, Jared found himself fastidious about touching him. As he looked down at his foot, he saw that one of Dash's eyelids was still fluttering. A wound shaped like an apostrophe gaped under the right side of Dash's jaw, and for just a second Jared

332 — ALEXANDER C. IRVINE

was embarrassed at having hit him in the neck when he was aiming for the center of Dash's back. Then he was a little bemused at his marksmanship concerns, and then he caught the full force of the stomach-churning realization that he had murdered a man who meant him no harm. Dash's blood pulsed out of the wound and pattered onto the two fire-escape landings between his body and the alley pavement.

A spy, but I shot him in the back, Jared thought. Far away the riot raged, the handiwork of the man whose body lay dripping its blood through the iron grate at his feet. Jared got his balance on the landing and leaned against the railing, feeling it give a little at his weight. Remorse was as tangible as love or hate: a knot in the base of his throat and a spreading molten pain in his gut. It would have been different on Guadalcanal, he thought.

A gust blew across the back of his neck, moist and smelling of age and death and salt. Jared closed his eyes. There was motion all around him, a rattling scrape like the sound the gurneys made swinging into the Tabernacle, or that pebbles made running up and down with the tide on the rocky shores of Maine. Jared turned to his left and looked into the glittering eye of the dragon. Its tongue flicked out, ghosting across his face. He saw its claws hooked through the fire-escape stairs above him, followed the undulating line of its body up to the roof, where another of its feet bit into the sandstone cornice. Its tail wove down the wall, all the way to the ground, scraping along the brick walls and flicking bits of trash around in the alley below. All around Jared the shadows unspooled and became the body of the dragon.

All of the voices that speak to me are dead, the dragon said. It shook its head with a rattle like falling dominoes. I am drawn to you.

"You dug all the way from Ypsilanti because you're drawn to me?" Jared said.

Ypsilanti. The syllables drew out as the dragon tasted them. *That is the name of my birthplace.*

"Yeah. The Willow Run factory in Ypsilanti."

None of my ancestors knew.

"You're an immigrant," Jared said. "My great-grandparents never heard of Detroit, I don't think." Jared couldn't decide whether the dragon was speaking out loud; his ears responded, but its voice whispered from his mind.

Like yours did in my mind, it said.

"You talk to the Dwarf, too?"

My ancestors warned me to be wary of dwarfs.

"They got that right."

The dragon regarded Jared. Its eyes were perfect teardrops of black incised by crescents of reflected moonlight. Twin skies in miniature.

"I shot a man in the back," Jared said. "And Moises is still dead."

He might have done the same to you.

"But he didn't. I did. Now I have to live with it."

Would you rather explain to your daughter that you shot a man in the back, or have your wife explain to your daughter that someone did the same to her father?

Jared could not answer.

All killing is revenge for something, the dragon said.

"What the hell do you know about it?"

It shook again, snuffling out a blinding plume of smoke. *I will know,* it said. *I am meant to know.*

"You and me, dragon, we have something in common. Both of us are OEI patsies. Difference is I know it and you don't." Jared remembered the pride he'd felt walking through the corridors of the Rotunda, nearly three years ago. *Made myself an easy mark,* he thought. *They needed me, I needed to be needed. Presto. They probably already had the dragon.* "Had you," he said out loud, in case it wasn't paying attention. "My old man was right. How about that? Marty Cleaves was right about something that mattered. They picked up on my mom, they found out about the dreams. They figured that the dreams would put me in touch with you because you're the catastrophe the Dwarf wants tonight. It's got nothing to do with the riot; they just wanted to get at the Dwarf, and if I had some kind of control over you, that was gravy. That make sense to you, dragon? You like being a means to an end?"

The dragon's mouth opened, and it raised its head to the sky. *I want*, it said. Jared felt its need like an ache in his own body.

"You're supposed to want," Jared said. "So was I. Why do you think you went through the salt mine?"

The way was there.

"The way was put there. My father works in that mine. You want to talk about ancestors? My mother is a witch, and my father worked the mine you used to get out into the world. You went and dug through twenty-five miles of bedrock and salt just so you could talk to me. Well, here I am. I'm Jared Cleaves, and I've been played for a sucker just like you have. The rabbi in there, he knew. All of it was falling apart, and he knew it."

The vast body shifted. Pieces of brick and concrete from the roof broke loose, and the entire cornice tumbled down to burst in the alley. The frame of the fire escape squealed and settled into a new equilibrium. Jared adjusted his balance, and John Dash's body shifted, coming to rest with his face pointed toward the talons hooked through the railing next to Jared's legs. One of Dash's eyes was still open a little. No more blood was coming out of his neck.

"Christ," Jared said. "Anyone can set a fire. Putting one out, now, that's the trick."

The dragon adjusted its grip on the fire escape, and Jared saw the way that the outer two talons didn't move with the others. A kind of peace came over him. *Yes*, he thought. *It all comes down to this.* "Dragon," he said, and raised his right hand. "Look."

Moon and stars disappeared as the dragon spread its wings and held them out. God, Jared thought. A hundred feet, maybe, from tip to tip? More? It straightened its neck and roared at the sky, then beat its wings once, the downdraft thundering through the alley, driving Jared to his knees and rolling John Dash's body up against him. He kicked the body away and hauled himself to his feet, feeling another shift in the frame of the fire escape at his feet.

"Did your ancestors say anything about being a cat's-paw for a bunch of humans? A bunch of bureaucrats scared that their next appropriation won't come through?" Jared asked it, and in the raging instant when he stopped caring about whether he lived or died cuffed the dragon along its flared nostrils. "You're not from this world, dragon. What's your name?"

Silence. Revelation is cheap, is what Jared understood right then.

"That's the difference. I'm Jared Cleaves. My father is Marty Cleaves. My mother is CeeCee Magruder Cleaves. I shot John Dash in the back. My wife's name is Colleen, and she'll come back to me. I have a daughter named Emily, and I'll kill you to be able to see her again. Go on, you nameless orphan son of a bitch. If you're going to burn my town, you burn me first. Let the Dwarf sucker you, too."

Silence, broken by sirens from the east. Intake of the dragon's breath. Taste of salt and fire in its exhalation. Pebbles, running up and down with the tide. Maine, Jared was thinking. I shot the rapids. The motion of the dragon's body stormed in the alley, dragging trash and dust in its wake, and Jared heard the beat of wings. Another downdraft that drove him to his knees, and then another, amid a rain of shattered chips of brick and sandstone. His ears popped. Trash cans clattered up and down the alley, and a window broke. Then silence again.

Jared waited for the roar of fire.

When it did not come, when he looked to the east and saw only the flicker of burning cars, when he looked to the southwest and saw the vaster and infernal glow of a pour at the Rouge, Jared knew. He looked around for the Dwarf. Where are you now, you hunchbacked little fucker? Jared thought. I got you. He was crying. I got you.

EPILOGUE

Jared stepped back from the Christmas tree, brushing needles from his shirt and rolling his shoulders to get them out of his collar. "Damn thing takes up the whole room," Marty Cleaves said, half hidden by the branches. "You should do like your mother and I do. Artificial trees they got, you can put 'em right on the kitchen table."

"Lean it just a bit to the right. No, your right, Pop." Jared eyeballed the tree, then got back on hands and knees to retighten the bolts holding it in the stand. He backed out and took another look. "There we go."

Marty let the tree go and came over next to Jared. "Yep," he said. "There we go." He went into the kitchen and popped a beer.

"Out, Marty," Colleen said. "I'm trying to cook here."

Emily and CeeCee came in the back door, flushed and dusted with the snow that was coming down in big flakes only three or four degrees from being rain. Claude trotted in after them. The Philco was playing "O Come, All Ye Faithful." Emily ran to Jared and banged into his legs. "Daddy!" she said. "Christmas tree!"

"It sure is," Jared said. The song ended and WWJ picked up a national news feed. The announcer said that bombers had flown successful missions in Osnabrück, Kwajalein, and Cape Gloucester, with other action over Canton. The Fifth and Eighth armies were hacking their way across Italy. In local news, the last of the troops called in to occupy Detroit in the wake of the riots had returned to their bases or been demobilized. The Arsenal of Democracy was humming, and doing it without the oversight of National Guard boys from Toledo. Doing it without Jared Cleaves, too; after the mothballing of the Frankenline, he'd wangled another job at the Rouge, fitting axles onto Willys jeeps. Swerdlow's replacement, another ex–Special Service skullcracker named Stu Roberson, treated him no better or worse than anyone else—with the exception of periodic snide insinuations about Swerdlow's murder, which had been pinned on one Wilhelm Werner, found in Elmwood Cemetery on June 22 with a knife that Wayne County medical examiners had no trouble matching to the fatal wound under Carlton Swerdlow's left arm. Jared knew somebody had called in a favor, and never asked who; the last thing in the world he wanted was to talk to anybody in the OEI again. If that was possible—a month ago, he'd been wandering past the building and found the OEI plaque gone. The same sergeant was in the office, but he claimed to have been an attaché to the War Mobilization Office since the day that body was formed in late May. Then he gave Jared a carton of Pall Malls and told him to hit the bricks. Jared walked back out scanning the trees and phone wires for notable crows.

He hadn't seen a golem since the group that carried Moises away.

What did they do? he wondered. Did they bury themselves with him in an empty lot? Did they walk down into the river and let the current carry them away, a billion silty bits of Europe returning home? Or had they just gradually run down, done their normal rounds and fallen inert one fall day in the alley off Twelfth Street just south of Clairmount, where John Dash's blood still darkened the pavement and if you looked more closely than Jared Cleaves ever would you might find the scale of a dragon in the shadow of the fire escape?

For a while Jared worried about this. Lately it had occupied him not at all. For the first time, this past week or so, he'd lost the urge to tell people about the Frankenline. I did what I did, he thought. So did the other guys. Now we do something else. He wondered where Jem and Felton were, and Ferenc and the molders. Felton's name hadn't been listed among the victims of the riot, which was some solace—but Moises' name wasn't there, either. Or John Dash, if that had been his name.

The doorbell rang. Before anybody could answer it, Theo and Deirdre came in, Theo heaped with packages and Deirdre's arms strategically empty in anticipation of her granddaughter's assault. While Emily bounced in Gamma Deeda's embrace and told her everything there was to know about cutting down a Christmas tree at a tree farm in a place called Canton, Theo set his load down and shook the hands of both Jared and Marty Cleaves. "There's pies out in the car," he said then, and went back out to get them.

"There *are* pies, Theo. Good Lord, how is this little girl going to learn to speak properly?" Deirdre called after him. She saw Jared watching her and winked at him.

"*Are* pies, Feo!" Emily crowed.

Jared helped Theo get the pies in: two each of apple, pecan, pumpkin. "We're going to be eating pie for a week," he said.

"Could be worse," Theo said.

Marty was on the couch finishing his beer when they came back in. "You believe that dog?" he said. "Took one look at the tree and lifted his leg like we'd just put in a bathroom for him."

"Are you serious? Where is he?" Jared asked.

"Out," Marty said, jerking a thumb toward the back door. "In the doghouse." He looked around, taking in the scene with evident pleasure. "See this?" he said. "This is a Christmas, right here. Should have done this years ago." He was effusive for the best reason Marty

Cleaves ever had, which was that this gathering had been his idea. "Hey, Theo," he said. "Let's you and me go out to Olympia sometime. Catch us a hockey game."

"For chrissake," Theo said. He got a beer and sat next to Marty, who engaged him in a lively discussion about the merits of ice hockey. The Red Wings were charging through the season again, Carl Liscombe and Syd Howe leading the way. As soon as Jared heard the name Mud Bruneteau, he evacuated to the kitchen, where Colleen put him to work mashing potatoes. Moving with and around her in the kitchen, Jared felt hope. The war was turning. She had come back to him. Cleaveses and Stuarts argued about hockey in the living room, and Emily begged Colleen to grant Claude clemency.

Marty came into the kitchen and sidled up next to Jared. "You getting the lumps out of those spuds?" he asked.

"You want to do it?"

"Shoot," Marty said. "Hey, tell me something. Too goddamn many triangles around here. When do we see a square?"

"Out, Marty," Colleen said. When he was back on the couch, she came up to Jared and pointed a spoon slick with cranberry pulp at him. "Keep your father out of this kitchen," she said, with such a pathetic attempt at hiding a smile that Jared almost cracked up himself.

"Yes, ma'am," Jared said. He glanced out into the living room and saw his mother watching him. "Ma," he called. "You want to check on my potatoes here?"

With Emily on her lap, CeeCee Cleaves wasn't going anywhere. "This is your house, Jared," she said. "You make the potatoes however you like."

"However you like," Deirdre said to Theo. "I hope you heard that." Leaning over to confide in CeeCee, she added, "Theo always says *however you want*."

"For chrissake," Theo and Marty said together as CeeCee nodded gravely.

Emily *ha-ha-ha*'ed.

Before dinner, Jared took Claude for a walk. He wound through the neighborhood, let Claude romp off his leash in the cemetery for a while, then came back the long way. At the snow-covered ruin of Plenty Coup's house, he stopped for a while to think. "So where's it all get you?" he asked Claude, who just wanted to get to the next bush he could water. Every so often Jared got caught up in an internal debate over what he should do about Moises. The news out of Europe grew more and more horrific if you were paying attention to more than the Eighth Army's steady march north, and Jared found himself divided straight down the middle over the Moises question. What did you do to memorialize a guy killed on his couch in Detroit by a Nazi spy when you were the only witness? A thousand people died every day in Europe and the Pacific, and most of them went out harder than Moises had. John Dash was a killer, but a clean killer. Moises could have suffocated in a boxcar or burned to death in an oven; instead he'd made six thousand golems and died of a bullet. What the hell kind of world was it, though, when that was mercy?

I did what I could, Jared thought, watching snow fall on Plenty Coup's house and devoting everything he had to squelching the remnants of the despair he felt. The war and its machines ground on. Jared Cleaves did what he could. I put in my hours, he thought. I hold my marriage together. I try to bring my daughter up right.

Claude strained at the end of his leash. When no revelation came, Jared quit fishing for it and followed his dog home.

ABOUT THE AUTHOR

ALEXANDER C. IRVINE has won the Crawford Award for best new writer, which is given by the International Association for the Fantastic in the Arts. He also won awards for best first novel from *Locus* magazine and the International Horror Guild, and he was a finalist for the Campbell Award for best new writer. His short fiction has appeared in Salon.com, *Vestal Review, The Magazine of Fantasy & Science Fiction, Alchemy,* and *The Year's Best Science Fiction,* among others. He has been nominated for a Pushcart Prize for his short story "Snapdragons." Irvine lives in Maine with his wife and two children.

ABOUT THE TYPE

This book was set in Perpetua, a typeface designed by the English artist Eric Gill, and cut by the Monotype Corporation between 1928 and 1930. Perpetua is a contemporary face of original design, without any direct historical antecedents. The shapes of the roman letters are derived from the techniques of stonecutting. The larger display sizes are extremely elegant and form a most distinguished series of inscriptional letters.